WHEN THE STARS FALL

EMERY ROSE

Cover Design: Lori Jackson at Lori Jackson Designs

Photographer: Michelle Lancaster

Editors: Jennifer Mirabelli (Content Edits); Ellie McLove, My Brother's Editor

For Jennifer Mirabelli.
This book wouldn't be what it is without you. Thank you times a million. xoxo

"When it is dark enough, you can see the stars." – Ralph Waldo Emerson

ALSO BY EMERY ROSE

THE BEAUTIFUL SERIES

Beneath Your Beautiful

Beautiful Lies

Beautiful Rush

Love and Chaos Series

Wilder Love

Sweet Chaos

Lost Stars Series

When the Stars Fall

When the Storm Breaks

When We Were Reckless

When Wrecked Meets Ruined

PLAYLIST

"Lost" – Dermot Kennedy
"Shiver And Shake" – Ryan Adams
"Howlin' For You" – The Black Keys
"Losing My Religion" – REM
"Love Runs Out" – One Republic
"Already Gone" – Sleeping At Last
"The Ending" – Wafia, FINNEAS
"All My Friends" – Dermot Kennedy
"I'm A Liar" – Amy Shark
"Wild Horses" – Alicia Keys, Adam Levine
"Lost Stars" – Adam Levine

PROLOGUE

Lila

I clawed at his hands, my eyes wide. He was choking me with his bare hands, cutting off the air to my windpipe.

Was this how it was going to end?

Was I going to die at the hands of the man I loved?

But this wasn't him. This was a man I didn't recognize. His blue eyes were wild and unfocused like he was somewhere else. I gasped for breath, tears streaming down my face.

I saw the moment when it registered with him that I was on the bedroom floor in a chokehold, his hands wrapped around my neck, making it impossible for me to breathe. He released me and sat back on his heels, tugging at the ends of his hair. I tried to breathe through the pain, my hand reaching up to rub my bruised neck.

"Lila," he said, his voice raw. The moon was so bright tonight I could see the pain etched on his face. "Fuck. Lila. I'm so sorry, baby. I'm so sorry."

He gathered me up from the bedroom floor, pulled me into

his lap and held me in his arms, his forehead pressed against mine. His tears mingled with my own.

How had we gotten to this place?

"Talk to me," I pleaded for the hundredth time since he'd returned home a year ago. Naively, I had believed that when he came home, we could resume our regularly scheduled life. I'd been wrong. So fucking wrong. Even though I was trembling on the inside, I fought through it. I had to ask. "Tell me what happened to you," I pleaded again. "Please, Jude, I'm begging you."

He buried his face in the crook of my neck and said nothing. It hurt that he couldn't talk to me about anything when we used to confide in each other. Now, I was walking on eggshells. Constantly on the lookout for his triggers. Dirt roads. The Fourth of July fireworks. A rustling in the tall grass behind the barn. He saw danger in places where it didn't exist.

And tonight, all I'd done was wrap my arms around him while he was asleep. I'd done it on instinct, reaching for him in the middle of the night like I'd done so many times before.

Nights were the worst. The circles under his eyes were testament to his lack of sleep.

"I love you," he said, the words ripped from his throat like they were painful. "I love you so fucking much."

"I love you more. I... Jude..." I clung to him.

Don't go.

Don't leave me.

But I knew that he was already gone. I'd lost him somewhere on the other side of the world. "We need to find someone who can help you."

He didn't say anything. He'd been seeing a therapist but it wasn't helping. He was convinced that no one could help him. He was giving up. I could see the defeat in his eyes.

"I'm sorry," he said over and over. He kept saying it like that would make everything okay. But I knew that nothing would ever be okay again.

Jude McCallister was the strongest man I'd ever known. He'd survived three deployments to Afghanistan. Five years of active duty in the US Marine Corps. He'd been shot in the head and he had survived. I kept his helmet in my closet. A huge hole had ripped through the material, but the Kevlar had stopped the bullet and had saved his life. My photo was taped inside that helmet and he said he'd carried me with him everywhere he went.

I used to think our love was strong enough to survive anything. Even a combat zone.

I was wrong.

What I hadn't counted on was the injuries that left no scars. The broken parts that no doctor was able to fix. He'd brought that hell home with him, and I had no idea how to help him. But I would keep trying.

I couldn't lose Jude.

He was supposed to be my forever and my always.

Jude

I sat on the edge of the mattress and I watched her sleeping. She looked so peaceful. So fucking beautiful, her wavy brown hair all messy and disheveled, her long lashes resting in the hollows beneath her eyes. Those green eyes, the same shade of green as the grass in the meadow. My gaze lowered to the purple marks on her neck that I'd put there two days ago. She used makeup to cover them, but they were still there, clear as fucking day for everyone to see. No amount of makeup could hide the truth.

I had done this to her.

I had inflicted pain on the person I claimed to love above all others.

A few months ago I'd almost broken her wrist in the midst of a night terror. I hated myself for the hell I'd put her through. The shouting, the unfounded accusations, the drinking and the times I couldn't bear to be touched. This wasn't what she'd signed up for. Love shouldn't have to hurt this much. She'd tried to convince me otherwise, but she was blind to the truth. And I'd be damned if I would continue dragging her down with me. Lila was tough and she was strong, but her love for me made her weak. She had stayed by my side, through thick and thin, when she should have left my ass.

Hell, she should have left my ass the day I went off to boot camp at the ripe old age of eighteen. Back then I'd had it all figured out. So cocky. So confident that I was strong-minded enough to handle anything. That was only six years ago, but it felt like another lifetime.

Now, she was scared of me. Scared for me. Afraid to leave me alone. Afraid I wouldn't make it to my twenty-fifth birthday.

Look what you've done to her, asshole. Can you really expect her to love you for better or worse?

She deserved so much better than a psycho who had almost choked her to death. The list of shit I'd done to her—to my entire family—was long and unforgivable. Not just the past year since I'd been home, but the years she'd spent waiting and worrying about me while I was off fighting a war she'd begged me to stay out of. Lila would claim that she hadn't made any sacrifices to be with me, but it was bullshit and we both knew it.

I stood up and set the note on the bedside table then walked out of the bedroom before I could change my mind. I hoped she would understand that I was doing this because I loved her. It was time to set her free. I couldn't be the man she needed. That man was gone.

The sun was starting to rise as I drove away. I left my home. I left Texas. I left my family. And I left the love of my life. If I could have crawled out of my own skin, and out of my head, I would have left them behind too.

I cranked up the volume on a classic rock song—"Carry On Wayward Son"—and I drove.

Lifting the bottle of whiskey to my lips, I took a long swig.

"You fucked up, McCallister." I turned my head to look at my buddy Reese Madigan, sitting in the passenger seat of my Silverado. He rubbed his hand over his buzzed cut, his other hand tapping out the beat to the music. Reese loved this song. Used to belt it out at the top of his lungs just to piss everyone off. Dude had the worst singing voice. Couldn't carry a tune to save his life. "You should have known."

"He was just a boy," I argued. "We played football with him. Gave him candy. How could I have known?"

"You telling me you didn't see the cell phone? You saw it but you hesitated, didn't you?"

I wiped the sweat off my forehead with the back of my arm. My heart was hammering against my ribcage, fear and dread crawling up my spine.

I checked the passenger seat again. Reese was gone. Because Reese was fucking dead. I was talking to dead men now.

I took another swig of whiskey. And I kept driving.

She'd be better off without me. My girl was a fighter, and she was resilient. I didn't believe in much of anything anymore, but I still believed in her.

PART 1

CHAPTER ONE

Lila

"Why do I have to wear a stupid dress?" I grumbled as my mom brushed the snarls out of my hair. I scowled at my reflection in the mirror. The sundress was yellow with white embroidered flowers. *Flowers*. Barf.

"Because the McCallisters invited us over for a barbecue."

The McCallisters lived right up the road from our new house, so I guess that made them our neighbors. Yesterday, Kate McCallister stopped by to welcome us to the neighborhood and it turned out that she and Mom had known each other in college. Small world, they'd said, laughing and hugging like long lost friends.

"I can't see why it should matter what I wear."

"Stop being a grouch," Mom teased, dividing my hair into three sections so she could braid it. She was smiling. Had been since Derek agreed to leave Houston and move to Cypress Springs, a small town in the Texas Hill Country. Mom was a nurse and would be starting her new job next week. Derek was an electrician and since he was self-employed, it didn't matter where we lived, he could work anywhere.

"Two of the boys are the same age as you," she said. "Maybe you can be friends."

"I doubt it. Not when they see me in this dress. I look stupid."

"You look pretty." She tugged at the end of the French braid she'd just put in my hair. My eyes met hers in the mirror. They were the same shade of green as mine and we both had dark brown wavy hair. Everyone said I was the spitting image of her.

I stopped and thought about what she'd said. "Wait a minute. How could they both be my age?" My eyes widened. "Are they twins?"

"No. They're cousins."

"Oh." My shoulders sagged in disappointment. Twins sounded like a lot more fun. They could fool people by pretending to be each other.

"Well, don't you look pretty as a picture?" Derek said with a smile.

I forced a smile even though I was still annoyed about having to wear a dress.

"Derek gets to wear jeans and a T-shirt." I scowled at the sunflowers on my flip-flops as we headed out the front door. I'd rather be wearing my Converse high tops. "How's that fair?"

"Life ain't fair, sweetheart," he said with a chuckle. "You'll learn that soon enough."

Wasn't the first time I'd heard that but I decided to stop complaining about it. Wouldn't change anything. This was our new home and my mom insisted that I was going to love it here. She made it sound like one great big adventure. But she wasn't the one who had to leave her best friend behind. I spun the purple friendship bracelet on my wrist around and around, wondering what Darcy was doing right now. Probably swimming in the pool at our apartment complex. I sighed longingly, thinking about the summer we'd planned during countless sleepovers. The summer that had been ruined when my mom announced we were moving.

Derek wrapped his tattooed arm around my mom's shoulders and kissed the top of her head as the three of us walked up the road to the McCallister's with me huffing along beside them. For seven whole years, it was just me and Mom, and that was just the way I liked it. Until she married Derek two years ago.

Now that she had him, I felt like the third wheel.

Life ain't fair, sweetheart.

Ain't that the truth.

The McCallisters lived in a big stone farmhouse with a wraparound porch on a couple acres of land. We ate on the back porch overlooking a field and a barn with rolling hills in the distance that Patrick McCallister said belonged to a ranch. He was a general contractor and owned a construction company. Judging by the size of their house and all the land, I got the feeling they were a lot richer than us. Within five minutes, the adults were laughing and talking like old friends while I was stuck at the kids' table with the boys. All four of them.

Over burgers, corn on the cob, and potato salad, I learned quite a few things about the McCallister boys.

Number one: Jude McCallister was the most annoying boy in the world. A show-off and a know-it-all, he acted like he was the boss of us.

Number two: Jude's cousin Brody had the worst manners

of any boy I'd ever met. He chewed with his mouth open and ate his food so fast you'd think it was the first meal he'd had in years. When Jude reached for another ear of corn, Brody stabbed his hand with a fork.

Number three: Brody had just moved in with the family last month and hadn't even met his cousins before that. I didn't know the full story because when I asked where his mom was, Brody said, "It's none of your damn business."

Which had shocked me into silence. A nine-year-old wasn't supposed to cuss and I told him so.

"I'm not nine," he said around a mouthful of food. "I was ten on April tenth."

"And I'll be ten on August twentieth," Jude said. "When's your birthday?"

"May fifth," I said reluctantly. I'd just turned nine, which meant they were both older than me. Jude, the know-it-all, was quick to do the math.

"You're nine months younger than me and thirteen months younger than Brody."

Like that made them so superior. It didn't. They were both going into fourth grade, just like me.

Gideon was six and all he wanted to do was go inside and watch movies, but his parents said he wasn't allowed. So he was sulking. Jesse, the baby of the family, was four and all kinds of adorable. He was cute and funny and had us laughing at the goofy things he said.

Now we'd all finished eating—except for Brody who was on his third helping of strawberry shortcake—and the adults told us to go off and play. Brody wanted to ride the horses but we weren't allowed to do that without adult supervision so we had to come up with our own fun. Which was how we'd ended up in the field behind the house playing football.

"You won't be able to catch it," Jude the know-it-all said.

"Brody just caught it. I can too." I eyed Brody. He was a lot smaller than Jude and kind of scrawny. He had knobby knees and sharp elbows and dark blond hair. Even though he had the same last name, Brody didn't look like the rest of the blue-eyed, brown-haired McCallister boys.

Jude shook his head. "Brody's tough. He's used to catching a football. You're a girl. In a dress," he scoffed, tossing the ball high into the air and catching it in his hands.

"It'll knock you on your butt," Brody said, picking at a scab on his knee. Blood trickled down his calf. *Gross.*

"That's if you can even catch it," Jude said.

I wasn't looking forward to fourth grade at my new school if it meant I'd have to see them every day. Jude was stalling, acting like it was a big deal when it really wasn't. It was just a football, not a bomb.

"Just throw the stupid ball. What's the matter? You scared a girl will catch it?" I taunted.

Jude snorted like the very idea was ridiculous. "You're not gonna catch it."

I hated the way he sounded so sure, like he knew everything. "Just throw the stupid ball," I repeated, getting more annoyed by the minute.

"Okay. But just remember. You asked for it."

I rolled my eyes, kicked off my flip-flops and streaked across the field, putting distance between us just like Brody had. "That's far enough," he yelled.

I ignored him and kept on running. He wasn't the boss of me. When I was good and ready, I stopped running and spun around to face him. Whoa. I'd covered some distance. He was pretty far away. He probably couldn't even throw a football this far.

I smirked, imagining the ball falling short. That would teach him to gloat.

"It's gonna hurt," Gideon warned, not even lifting his head from the comic book he was reading. I didn't think he could read yet, so he was just looking at the pictures. His lips were purple from the grape popsicle in his hand, juice dripping down his arm.

"That's if she can catch it," Jude snickered.

I'd catch it if it killed me. Besides, I doubted he could throw a football as hard or as far as what they were claiming he could. The ball left his hand and spiraled through the air like a missile headed directly toward me. The sky was so blue and I was staring up at the sun which made it hard to see the ball. Jude's annoying voice was yelling something but I didn't hear his words. I was too focused on catching this ball. Concentrating like my life depended on it.

Next thing I knew, I was flat on my back, all the air knocked out of my lungs. There was an elephant sitting on my chest making it hard to breathe or even move.

"Is she dead?" That sounded like Jesse. A finger poked my ribs. I played possum.

"Jude killed Lila?" That would be Gideon. "We're gonna be in so much trouble."

"Let's get another popsicle."

"Yeah. This is boring."

A shadow blocked the sun on my face. I opened my eyes and blinked a few times. Blue eyes the color of the wildflowers in the field peered down at my face, too-long brown hair falling over his forehead, his brows drawn together. "Are you okay?" Jude asked, his voice softer than before, tinged with worry.

I wheezed, trying to catch my breath so I could speak. "I'm fine."

"You caught the ball."

My eyes widened in surprise. "I did?"

He nodded and gave me a smile that put dimples in his

cheeks. "Sure did," he said, and I heard the pride in his voice. My stupid heart inflated like a balloon. "Held on to it too."

I tilted my chin down to look at the football I was still clutching to my chest. Now it was my turn to gloat. "Well, of course I did. Told you I would."

"Your underwear says Saturday," Brody pointed out, and I couldn't decide who was more annoying. Him or Jude. "Today's Sunday."

"Pull down your dress," Jude said gruffly, smacking Brody upside the head. "Don't look at her underwear."

Brody shrugged. "Not my fault she's wearing a dress to play football. Not my fault she doesn't change her underwear."

I most certainly did change my underwear every day and opened my mouth to protest. But Brody had already darted away and I shut my mouth, not bothering to correct him.

I vowed to never ever wear a dress again. Ignoring Jude's outstretched hand, I got to my feet and smoothed my hand over the skirt of the stupid dress.

"There's no Sunday," I mumbled.

"What?" Jude asked.

"The underwear. There's only six in a pack. They skipped Sunday."

"That's messed up."

"Yeah." My cheeks flushed with heat. This was so embarrassing. I cast around for something to do, other than playing football. My hands still stung from catching the ball and my chest was still sore from the hit, but I wasn't about to admit that.

"You wanna race?" Last year, I was one of the fastest runners in the third grade, and I knew I could beat Jude and Brody, even in a dress and bare feet. That's how sure I was.

"What are we betting?" Brody asked.

"Question is, what are you willing to lose?" Jude smirked

at me.

So. Annoying.

"Since you're gonna lose, let's make it good." In my head, I was running through a list of my prized possessions, ready to offer one of them up to the winner. Since I would be the winner, I wouldn't have to part with anything.

Jude tilted his head and studied my face. "Truth or Dare?"

"What?"

"Pick one."

"Dare," I said quickly, without even stopping to think about it.

Jude and Brody chose dare too, big surprise. We lined up and Jude checked that the three of us were even.

Then he snapped his fingers like he'd just remembered something. "Oh hey, you're not scared of crocodiles, are you?" I searched his face for signs that he was joking but he looked dead serious.

"I'm not scared of anything," I said bravely. I was only scared of one thing. Thunderstorms. But I wasn't about to tell him that. "Why?" I asked, immediately suspicious. I looked around for a swamp or whatever it was that crocodiles lived in but I didn't see one.

"Just make sure you win and then you won't have to worry about it."

I followed his gaze to the fence at the bottom of the field. Our finish line. It was pretty far away but I wasn't too worried about the distance.

"Are you sure you wanna do this?" he asked, giving me an out.

I nodded. "I'm positive."

"You can have a head start, on account of being a girl and all," Jude offered.

"No, thank you." I crossed my arms over my chest and kept

my feet planted on the ground. "I'll stay right where I am."

"You're not wearing shoes," Jude said, pointing out the obvious.

"So what?"

"That doesn't make it a fair race."

"You're just scared of getting beat by a girl. I'm fine right here. Even without shoes."

Jude looked at me for a minute, then he toed off his sneakers and peeled off his socks so he was barefoot too. Brody did the same. I looked down at their bare feet. "Now it's fair," Jude said, and I was surprised he even cared about playing fair but the way he said it made me think it was important to him.

"On your marks, get set, go!"

I was off like a shot and I could see from the corner of my eye that I was in the lead. I ran faster than I'd ever run. My lungs were burning, legs and arms pumping. The rough grass and small rocks dug into the soles of my feet, but I ignored the pain and pushed myself to go faster. The fence was within my sights when Jude overtook me. He sprinted past me, running so fast I felt the breeze.

I lost to Jude by a mile and Brody by a neck. When I reached the boys, Jude was sitting on top of the fence, looking cool as you like. As if he'd been hanging out there for hours and had already gotten bored waiting. He wasn't even out of breath. Brody threw himself onto the ground and panted like a dog. My legs gave out and my knees hit the ground. I leaned over, my hands planted on the ground, and I tried to breathe.

I felt like I was going to throw up.

Mom always said it's important to be a gracious loser but it stung. Left a bitter taste in my mouth. And now I'd have to pay the price.

"So what's the dare?" I'd show them. I'd never back down from a dare.

CHAPTER TWO

Lila

JUDE JERKED HIS THUMB OVER HIS SHOULDER. I MOVED closer to the fence and stared at the creek just over the hill. My stomach dropped and I swallowed hard, trying to push down my nerves.

"Me and Brody will go with you." Brody bobbed his head in agreement and climbed the fence, jumping down on the other side and ambling down the hill to the creek.

"I'll show you what you need to do," Jude said, hopping down from the fence to stand beside me.

I looked over my shoulder to see if our parents were watching but couldn't see them from here.

"You need help climbing the fence?" he asked.

I shook my head. I didn't want him to think I was a big baby. With a shrug, Jude hopped the fence, making it look so easy. He peered at me through the slats from the other side. "Just crawl through here."

"But you didn't do it that way."

"Doesn't matter how you get to the other side, Rebel. Just as long as you get here."

"Rebel?"

"Yeah. Rebel." He scowled at me, and I bit the inside of my cheek to keep from smiling. I liked that nickname. Made me sound cool. "Everything I say, you're always saying the opposite. It's annoying."

"You're pretty annoying yourself, Mr. Know-It-All."

"What I know is that you're gonna get a splinter." He eyed my hands as I gripped the rough wood. Ignoring his warning, I pulled myself up and then I realized I had a problem. I was wearing a dress and I needed to straddle the top of the fence to get to the other side.

"Turn around," I ordered. "Don't watch."

Surprisingly, he did as I asked. Using all my strength, I tried to pull myself up and sling a leg over the top like he had. But it wasn't as easy as it looked. I was too small and my arms weren't strong enough.

"Oomph." The wood was digging into my stomach. Not sure how I managed to get in this position with my butt sticking up in the air and my body folded over the fence. All the blood rushed to my head and my feet were dangling down one side, my arms on the other. I reached with my fingers as if I could touch the ground from way up here.

I heard Jude laughing. "Rebel. That's no way to climb a fence. Touch your feet back down on the other side and crawl through like I said."

Did I listen? Of course not. Instead, I shimmied over the top, kicked up my legs and dove for the ground. Which left me sprawled at his feet with him laughing his head off and all the wind knocked out of me. He was laughing so hard he was doubled over.

When he finally stopped laughing, he helped me to my feet

and I looked down at the scrapes on my knees as I dusted off my hands, hiding the evidence by clasping them behind my back.

"How big's the splinter?"

"I didn't get one," I lied.

He just cocked a brow, not believing me for a minute.

"Are we allowed to be here? We're trespassing."

Jude grinned, mischief dancing in his blue eyes. "That's what makes it a dare."

"Oh. Right." I pushed away my fears and followed him down to the creek where Brody was skipping rocks, a tall piece of grass dangling from the corner of his mouth like a cigarette.

Jude unwound a rope that was wrapped around the thick tree branch and held it out to me. "You have to swing out as far as you can over the water and then come back. Easy."

"Watch out for the crocodiles," Brody said, eying the dish-water brown and bottle green water. The creek was wide, the water running between two dirt banks with scrubby grass and loose gravel.

"We had a lot of rain. Sometimes the creek gets flooded," Jude said, scratching his head as if he was puzzled about something. "Not sure how the crocodiles find their way here but they do."

There was a loud splash and I jumped back, my hand over my racing heart as Brody doubled over, laughing, a big rock in his hand about the size of the one he'd just thrown.

"Pretty sure it's feeding time. Snap snap," Jude said, moving his hand like it was the jaws of a crocodile.

I yanked the rope out of Jude's hand and kept telling myself that they were lying. Just trying to scare me. The rope was thick and knotted and I studied it in my hands, trying to figure out how to get from where I was, out over the water, and back again. I gulped, not wanting to let on that I was scared and had no idea how to do this.

"Here," Brody said, wrestling the rope out of my hands. "I'll show you how it's done."

"If you want." I shrugged like it was no big deal. But secretly, I was relieved. Happy that I wouldn't have to go first.

Brody backed up until the rope was stretched taut, his hands wrapped around one of the knots. Then he ran and just before he reached the water's edge, he pulled himself up and wrapped his legs around the rope, swinging wildly above the creek with one arm raised in the air as he whooped and hollered before he flew back and landed on his butt, sending up a cloud of dust that nearly choked me.

Jude took the rope from him and I watched him do the same thing Brody just had. But Jude's style was different. He flew like a cannonball, so fast he was a blur and then he was back by my side, both feet planted on the ground, offering me the rope. I got the feeling that there was nothing Jude couldn't do.

I'd later learn that he was one of those boys who was good at everything and made it all look easy. Even when it wasn't.

My hands were all sweaty and I wasn't sure what scared me most. The crocodiles or the fear of embarrassing myself by not being able to do it.

"Can you swim?" Jude asked, his voice low like he didn't want Brody to overhear.

I nodded and swallowed hard, tightening my grip on the rope.

"If you're scared, it's okay," Jude said quietly.

I turned my head to look at him, trying to decide if he was just being nice or if he was making fun of me. "I'm not scared."

"Okay." He crossed his arms over his chest and smirked. "Whatever you say."

I backed up so I had a good amount of space to take a running jump. If I fell I'd end up in the creek. In a dress. With hungry crocodiles ready to eat me. But I couldn't back down from a dare. Not now that the boys were watching and waiting to see what I'd do.

So I took a deep breath and I ran and then I was flying through the air. The rope slipped from my sweaty hands and I hit the water with a splash and went down, down, down. This creek was a lot deeper than I'd expected. My arms flailed as the current carried me away.

Gripped by panic, I forgot how to swim.

Arms wrapped around me and my head emerged from the water. I coughed, my nose burning from all the water I'd inhaled. My body thrashed, struggling to break free.

"Stop fighting me."

He was treading water, keeping us both afloat, hanging on to me for dear life. His grip was so crushing, it squeezed all the air out of my lungs and I was struggling to breathe.

"Let me go," I wheezed. "I can swim."

He loosened his hold but still didn't let go. "Sure could have fooled me. You looked like you were drowning."

"I wasn't drowning. Just let me go."

No sooner were my words out when Brody came flying through the air and landed in the water with a big splash that rained drops of water down on our heads.

Jude released me and I got my wits about me, treading water while the boys horsed around, dunking each other and laughing. I couldn't help it, I was laughing with them. All thoughts of hungry crocodiles flew right out of my head.

We took turns swinging from the rope and dropping into the creek. The more times I did it, the easier it was and the braver I got. Jude cautioned me to drop into the water at the deep part or I'd get hurt.

This time I heeded his advice.

"Jude McCallister! You have some explaining to do."

I pushed my wet hair off my forehead and looked over at Jude's mom, who was standing on the other side of the fence with her hands on her hips, a look on her face that said she clearly wasn't happy. My mom was right next to her and wore a similar expression.

We were in so much trouble.

———

The three of us trudged to the back porch to face our punishment, creek water dripping from our clothes. We were all questioned. I kept my lips sealed. I wasn't a tattletale so I didn't mention it was a dare. Brody didn't say a word, just stood there looking bored with the whole thing.

Jude stepped forward. "It was all my fault. My idea. I talked them into it." His voice never wavered, it was strong and sure, his shoulders squared as he stood tall in the face of the four adults who were acting as our judge and jury.

"It wasn't his fault," Brody said, stepping forward. "I dared him to do it."

"Nuh uh." Not wanting to be left out, I took my place right in the middle of the boys. "It was all my idea. I wanted to see what was on the other side of the fence." I jerked my thumbs at the boys. "They followed *me*."

Jude snorted. "I'm not a sheep, Rebel. I *lead*. I don't follow."

"I'm not a sheep either, and I wouldn't follow you anywhere."

"Pretty sure I was the first one down at the creek, waiting on you two," Brody chimed in.

We were so busy squabbling over who followed who that

we barely heard our punishment. The boys were given chores around the house and so was I. I didn't even care though. It was worth it.

After that first day, Jude, Brody, and I were thick as thieves. I spent more time at the McCallister's house than at my own. Kate stayed home with the kids and didn't work so she told my mom she'd be more than happy to watch me too.

That wouldn't be the last time we got into trouble either. We ran wild and we ran free, and by the end of the summer my skin was tanned to a nut brown and my arms and legs were covered in cuts and bruises.

One time, Brody found a wasp nest on the side of the barn and got the bright idea that he'd squirt it with the hose. Sure enough, he angered the wasps and they chased after us. All three of us got stung and my arms and back were covered in welts.

That was the summer I learned how to ride a horse. How to skip rocks in the creek that we weren't supposed to be anywhere near. How to climb a fence and swing from a rope. On the Fourth of July, we set off fireworks in the back yard and had a bonfire party. We stole a beer from the cooler and hid in the barn, passing it around and taking turns drinking. We'd only taken a few sips each when Jude's dad caught us and hauled us up to the porch. My mom gave us a lecture about underage drinking and how many brain cells we'd just killed off by drinking those few sips of beer and once again we got punished.

It seemed like we spent most of that summer shucking corn, peeling potatoes, and cleaning beans while we tuned out yet another lecture.

One night in August we talked our parents into letting us camp out in a tent in the McCallister's back yard. Brody slept with a flashlight and I got the feeling he was scared of the dark, even though he'd sooner cut off his arm than admit it. We got sick on junk food and stayed up late telling ghost stories, passing the flashlight around and holding it under our chins to make the stories that much scarier.

Halfway through the night, I woke up to the sound of thunder and ran to the house so fast, I surely would have beaten the boys if it had been a race. I dove under Jude's covers on the bottom bunk, my body trembling, and he and Brody joined me not long after. Jude slept with his feet by my head and I complained about how smelly they were. Which prompted him to move his feet right under my nose.

Secretly, I didn't care about his smelly feet. I was just glad he and Brody were sleeping in the same room with me. It made the storm less scary and they took my mind off it by telling pickle jokes that were so stupid all I could do was laugh.

I never wanted that summer to end.

But like all good things, it did.

CHAPTER THREE

Jude

"Summer's over. She'll be coming back soon," Brody said, trying to wrestle the suitcase out of my mom's hands. "I don't want her to get upset if I'm not ready to go."

"Brody," my mom said with a soft smile. "If your mom comes back, I'll help you pack—"

His hands balled into fists. "Not if. When. You said if."

"I'm sorry. You're right," she said. "When your mom comes back, we'll pack up your things. But until then, you and Jude are sharing a room and we don't need this suitcase in here, honey. How about we just move it into the attic until you need it?"

"Yeah, okay. I guess," he mumbled. "Can I ride Maple Sugar tomorrow?"

"Of course you can. You can ride her when you get home from school."

She tousled his hair like he was another one of her sons and not her nephew.

I didn't know where Brody was before he came to live with us but just after Memorial Day weekend, Dad went and picked him up and brought him back to our house. Nobody had heard from his mom since then. But he kept thinking she'd come back to pick him up. Every now and then he'd pack his suitcase so he'd be ready for her. I had a bad feeling that she wouldn't be coming back and I could tell by the look on Mom's face that she thought the same thing.

I'd overheard my parents talking about Dad's younger sister, Shelby. Dad said she'd gotten messed up with drugs when she was a teen and had always been trouble. He said that Brody was better off living with us and that he'd do everything in his power to make sure we could keep him here.

But I wasn't supposed to know any of that, and I wasn't about to tell Brody that I knew stuff that he didn't. He missed his mom, I guess, and I couldn't blame him for it. I'd miss my mom something fierce if she just up and left me like that. It wasn't something I could ever imagine my mom doing. She loved us too much and said so all the time.

My mom hugged us and kissed us goodnight and Brody climbed into the top bunk which used to be mine. Mom made me give it to him because she could tell he wanted it. Not gonna lie, that had pissed me off. We had a spare bedroom that he could have moved into but Mom thought he'd be scared to be on his own so now I had to share.

After making sure the nightlight was on for Brody who claimed he wasn't scared of the dark but really was, Mom turned off the lights. "Sweet dreams," she said like she always did before the door closed softly behind her.

"Jude?" Brody said a few minutes later.

"Yeah?"

"You don't think my mom's coming back, do ya?"

I tucked my arms under my head and stared up at the bunk

above me even though I couldn't see him. My mom and dad were always saying that you should never lie. And usually, I prided myself on telling the truth. But something about his tone of voice stopped me from being honest. "Sure I do. She just needed a vacation is all."

"Yeah," he said, letting out a breath as if he'd been holding it, waiting for my answer. "That's what I think too."

We were quiet for a few minutes and I was just drifting off to sleep when he said, "You think Lila's pretty?"

I snorted. "No."

It was the second time that night I'd lied and I had no idea why I'd done it. I just didn't want to admit it to Brody, I guess. Lila Turner was a whole lot prettier than Ashleigh Monroe, and all the boys thought Ashleigh was the prettiest girl in our class. But Lila was our friend, she was one of us, and she was mine to protect.

I'd decided from the day I met her, scared to death that she was going to drown in that creek, that I'd always be there to rescue her and keep her safe. So I didn't want to think about if she was pretty or not.

The next day we started school and Lila showed up at the bus stop in a dress. I could tell by the look on her face that she wasn't happy about wearing it. All summer, except for that first day, she'd been wearing shorts and T-shirts. So it was strange to see her in a light blue dress with white butterflies all over it. Her hair had been brushed which was a big change from the way it usually looked and she was wearing a headband to keep it off her face.

She looked like... a girl. I was staring, my mouth gaping open.

"Trying to catch flies?" she asked.

My mouth snapped shut but I was still staring. No idea why.

"Stop looking at me," she snapped, elbowing me in the ribs. The girl had the sharpest elbows. "I look stupid," she muttered.

I guess she was waiting for me to say she didn't but the school bus pulled to a stop in front of us and I didn't say a word. I climbed onto the bus in front of Brody who tried to shove me out of the way to get on first. Not happening.

"Jude!" Reese called, his hands cupping his mouth as he shouted to me. "Saved you a seat."

I took my seat next to Reese and pretended I didn't notice that Lila sat at the front by herself. Brody sprawled out on a seat in the back, his feet hanging in the aisle which earned him a smackdown from a few of the older boys. He didn't back down, so I waded in to help him out and got told off by the bus driver for causing trouble. That was just the beginning of the day, and things went downhill from there, thanks to Brody.

By lunchtime, all the boys in the fourth grade were talking about Lila's days of the week underwear and saying she never changed them. I tackled Brody in the playground and he was kicking and punching, laughing like a hyena. He punched me in the face and I punched him back. We both got sent to the principal's office.

That night we got lectured at the dinner table.

"Fighting is not the way to solve problems," my mom said, looking to my dad for backup. "Isn't that right, Patrick?"

My dad looked up from his bowl of chili. "That all depends on the reason for fighting."

I smirked. Brody grinned. He was an idiot. He had a black eye and a split lip but he didn't seem to care. Brody loved to fight and in the short time he'd been here, he'd already picked plenty of fights with me. Now he grabbed another piece of cornbread, slathered it with butter and stuffed half of it in his mouth.

"Patrick. You're supposed to be backing me up here."

"I seem to remember a time when I got in a fight over you at that bar—"

"Patrick," my mom hissed, giving him the eye. "We can't allow them to fight."

My dad nodded and murmured that she was right before he focused on Brody who was always watching my parents like they were an alien species. He didn't know who his dad was and hadn't grown up with one so I guess this was all new to him.

"Brody. No more spreading gossip, you hear? In this house, we treat the ladies with respect. And that goes for anything you say and do outside this house. Understood?" my dad questioned, his voice stern.

"Yes, sir," Brody said, a surly expression on his face as he side-eyed me.

"And Jude..." My dad looked at my mom's face and repeated the words she always said. "Use your words next time, son."

I tried to keep the grin off my face. "Okay."

"What's for dessert?" Gideon asked. "Can I watch TV now?" That was all my brother cared about. Dessert and TV.

"Can I have ice cream?" Jesse asked, crawling into Mom's lap and smacking his hands against her cheeks before he kissed her. "You're so pretty, Mommy."

"Such a charmer."

"Does that mean I get ice cream?"

She laughed. "Yes, you two can have ice cream."

"What about me?" Brody and I said in unison.

My mom's lips pressed into a flat line. She wasn't happy with us and I knew we hadn't heard the end of it yet. "You two can clear the table and stack the dishwasher."

I jostled Brody out of the way and stacked the plates before he could get to them. I ignored my mom cautioning me to make two trips. I could handle it.

Brody scowled as he collected the silverware and stabbed me with a fork on our way to the sink, a teetering pile of dishes in my hands. When I didn't react, he stabbed me again, harder this time. I gritted my teeth as a plate crashed to the terracotta tiles and shattered at my feet.

"Boys!" my dad shouted, coming to stand in front of us. He took the pile of dishes out of my hands and set them in the sink, then crossed his arms over his wide chest and gave us both *the look*. The one that said we were testing his patience and if we didn't stop, there'd be hell to pay.

"What did your mother say?" he asked me.

"To make two trips," I muttered.

"No allowance for either of you this month. Money doesn't grow on trees and these plates cost money."

"Does that mean we don't have to do our chores? Since we're not getting allowance?" Brody asked, his voice hopeful. Like I said, he was an idiot. My dad was a former Marine and when he laid down the law, you didn't argue with him unless you wanted double the punishment.

Sure enough, my dad said, "It means you'll be doing double the chores you usually do. Now do as your mother asked. And try not to break anything."

I exhaled loudly as my dad strode away then narrowed my gaze on Brody. He tossed the silverware in the sink, the stainless-steel clattering against the enamel and we trudged back to the farmhouse table to collect the glasses. The rest of the family was on the back porch eating ice cream sandwiches. My favorite.

"You know why I did it?" Brody asked as I rinsed a plate and handed it to him, not fully trusting that he would get the job done correctly.

I shrugged like I didn't care, not wanting to let on that I was curious.

"Just to prove my point."

"What was your point?"

"You *like* Lila."

He made it sound like I was in love with Lila or something. I scoffed. "No, I don't."

"Sure you don't." He snickered. "That's why you punched me in the face. You wanna hear the funny part?"

"No."

"She thinks it was you." He cracked up over that one. Unfortunately, it was true. Brody had started the rumor and I'd gotten the blame for it.

Nobody seemed to care that *she* had come after *me* and kicked me in the shin. Just because she was a girl, she got away with it. How was that fair? When I'd laughed in her face, it had only made her angrier.

Her little hands balled into fists. "I'm going to punch you, Jude McCallister."

"Punch me. I won't even feel it, Minnie Mouse."

She'd punched me and I laughed even harder. She was so funny when she got all fired up and sometimes I just pushed her buttons to see what she'd do. Getting Lila all riled up was one of my favorite forms of entertainment. She never failed to deliver.

That night after Brody fell asleep, I hid all the nightlights in the attic where he'd never venture. I didn't know why he was such a big baby about the dark.

In the middle of the night, he woke up screaming and crying and covered in sweat. Dad was the only one who could calm him down. I'd never seen my dad so angry with me as he was that night and I didn't even understand why. All I'd done was hide the nightlights. It was payback for what Brody had done at school, not to mention making me drop a plate. Seemed only fair.

Dad told me that Brody had been through a lot of bad stuff in his life and I needed to keep that in mind before pulling pranks. Nobody bothered telling me what kind of bad stuff he'd been through. I was just expected to understand something that made no sense. But after that, I made sure we always had a nightlight in our room.

I guess you could say that Brody was like a brother to me. Annoying as hell, but he was family. Whenever he got in fights at school, which was often, I was right there by his side. I always had his back, no questions asked. And whenever I needed to work on my passing skills, he spent hours in the back yard with me, going long to catch a pass without once complaining about it.

And as for Lila... it turned out that Brody was right. I did have a crush on her. But it took me years to admit it or even realize why I acted the way I did around her. In my defense, I was just trying to look out for her like I would for any friend.

The fact that she happened to be a girl made everything a whole lot more complicated.

CHAPTER FOUR

Lila

"Jude McCallister, you are the bane of my existence," I shouted, slipping into the barn and sliding the heavy wood door shut before he could reach me. Leaning my back against the door, I panted from the exertion of running. The only reason I'd beaten him was because he had a limp after getting hit with a foul ball. Served him right. He'd been too busy causing trouble for me to keep his eyes on the game. It wasn't like him to get so distracted but when he took the pitcher's mound he redeemed himself.

My gaze settled on Brody. "How come you weren't at the game?"

"Had to clean out the barn." He was chewing on a long piece of straw as he saddled up Whiskey Jack, the quarter horse he practiced barrel racing on.

"Are you okay?" I asked.

He shrugged. In Brody speak that was a no. A few weeks

ago, his mom had come back and caused a scene. Now she was fighting for custody. "What are you going to do?"

Another shrug of the shoulders followed my question. "Uncle Patrick told me to speak my own truth. But I don't want to get her into trouble, you know?"

"Yeah," I said, although I didn't know. Not really. "Do you want to... I mean, do you want to live with your mom?"

He shook his head and my relief was instant. I didn't want him to go, I didn't want him to leave us. "I don't want to go back to the way things were. But I want her to be okay."

I nodded, not exactly sure what to say about that. Patrick said his sister was an unfit mother who didn't deserve her son. I agreed. From what I'd overheard, she'd been a bad mother. She had locked Brody in a closet and left him there for days with no food or anything. He'd ended up in foster care and thankfully the social worker tracked down Patrick who went to get him. We didn't know what all Shelby did to Brody but I guessed none of it was good because my mom sat me down and lectured me about drugs and how bad they were.

"What's Jude done now?" he asked, making it clear he didn't want to talk about his mom or the custody battle.

"Doesn't matter." It was nothing compared to what Brody was going through and it was good to remind myself that people had bigger problems than I did. I pushed off from the door and walked over to the stalls, sizing up the black and white Appaloosa, Raven. A wild horse if there ever was one. Brody had begged the McCallisters to buy this horse from the ranch owner and as payment he was doing extra chores.

"Mind if I ride with you?" I didn't usually ask for permission, but ever since Shelby turned up, he'd been wanting more time alone and I didn't want to intrude.

His eyes scanned my tank top, shorts, and Converse. "You need to put on some jeans."

"I'll be fine." It wasn't the first time I'd ridden in shorts.

"You can ride with me. I set up the barrels."

I smiled at the invitation. "Yeah, I saw."

He narrowed his eyes on me as I stroked Raven's head. The horse's eyes flared and he nickered, tossing his mane and showing his teeth. I dropped my hand to my side and took a step back. "Not that one, Lila."

"I'm a good rider. I can handle him."

"He gets mean and ornery. I'm the only one who can ride him."

Normally, I'd argue if it weren't for the fact that it was true. Kate called Brody a horse whisperer and said he had a gift.

"How'd you learn to be so good with horses?" Nobody could handle a horse like Brody could. At fourteen, he wasn't that same scrawny kid I'd first met either. He was still lean and wiry but he had muscles now. And it didn't go unnoticed by the girls at school either. Girls drooled over the McCallister boys. It annoyed me to no end.

"Dunno. Just comes naturally, I guess. Like Jude and ball sports."

"Yeah." I smiled, forgetting that just minutes ago I was calling Jude the bane of my existence. He pushed my buttons like nobody else did. But man oh man, did he ever have a gift when it came to football. He played football, basketball, and baseball and he was good at all of them. Not just good. *Really good.*

Even though he was only thirteen, two months shy of fourteen, everyone was already saying he was destined to go all the way to the pros. When I asked him if playing in the NFL was his dream, he said no. He wanted to enlist in the Marines just like his dad had done. It was all he ever talked about. Sometimes I wished he had a different dream. I didn't want to think about him fighting in a war. But I didn't tell him that. It would make it look like I cared about what he did. And I didn't. Not even a little bit.

While I adjusted the stirrups for my shorter legs, Brody led Raven out of the stall and talked to him quietly as he put the bridle on him. Raven's ears pricked up as if he was listening to every word.

When I turned around to get the crate and drag it over so I could climb onto Whiskey Jack's back, I slammed into Jude. He was still wearing his blue and white baseball uniform with clay and dust stains on the knees. Strands of chestnut brown hair poked through the snapback of his backward ball cap. He smelled like boy sweat and Double Mint gum. "What are you doing, sneaking up on me like that?"

"I'll give you a leg up."

I narrowed my eyes on him. "Last time you gave me a leg up you tossed me right over the horse's back."

He and Brody snort-laughed. I rolled my eyes and tried to shove him out of my way but he blocked my path and wouldn't budge an inch. He'd gotten so much taller than me that I had to look up to see his face. I planted my hands on my hips and raised my brows. "Do you mind?"

"Come on, Rebel. I promise I'll play nice."

"Why should I believe you?"

"Have I ever lied to you?"

I snorted. "Only about a million times. You lied about the crocodiles in the creek. And I'm sure if I gave it some thought, I'd come up with plenty of other times you lied."

"Well, I'm not lying now." He gave me a smile that I knew was genuine. I knew all his smiles. This one was real and it showed off his straight white teeth. I ran my tongue over the clear braces on my teeth, counting down the months until they came off.

"Why are you being so nice all of the sudden? Is your guilty conscience troubling you?"

"I've got nothing to feel guilty about."

"You told Kyle Matthews I had head lice." I shoved his chest. It was like a wall. When had he gotten so big and strong? "Another lie."

He shrugged and chewed on the gum in his mouth. "I thought I saw something moving in your hair." He held up both hands like he was innocent. "An honest mistake."

An honest mistake, my ass. "He won't get anywhere near me now."

"Good. I don't like the guy. Didn't like the way he was looking at you either."

Brody snickered. Jude and I ignored him. "How was he looking at me?"

"Don't worry about it." He crossed his arms over his chest. "I'll take care of Kyle Matthews."

"I don't want you to *take care* of him. You can't keep messing with every boy that so much as looks at me."

"Can't I?" he asked, with that smug look on his face that made me want to punch him. Too bad my mom made me promise I'd never punch him again.

I glared at him. "No. You can't. You need to keep your nose out of my business."

"Well, you see, I can't do that because you keep making stupid choices."

My jaw dropped. "I don't make stupid choices."

"Talking to Kyle Matthews is a prime example."

"He seems nice enough," I said, not sure why I was forcing the point. I didn't give two hoots about Kyle Matthews but it annoyed me that Jude thought he could dictate who I could and couldn't hang out with.

"Oh wait. Do you like Kyle Matthews? Do you have a *crush*

on Kyle Matthews?"

"So what if I do?" I said, goading him just to see what he'd do. It was my favorite sport and he always played along.

"Well, let me tell you something. Even if you had bugs in your hair, I wouldn't even care."

"You wouldn't care if I had head lice?"

"Nope."

"What am I supposed to say about that?"

"Thank you would be a good start."

"I'm supposed to thank you?"

"Yeah." He gave me a look like Duh.

"Why?" I asked, confused.

"Because Rebel... if a guy is worth it..." He leaned in close, close enough that I could smell his minty breath, and wrapped a lock of my hair around his fingers, tugging it gently. It was playful but it felt like something else, especially with the way he was looking at me, his blue eyes darker, focused on my mouth. I wet my lips with my tongue, noticing the way his eyes followed and his breathing got shallow.

"If he *really* likes you, he won't even care if he has to shave his head because of you."

"That's um..." I shook my head. Sometimes he made absolutely no sense. Was he saying he liked me? As in *liked* me? "You're ridiculous, you know that?"

"Why don't you two just kiss and get it over with?" Brody said over his shoulder.

My eyes widened in horror. "I wouldn't kiss him if he was the last boy on earth."

"Sure you wouldn't." Brody rolled his eyes then walked his horse out of the barn.

I watched him a minute to make sure he was okay on that mean, ornery horse. It was a bit skittish but instead of reining him in, Brody gave him the lead, leaning over his neck and talking in his ear, his voice too low to hear, as if he really was a horse whisperer and that horse understood his every word. Not only that, but Brody was riding him bareback. Raven wasn't so crazy about getting saddled up.

When I was sure that Brody had it under control, I returned my gaze to Jude. He gave me a slow, lazy grin that made my stomach flip-flop.

It was only in that moment that I realized that my best friend slash bane of my existence was beautiful with his suntanned skin that made his blue eyes bluer and his dimpled smile and square jawline stand out.

Now I understood why girls fell all over themselves trying to get his attention.

I hated it. I hated the way they talked about him and ogled him and passed him notes at school. The way Ashleigh Monroe flipped her blonde hair over her shoulder and licked her pink-glossed lips whenever he looked her way.

How could I have been so blind not to notice what was right in front of me? I just stood there, staring at him like it was the first time I'd ever seen him.

"Now who's lying?" he said before he strode out of the barn having gotten in the last word. He *always* got in the last word but this time all I could do was stare at the door he'd just walked out of while my pulse raced and my heart pounded so hard I could feel it in my throat.

What had just happened?

CHAPTER FIVE

Lila

"Just have a good time," I heard Kate telling my mom on the phone as Jude dealt our cards. She had it on speaker so we could hear my mom from our spot on the back porch. She and Derek had gone away for the weekend to celebrate their sixth wedding anniversary. "You know we love having Lila. She's like one of the family."

It warmed me from the inside to hear those words. I liked thinking that I was one of the family, like I was a part of something bigger, and had a special place in the McCallister's lives. It didn't make me feel so lonely being an only child. Not when I had four boys who were like brothers to me.

Kate came out to the back porch and handed me the phone. I took it from her with a smile. My hands were sticky from the watermelon we'd just eaten so I set the phone on the picnic table. "Hey Mom."

"Hey sweetie. Everything okay?"

"Yep. I'm playing poker with Jude and Brody."

"Stakes are high," Jude said, watching my face as I checked my cards. Ugh. It was the worst hand ever. I laid it on the picnic table, face down. I was going to lose. *Again.* "Lila's about to lose her nuts."

"Too bad she doesn't have any. Now me... I've got nuts to spare," Brody said, making himself and Jude crack up and me roll my eyes at their stupid, dirty jokes.

We were using monkey nuts for currency. Last week, we tried using M&M's but we kept eating them and didn't have anything to bet with after the second hand.

"That'll be enough from you boys. Mind your manners," Kate said, shaking her head as she walked back inside the house. She was always telling them to mind their manners. Not that they listened.

"We're playing for peanuts," I told my mom before she got the wrong idea. Nobody needed to hear another one of her talks on puberty. Lately, she'd taken it upon herself to give us sex education talks which were beyond embarrassing. "Are you having fun?"

"We are," she said, her voice hesitant. "Derek and I were talking about his teenage years."

Oh no. I'd heard a few stories about Derek's teenage years and his early twenties. He'd been a biker and a bad boy with no real direction in life until he'd met *an angel who had helped him turn his life around.* Those were his words.

"When I get home, we need to discuss safe sex practices."

My cheeks flushed and I squeezed my eyes shut, not wanting to see the look on Brody and Jude's faces. One of the pitfalls of having a mother in the medical profession meant that no topic was off-limits.

"Mom, you're on speaker," I hissed, jabbing a finger at the button that took her off it. Jude grabbed the phone from my hand and held it up to his ear, smirking at me. "Hey Caroline. It's Jude. Mind if I sit in on that discussion?"

Brody hooted with laughter. "Me too. I could use some tips."

My cheeks were flaming. Could my mom get any more embarrassing?

Jude handed the phone back to me as Jesse and Gideon ran up to the porch, slip-sliding on the tiled floor, leaving puddles in their wake from the sprinklers they'd been running through. Thankfully, they'd missed the reason Jude and Brody were still laughing.

"Bye Mom. We're in the middle of a card game so yeah, gotta run."

"Okay, honey. Be good and we'll see you tomorrow. Love you."

"Love you too," I mumbled, cutting the call and walking the phone back into the house. I set it in the cradle on the kitchen counter and turned as Jude came inside. I watched him reach for a mason jar from a high shelf in the oak cupboard. The hem of his green T-shirt rode up and exposed a strip of suntanned skin.

"Hey," I said, tucking my hair behind my ears, trying to act cool and casual.

He grinned. "Looking forward to the sex talk with your mom. Not sure how she's going to top the teenage hormones talk though. How's puberty been treating you, Rebel?"

His eyes lowered to my boobs. Which weren't really boobs at all. I still looked like a ten-year-old boy and hadn't even gotten my period yet. Unlike Ashleigh Monroe who got hers last year and had boobs.

"Better than it's treating you. At least I don't smell bad."

"I don't smell bad," he said, offended. "Come on. Smell me, Rebel."

"I don't want to smell you."

"Yeah, you do." He moved closer, crowding me. My back hit the edge of the counter, his arms caging me in so I had no choice but to smell him. He didn't smell bad. He smelled like freshly cut grass and the woodsy scented shower gel he used. He smelled like summertime and boy. Not bad at all. But it made me a little dizzy being so close to him, and I didn't like that or understand why it was happening.

This was Jude, the most annoying boy in the world. So why did it suddenly feel like I couldn't breathe with him standing so close to me?

"Rebel."

"Yeah?" My voice sounded all breathy.

"Unless you want to lose your nuts, you're gonna have to work on that poker face of yours." He scrunched up his whole face, a pathetic attempt to mimic my expression.

Like I said. *Annoying*.

I ducked under his arm and returned to the porch, his laughter following me as I threw myself into a wicker chair and tipped my face up to catch the breeze from the ceiling fans. It was baking hot out here in the August heat.

Brody was eating sunflower seeds and spitting the shells over the railing. He had that sullen, moody look on his face that he got sometimes.

It had been two weeks since Patrick got custody of Brody and he hadn't said one single word about it. I wanted to ask how he was doing, and what he thought about it, but I wasn't sure how to do that.

Wrapping a string from my cut-offs around my finger, I pulled it so tight it cut off the circulation as my eyes bored a hole in Jude's back. He was sitting on the top porch step, poking holes in the lid of a mason jar with the Swiss Army knife he'd gotten for his birthday last week.

"Here you go," Jude said, handing the jar to Jesse. "Your very own firefly catcher."

"Cool." Jesse grinned at his big brother, a look of adoration on his face like Jude had just handed him the sun, the moon and all the stars in the sky. At eight, Jesse was still the most adorable and lovable McCallister. "Thanks, Jude."

"Anytime."

"You gotta set them free though," Brody said, his voice brusque. "After you're done looking at them, you need to open the lid and let them fly away."

"Why?" Gideon asked, pointing his remote at the Formula One car he got for his tenth birthday. It raced across the porch and he hit stop before it flew down the steps.

"Because no living creature should ever be put in a cage or a jar. It ain't right. How would you like it?"

"That would have to be a really big jar," Jesse said, snorting laughter and slapping his thigh like that was hilarious.

"You keep your horses in a stall." Gideon pointed out as his remote-control race car crashed into the railing, its wheels spinning.

"Yeah, and I don't like that either. Someday I'm gonna have wild horses and a lot of land for them to roam free."

Gideon wandered into the house, the screen door slamming behind him which had Kate hollering from inside the house, "How many times have I told you not to slam that screen door? Sometimes I feel like I'm talking to a brick wall."

Clutching the jar like a football, Jesse jumped off the top railing of the back porch and landed on his butt.

"How many times have I told you not to jump off the top railing," Kate said from the other side of the screen door. "Use the stairs."

Jesse grinned and waved at his mom then raced across the back yard in search of lightning bugs even though it was too early for them to come out. The sun was just setting over the field, the late summer sky streaked pink and orange. The air was already starting to smell different. Like freshly sharpened pencils and apples from the orchard. We only had one more week of freedom before school started and I was already feeling sad to see it end.

Summertime meant long, hot days and all-day baseball games. Staying up way past our bedtime. Jumping off the rocks into the cool, bottle green water at the swimming hole. It was the three months of the year when I had my boys more or less to myself. And that was the way I liked it.

"Keep an eye on Jesse," Kate told us. "We're about to start a movie. It'll be a miracle if we get past the opening credits before your father falls asleep."

"If you picked an action movie, I'd stay awake," Patrick grumbled.

Kate laughed and their voices got muffled as they headed into the family room to watch a movie.

I side-eyed Brody, thinking about what he'd said about the wild horses. "Sounds like a good dream," I said. "The wild horses and the land."

Brody cracked the sunflower seeds between his teeth and said nothing. Some days it was a chore, trying to navigate all these 'boy hormones.'

"What's yours?" Jude asked me. "You know mine. You know Brody's. What's your dream?"

My dream was that everything would stay exactly as it was. I didn't want anything to change. I didn't want *us* to change. But I couldn't say that. It sounded stupid. Besides, that wasn't a dream. It was a wish. And we were already changing. I saw it in the way Jude sometimes looked at Ashleigh. I saw it in Brody's swagger whenever girls were watching him, and the way he'd wink at them as he passed by, causing them to blush and giggle.

"I don't know. I guess I want to do something with nature. Like... a landscaper or something."

"That's cool," Jude said, and for a change, he wasn't even teasing me about anything.

"Why do you want to be a Marine so much?"

"I want to fight for our country. I want to do my part to protect our freedom." When he talked like this, he sounded older than thirteen, like he had the future all figured out.

"I want to feel like I made a difference," he said quietly.

"You just want to fight," Brody said, throwing down his cards face up. I glanced at his hand. It was a full house. "Stop acting like you know anything about war or what it would be like to have a gun pointed at you. You know nothing about the real world because you live in this perfect little world and that's all you've ever known."

Having said his piece, Brody jumped off the porch and stalked away. I stared at his back, dumbfounded, and tried to figure out what had just happened and why Jude's words had made him so angry.

Jude strode after him and grabbed his shoulder, turning him around to face him. I moved to the porch steps and sat on the top one so I could watch.

"What the hell was that about?"

Brody shook his head. "Just speaking my truth, like your dad said I should."

"Your truth? Have you been to war?"

"There are all kinds of wars, Jude, and you don't know shit about any of that."

"Why don't you tell me since you seem to be some kind of expert."

They faced off, their shoulders squared, their eyes narrowed like they were about to rip each other's heads off.

"Why are you coming down so hard on Jude?" I asked Brody. "It's not his fault..."

Neither of them looked at me or even paid attention to my words so I didn't bother finishing my sentence. They were angry about something I wasn't privy to. It wasn't the first time I'd seen them disagree. They fought a lot in private but at school, and in public, they were always on the same team and they always stood up for each other.

As Jude always said, they were family and family always came first. It was the McCallister motto.

"I thought you wanted to stay with us," Jude said, his voice low and angry. I got the feeling that the thought of Brody not wanting to stay cut Jude to the core. He was hurt but trying not to let it show. That's what boys did. They locked down their emotions. Patrick was always telling them to 'tough it out.' "I thought you liked living here."

"Let me put it this way. I had two choices. Shitty. Or shittier."

"What's so shitty about living with us?"

"I'm the stray dog your family took in because my mom is too fucked up to stay clean and my dad..." Brody hung his head and left his sentence hanging.

"What about your dad? I thought you didn't know him."

"I know enough."

Brody turned to go. Jude grabbed his arm to stop him. "What do you know?"

"That's the thing about speaking your truth. You get to hear everyone else's truth and it ain't always pretty."

"Where's your dad?" Jude asked again, not about to let this go.

"Prison. Locked up in a cell. *For life.* Happy now?"

Oh, my God. My eyes widened. His dad was in prison? For

life? That had to mean he'd done something really, really bad. Like kill someone.

Stunned by Brody's answer, Jude released his cousin's arm. For once, Jude had nothing to say. He rubbed the back of his neck, a look on his face like he was sorry but didn't know how to say it or what to do to make this better.

"Yeah," Brody said, shoving Jude's chest. "So think about that when you're off fighting a war for our *freedom*."

With those final words, Brody turned and strode away.

"Brody." I went to chase after him but Jude grabbed my arm and held me back.

"Let him go. He just needs some time on his own. He'll be back." Jude sounded so confident that I wanted to believe him.

I watched Brody cross the field and then he leaped the fence and I lost sight of him. Maybe Jude was right. Maybe Brody needed space. But what if he needed to know we were there for him?

About an hour after he left, Kate came to the screen door and asked us to get Jesse to come inside for his bedtime. We found him next to the barn, playing with a tiny green lizard he'd found.

"Set it free," Jude said. "Put it in the grass."

"But the lawnmower might get him."

So we took the small lizard down to the fence and set it free in the tall grass on the other side of it.

"Have a good life, Bug Eyes," Jesse said, waving goodbye before he turned and ran up to the house.

Jude and I looked at each other, both of us thinking the same thing. Without saying a word, we climbed the fence and went in search of Brody.

It was dusk, the fireflies were out now, cicadas chirping loudly as we followed the creek. I looked out over the rolling hills and trees on the other side. Brody could be anywhere. "Maybe he's on the ranch somewhere."

I stumbled on the uneven ground, and Jude caught me by the elbow before my knees hit the ground then took my hand in his bigger one and guided me along the creek bank. I looked down at our joined hands. It was the first time we'd held hands like this. It felt a lot nicer than I would have thought.

Being with Jude always made me feel safe. Like he could protect me from anything. He made me feel braver and I liked that.

"I know where he is," Jude said.

We walked for another ten minutes before I caught a glimpse of Brody through the trees, sitting on top of a rust-red cargo container.

My body flooded with relief that he was okay but at the same time, jealousy reared its ugly head. The boys had obviously known about this place but had kept it a secret from me. I yanked my hand out of Jude's.

"You never told me about this place."

"Well, now you know," he said, his eyes searching my face.

I remembered what he'd said about my poker face and averted my gaze so he couldn't see the hurt. "Whatever. It's not like you guys have to tell me every little thing." Hurt and annoyed, I strode ahead.

"Hey." He tugged my elbow and spun me around to face him.

"What?" I folded my arms over my chest and tapped my foot on the ground.

"It's kind of Brody's secret spot. He likes to come down here and just chill."

"Oh. Well... I guess..." I chewed on my lip, mulling it over. "He has a lot to think about."

Jude nodded. "Yeah. It's been hard for him."

I looked over my shoulder at Brody then back at Jude. "Do you think he wants us here?"

"I don't know if he *wants* us to be here, but I think he *needs* us to be here."

"What's the difference?"

He gave it a moment's thought before answering. "Sometimes we think we want one thing but what we need is something completely different."

Sometimes Jude was smart. Smarter than you'd expect a just-turned-fourteen-year-old annoying boy to be. And sometimes he wasn't annoying at all. Not even a little bit.

He jerked his chin. "Come on."

We closed the distance between ourselves and Brody. He saw us but didn't tell us to get lost. He didn't say a single word.

Jude was standing behind me as I tried to figure out how to scale the side and get to the top where Brody was. Climbing still wasn't my strong suit. Before I'd worked it out, Jude's hands wrapped around my waist and I was lifted off the ground like I was featherlight.

"Grab the rail."

I reached for the railing and grabbed hold with both hands as he gave me another boost. Gripping the corrugated metal with the toes of my sneakers, I pushed myself up and over while Jude scaled the wall of metal with no problem and sat on the edge, with his legs dangling over the side.

I took my place between the two boys and the three of us sat in silence. It wasn't the bad kind of silence. It was comfortable. Like we didn't even need words.

The sky grew dark and we lay on our backs under a blanket of stars. Jude knew all about the stars and constellations and on clear nights like this, he could trace them with his finger. Aurora Australis, he said, and I took his word for it because astronomy was one of his things.

One time I asked him why he was so obsessed with the stars. He said it was cool that they were thousands of light years away but we could see them with the naked eye. And that our planet was nothing more than a speck of dust to whoever was watching us from the stars. I told him that made me feel small and worthless. He said it was the opposite, that we were a part of something bigger.

And I guess that's how Jude looked at life, like we were all here for a purpose and it was our responsibility to do our part. He truly believed that by fighting for our country, he'd be doing something for the greater good, and that he could protect the people he loved.

"Did you know the stars shine brighter here?" Jude said. "On account of not having light pollution. In the cities, they're harder to see."

"It's true," Brody agreed. "I could never see the stars where I used to live."

I thought about a sky with no stars and couldn't imagine anything sadder. Where we lived, the sky was bigger. The days were glaringly bright and the night sky was inky blue, so dark you could see millions of stars.

"Sucks to be you," Jude teased, an attempt to lighten the mood.

"Yeah," Brody said with a laugh, tucking his arms under his head. "Guess it's not so shitty here after all."

"Guess not. But sometimes it smells like shit. Did you know that cow manure is worse for air pollution than cars? And when they fart, they emit enough gas to fuel a rocket."

We all laughed and everything was back to the way it was supposed to be. But when your two best friends were boys, there were times when it got complicated. I wanted to be one of them, but at the same time, I wanted them to see that I was a girl. I didn't like it when they looked at other girls. I especially didn't like it when Jude looked at other girls.

But as it turned out, that would be the least of my problems.

As Brody had said, there were all different kinds of wars, and there were some wars that no matter how hard you fought, you couldn't win.

That was the year everything changed.

That was the year when one word put more fear into me than I ever thought a word was capable of doing.

Cancer.

"We're going to beat it," Derek said, his voice ringing with conviction.

My mom just smiled as he pulled her into his arms and kissed her forehead. She reached for me and pulled me into their circle so I wasn't on the outside looking in.

I wish Derek had cancer instead of my mom. I squeezed my eyes shut and pressed my lips together, not giving a voice to my horrible thoughts.

Nevertheless, I couldn't stop myself from thinking it and the years marched on and my mom was losing the battle, I wished it with all my heart.

But some wishes don't come true.

CHAPTER SIX

Jude

THE GARDEN WAS LILA'S IDEA, A SURPRISE FOR HER MOM who had been talking about it since they'd moved into the house but had never gotten around to doing it. It was the first day of our spring break, and I'd gotten here early this morning, right after Derek took her mom to chemo. Ever since I'd arrived, Lila had been bossing me around, barking out orders like a drill sergeant. Now she flew out of the house and ran across the yard, flapping her arms like an angry bird. A laugh burst out of me. I couldn't help it. She looked so funny when she was mad.

After she wrestled the shovel out of my hands, I crossed my arms over my chest, feeling the heat of her glare.

"This is all wrong," she wailed.

She looked like she was on the verge of tears. I was on the verge of telling her to dig up her own damn flower beds. But I wouldn't. This was for Caroline but mostly, it was for Lila. She needed this and I wanted to be the one to give it to her. Even if it meant sweating my balls off in the April sunshine and being shouted at by Minnie Mouse.

I took a few deep breaths so I didn't lose my shit. "You said you wanted flower beds. I'm digging flower beds." I looked down at all the soil I'd dug up. The flower bed was a long rectangle, exactly as she'd specified and as far as I could tell, it was damn near perfect. "What's wrong with it?"

"I can't see it from my parents' bedroom window. That's what's wrong with it." Her shoulders sagged, all the fight drained out of her. "My mom won't be able to see the flowers."

I didn't bother pointing out that her mom would have a clear view from the kitchen window or that she'd be able to see them while she sat on the back deck and drank her coffee like she did every morning. I kept my mouth shut and wiped the sweat off my forehead with the back of my arm as Lila paced across the yard and stopped about ten feet from where I'd been digging. "It needs to be here."

Would have helped a hell of a lot if she'd decided that before I'd dug an entire flower bed. When I'd arrived, this was where she said the flower bed needed to go. While I'd been digging up the yard and removing the rocks from the soil, she'd been using a trowel to make holes for the plants and flowers. So we'd wasted hours of work on something that she now deemed all wrong.

"You sure?" I asked before I dug up more of her lawn. Wasn't so sure how happy Derek would be when he saw what I'd done to his grass but unlike my dad, Derek wasn't concerned with having straight lines when he mowed it. I'd never noticed that before but today it had really bugged me when I saw his uneven lines like he didn't really give a shit how it looked. I was tempted to take over the lawn mowing myself so Caroline would have straight lines to look at. It was the same with a lot of things at their house.

I'd already made a mental list of things I would fix. WD40 for the squeaky door hinges. The deck needed to be re-stained, and the paint on the railings was flaking. The Weber grill on the deck was rusted and I suspected he didn't even keep it covered. I wasn't a big fan of Derek's and I didn't think my parents were either but none of us would ever say a word. We all loved Caroline, and Derek was Lila's stepdad. So even though he had shifty eyes and I didn't trust him, I needed to keep my opinions to myself.

"I'm sure. That's where it needs to go," Lila said, referring to the place where the flower bed needed to be.

I took off my ball cap, ran my hand through my sweaty hair and put it on backward. Her lips curved into a smile that caught me off guard. It wasn't the first time I'd noticed how pretty my best friend was or how green her eyes were in the sun or how full and kissable her lips looked. But there was something about her smile at this moment that made my chest tight. "What's the smile for?"

"You," she said softly, laughing a little, her eyes lowering to her dirty white Chucks. "Thanks for doing this. And thanks for putting up with me. I know..." She lifted her eyes to mine and took a deep breath. "I guess I've been kind of bitchy lately."

I shrugged one shoulder, mesmerized by the way she tugged her lower lip between her straight white teeth. No more braces. No more skinny little girl in a yellow sundress. She was still small and petite, short enough that she had to tip up her chin to look me in the eye. I'd shot up to five-eleven while she was still five foot nothing. But she wasn't a little kid anymore. Her wavy brown hair was in a messy bun and the strands of hair that had escaped it framed her perfect face. She never wore makeup like the other girls in our class did and I was happy about it. She didn't need it.

Lila had five freckles on her nose. I knew because I'd counted. "It's understandable. I'd be much worse."

"What would you do? If you were me?"

"I'd plant a garden and make sure it was perfect."

She looked at a spot over my shoulder and blinked back her tears. Lila didn't cry. Ever. "What else would you do?"

I wasn't sure exactly what she was asking but I tried to put myself in her shoes, and I gave it a minute's thought before answering. "Guess I'd just try to be there for her by doing stuff I know she'd like. Stuff that's important to her so that she knew I loved her."

Lila reached up with her hand and touched my cheek. "You have dirt on your face," she said by way of explanation, her eyes locked on mine as she rubbed her thumb across my cheekbone.

She moved closer, just a step but she was close enough that I could smell the scent of her shampoo. Spring rain and honey-suckle. Inhaling deeply, I filled my lungs with the scent of Lila. It made my head swim and the ground tilt underneath me.

I could kiss her. I could steal her first kiss right now. Just dip my head and claim her lips. Would they be soft? Would she taste like the Dr. Pepper she'd been drinking earlier? Would she kiss me back?

I wanted to be her first kiss. I wanted to be her first everything.

"Hey, hey, hey," Reese said, rounding the side of the house with our other friend, Tyler in tow. Lila jumped back, snatching her hand away as if she'd been doing something illegal then walked away from me.

Normally, I would laugh but I was too busy watching her as she drew a chalk line in the grass for where she wanted the flower bed to go. From here, I had a perfect view of her ass in those little denim cut-offs she always wore.

Tyler gave me a slug on the shoulder, snapping me out of it. "Enjoying the view?"

"Shut up," I growled, hoping she hadn't heard him.

"So this is why you told us to come later," Reese said, wagging his brows. They were a paler shade of red than his hair.

Now I regretted having called in reinforcements as they greeted Lila who acted like they were sent from heaven above.

"Thanks, you guys, I really appreciate it," she gushed.

Tone it down, Lila. They haven't even done anything helpful yet.

"Anytime." Reese rubbed his hands together and looked over at me, ready to be put to work. "What do you need me to do?"

I tossed him a shovel. "Start digging."

A few minutes later, Brody showed up with a wheelbarrow filled with bags of wood chips and mulch that I suspected he'd stolen from our shed. My dad was anal about his garden and kept an inventory of his tools and supplies but since it was for Caroline, I knew he wouldn't mind. Right behind him was Ashleigh and Megan. The two blondes were carrying Tupperware containers and bags of junk food. Supposedly, they were Lila's friends but I didn't trust them. They weren't true friends. They hung out with Lila to get closer to me, but if I told her that, she'd just get pissed and call me cocky.

"I made those cupcakes you like," Ashleigh said, her smile aimed at me. She was wearing a short T-shirt dress that clung to every curve of her body. I couldn't help but notice her tits because they were big and right there in my face. Every guy in our class ogled them and Reese and Tyler were practically salivating.

"Devil's food," Ashleigh said, referring to the cupcakes that she always brought to my baseball games.

Lila glanced over at me, her eyes narrowing to slits. "Figures you'd like devil's food," she muttered.

I laughed. Ashleigh looked from me to Lila, not sure what was so funny or if I was laughing at her expense. I wasn't. I liked it that Lila got jealous. Not that she'd ever admit it.

"Mom's here," Jesse bellowed as he ran along the side of the house.

"You need to unload the plants and flowers," Gideon said, stressing the 'you' and pulling a face at the mere thought of touching anything green. It was like Gideon was allergic to the outdoors. He hated nature. Hated living in a small town. Even claimed to hate Texas. In short, Gideon hated everything about his life and was constantly talking about getting away and living in a big city.

Mom said he was going through a 'phase' but as far as I could tell this phase had lasted the entire eleven years he'd been on the planet. Dude was cold. If he had any emotions, he never let them show.

His hair was darker than mine, almost black and his skin pale like it had never seen the sun. Dude looked like a Greek statue carved from marble. It was hard to tell if a beating heart lived under that cool exterior.

"Your brother looks like a sparkly vampire from the book I'm reading," Megan said, staring at Gideon.

"Oh my god, he totally does," Ashleigh said. "He's kind of hot."

"He's *eleven*," Lila said, a look of disgust on her face that I completely agreed with. "So that's just creepy."

Not to mention he was ice, not fire.

Ashleigh just shrugged and twirled her hair around her finger and I knew she wouldn't lift a finger to help today. She could hang out with Gideon. As predicted, Gideon threw himself into a lounge chair on the deck and played on his

Nintendo while Jesse performed 'death-defying acts' on Lila's trampoline.

"Watch this. I can do a double flip," Jesse said to Ashleigh and Megan, his captive audience who kept saying how cute he was. Which meant he'd knock himself out to put on a show for them.

Reese and Tyler trailed me and Brody to my dad's truck parked in the driveway. McCallister & Sons Construction was painted on the door. It always made me laugh. None of my dad's sons worked for him, although he always said that one day the business would be ours.

By the time we unloaded the truck, the back yard was filled with potted plants and flowers that my mom deemed perfect for the subtropical climate. She claimed they would be low maintenance but beautiful to look at.

Lila hugged my mom and thanked her profusely, so touched by the gesture that she might have been crying. I couldn't tell. My mom eyed me over Lila's shoulder and gave me a sad smile. I averted my gaze and got back to work where at least it felt like I was doing some good rather than sitting around feeling helpless that I didn't have a cure for cancer.

Unlike my mom, I didn't believe in praying for miracles. But I'd never say those words to my mom or Lila or anyone else. I just planted a garden with my friends in the hope that it would put a smile on Lila's face.

Lila threw herself into the job, planting the flowers like it was her sole mission in life to make this garden spectacular.

Later, when Caroline got home, she sat on the back deck with my mom and they talked quietly while we worked. Even though she looked tired, Caroline had a smile on her face, so I knew it was worth it.

Spring faded into summer and before I knew it, it was August, and only two days until my fifteenth birthday.

Yesterday, we'd started pre-season football training and Lila had shocked me by announcing that she'd tried out for the cheering squad and had gotten onto it. It was the first I'd heard that she had any interest in being a cheerleader, but I suspected it had something to do with her mom, who had been a cheer-leader back in high school.

"She let me get to second base on the first night," Reese said as we stashed our bikes behind a tree at the swimming hole. "On the last night of our vacation, she gave me a blowie. Thought I'd died and gone to Heaven."

"No shit. Did she swallow?" Tyler asked.

"Nah. I jizzed all over her stomach though. Got to finger-bang her too." He pointed a finger gun and swiveled his thumb. "It's all about dat thumb."

"What do you do with the thumb?" Tyler asked, his thumb poised over the keypad of his phone. Wouldn't be surprised if he was taking notes.

"You stroke with it and it sets off an explosion bigger than the Fourth of July fireworks. She said she was seeing stars." He walked toward the water with a little more swagger than usual. Tyler's older brother had a stash of porn that he kept under his bed and one night back in June we had a porn marathon. I suspected that was the source of Reese's information rather than actual experience.

"I call bullshit," I said. I'd never even seen him talk to a girl, let alone find one who would let him do everything he claimed to have done. He stripped off his T-shirt, exposing his pale, freckled chest. Reese was smaller than me and Tyler but he was fast which made him a good running back.

"Call it what you want but it happened."

"It's kind of suspicious that shit always happens when

you're out of town and there are no witnesses to back up your story," Tyler said, roughing his hand over his spiky black hair. "How about you show us how it's done?"

Reese's face visibly paled and his Adam's apple bobbed when he swallowed.

"Sounds fair. Pick a girl. Any girl," I said, feeling generous. Let's face it, dude had no game. "And make your move."

"I don't need to prove anything."

I shrugged. "Okay. Then my verdict stands. Your story was bullshit."

"It only happened in your overactive imagination," Tyler said.

"It happened, I'm telling you. Okay. Say I go along with this. When I succeed, you two boneheads need to do the same," he said, challenging me and Tyler.

"Nah. We weren't the ones bragging about getting a BJ." I tossed my T-shirt on top of my towel on a flat rock and chugged the rest of the water in my bottle, wiping my mouth with the back of my hand. It had to be a hundred degrees today. The cool water beckoned but now I had to see this through before I could go for a swim.

"Or using our trigger finger." Tyler shot a finger gun and we laughed. Reese's face turned so red it matched his hair and for a minute I felt almost bad about teasing him. That quickly changed.

"Okay. You're on." He smirked. "I've got just the girl in mind." I followed his gaze to a group of girls at the picnic table in a grove of trees dancing to a Black Eyed Peas song. My eyes zeroed in on Lila just like they always did whenever she was in my vicinity. She was wearing a green striped bikini that showed off... well, everything. Her taut stomach, suntanned legs, and boobs that hadn't been there last summer. I watched, mesmerized as her hips swiveled to the beat and her long, wavy hair flew out around her.

I'd never seen her dance before, and now I couldn't drag my eyes away. Before, I'd thought of her as girl-next-door pretty. But now what I saw was something different. Girl-next-door hot.

Watching her dance like this confirmed something I'd suspected for a while now. She'd become more to me than just my childhood friend.

I grabbed Reese by the shoulder as he lurched forward, ready to make his move. "Lila is off-limits. Any other girl but her."

"Pretty sure your words were 'Pick a girl. Any girl.' Are you backing down now, McCallister?" He puffed out his scrawny chest. "Scared she'll see that I'm the guy for her?"

"You're not the guy for her." I widened my stance and crossed my arms over my sweaty chest, confident that *I* was the guy for her. Not Reese. Not Tyler. Not that douchebag Kyle who was always sniffing around like a dog.

"Guess we'll see about that. Hey Brody," Reese yelled as my cousin climbed out of the bed of a truck I didn't recognize and ambled down the hill toward us. Even in boardshorts and a T-shirt, he walked, looked and acted like a cowboy. He'd gotten involved in the rodeo and this summer he'd been competing in bronc riding. Which just went to show how crazy he was.

He ran his fingers through his longish dirty-blond hair and stopped in front of us, squinting against the sun. "What's up?"

"Reese here claims he got a BJ from some chick on his family vacation," Tyler said.

Brody snorted. "Sounds like a tall tale to me. You've got no game, dude."

My thoughts exactly. Sometimes Brody and I were on the same page.

"I'm about to prove you all wrong. Watch me make my moves on Lila Turner." He cracked his knuckles and rolled out his shoulders, psyching himself up for what I was sure would be a massive defeat.

Brody's eyebrows shot up to his hairline. He gave me an inquiring look that asked if I was cool with this. Pretty sure he could tell that I wasn't.

When it came to Lila, we were in complete agreement. Nobody got to mess with her. Not any of the guys or the girls. We made sure of it. She was ours to protect.

"He's going to get shot down," Brody said. "Might as well enjoy the show."

"Too bad he missed the memo that she belongs to Jude."

"Not sure how he could have. Jude might as well have announced it over the school loudspeaker, it was that loud and clear."

Couldn't deny it. It was the damn truth. But Reese wasn't overly bright. Nice guy, a few screws loose but he wasn't a douchebag. Which was the only reason I stood back and watched from the sidelines, eyes narrowed, arms crossed over my chest, as Reese moved in on Lila.

"Oh, look at that folks, he's going in. They're looking this way," Tyler said, narrating the play-by-play as if I couldn't see it with my own two eyes.

Reese cupped his hand and whispered something in Lila's ear. She glanced my way and smiled. I knew that smile. It was the devious smile she used when she was about to do something to piss me off. She leaned in and whispered something in Reese's ear that put a smile on his face. He took the bottle of suntan lotion from her hand and she turned her back to him, sliding her hair over one shoulder to expose her suntanned skin. Only a string tied at her neck and her back held the bikini top in place and she was offering it up to Reese Madigan on a silver platter. Like her skin was his to touch.

Oh hell no. Not happening.

Before I could stop myself, I was striding toward them, ready to put an end to this little game they were playing.

"Hey Jude." Ashleigh stepped in front of me, blocking my path to Lila. She flipped her blonde hair over her shoulder and smiled at me. "You looked really good out there today. At practice," she added.

"Thanks."

"So I'm throwing a pool party next Saturday. You should come. Bring whoever."

"Yeah, maybe," I said, distracted by Lila whose back was being slathered with suntan lotion compliments of Reese who was doing a shitty job of it, might I add.

But his hands were touching Lila. I was having trouble breathing.

"I've invited the girls from the squad. We'll just hang out and chill by the pool." Giving me another smile, she swept her tongue over her pink glossy lips and placed the palm of her hand on my bare chest, looking up at me from under her long lashes. "It'll be fun. Even more fun if you're there."

I looked straight into Lila's eyes as she watched us over her shoulder. She averted her gaze quickly but not before I saw her face fall. Disappointment? Hurt?

Meanwhile, she was sitting on top of the picnic table next to Reese, talking now. They were shoulder to shoulder, thighs touching, and he was listening to every word that came out of her mouth like she was the most fascinating creature on the planet.

No part of her should be touching any part of him.

There were a few different ways to put the brakes on this,

but I knew Lila well enough to know that if I shut it down she'd push back so I opted for a different tactic.

Improvise. Adapt. Overcome.

"Hey Lila," I said casually.

"Yeah?" Her brows raised, a look of practiced boredom on her face to hide the curiosity. I knew this girl so well, I could practically read her mind.

"You up for a race?"

"What kind of race?"

I jerked my chin toward the water. "First one to the waterfall wins."

"What are you willing to lose?"

How laughable that she actually thought she could beat me. Gotta love that kind of optimism. "The *winner* gets a slave for the day."

"So when you *lose*, you'll be at my beck and call for an entire day."

I bit the inside of my cheek to keep from laughing as she jumped off the picnic table faster than you could say Rebel, earning me a scowl from Reese. Hey, I'd warned him. Fair is fair. "You're on. Get ready to eat my dust."

Lila never could resist a dare or a chance to compete with me. Even though she never won, she still believed that one day she would.

She sprinted toward the water, and I gave her a head start before I chased after her just like I'd been doing since we were nine years old.

As usual, she lost and I was waiting for her when she reached the waterfall.

She pushed her wet hair off her face with both hands. "You did that on purpose," she accused, green eyes narrowed on me, water spiking her long lashes. The sunlight picked up the flecks of gold in her eyes. She was beautiful. Full of fire and sass. And I didn't want anyone else to have her.

I wanted to kiss her. Lick the beads of water off her face. Suck on her plump bottom lip.

"Did what?" I played dumb. We were treading water, circling each other, her long dark hair slicked back from her summer sun-kissed face and I was loving the idea that she'd be my slave for a day. My imagination was running wild with the possibilities of having Lila at my beck and call.

"Challenged me to a race, knowing I can never resist."

"You can never resist me?" My leg brushed hers under the water and I wondered if she felt it too, that current of electricity that zinged through my body.

She rolled her eyes. "That's not what I said."

"It's what you meant." I spread my arms. "I'm irresistible."

Which was the only invitation she needed to launch herself out of the water and dunk me. I wrapped my hands around her waist, lifted her clear out of the water and tossed her in the air like she weighed nothing. The look on her face was priceless when she emerged from the water, spluttering.

I laughed. She was so cute. It only took her a few seconds to pounce on me again. "You just never learn, do you?"

I tossed her. She flew through the air. And we played this dunking game a few more times until we were both laughing so hard we couldn't breathe. I didn't even know what we were laughing about and I doubted that she did either. It didn't matter.

She was my favorite person. Even when she got bitchy. Even when she shot me dagger eyes when I talked to other girls. *Especially* then.

She was the only girl who made me angry. Frustrated. Jealous. The only one who made me want to protect her from all the bad things in the world. The only girl I wanted to spend my time with. The only girl I wanted to talk about everything and nothing with.

Late at night, we texted. Sometimes we'd text for hours. Sometimes we just talked about stupid stuff like which super-power we'd choose or how wrong it was to mix Skittles and M&M's together like Brody did.

It didn't matter what we talked about. It didn't matter if it was two in the morning and I had to get up early for football practice. I wanted to be her two in the morning person. The one who was there for her no matter what.

Lila was mine. End of story.

CHAPTER SEVEN

Lila

I RIPPED OUT THE WEEDS IN THE FLOWER BED LIKE THEY
were responsible for the cancer that was killing my mom. It had
only been one year since we'd planted this garden but everything had changed. For the worse.

I looked over my shoulder as Jude did another lap with the
lawnmower. Our back yard wasn't that big so he used the
mower from the shed instead of his dad's riding mower. The
muscles in his arms flexed and I took a moment to appreciate
his muscular calves and the broadness of his shoulders while
his back was turned to me.

The ends of his brown hair curled a little where it hit the
collar of his sweat-stained white T-shirt. Kate was always on
him to get a haircut but I liked it when his hair was a little bit
too long.

He'd made it his mission in life to give my mom straight
lines on the back lawn. Derek had just laughed, and said,
"Whatever floats your boat."

Now he came out onto the back deck and called my name. "I'm going out. Just checked the fridge. Looks like you're all set for dinner."

Jude cut the lawnmower engine and stared at him with a stony expression. Our refrigerator was filled with food in Tupperware containers that Kate brought over. Her way of trying to help out in any way she could. When my mom was too weak to do the cooking, cleaning and laundry, Kate and my mom's friends from the hospital took care of it. Until I told them I could take care of everything.

And I could. I wanted to do it for my mom. I wanted to be there for her in any way I could. I didn't want her to have to worry about the house being clean or the laundry or anything that drained what little energy she had left.

"Yeah, sure, whatever," I told Derek, my expression neutral so she couldn't see how much I hated him.

"Where you headed, Derek?" Jude asked, as if he had the right to question an adult.

Derek stroked his black beard, leveling Jude with a look. Jude called him shifty and I think it was his beady eyes that made him look like that. My mom was so smart with such a huge heart. How could she have fallen for a man who had only been there for her when times were good? That wasn't love. He vowed to be there for her in good times and bad, in sickness and health.

"I'm going out," he said. "Catching up with some friends." That was code for: I'm going to a bar where I'll pick up a bimbo and give her a ride on my Harley because I'm the asshole who bought a motorcycle when my wife got sick with cancer. "Is that okay with you?"

Jude looked up at my mom's closed bedroom window—she'd gone upstairs to take a nap earlier—and just shook his head in disgust, muttering something under his breath. The lawnmower rumbled to life again and he continued mowing our back lawn.

After he mowed the lawn and returned the mower to the shed, I helped him gather the grass clippings and bag them which he said was part of the job.

When we finished, the back door slid open and my mom stepped onto the deck. Her hair was starting to grow back but it was fine, baby hair like peach fuzz on her scalp that made her eyes look enormous. Now they were covered in oversized sunglasses to fight the glare of the spring sunshine.

Jude was by her side before I could even reach the deck. He wrapped his arm around her waist and helped her into a cushioned lawn chair. He looked so much bigger and stronger than her. The picture of health. While she was disappearing a little more each day.

"Thank you, sweetie."

Whenever Jude was around he insisted on helping her. It was kind of sweet.

"Sorry, I'm all sweaty." He gave his armpits a sniff test and pulled a face that made me snort-laugh.

"You stink. I can smell you from here," I joked, darting out of his reach when he tried to pull me into a hug and smother me with boy sweat.

My mom was laughing at our antics.

"The back yard looks beautiful," she said. That put a smile on Jude's face. He was proud of his handiwork and I knew this was his way of trying to do something to make my mom happy. He was always showing up with his toolbox to fix whatever was broken in our house. So handy.

"I need to get this smelly boy some water."

"Hurry up," he said, panting like a dog. "I'm dying of thirst out here."

"Drama queen."

I went inside and grabbed the pitcher of cold water from the fridge that I'd garnished with lemon slices the way Kate always did because I knew that was how Jude liked it. I carried the pitcher and three glasses out to the deck and set them on the teak table between my mom's chair and mine.

After I poured us all a glass of water, I sat on the other lounger while Jude leaned against the railing facing us. A few weeks ago, he had sanded down the railings and repainted them. They looked fresh and clean now, the paint glossy and white. My mom had insisted on paying him but he refused to take the money.

"I love you, baby," my mom told me. She said it often now, as if she wanted to make sure I knew it.

"Love you too, Mom."

She smiled at me then turned that smile on Jude. Lately, she'd been giving us 'talks' as if they could ever prepare us—*me* —for losing her. But nothing could prepare me for that.

"Every time I look at you kids, you look more grown-up. Slow down. I don't want you growing up so fast."

She blinked away her tears and Jude and I pretended not to notice.

"So... have you two kissed yet?"

Water sprayed from Jude's mouth and he coughed, pounding his fist against his chest. My cheeks flamed. My mom just laughed. Sometimes she was so embarrassing.

What was I going to do without her?

"So, you and Jude are just friends, right?" Ashleigh asked me, twisting a lock of blonde hair around her finger as she leaned against the locker next to mine.

I stuffed the books I'd need for this weekend's homework

into my backpack and slammed my locker shut. The sound rang out in the almost empty hallway, everyone in a rush to get out of the school and start the weekend.

My stomach hurt. I felt like screaming.

"I mean, I've been crushing on him for ages. And you guys are like, just friends on account of your moms being friends and being neighbors..." Ashleigh said, making me feel all stabby. Like the fact that our moms were friends was the only reason Jude would hang out with me.

Granted, he was Mr. Popularity. Ever since we started high school this year, I'd been noticing how people acted around him. Jude was an athlete, he had a lot of friends and made them easily, and everyone liked him. Even the teachers liked Jude and cut him more slack than they did for the other freshmen.

Jude was cool without even trying, and he had that charisma that made people gravitate to him. Like they were ready and willing to follow him anywhere. But unlike some of the guys on the team, he never abused his power or his popularity and I think that's what made him so special. Like, he *could* act like an asshole and treat other kids like crap and still get away with it but he never stooped to that level of leadership.

"Are you cool with it?" she prompted. "If I go for him?"

This was my chance to say no. She was asking for my permission. Jude and I were so much more than just friends. And yet... we were *just friends*.

"Yeah, sure. Whatever. Jude and I are just friends." She gave me a big Colgate smile like she'd just won a prize. I wanted to punch myself in the face but instead of shutting up I kept talking. "Why wouldn't I be okay with it?"

"Okay with what, Rebel?" His voice was low in my ear. He was standing right behind me, having crept up behind me like some kind of Ninja.

I spun around to face him. "You need to stop sneaking up on me."

His eyes narrowed to slits. "What are you okay with?"

"Nothing." I shook my head. "It's... just... nothing."

"Hey. I'll see you guys tomorrow." Ashleigh gave us a little wave and an extra special smile just for Jude. Tomorrow she was having another pool party. I had no intention of going.

"You wanna tell me what that was about?" Jude grabbed my backpack and slung it over his shoulder. He was already carrying his own backpack and his heavy sports bag.

"You don't have to carry my bag." I tried to wrestle it away from him but he swatted my hand away and strode down the hallway like he owned the place.

"It weighs more than you do." He slowed his pace to accommodate my shorter legs so I didn't have to jog to keep up with him. "What do you have in here anyway? Bricks?"

"Just textbooks."

"There's only a few more weeks of school left."

"I know. But we still have homework." I'd been working hard, determined to get straight A's to make my mom proud. We'd been talking about college and I told her I wanted to go to University of Texas in Austin just like she had.

Behind me I heard some guys snickering and talking shit. Without having to look, I recognized one of the voices as Kyle Matthews. Pretty sure he was still annoyed with me for shooting him down. Back in October, he invited me to the homecoming dance. Actually, it wasn't even me who shot him down. It was Jude and Brody who were pissed that anyone would actually dare to ask me out.

Ugh, boys. Sometimes Jude and Brody treated me like a little sister. Was that how Jude saw me too?

Tuning out Kyle's lewd comments, I sped up. My stomach

really hurt now and all I could think about was how I'd given Ashleigh permission to go for Jude. Why hadn't I told her... told her what, exactly?

Not about to let the insults go, Jude turned around and walked backward, shooting a glare in Kyle's direction. "You got a problem, asshole?"

"No. But your little girlfriend does. First head lice and now this. Damn. She's a real catch, McCallister. Bet she gets bitchy when she's on the rag, doesn't she?"

Oh my God. *What?*

Jude slammed Kyle against a locker. I didn't hang out long enough to see what was happening. I sprinted to the nearest girls' bathroom and locked myself in a stall. It was a massacre. Blood everywhere.

Why had I worn a white denim mini today? *Why?* The floral top I was wearing was blousy, the elastic skimming the bottom of my waistband. It did nothing to cover the damage. Kate took me shopping last weekend and bought me this outfit for my fifteenth birthday. At the time, I thought it was so cute. An attempt to move on from my usual jeans, T-shirts and Converse.

How many girls didn't get their period until they were fifteen? Me. That's who.

I wanted my mom.

Please get better, Mom. I need you. But she wasn't going to get better. The cancer had metastasized, and there was nothing the doctors could do now.

And I was locked in a toilet stall without my bag. Not that anything in my bag could have helped this situation. I tried to do what I could with wads of toilet paper but it didn't help. I flushed the toilet and leaned against the door, staring at the ballet flats on my feet as if they had a solution for my problem.

I couldn't go out there until I was sure everyone was gone. I was going to miss the school bus. Then I'd have to walk home. Why me?

Tears of frustration blurred my vision but I blinked them back. Tears couldn't help me now.

"Hey. Are you okay?" a girl's voice on the other side of the toilet stall asked.

I didn't recognize the voice but if I spoke up she might be able to help. I took a few deep breaths, trying to find my voice. "Um. I just got my period..." I sighed, my shoulders slumping.

"Oh man, that sucks. You need something? I think I have a tampon. Hang on. Got it."

I looked down as a tampon appeared under the door and I took it from the girl's fingers. "Thanks. I..." I stared at the tampon in my hand then ripped off the paper wrapper and stared at it some more. Of all the things my mom had taught me, inserting a tampon wasn't one of them. God, this was so embarrassing.

"I've never used one before." I cringed.

"Okay. It's cool. I'll talk you through it. My older sister helped me. It's kind of weird the first time but you'll get used to it."

She talked me through it and if she hadn't been so cool about it, I would have been more humiliated than I already was. Not to mention that it felt weird and I wasn't sure how I'd ever get used to it. "I'm Christy, by the way. Christy Rivera."

I put a face to the name. Long, sleek dark hair, big dark eyes, funky clothes. She hung out with the artsy kids. "Lila Turner."

"We have a couple classes together."

"Lila?"

My eyes widened at the sound of Jude's voice.

"Oh hey. She's in here. You're Jude, right?"

"Yeah. Christy, right?"

"That's me."

"You okay, Rebel?" he asked, his booming voice echoing off the tiles.

"You shouldn't be in here," I hissed.

"Come out," he said, sounding unfazed by the fact that he was in the girls' bathroom and that I was locked in a stall with blood on my white denim skirt.

"I..." I exhaled loudly. "I can't."

"Hang on." His sports bag dropped to the floor with a thud and under the door I saw him rummaging around in it. A few seconds later, he tossed his faded blue hoodie over the door.

"Hey. I'll see you guys later," Christy called. "Have a good weekend."

"Thanks. For everything."

"No problem." I heard the door close behind her and then it was just me and Jude. Alone. In the girls' bathroom.

"Jude... you should go. You're going to miss the bus."

"Already did. I called my mom to pick us up. Just put my hoodie on. It'll be long enough to cover..." He cleared his throat. "... you know."

My cheeks flamed with mortification.

Every other girl I knew had already gotten their period. I'd gotten mine at the end of my freshman year in the middle of the school hallway. And who had seen it? Besides the guys who had laughed at me, of course. Jude. I wished the ground would swallow me up. No such luck. I was still standing on terra firma.

"Thanks," I mumbled when I'd pulled on his oversized hoodie that reached mid-thigh and covered the evidence. The sweatshirt smelled like the fabric softener his mom used and his woodsy shower gel and peppermint gum. It smelled like him.

I stepped out of the stall, unable to look at him and washed my hands at the sink. "This is so gross."

"Nah. It's no biggie."

Easy for him to say. I side-eyed him as we exited the bathroom. He didn't look grossed out. He gave me a little smile and didn't even tease me.

"I'll um... wash the hoodie and get it back to you tomorrow."

"Keep it," he said, holding the front door open for me.

I stepped outside and took a deep breath of hot, muggy air. "But it's your favorite."

"That's why I want you to keep it." He came to stand next to me and dropped all three bags onto the sidewalk while we waited for his mom to arrive.

"But why?" I asked, not understanding his logic.

"Because, Lila... if a guy won't give you his favorite hoodie, he's not worth your time."

I turned my head to look at his face. He smiled, his dimples on full display. My breath caught in my throat as he tugged on one of the strings of his hoodie. "I like you in my hoodie. Looks better on you."

It didn't. It looked good on him. Just like the basketball shorts and T-shirt he was wearing. Everything looked good on Jude because he was like a young god with tousled chestnut hair and full lips and piercing blue eyes that could read my face and see straight into my soul.

For a few long moments, we just stood there staring at each other and I wanted to take back all the stupid things I'd said to Ashleigh.

Because Jude was mine and I didn't want anyone else to have him.

Because that was the day I fell in love with Jude McCallister. Six days after my fifteenth birthday. The first time I got my period. The day he strode into the girls' bathroom and came to my rescue by giving me his hoodie.

"My mom's here," he said, breaking the spell I was under.

CHAPTER EIGHT

Lila

ANOTHER YEAR HAD COME AND GONE AND I'D CELEBRATED my sixteenth birthday by blowing out all the candles on a cake that Kate baked for me and wishing for a miracle. I bargained and bartered and pleaded with a God who wasn't listening.

If I get straight A's on my report card, my mom will get better.

If I clean the house from top to bottom, my mom will get better.

If I push myself to run one extra mile, my mom will get better.

Spoiler Alert: She wasn't going to get better.

Now I was huddled on the sofa, trying to get lost in a stupid vampire book while a summer storm raged outside. Stupid Bella. She was so freaking annoying that I was tempted to throw the book across the room but I kept reading to see if she'd develop a spine. Edward didn't even sound that great. What was all the fuss about?

I kept hoping he'd bite her and turn her into a vampire. Then maybe we'd have a fun story.

"Hey Rebel. You good?" Jude asked when I answered my phone.

"Checking up on me?" I asked. "Or do you just want to get in on the pizza I'm ordering?"

"Pizza. Why didn't you say so?"

A bolt of lightning lit up the sky outside my living room window and I squeaked, hoping I couldn't be overheard over the rumbling thunder.

"I'll be right over."

Guess he'd heard that squeak.

I hadn't seen much of him this summer but I'd heard plenty of things I'd rather not know. He was working construction for his dad and I spent most of my time at home, tending to the garden and doing the laundry and cleaning and cooking. Not that my mom ate much these days.

Minutes later, I opened the front door to Jude who stepped inside, all six foot two inches of lean muscle and broad shoulders and it was weird to think that I'd known him when he was just a little kid with a mischievous grin and shaggy hair falling into his eyes. He shook his head, spraying droplets of rainwater all over me. I jumped back, laughing.

"You're like a wet dog. Smell like one too."

No, he didn't. He smelled good. Like fresh rain and the shower gel he used and the Double Mint gum he always chewed.

"Where's the pizza?"

"I haven't called in the order yet."

He strode into the kitchen and picked up the phone to call in the order. I let him take charge because outside a summer storm was raging. After he placed an order for a pepperoni pizza he helped himself to a clean towel from the downstairs bathroom and ran it over his hair before he hung it on the hook on the back of the door.

"Let's see what's on TV." He nudged me forward, his hand on my lower back.

"We can't watch TV..." I jumped at a clap of thunder and covered my face with my hands. "I'm such a wimp."

"Nah. Everyone's scared of something."

I plopped down on the sofa next to him and he leaned forward, grabbing the remote from the coffee table and pointing it at the TV.

"What are you scared of?" I asked.

"Nothing."

I swatted his arm and he laughed as he flipped through the channels. He stopped at a baseball game and I tried to wrestle the remote out of his hand but he held it up in the air out of my reach.

"My house. My choice," I said, trying to grab the remote.

"Fight me for it," he said, holding it out of my reach. I jumped onto the sofa and lunged for the remote. My hand wrapped around it and I held it in the air triumphantly, but my victory was short-lived. He tackled me, pulling my legs out from under me and pinning me to the sofa, his face mere inches from mine.

I stared at his mouth, at his slightly parted lips, his stupid perfect lips. Then I remembered where that mouth had been.

I shoved his shoulder. "Get off me," I snarled.

He smirked and sat up, not even putting up a fight. "Whatever you say, Rebel."

The remote was back in his hand, a smug smile on his face. I hated Jude McCallister. I really, really did.

The lights flickered and died just as the TV did, plunging us into darkness.

"I need to check the fuse box."

"No." Don't leave me alone in the dark with a storm raging outside. I grabbed his arm to stop him from leaving the sofa. "You can't do that."

"You want us to just sit here in the dark?"

"It's in the basement. The fuse box."

"Uh yeah, that's usually where they are." He shook off my hold on him and stood up. Another bolt of lightning lit up the dark room and illuminated his face for a fraction of a second. "I'll be right back."

"Wait." I jumped up from the sofa. "I'll come with you." He used his phone flashlight to guide the way and I stayed close behind him, stopping short of hanging on to the hem of his T-shirt. I had my limits. I wasn't *that* big of a wimp. I could hold my own and didn't need a guy to take care of me. *Most of the time.*

"This is the kind of thing that happens in horror movies," I said conversationally as we descended the stairs to the basement. "Like, don't go down there and then the person ventures down and boom..." I clapped my hands together for effect. "It's a zombie attack or a madman with a machete jumps out and chops up the unsuspecting victim and stores the body parts in the refrig—"

"Lila."

"Hmm?"

"You can stop now."

I took a deep breath and tried to contain my crazy. "Okay."

When we reached the bottom of the stairs, he had to duck his head because the ceiling was so low. He took my hand in his and arced his flashlight around the basement, searching for the fuse box. I hated it down here. It smelled musty and not even the dehumidifier that I emptied daily took the moisture out of the air.

"It's over by the washer and dryer," I told him and he zeroed in on it with his flashlight.

"You know what I don't get."

"What?" There were a lot of things I didn't get but I'd love to know what he didn't understand.

"Why do you love watching horror movies so much? You never even get scared when we watch them. You're totally fine. But you're scared of basements and thunderstorms?"

"Because the things that happen in horror movies aren't real so they don't scare me. Thunderstorms are real." Cancer is real.

"I'd never let anything happen to you," he said, his voice low and deep, so confident that he could protect me from unseen dangers. "You're safe. We're safe. Everything is okay."

"Okay." Except that everything wasn't okay. While I was trying so hard to hold everything together, it was all falling apart, and so was I. Not that he needed to know that.

As if he could read my thoughts, he gave my hand a gentle squeeze, a reminder that he was right there next to me. We crossed the concrete floor and when we stopped in front of the fuse box, he handed me his phone.

"Hold it up for me so I can see the box." I did as he asked, training the light on the fuse box so he could see what he was doing.

He studied it for a moment then flipped a few switches and looked up the basement stairs. It was still dark. "It's not the fuses. Power must have gone out."

"Great," I said, my shoulders sagging. "So we're stuck without electricity in the middle of a storm?"

"Looks that way. Have you got any candles?"

. . .

I tossed my crust in the box and Jude grabbed it and ate it in two bites. We'd demolished the pizza and now there wasn't even a piece of crust left.

"So, why did you quit the cheering squad?"

I shrugged one shoulder and took a sip of my Coke, letting a curtain of hair cover the side of my face that was turned to him. "It wasn't really my thing."

He flicked my arm. "What's wrong?"

"Nothing."

"Nothing always means something."

"Did you learn that in Psych 101?"

"I learned that in Lila 101. I know you like a book."

"Oh really." I turned in my seat and sat cross-legged, my back against the armrest. He kicked back and propped his Nike-clad feet on the coffee table. The flicker of the flames from the candles danced across his face. "So you think you can read me?"

"Yep," he said, so sure of himself.

"Then why do you need to ask if you already know me like a book?"

He carved his hand through his hair and turned his head to look at me. I forced myself to meet his gaze. He licked his lips and for a moment I saw a flicker of guilt cross his face. So fleeting I might have imagined it.

Not like we'd ever promised to be each other's first. Not like we were anything more than just friends.

"What did you hear?"

"Pfft." I waved my hand in the air. "I don't have time for idle gossip."

"It didn't mean anything. The kiss," he clarified.

From what I'd heard, it wasn't just a kiss. By the sound of it, they'd done a lot more than just kiss. I'd missed that stupid party. I'd missed the fruity vodka drinks and the shots and the kissing and the sex or whatever else had happened at yet another of Ashleigh's infamous pool parties.

I didn't go to parties anymore because I needed to be here. Just in case.

Most of the time, my mom was asleep. She slept more than she was awake these days. But still. I didn't want to miss any of the time when she was awake and wanted to pass on her wisdom to me.

"Oh. You think I care that you kissed Ashleigh?" I laughed like that was the most ridiculous thing I'd ever heard. "Why should I care?"

"Because if you kissed someone, I'd care."

I snorted. "You don't want to kiss me but you don't want anyone else to kiss me."

"What makes you think I don't want to kiss you?"

"Do you?"

He shifted as if he was going to move in and kiss me. Which was when the lights came on and the TV blared so loud, I nearly jumped off the sofa. Jude grabbed the remote and lowered the volume and we sat back and watched TV just like nothing had happened. Because nothing had happened. He glanced at me but I kept my gaze focused on the TV. We were watching a movie but I didn't even know what it was or what it was about.

"You can go now. The storm has passed."

"Okay," he said but he stayed right where he was, sitting next to me on the sofa, close enough that I could feel the heat from his skin and smell his boy scent. Close enough that I could hear his inhales and exhales, feel the rise and fall of his chest. Was his heart beating wildly like mine was? Was his pulse racing? I felt like I could barely breathe. Neither of us dragged our eyes away from the screen.

"You told Ashleigh we were just friends. Figured you wouldn't care what I did with her."

That was a year ago when I was younger and stupider. "What exactly did you do with her?" Using my middle finger, I chipped away at the indigo blue polish on my thumb.

"I don't kiss and tell."

I used my middle finger in a different way. He chuckled under his breath. "Is that for me... or Ashleigh?"

"You."

It was for the best. Even worse than knowing where his mouth had been was knowing where *hers* had been. I punched a throw pillow in frustration which made him laugh even harder. I was a source of entertainment for him.

I was sixteen, and I'd never been kissed. It was all Jude's fault. He'd staked his claim and all the other guys thought I was off-limits.

"He's the most amazing kisser. Oh my god, he's so hot," Ashleigh gushed. *Pretty sure she only called me to gloat and rub it in my face.*

How amazing could it have been? Not like he had tons of experience. How had he even known what to do? Maybe he'd been hooking up with girls left, right, and center and I just hadn't known about it. In the past year, he'd gone to a lot of parties that I'd missed.

I'd never be his first kiss now. Not that he even wanted to kiss me. Ugh, I didn't know.

I didn't know what Jude and I were to each other anymore. It used to be so simple. He was my neighbor. My best friend, sometimes enemy, but not really. The boy I grew up with. The most annoying boy in the world. Mr. Know-It-All. He was the boy who taught me how to climb a fence and skip rocks and swing from a rope tied to a tree. He was the boy I'd gotten skinned knees with. He was my summertime. My childhood memories.

The boy who knew I was scared of thunderstorms and ran down to my house in the pouring rain to make sure I was okay. If he hadn't been here, I would have been huddled on the sofa, alone and in the dark.

His pinkie linked with mine and we just sat like that, our eyes glued to the TV screen.

Me and the boy who gave me his favorite hoodie when I got my period, and he hadn't made fun of me or made me feel like a freak.

When I told my mom the story, she'd smiled and said, *"That's what I call a true love story."*

"I wouldn't go that far."

"It was an act of chivalry. Not all men are honorable. And I don't know of many teenage boys who would have handled that situation quite so well. When you fall in love, make sure he's worthy."

The front door opened and I looked up as Derek stepped inside the living room, his gaze darting from me to Jude.

"Thanks for keeping Lila company during the storm," he said, roughing his hand through his dark hair just as if he cared about my safety and well-being which I was pretty sure he didn't.

"Yeah. Sure. Anytime." Jude's jaw was clenched and I knew he was fighting the urge to tell my stepdad what he thought about him not being here. It was nothing new though. He was never here anymore, and that was just fine by me.

But the question that kept nagging me was, *What would happen when my mom wasn't here?* I wasn't Derek's kid, and my real dad had never been in the picture. I'd never cared because I always had my mom and she was like two parents rolled into one. But now I had no idea what would happen. My mom assured me that Derek would look after me and he had promised he would.

But promises were made to be broken and I'd seen him break too many to rely on his word alone.

Distracted with his own thoughts, Derek said goodbye and wandered into the kitchen, his footsteps heavy. I heard the refrigerator open and then the sound of him flipping the tab on a beer can before the patio door slid open and shut. This was his new nightly ritual. Drinking beer on the back deck until he passed out. Sometimes I'd find him there in the morning.

It was like he'd already checked out. I rarely saw him and when I did, we didn't talk about anything important. Sometimes he tried to make small talk but it was so awkward that I'd prefer he said nothing at all.

Jude's brows raised in question. "What's Derek doing?"

"Drinking a beer."

He looked up at the ceiling as if he could see directly into my mom's room. "Doesn't seem right." He hesitated a moment and I thought he might say more but he rose to his feet and I walked him to the front door.

"'Night, Lila."

"'Night."

I watched him jog in the direction of home until the darkness swallowed him up and I lost sight of him.

Then I went upstairs, got ready for bed and slipped into my mom's room, closing the door quietly behind me so I didn't disturb her. What Jude didn't know—what I hadn't told anyone—was that Derek slept in the spare bedroom and had been doing so for the past two years.

I crawled into bed next to my mom and listened to her breathing. Reassured by the sound, knowing that she was still here, I drifted off to sleep.

CHAPTER NINE

Lila

THE BOOK SLID OUT OF MY HANDS AND HIT THE FLOOR
with a clunk. I sat up and blinked, disoriented. Dread settled in
my stomach. When my eyes adjusted to the darkness, I made
out the sleeping form of my mom.

"Go on and get some sleep, honey," the night nurse, Marge,
told me. She must have turned off the lights.

Her job was to keep my mother as comfortable as possible.
Which meant that she dosed her with medication for the pain.

"Mom, I'll be back later, okay?" I said quietly, wanting her
to know but not wanting to disturb her in case she was asleep.

"Goodbye, baby," she said, her voice barely a whisper.
"Love you."

Marge ushered me to the door as if she was in a hurry to get
rid of me. "I'll look after her." Sensing my reluctance to leave,
she tried to reassure me with words that we both knew was a
lie. "Everything will be okay."

With one last look at my mom, I crept out of the room and

stood in the hallway for a few seconds. I wasn't tired anymore. I was keyed up.

In my room, I put on my sneakers and pulled my hair into a ponytail, checking the time on my phone as I slipped out of the house. It was ten o'clock. A crazy time to go running but I'd been doing it every night.

A shadowy form came from the side of the McCallister's house, the big orange October moon lighting his way. Like he'd been waiting for me. Expecting me.

"You need to stop running so late, Rebel." He turned on his phone flashlight and trained it on the ground in front of us so we wouldn't stumble or twist an ankle in a ditch or pothole. "It's dangerous."

"You don't have to come with me."

He snorted. "Like I'd let you go alone."

Nobody knew we ran late at night. Every night for the past few weeks, Jude had been climbing down the trellis from his bedroom window and there he'd be, waiting for me, even on a school night. Even when he was tired after a full day of school and football practice.

Jude was the starting quarterback this year and had been since our sophomore year. Which was a big deal in a football-obsessed town. He was carrying the hopes and expectations of an entire town on his shoulders but if he felt the pressure, he never let it show.

I used to think that everything came so easily to Jude. Sure, he had natural talent. But nobody on the team worked harder than Jude. He gave it his all and left everything out there on the field. It was the same for everything he did. Once Jude committed to something, he gave it a hundred and ten percent.

In the distance, a dog howled but other than that, it was quiet except for the sound of our breathing and our feet pounding the dirt lane. The crisp fall air smelled like wood smoke and decaying leaves.

"How's your mom?" Jude asked as we crested a hill.

"Same," I said, effectively ending our conversation.

There was nothing else to say, and unlike him, I couldn't chat while I ran because I needed to breathe so Jude didn't push me for more.

Waiting for someone to die was the cruelest form of punishment. Every morning before I went to school, I worried that she wouldn't be there when I got home. Every night when I went to sleep, I worried that she would be gone when I woke up.

I wanted to keep running, to the end of the world. Or back to a time when my biggest problem was having to wear a dress to meet the McCallisters. Before my mom got sick and Derek checked out. Had he been a good guy when I was younger? I couldn't really remember. Maybe it was my fault for never treating him like a dad. But I was only seven when he married my mom, so shouldn't he have made the effort?

"You good?" Jude asked.

Not even close. But I knew he was talking about running and if I said I wasn't fine, he'd slow his pace or turn around and head home. I wasn't ready to go home. Running had become my addiction and I needed it. I needed it to help me forget. To make me so tired that I'd eventually fall asleep.

"I'm good." To prove my point, I shot forward with a burst of speed. For me, it was an effort to run this route and I had to push my body to keep going even when I felt like quitting. It wasn't flat. It was hilly and rugged. For Jude, it was a cakewalk.

He was the bionic man, his stride so strong and sure, and his breathing measured, not the least bit winded. He didn't look like a boy anymore. At six foot two, he was the same height as his dad who had always seemed like a giant to me. He had a six-pack and washboard abs, and I knew this because when he mowed our lawn in the summer he sometimes went shirtless.

By the time we got back to his house and did our stretching exercises, I still wasn't ready to go home. I knew sleep wouldn't come.

"Tired yet?" he asked as if reading my mind.

I shook my head. "It's okay though."

I turned to go. He grabbed my wrist and dragged me along the side of his house. We stopped in front of the trellis. It stopped a few feet short of his bedroom window which he'd left open, waiting for his return.

"Come on." He jerked his chin at the trellis. "Let's go sit on the roof."

"The roof?" I tipped back my head, looking up at the gabled roof. How did he propose we get to the roof?

"Yeah, Rebel, the roof. It's closer to the stars. Trust me," he said, noting the way I chewed on my lip, worried about how in the hell he expected all five foot three inches of me to get on the roof. "I'd never let you fall."

It was the way he said it, like he'd die before letting me fall, that had me doing as he asked. Sometimes I thought I would follow this boy to the fiery pits of hell if he asked me to. And sometimes that scared me. I didn't want him to have that kind of power over me. It was the reason I pushed back so hard, not wanting him to give an inch, knowing he'd take a yard.

Getting onto the roof was no easy feat but Jude stayed true to his word and now here we were, lying on the roof under a sky full of stars, our knees bent, feet planted on the cedar shingles. And all we'd had to do to get here was climb up the trellis, tightrope walk across the drainpipe, and scale the stone wall then pull ourselves up and onto the roof.

"Next time we should use a ladder."

"Where's the fun in that?" Jude asked and I laughed.

From this vantage point, the stars looked so close it felt like we could reach up and touch them.

Everything was changing and I hated it.

"My mom is dying, Jude. She's going to die." He didn't even bother trying to deny it. He couldn't because he knew it was true. She was going to die and there was nothing that anyone could do about it.

Jude reached for my hand and clasped it in his and we were silent for a while, lost in our thoughts, our gazes focused on the stars and I couldn't tell if it really happened or if my eyes were playing tricks on me but I could have sworn I saw a falling star in my peripheral. When I turned my head, it was gone.

"What happens when the stars fall, Jude?"

"I'll put them back in the sky for you," he said, sounding so confident. As if he had that kind of power. As if he were a god, and not just a seventeen-year-old boy. "I'd do anything for you, Lila."

"Anything?"

"Anything." There was no hesitation in his response, not even for the briefest moment. He was so sure of himself. How brave and how foolish he was to make a statement like that. What if he couldn't deliver? What if I asked him to give me the sun and the moon and all the stars? What would he do then?

"Okay. Then kiss me," I challenged with false bravado, like this was one of our dares.

"You want me to kiss you?" he asked as if he wanted to make sure he'd heard me correctly. And this time I heard the hesitation in his voice. Maybe he didn't even want to kiss me and I'd just made the biggest fool of myself.

"Lila," he prompted, his voice low and husky. "You want me to kiss you?"

I shrugged one shoulder like I didn't care one way or the other and pressed the palms of my hands against the shingles to stop them from shaking. "Do you want to?"

He was quiet and made no move to kiss me. I stared at the night sky, too scared to see what I might not want to. He hadn't even said yes. God. How much more could I embarrass myself?

He was only nine months older than me and I never used to notice the difference in our ages but now I did. While he was going to parties and drinking beer and letting girls kiss him and give him blow jobs, I was sitting at home watching my mom die.

I wanted to go back to my carefree days when nothing scared me. I wanted to be reckless and daring again. And I was determined to do it with or without him.

"Fine." I pushed myself up on my forearms. "If you won't kiss me, I'll find someone who will."

The words were barely out of my mouth and then I was caged in his arms, his face so close to mine, all the edges were blurry. This wasn't like the times we used to wrestle. My body was humming and I could feel the trembling in his arms as he used them to brace himself so he wasn't pressing his full weight on me.

"You're going to fall off the roof."

"Worth it," he said.

And what I heard was that *I* was worth it. He'd willingly fall to his death for me.

His soft breath mingled with mine and I could smell his sweat and the fabric softener his mom used and the scent that was just him. The scent that made me slightly dizzy. I was so lightheaded that I might have floated away if he didn't have me pinned to this roof.

"Am I your first kiss?" he asked quietly, studying my face in the moonlight, his gaze darting from my eyes to my lips where it stayed.

I pursed my lips, not wanting to acknowledge it and shook my head. "No."

He smirked. "Yeah, I am." He shifted so he was leaning on one forearm and lightly ran his fingertips over my lips. So gently it felt like a soft breeze not the touch of a boy who promised to put the stars back in the sky. "Nobody else is allowed to kiss you."

And that was the problem. He'd decided that I was his but he could kiss anyone he wanted. The hypocrisy incensed me and I steeled myself against his soft touch that made delicious shivers run up and down my spine. "I changed my mind." I tried to shove him away and get out from under him but he just laughed. "I don't want to kiss you."

"You wanna kiss me. I'll make it good for you."

"I heard you're a lousy kisser."

"Say yes, Rebel." His mouth hovered mere inches above mine. He licked his bottom lip and he waited to hear the word coming from my mouth and I knew he'd wait until the stars died if that's how long it took. He'd never do anything without my consent but even so it still felt dangerous. "Do you want me to kiss you?"

I wanted it more than I'd ever wanted anything in my life. Should I really deny myself this pleasure? I nodded. "Yes."

When his lips met mine, he was smiling. His lips brushed against mine, sending a shockwave through me, and this wasn't really a kiss, just the prelude to one. As if he had all the time in the world and he wasn't risking life and limb to kiss me on top of this roof. I wound my arms around his neck, thinking maybe I could save him from falling.

And that's when he kissed me. He kissed me hard. I gasped, and he took that opportunity to deepen the kiss. His tongue stroked mine and it felt so strange yet so wonderful all at the same time. He groaned and I made a little sound that was close to a whimper.

I can't lie. It was a perfect kiss.

I'd gladly fall off the roof if it meant I could keep kissing him like this. I never wanted this kiss to end.

CHAPTER TEN

Jude

Kissing Lila was like nothing I'd ever experienced before. I never wanted to stop kissing her. My dick was so hard I knew she had to feel it prodding her thigh. Her back arched off the roof and her fingers dug into my shoulders and when she rocked her hips, I didn't even stop to think. I was thrusting against her, the thin silky material of our running shorts the only barrier preventing me from burying myself inside her.

This was quickly turning into a hell of a lot more than a kiss. We were dry humping on a roof and my mouth was on her neck, my teeth grazing her collarbone, her fingers tugging at the ends of my hair while in my head I was coming up with a million different ways to make her feel so good she'd never want to kiss another guy for as long as she lived.

But we couldn't keep doing this. Not now. Not here on a roof while her mom was dying. Not after the promises I'd made.

"You're a good friend to Lila. She's going to need you to help her through this."

"I'll be there for her. I'll always be there for her."

"I know you will, sweetie. She's lucky to have you. Just do me a favor, okay?"

"Anything."

"Make her first time special."

I coughed, not sure I'd heard her right. "Her first time?"

She laughed. "Sex, Jude. Don't act like you haven't thought about it. I might be dying but I'm not blind. I see the way you look at her. But there's no rush. You're both young. Wait until the time is right."

"I..." I chuckled. "This is awkward."

"Sex is natural. No need to make it awkward. I'm glad you found each other. Sometimes I wish... well, never mind. It's good to wait until the right person comes along and when that right person comes along when you're nine years old, that's magical."

With every ounce of willpower I possessed, I forced myself to stop and I pulled away, trying to get my raging hard-on under control. No easy feat. I wanted her so badly I couldn't see straight. Bracing my arms on either side of her head, I looked down at her swollen, kiss-bruised lips. I wanted to mark her like those stupid vampires in the books all the girls were reading.

She looked up at me, her lips parting and I dipped my head and kissed her neck, sucking on the sensitive skin until I was sure it would be bruised and purple tomorrow.

Mine.

"Did you just give me a hickey?" she asked when I rolled off her and sat next to her.

"Yep."

I leaned back on my elbows, pretty damn proud of my handiwork and she rolled her eyes and said *gross* but there was a smile on her lips and I didn't think she minded it that much.

"How was your first kiss?" I asked, wishing I'd just kept my mouth shut.

"Not bad. It was kind of nice."

"*Kind of nice?*"

"I don't want to give you a big head or anything." She tugged her bottom lip between her teeth, suddenly shy. It was cute. "Are all kisses like that?"

I laughed and scrubbed my hands over my face, stifling a groan. "No. Definitely not."

She smiled, triumphant, like it was a contest and she'd won. Which she had. Hands down best kiss I'd ever had. Because it was Lila. And I'd been dying to kiss her for longer than I could remember. We'd had so many almost kisses which had made this one even sweeter. The waiting. The wanting. The longing.

I wanted more. Of everything.

"Good," she said.

The smile slipped off her face and I saw the sadness that had been there for months. I reached for her hand again and held it in mine. "I took her for granted. I thought she'd be here forever, you know?"

Sometimes I forgot how small Lila was but right now she looked so tiny. So fragile. "Come here."

I sat up and pulled her against my side, wrapping my arm around her shoulders, trying to let her know that I was there for her. I could feel her breaking. She was crying. Just these big fat silent tears rolling down her cheeks and all I wanted to do was take away her pain and make it my own. I wanted to fix this for her and it made me angry that I couldn't.

I swallowed hard. Lila was talking about her mom as if she was already gone, and maybe that was what she had to do. Contradicting her, telling her that there was still a chance her mom would be okay, would be a lie.

"She was the best mom."

I nodded in agreement. She was right up there with my mom who was pretty damn great.

"Tell me something good, Jude."

I wracked my brain trying to think of something good and opted for something funny instead. Having Jesse around ensured that there was always plenty to laugh at. "If you put grapes in the microwave, they explode. We found this out yesterday when Jesse conducted an experiment."

Lila laughed. "He's crazy. What did your mom do?"

"Just kind of shook her head and tried not to laugh. He said it would be easier to make jelly now and he smashed up all the exploded grapes and slathered them on his peanut butter sandwich."

Lila was really laughing now. "Jesse is obsessed with exploding food. Remember the time he tested the Pop Rocks and Coke myth?"

I snorted. He'd been so disappointed when his stomach hadn't exploded. It just made him burp. "Did you know that Cap'n Crunch has a real name?" I said, sharing more Jesse trivia.

"No. What is it?"

"Captain Horatio Magellan Crunch."

"It is not. You're making that up."

"Nope. True story. And Minnie Mouse's name is Minerva." I side-eyed her. "You kind of look like a Minerva."

"Sure I do. With a name like that, I can understand why she goes by Minnie."

"I bet you can, *Delilah*."

She scrunched up her nose. "Ew, don't call me that."

"Why not? I think it's cool."

"Oh yeah?"

"Mmhmm. She was a biblical temptress."

"Samson's downfall."

"You'd better not cut your hair," she said.

"You'd better not cut it while I'm asleep."

"Tempting."

"Wouldn't put it past you."

She laughed and I kissed her again. And again. And again.

I blinked up at my mom as she entered my room and sat up, rolling out my shoulder that was stiff from sleeping on the hard floor. By the look on my mom's face, I could guess why she was here.

"Oh honey. Was she with you all night?" my mom whispered.

I sat up and roughed my hand through my hair and nodded, my gaze seeking out Lila. She was still asleep in my bed and I got the feeling it had been a long time since she'd slept so soundly. Which was why I'd suggested it last night—or rather, in the early hours of the morning. As soon as she'd toed off her sneakers and her head had hit my pillow, she'd fallen sound asleep. I'd debated whether to climb in bed and sleep with her but had opted for my sleeping bag on the floor instead. Not that I was being noble. I was seventeen and I was a guy and she gave me a raging hard-on that was impossible to hide. If I'd crawled into bed behind her, I couldn't trust myself not to dry hump her in her sleep.

"Don't wake her," I said, my tone hushed.

My mom nodded, her smile sad and for a few seconds we both watched Lila sleeping before I followed my mom out of the room. I'd gotten as far as the door when Lila's sleep-groggy voice stopped me.

"Jude?"

My mom paused in the hallway. Reluctantly, I returned to

my bedroom, hating that I would be the first face she saw when her entire world was destroyed. On the other hand, I was glad I could be here for her. My mom and I didn't have to say the words. Lila sat up in bed, her wavy hair wild, and the look on her face... the devastation on it was something I'd hope to never see again in this lifetime.

"Lila, honey." My mom's voice was soft. "Derek's here, sweetie. I'm so sorry." My mom's voice cracked on the words and I could see that she was barely holding it together.

Lila didn't cry. She didn't shed one single tear. She shot out of bed and jammed her feet in her sneakers. "I should have been there. I should have been there for her."

I reached for her, trying to pull her into a hug but she shoved me away and darted out of my room. I chased after her and collided with my dad in the hallway.

"Let her go. Derek's here for her."

Physically, he was here but from what I'd seen, he hadn't been there for Lila or for Caroline. He wasn't even Lila's dad but now he was all she had for a parent. A shitty excuse, if you asked me.

Downstairs, I heard the door close then stillness settled on the house and it was so quiet.

Brody's door opened, and he joined us in the hallway in his boxer briefs, scrubbing his hand over his face. His dirty-blond hair was matted down on one side where he'd slept on it. "What's going on?" he asked and in the next breath he said, "Oh shit," reading the situation without having to be told. "Lila's mom."

"Watch your language," my mom told him, more out of habit than anything.

"What happened to Lila's mom?" Jesse asked, his panicked voice rising a few octaves higher.

I shouldered past my dad, leaving him to deal with my brother. Lila needed me.

In my bare feet, running shorts and T-shirt that I'd slept in, I jogged to her house, the fallen leaves crunching under my feet and walked through the front door that was left wide open.

"Where is she?" Lila screamed from upstairs.

"Calm down."

"Where is my mom?" Upstairs, a door slammed shut and I heard the sound of something crashing.

"Lila. Stop it!" Derek shouted.

"How could you let them take her?" she shrieked. "I didn't even get to say goodbye. Get. Off. Me. Let me go."

That son of a bitch.

My hands balled into fists and I took the stairs two at a time. Without even stopping to think, I ripped Derek away from her, spun him around and flung him across the hallway. He slammed into the wall, knocking a picture from a hook and it crashed to the floor, the glass in the frame shattering.

I pinned him to the wall with my arm and got right in his face. "Did you touch her?" I asked, my voice shaking with anger.

"Get the hell away from me." He tried to shove me away but he was no match for me. I had a good three inches on him and had muscle in the place of his beer gut.

I fisted his T-shirt in my hands and looked him in the eye. His face had turned an alarming shade of beet red. "I'm asking you a question," I seethed. "Did. You—"

"Jude. Stop. He didn't do anything. Just... stop making a mess of everything." She grabbed my arm and pulled me away from Derek who glared at me and rolled out his shoulders.

Not entirely sure what had just happened, I looked to Lila who was down on her knees, holding the picture that had fallen from the wall. In the photo, Lila was blowing out the four candles on her birthday cake and her mom was right next to her with a big smile on her face. Caroline looked so young and so healthy, her green eyes vibrant and her dark hair glossy, and there was so much joy and love on her face while she watched Lila that I nearly cried just looking at it.

"Go home, Jude." Her voice was quiet. Resolute.

"Was he—"

"He wasn't doing anything. Just go. I want to be left alone."

I took a few steps back from Derek. "Sorry," I mumbled, running my hand through my hair. I cleared my throat. "I thought..."

He shook his head in disgust. "I know what you thought. You heard her. Go on home."

But I couldn't go home and just leave her so I followed the trail of blood down the gray-carpeted hallway to her bedroom. Her knees were bleeding from where she'd knelt in the broken glass. "Lila. I'm sorry. I—"

The door slammed in my face. I pressed my forehead against the wood and heard the lock turning on the other side like she was so desperate to keep me out that she had to lock herself inside. My eyes drifted shut and I placed the palms of my hands flat against her door.

"Let me in, Lila. Please." I was pleading. Begging. And I knew I sounded pathetic but fuck that. She couldn't shut me out. I was her best friend. I was the guy who loved her more than anyone on this planet. Caroline was gone but I was still here, begging for her to let me in.

And I did. I loved her. I'd loved her forever. I'd loved her since we were nine years old and I was scared she was going to drown in the creek. I'd loved her when she punched me in the fourth grade.

I'd loved her when I gave her my favorite hoodie in ninth grade.

I'd loved her in tenth grade when she cheered for me from the bleachers at my football games even though she was the sad girl.

After she quit the cheering squad, she still went to the games because the entire town went. She usually sat with my family or with Brody if he wasn't away at one of his rodeos. One Friday at school, on a game day, I tried to give her one of my jerseys to wear to the games but she'd thrown it back in my face.

"Is this supposed to mean something?" She looked down at the blue jersey in her hand, my name and the number ten emblazoned in gold.

"Uh, yeah. It means you're on my team." It means you're mine and nobody else's. How could she not have figured that out?

She'd tossed the jersey back in my face and walked away.

But I'd loved her anyway.

Unfortunately, dumb shit that I was, I'd let my dick do the thinking and somehow it had found its way inside Ashleigh's mouth and somehow my mouth had found its way to... yeah, you get the picture. I'd like to say that was a one-time thing but I'd be lying.

Goddammit.

"Rebel. Open up." I smacked the palm of my hand against her door. "Let me come in."

You need me.

Lila didn't answer. She didn't unlock the door. I stayed where I was, glued to her door and I waited. And I listened for signs of life inside. My heart thrashed in my chest when I heard her footsteps crossing the room, getting closer. I breathed a sigh of relief and took a step back from the door, waiting for it to open.

My hopes were dashed when two seconds later, "Move

Along" by the All-American Rejects blasted from her speakers. I jumped back realizing why her footsteps had come so close to the door. She'd put a speaker right on the other side of it and had cranked up the volume. Her music was so fucking loud it shook the walls.

Move along. Cute, Rebel, cute.

"I'll camp outside your door until you let me in," I yelled over the music.

"Go. Home."

I sat outside her door and leaned my forearms on my bent knees. I was still sitting there, listening to her angry-girl emo music when my dad's work boots appeared in front of me. I lifted my head and met his glare. His jaw was clenched and he looked as if he was two seconds away from losing his shit.

"It's time for school."

"I'm not going." I kicked my legs out in front of me, crossed my arms over my chest and leaned my back against the door, settling in for the long haul.

"Jude." He pinched the bridge of his nose and spoke through clenched teeth. "Get the hell off the floor and get your ass home now. Or there will be hell to pay. Understand?"

"I can't go to school. Not now when..." I jerked my thumb at the door behind me. Fill in the blanks, Dad. Sad girl was on the other side, maybe crying her heart out and how was I supposed to just leave her like this?

I couldn't.

I wouldn't.

"It's game night. You're the star quarterback." Like football was the most important thing at a time like this. "You need to go to school and you need to tough it out. Everyone's expecting a win tonight."

Tough it out. My dad's catchphrase. *McCallisters are*

winners, not quitters. That was his other famous line. Nothing short of victory was acceptable.

If I didn't go home with him now there really would be hell to pay.

So I took a few deep breaths through my nose then got to my feet. It was a Friday. Game night. And I had no idea how I was going to lead my team to victory after Lila had just lost her mom. But that was what was expected of me.

Every single Friday night during football season I went out on that field and I left it all out there. My blood, my sweat, and my mother's tears when I got sacked and ended up with a concussion three weeks ago. The following Monday I was right back out there on that field for practice. Because that's what winners did. They got back in the game no matter what.

Coach expected me to deliver. My teammates expected it. Hell, the whole goddamn town expected it.

But no matter how well I played, my dad would still point out what I could have done better. I always dreaded Saturday morning breakfast because that was when he went through the game, citing play-by-play and pointing out any weaknesses in my game.

Don't get me wrong. I loved football and I loved my dad. But sometimes he was a hard ass and a taskmaster who demanded nothing less than excellence from me. Tough love, he called it when he had me doing drills at six in the morning on weekends. He was the same with Jesse, who had gotten into motocross this past summer. And the same with Brody's rodeo competitions.

We had to be the best, and nothing less would suffice.

With Gideon, my dad didn't know what the hell to do. Gideon hated playing sports. The funny part was that he had a lot of natural ability but he hated the way my dad got all competitive so he half-assed it which always led to arguments and slammed doors.

Now, my dad and I crossed the Turners' front lawn, the soles of my feet stinging from the cuts I'd gotten on my barefoot jog to her front door.

"What the hell were you thinking, punching Derek?" my dad asked.

He told my dad I punched him? That fucking weasel. "It was a misunderstanding." He raised his brows, waiting for an explanation. "I thought he was..." I cleared my throat, embarrassed about my assumptions but not entirely sorry for my actions. "... being inappropriate with Lila," I finished, trying to put it delicately and not paint myself as the world's biggest asshole. But hey, I was just trying to defend her.

"Ah." My dad nodded like he understood and said nothing more as we strode up the street to our house, the trees a riot of color, the fall leaves at that point where they were still vibrant orange, and red, and gold just before they withered and died.

Withered and died.

I looked over my shoulder at Lila's brown-shingled house before we reached the bend in the road and the trees obscured my view. I thought I saw her face in the second-story window, watching me. But most likely she wasn't thinking about me at all, much less watching me from her window.

"Do you think he was? Is that something I should be worried about?" my dad asked when we reached our front porch. My mom had decorated it with pumpkins and cobwebs and a scarecrow in a straw hat with a plaid shirt under overalls.

"I don't think so, but I don't trust the guy."

"If you notice anything, you tell me, you hear? Don't take it upon yourself to deal with it on your own. If worse comes to worse, I'll take care of Derek and we'll move Lila in here with us."

Say what? "Can you do that?"

He nodded. "Caroline made provisions in her will. Just in case it became necessary."

Well, shit. I didn't know about that and I doubted that Lila did either. But my dad asked me to keep it to myself so I did.

Not that it mattered. Lila ignored me. Went out of her way to avoid me. The seasons came and went and the sad girl found new friends and went to parties with the artsy kids where guys played fucking guitars and girls wore Birkenstocks and didn't shave their armpits.

Pretty sure she was a lesbian now.

I stopped leaving notes in her locker. I stopped trying to talk to her. Stopped sending texts that went unanswered.

I stopped giving a shit what she did or who she did it with. Which would have all been fucking peachy if only it were true. I missed her spring rain and honeysuckle scent.

I missed the way she kissed me. Like I was her oxygen and she couldn't breathe without me.

I missed her laugh, low and throaty, and kind of dirty. I missed her smile. All her smiles. The devious ones and the happy ones and the sweet and shy ones.

I missed the way she used to fight me and argue with me.

I fucking missed *her* but instead of dwelling on it, I hooked up with girls who wanted to be with me. The generically pretty ones with names like Ashleigh and Megan and Kylie. Okay, I hooked up with all three of them.

But what the fuck? Rebel was making me crazy.

The only way to keep my mind off of her was to pretend she didn't exist.

CHAPTER ELEVEN

Lila

SEVEN MONTHS. THAT WAS HOW LONG IT TOOK DEREK TO decide he had no interest in looking after his dead wife's kid.

One month after my mom died, Derek brought his girl-friend home to meet me. Ha, joke. He didn't bring her over to meet me. I just happened to be there when he pulled up on his Harley and she climbed off the back of it. Her name was Mindi with an i and she wore painted-on jeans, plunging necklines and acrylic nails. Her bleached blonde hair had two-inch roots and her heels left divots in our front lawn but Derek acted like she was the best thing since sliced bread. If he was trying to find the antithesis of my mother, he'd succeeded. Biker Barbie had moved into our house and into my mother's bedroom that she shared with Derek. For six long months I had to deal with Mindi, her makeup and cheap perfume littering the shelves of the bathroom, her cigarette smoke wafting through the screen door and polluting my air.

I'd dug up the garden that Jude had helped me plant because I didn't want Derek and Mindi to have a nice view.

I was small and petty and bitter.

Everything was dead and broken.

The only surprise was that Derek had hung in there for as long as he had. He'd waited until the day after my seventeenth birthday to inform me that he was putting the house on the market and moving to another town with Mindi.

I didn't even know where Derek was moving nor did I care to ask.

Now it was June, school was out, the house was sold and my life had been packed into a few boxes that were being shuttled over to the McCallister house.

The one bright spot in my junior year was Christy Rivera who jokingly called herself The Tampon Girl. I called her a lifesaver. Pathetic as it sounded, she was my first true friend who was a girl. As for my other two best friends... I missed them. So much.

Especially Jude. I missed him like a missing limb and as I watched him go from one girl to another, I knew I had no one to blame for our rift except myself.

I told myself it was for the best. I couldn't bear to lose another person I loved. Jude was leaving, he was going to enlist and leave Cypress Springs right after we graduated high school, so it was better to keep my distance. If I got too close, it would only hurt more.

But now, I was moving in with his family and I had no idea how to navigate this uncharted territory. Avoiding him would not be an option.

"How's it going, L?"

"Let's put it this way. I had two choices. Shitty. Or shittier," I said, using his words from four years ago. It felt like another lifetime ago.

"Yeah, I get that." Brody flopped down on my bed and tucked his hands under his head, staring at the ceiling. "You've got a sky full of stars though."

"What?" I asked, transferring my clothes from my suitcase to the oak chest of drawers.

This bedroom used to be the guest room and I'd heard that Gideon was supposed to move out of the room he shared with Jesse but now that I was here, he had to forfeit his own room. Which made me feel bad, just like so many other things about this living arrangement.

"You've got stars," he said, pointing at the ceiling.

I looked up but at first, I couldn't see anything.

"Turn off the light."

"Why?" I asked but I did as he said and turned off the lamp on the dresser. It wasn't that dark out yet but it was dark enough to see the stars glowing on the ceiling above my bed. I studied them, trying to work out the pattern and figure out which constellation it was but astronomy wasn't my thing. "Have they always been here?"

He chuckled under his breath. "Nope."

Jude. But would he have really done this? For me? He hated me now. I'd gotten my wish. He left me alone. Never tried to talk to me. Wouldn't even look at me when we passed each other in the hallways at school. He didn't bully me. Didn't go out of his way to make my life hell. Didn't even actively avoid me or ignore me.

He just looked right through me like I didn't even exist.

So why would he have put stars on my ceiling?

"Did you do it?" I asked Brody.

He just laughed. "You two deserve each other. You're both dumbasses."

I opened my mouth to protest but Kate poked her head in the doorway, stopping the words from coming out. "Hi honey. Need some help?"

"Oh, um... I'm okay. Thank you." I flicked the light back on and smiled at her. I loved Kate. I loved the whole family. But I knew how Brody felt now. Even though their intentions were good, I hated feeling like a charity case.

"Brody. Get your boots off Lila's comforter," Kate said.

His boots hit the floor with a thud and he got to his feet, leaving me with dried mud that had flaked off his boots and landed on my sunflower-patterned comforter. "Catch you later, L."

When Brody was gone, Kate brushed the dirt off my comforter and into the wastepaper can next to my desk then came to stand in front of me and held out her arms. "Come here, honey."

I took a step forward and she wrapped me up in a hug that was almost as good as my mom's. Almost. She stroked my hair and she held on tight and I hugged her back. I tried to swallow my tears but the lump in my throat was too big and something inside of me cracked. It was like a dam broke and all the tears I'd been holding rushed out of me.

I was sobbing so hard, I couldn't breathe. She held on tight and didn't let go.

"I know, sweetie. Let it out. Sometimes you just need a good cry."

Everything was broken and I didn't know how to put all the pieces back together. When my tears subsided, I pulled away and she handed me a pack of tissues from her shorts pocket as if she'd come prepared for my tears.

I wiped my eyes and blew my nose and when she asked if I

felt better, I nodded. In some ways, it was true. I felt hollowed out and empty but I felt a little bit better. My mom was gone and she wasn't coming back and I had to accept that. Derek was gone, our house was sold, and I had a few boxes of memories stored in the McCallister's attic. That was all I had left of my old life.

This was my new normal. I was an orphan taken in by the family of the boy I'd loved for so long. The boy I'd pushed away because I was too scared to let him get any closer. Instead of being with my mom when she died, I'd been kissing Jude on the roof. My mom died at one in the morning. Three hours after I left her. But I didn't find out until the next morning because Derek, the jackass, was with his girlfriend Mindi that night.

I hated him for that. I hated myself for leaving her. If only I'd stayed she wouldn't have had to die alone. If only I hadn't been so selfish.

From my peripheral, I caught a movement in the doorway but when I looked over at it nobody was there.

That night I slept under a sky full of stars.

"What happens when the stars fall, Jude?"

"I'll put them back in the sky for you."

CHAPTER TWELVE

Jude

TWO MONTHS INTO THIS NEW LIVING ARRANGEMENT AND I was already counting down the days until I could leave for boot camp. Which, let's face it, wasn't going to be for at least another year. I was still two weeks from turning eighteen. We still had to survive the rest of the summer and our senior year before we could get away from each other. Even then, she was part of the family now so I was stuck with her.

Turning off the shower, I scrubbed my hands over my face and stepped onto the tiles, reaching for a clean towel on the shelf.

"Oh my God. I... crap. I didn't know... um..."

I stood still, my hand holding the towel, her curious eyes roaming down my naked body. Her cheeks were flushed and she was just standing in the open doorway, earbuds in her ears, an iPod strapped to her upper arm, her music so loud I could hear it from here.

She was wearing tiny running shorts and a sports tank, her

hair in a high ponytail. Earlier, I'd seen her running and I had run right past her, leaving her in my dust, not even glancing in her direction as I passed. Lila was always running, she ran miles and miles every day, so of course my dad had talked her into joining the girls' cross-country team in the fall.

God forbid you lived with the McCallisters and didn't compete in a sport.

Meanwhile, she was still staring.

Let her take a good, long look. I had nothing to be ashamed of. In fact, I had everything to be proud of. I worked hard for this body. For the second summer in a row, I was working construction for my dad. I ran five miles a day. I lifted weights, swam, and punched the leather bag in the barn which no longer housed horses. Brody had moved his horses to the ranch where he worked. So my dad had set up a gym in there. And tomorrow pre-season football training was starting. I was fighting fit and no longer looked like the boy she'd grown up.

Yeah, baby girl, that's right. I've grown up. Just shy of six three, my shoulders were broad enough to carry the weight of the entire world and my washboard abs were so toned and rigid you could bounce a quarter off them.

My dick stood to attention and was instantly at half-mast. I might hate her but obviously my dick felt differently.

She squeezed her eyes shut. Then she spun around and ran out of the bathroom. Or she would have if she hadn't run into the door as it slammed shut in her face.

On the other side, I heard someone laughing their ass off.

Fucking Brody.

"Ow." She groaned and covered her face with her hands and this time I suspected it was in pain, not embarrassment. With a loud exhale to let her know that coming to her rescue yet again was a huge imposition, I wrapped the towel around my hips and in a few long strides, I was standing behind her. I turned her around to face me then took the earbuds out of her ears and looped them around her neck to assess the damage but I couldn't see a damn thing because her hands were covering her face.

"Rebel. The fuck are you doing?"

"I think it's broken."

"Let me see it," I said quietly.

Without meeting my eyes, she lowered her hands and I cursed Brody when I saw the blood. That idiot. I unspooled some toilet paper and dabbed the blood under her nose. She winced but let me clean it up. "We need to get some ice on it."

"I'm..." Her face drained of color and she swayed on her feet. I knew she was going down if I didn't stop her. My instincts kicked in and I held her by the upper arms to steady her. When I released my grip, she slid down against the door and put her head between her legs. "God. This is so embarrassing."

"Which part?"

"All of it." She lifted her head and leaned it against the door. I didn't think her nose was broken but it looked red and it was starting to swell and I knew it had to hurt.

"Are you trying to look up my towel?' I asked, now conscious of the fact that I was standing across from her in nothing but a towel.

"Ugh. No. I'm trying not to throw up."

"Are you two bumping uglies in there?" Brody yelled from the other side of the door. Might as well alert the entire fucking neighborhood.

I threw the first thing I could grab which happened to be a hairbrush. It hit the door above Rebel's head and bounced off. She ducked out of the way and covered her head with her hands before it could hit her on the way down. Good reflexes.

Then, for no reason I could fathom, Lila started laughing.

She was laughing so hard tears sprang to her eyes. "Ow," she said, covering her nose with her hands and then laughing some more.

"Are you high?"

She shook her head. "No." She snorted. "I don't even know why I'm laughing. But it's better than crying."

I wondered if she cried a lot. The only time I had ever seen her cry, *really* cry, was the night she moved in when I was skulking in the hallway outside her bedroom door. It had taken every ounce of self-restraint I possessed not to go to her and try to comfort her. That was what I would have done in the past but we weren't the same Jude and Lila anymore.

So I had to remind myself that she didn't want me. Which was something I had to do again now before I ended up making a fool of myself by telling her something stupid like *I miss you.* Or worse, *Why did you shut me out when all I wanted to do was be there for you?*

I'd temporarily forgotten that I was mad at her. I'd forgotten that I hated her for pushing me away and treating me like shit. And for destroying a friendship that I always thought was so rock solid nothing could ruin it. But that's life. You never know when it's going to throw you a curveball.

I was fed up and now I wanted to get out of this damn bathroom and forget the sad girl with the bloody nose.

"Move aside, Rebel." She scooted away from the door enough for me to open it and slip out into the hallway. "Hope you got a nice long look so you'll know what you're missing."

Petty? Maybe.

But I was done playing nice. This was all on her. If she wanted me back in her life, she'd have to beg, grovel, and plead before I'd even consider it.

CHAPTER THIRTEEN

Lila

TODAY WAS JUDE'S EIGHTEENTH BIRTHDAY AND EVEN though he hated me, I'd spent the past few weeks working on his birthday present. Now I wasn't sure if I should give it to him or if he'd even want it.

"He did give you his favorite hoodie," Christy said. "That's become the gold standard. If a guy won't give me his favorite hoodie, he's not worth it."

"What makes a girl worthy?" I asked.

"Red lipstick."

I laughed. Christy was bi-curious and had hooked up with both guys and girls.

"You should talk to him."

"And say what?"

"That you miss him and you want to jump his bones. You've already seen the goods. Might as well sample them."

I groaned. It had been two weeks since I walked in on Jude

and every time I closed my eyes, that was the only thing I could envision. Naked Jude. With his sun-kissed skin and lean muscles and... oh God, I had seen ALL of him. I was no expert but it looked... substantial. Like, how was that thing going to fit inside me? Not that he wanted me. Why would he when he had girls at his beck and call? Girls who were so much easier than me in every way.

It was pure torture living under the same roof with him. I saw him everywhere. In the family room on movie nights. At dinner on the nights when Kate insisted we sit down and eat as a 'family.' *In the bathroom.* Why hadn't he locked the door? Had he wanted me to walk in on him and see him?

There were two upstairs bathrooms but the other one had been occupied. Probably Gideon, whose showers lasted forever. I didn't even want to know what he did in there. Thankfully he always locked the door. He was the most private one in the family. While the other McCallister boys were rugged and rowdy, he was quieter and kept to himself. At fourteen, he already had the kind of good looks that were slightly intimidating. High cheekbones, dark hair, and arctic blue eyes that gave nothing away.

This evening, we'd had a family barbecue and cake for Jude and when he'd blown out his eighteen candles, I'd wondered what his wish was.

Everyone had given him their gifts except for me so he probably thought I hadn't bothered to get him anything. But it wasn't the kind of thing I wanted to give him in front of his whole family.

Now, I was lying on my bed, staring at the stars on my ceiling and waiting for him to come home from a party.

"He's probably going to come home drunk and smelling like another girl," I told Christy.

"He's not into any of those girls. They're vapid."

"And I'm a bitch. So where does that leave me?"

"No idea. Love is deaf, dumb, and blind," she said, making me laugh.

The sound of tires crunching over gravel drew me to my open window which conveniently overlooked the front lawn and the driveway. Headlights illuminated Jude and Brody as they climbed out of Tyler's Jeep.

They were home. Brody was definitely drunk but I wasn't sure about Jude.

"Hey Christy," I said. "I've gotta run."

"Call me tomorrow, bitch."

After promising I would, I cut the call and tossed my phone on the nightstand then took a few deep breaths. This was either going to make things better or completely blow up in my face.

Fortune favored the bold.

Clutching the gift to my chest, I crept down the dark hallway, praying that I wouldn't run into anyone along the way. I wasn't scared of his dad but I didn't want to give him a reason to get angry either. Sneaking into Jude's bedroom in the middle of the night could potentially get us both in trouble. Jesse was the one who told me the boys had been given a talk at the dinner table before I moved in.

"While Lila is living under our roof, you'll treat her like a sister. Have I made myself clear?" Patrick had said.

Apparently, Gideon had said, "So you're saying that Jude and Brody can't have sex with Lila while she's living with us."

Which had made twelve-year-old Jesse crack up when he told me the story.

Not that I was planning to have sex with Jude. I was just going to his room to give him his birthday present. It was perfectly innocent. I was wearing shorts and an old T-shirt, not the outfit of a seductress. No makeup. Hair in a messy bun.

Here goes nothing. I ducked into Jude's bedroom and quietly closed the door behind me, letting out a breath of relief that I hadn't woken anyone up. A sliver of moon lit up his bedroom and I debated whether or not to turn on the lights. Why wouldn't I turn on the lights? I was still standing in the middle of his room debating, when his head appeared in the open window. I slapped a hand over my mouth to stop myself from screaming.

Why was he climbing the trellis instead of using the front door?

I froze. This was a stupid idea. I should go. Slip out the door before he noticed me.

"That you, Rebel?" He didn't sound surprised. Or happy. His tone was flat like he really didn't care one way or the other.

"Yeah, it's me."

He turned on his desk lamp, casting a soft glow on the room, and dropped into the swivel chair then spun around to face me. His hair was messy and tousled as if someone had been running their fingers through it all night long and his eyes were glassy but I couldn't tell how drunk he was.

"What are you doing here?" he asked, his voice low as his gaze lowered to the wrapped gift I was clutching to my chest. Holding on for dear life, both arms wrapped around it tightly like it was my firstborn child and I couldn't bear to part with something so precious to me.

"I wanted to give you your birthday present." It came out sounding more like a question and I cursed myself for sounding so unsure. This had been a huge mistake. It wasn't the right time to give him this present, and I was starting to think there never would be a right time.

He hated me. Could I really blame him though? I'd hate me too.

He leaned back in the chair and linked his hands behind

his head, assessing me with cool disdain. I was under no illusions. He was in full command of this situation and he was going to use it to his benefit. His blue eyes were hooded as they roamed over my body from head to toe while I stood under his scrutiny. He didn't say a word. For a few long, excruciating moments it was so quiet I could hear my heart drumming in my ears.

He wanted to see me squirm. I didn't know why I was still standing there like an idiot. Why hadn't I walked out the door by now?

"You know what I want for my birthday?" he asked finally.

I shook my head and even though I knew I was setting myself up, I couldn't help but ask, "What do you want?" My voice sounded scratchy like I hadn't used it in a long time.

"You. Down on your knees in front of me." He licked his lips and closed his eyes as if he was savoring the taste. Then his eyes opened and locked onto mine and there was something different in them. "I want you *begging* me to let you suck my dick."

My jaw dropped and I had to pick it up from the floor. Who the hell did he think he was?

"Think you can handle that?" he taunted like this was one of our dares and he was challenging me to do it.

I spun around and headed for the door.

My hand was on the doorknob when his palm smacked against the wood above my head and my chest was pressed against the door, his body flush with mine.

He dipped his head, and shivers ran up and down my spine as his mouth moved close to the shell of my ear, his voice low and husky. "Stay, Rebel. See it through. *I dare you.*"

He took a step back, and I closed my eyes, my forehead pressed against the door. Then I squared my shoulders, turned the knob and heard him laugh. There was no trace of humor in his laughter.

"Go on. Do what you do best. Run, Rebel, run. But if you walk out that door now, don't bother coming back."

I released the doorknob and let my arm hang loose at my side. I'd never heard him use that tone of voice with me but I knew he meant what he said. If I walked away now, there would be no coming back from this.

Slowly, I turned around to face him. Setting my gift on the floor like it was an offering to the gods, I straightened my spine, lifted my chin and met his gaze. Something flickered in his eyes that set my pulse racing and my heart hammering against my ribcage. Like it was trying to break free.

I wasn't backing down. Challenge accepted. Jude would never force me to give him a blow job, I knew that, but I was volunteering. I was going to do this. "Where do you want me?"

When he didn't answer, I took a few steps closer until I was standing right in front of him. Placing my palms on his chest, I walked him backward until the backs of his knees hit his mattress. Curious to see what I'd do, he went along with it. With one more shove from me, he was sitting on the edge of his bed, watching and waiting.

I dropped to my knees in front of him and scooted closer, my knees scraping across the red and blue braided rug until I was kneeling between his spread legs. "Is this where you want me?"

I flattened my palms on his thighs, his rock-hard muscles flexing under faded denim. A thrill shot through me when I heard his sharp intake of breath.

I looked up at him from beneath my lashes and ran my tongue over my bottom lip. "Is this what you want?" Eyes locked with his, I took one hand off his thigh and slowly traced the outline of my lips with my fingertip, noting the way his eyes followed the movement. "You want these lips wrapped around your cock?" I asked, so boldly, so brazenly as if I said that word every day when in fact it was the first time it had ever left my mouth.

"Such a dirty mouth, Rebel."

I ran both hands over the tops of his thighs, inching closer and closer. There was no backing down now. I wouldn't and I could tell he knew that.

I had no idea how to do this. No idea how to give a blow job or seduce a guy or what to do to make him feel good. But I wanted to do this. I *needed* to do this.

"Take off your shirt," I said.

His eyes still on me, he did as I asked and pulled his shirt over his head then tossed it aside waiting to see what my next move would be. I wanted to touch his bronzed skin, run my hands over every inch of his bare chest and his abs and that V that dipped into the waistband of his jeans. Like it was leading to the promised land.

But instead of doing that, I dipped two fingers inside the waistband of his jeans and dragged them ever so slowly across his abdomen. He sucked in a breath when I stopped at the top button of his jeans. Because, of course, he couldn't wear jeans with a zipper. That would be too easy.

"Unbutton your jeans."

He shook his head, indicating that he refused to do it then adjusted himself in his jeans and smirked when my eyes lowered to his hand. I bit my bottom lip. He took my hand in his and guided it down so I could feel how hard he was. Knowing that he wanted me gave me confidence and spurred me on. My hands were trembling and I didn't know if it was from nerves or excitement, maybe both, but I was all thumbs.

And I was getting so turned on, it was ridiculous. My nipples had hardened into peaks and I squeezed my thighs together.

"Jesus Christ, Rebel."

My fingers fumbled with the buttons until he lost patience with my clumsy efforts and pushed my hand aside so he could do it himself. Then he pushed down the waistband of his boxer briefs and I swallowed hard because this thing right in front of my face was a lot bigger than when I'd seen him coming out of the shower.

I was staring. I lifted my eyes to his expecting to see amusement in them, but his blue eyes had darkened and there was no hint of amusement there.

"If you're not going to do it, I'll do it myself," he said, his voice strained.

I squeezed my eyes shut. "I want to do it."

"I'm dying here so anytime you're ready..."

All my bravado flew right out the window. I totally sucked at the art of seduction. "I don't know what to do. What if I do it wrong?" I winced. I was making myself so vulnerable, setting myself up for ridicule.

He chuckled under his breath. "Trust me. Anything you do will feel good right now. Just... wrap your hand around it."

I nodded. He hissed when I wrapped my hand around him. He was rock hard in my hand, the skin velvet soft and I was practically salivating. This was crazy. He moved my hand lower, wrapped his around mine and squeezed. Then his hand slid around the back of my head and he guided it down until my mouth was only inches from his tip.

My tongue darted out and I experimented, tentative at first, like this was a new flavor of ice cream and I wanted to test it before committing to an entire bowl. I licked the tip and he muttered a curse. Feeling bolder, I shoved his hand away and took control, licking and sucking, taking my cues from his responses. His hand fisted my hair and the guttural sounds coming from the back of his throat had me so turned on that I was rubbing my thighs together while I sucked him.

Thanks to the school gossip mill, I knew this wasn't his first, and I wanted this to be the best blow job he'd ever had. But what I hadn't expected was that I would love doing this for him.

"Lila. Fuck," he said, his voice strained. "I'm going to come. You don't want—"

It was a warning but I paid it no attention. I did want it. All of it. All of him.

I was all in and even as he tried to pull away, I kept my hand and my lips wrapped around him.

"Fuck, Rebel."

I lifted my eyes to watch him. I loved this. I loved watching him fall apart for me. With his lips parted and his eyes squeezed shut, he was so goddamn beautiful that I wish I had a photo to preserve this moment.

Warm, salty liquid spurted down my throat and I drank it all, swallowing every last drop.

When I released him, I couldn't help it. I pulled a face that made him laugh. "It's so salty," I said. That made him laugh harder, although it was silent laughter because we were in his bedroom doing something we shouldn't be doing.

"Happy birthday to me." He stripped down to his boxer briefs, turned off the desk light and climbed into bed then turned his back to me. "Close the door on your way out."

My stomach dropped but I gritted my teeth and balled my fists, forcing back the tears that stung my eyes.

If it weren't for the fact that his parents were down the hall, I would have slammed the door on my way out. But I didn't even get that satisfaction.

I brushed my teeth three times. Rinsed and spit. Rinsed

and spit. Trying to rid my mouth of the taste of Jude. But it didn't work.

I could still taste him on my tongue. This night had been an epic fail. And even worse than what I'd just done? I'd left the wrapped gift in his room.

I had to get it back before he opened it.

CHAPTER FOURTEEN

Jude

"DID YOU SEE THE WAY KELLY'S BEEN EYE-FUCKING ME?"
Reese asked when we stopped for a water break. A few of the
girls from the cheering squad were hanging out by the
bleachers watching our practice. Hated to break it to Reese but
Kelly wasn't interested in him.

"Kelly's looking at Austin Armacost who's standing right
behind you," I said, replenishing my electrolytes with the sports
drink that my mom bought by the case, ensuring that our
pantry was always fully stocked.

Reese looked over his shoulder for confirmation. "Goddamn. I thought she was looking at me."

"Dude. They're never looking at you," Tyler said, dousing
his head with water from the plastic bottle in his hand. "Face it.
You're gonna die a virgin."

"That's harsh. Brianna's still holding out on you, huh?"

"I've moved on. Your mother was up for it."

"You son of a bitch. Leave my mother out of it." A few of

the other guys on the team joined Tyler in ribbing Reese about his mom. By now he should be used to hearing shit like that. His mom was hot and all the guys teased him about her.

I tuned them out and checked my phone, chuckling under my breath when I read Brody's text.

L's searching your room. Turned it upside down. Did you steal something of hers?

Only her virtue. And her pride. I couldn't believe she'd gone along with it. But damn if it wasn't the sexiest thing any girl had ever done for me. Technique aside, it was the best blow job I'd ever had. Because it was Rebel, down on her knees for me. Which was something I never thought I'd see.

As an added bonus, she was now my foster sister. My dad had told me and Brody, in no uncertain terms, that she was off-limits to us. We were supposed to treat her with respect. Like she deserved my respect. She deserved nothing from me.

But let's face it, the forbidden aspect only made it that much hotter. What other boundaries could we push?

"Was she the one who gave you those crabs?" Austin asked Tyler, jolting me back to reality as I stashed my phone in my sports bag. Obviously, I'd missed something. "That shit was nasty. Did your pubes grow back yet?"

"Suck my dick and find out for yourself."

Austin gave him the finger.

"Come on, ladies," Coach said, clapping his hands together. "Enough gossip. Let's see how much talking you do after the next drill. Line up for sprint ladders. You know what to do."

"Goddamn, I hate suicides," Tyler grumbled as we lined up on the goal line. The whistle blew, loud and shrill, and we sprinted to the ten-yard line. Without stopping, we turned around and ran full speed back to the goal line. Then sprinted to the twenty-yard line. And so on and so on until my thighs were burning and buckets of sweat poured off me.

With soaring temperatures and the afternoon sun beating down on us, suicides weren't a lot of fun. But this was Texas. Football wasn't just a sport, it was a religion. So we worked our asses off for our coaches, for our town, for our team.

I didn't mind the conditioning drills. It was good training for boot camp. I was so ready for it.

Reese fell into step with me as I headed to my truck after practice. His face was an alarming shade of red and I couldn't tell if it was sunburn or heat stroke. "Can I bum a ride?" he asked, running a hand over his shower-damp hair that was more reddish-brown now than the orange shade it used to be.

"Yeah sure. No problem." Reese was always having to bum rides. His car was a piece of shit so it was out of commission more often than it was on the road.

"So I've been thinking," he said as I pulled out of the school parking lot and onto the two-lane highway, air con cranked up and music blasting. "I wanna enlist with you."

What the fuck? That had just come out of the blue. I'd known Reese since kindergarten and this was the first I'd heard of it.

"*You* want to be a Marine?" I asked skeptically.

"Yeah, I do. We can enlist together. They've got a buddy program so we'll be in boot together."

"Not sure that's how it works."

"We can talk to the recruiter. See what they say."

"When I enlist, I'm holding out for third MOS. That's Infantry," I clarified, trying to dissuade him. I had my future mapped out. I was planning to enlist within the next few weeks, on the Delayed Entry Program. I wanted to get into

Infantry and then Recon. I liked Reese. He was a good guy, but no offense, I couldn't see him being a Marine.

"Yeah, I know. That's what I want too. Girls go batshit over guys in uniform. I bet we'll get so much pussy—"

I cut him off right there. "You can't enlist in the Marines just because you're desperate for pussy." I swear, it was the only thing the guy ever talked about. He was so desperate he reeked of it and girls could smell that from a mile away.

"Yeah, I know. That's not the only reason I want to do it. It's just a bonus."

I shook my head. "You need a better reason. It's a huge commitment. It's not the kind of thing you can just walk away from or quit if you decide it's not for you."

"I know all this," he snapped. "I've been thinking about it for a long time. And it's what I want."

I side-eyed him. He looked determined but I wasn't so sure about this whole buddy thing. "We might not end up together. There's no guarantee."

"I'm doing it with or without you. But I'd still like to do the buddy program. I did the research. We'd go to boot together for sure and our names are close in the alphabet which would give us a better shot at ending up in the same platoon. We don't have to sign a contract until it has everything we want *in writing.*"

I was impressed that he knew all that so I guess he had done some research.

"You cool with that?" he asked.

I didn't know how to answer. I'd never considered going with a friend. For as long as I could remember, I'd wanted to be a Marine and everyone knew that. So I stayed silent, trying to formulate an answer to his question as I turned onto his dirt and gravel road flanked by scrubby bushes. There were no trees around to give it some shade and it always felt ten degrees hotter than other parts of town.

Reese lived in a double-wide on a patch of dirt and sparse grass that never seemed to grow. His mom bartended at The Roadhouse, a dive bar out on the highway, and it was just the two of them. He didn't take family vacations to the beach like he used to claim he did. In reality, he used to visit his dad in Galveston. But I got the feeling his dad didn't really want him around because he hadn't seen him since the summer before we started high school.

"If it's what you want, it's not like I can stop you," I said, pulling up outside his trailer. In all the years I'd known Reese, I'd never been invited inside. I suspected it was because he was embarrassed. Not like it was his fault. Not that I'd ever judge him on something as superficial as where he lived or how much money he had.

Brody hated this neighborhood. A few months ago, he'd had a run-in with Reese's neighbor who kept his hunting dogs in cages at the side of his house. When Brody confronted him and called it cruel and inhumane, the guy came after him with a shotgun. He claimed it was within his rights to shoot Brody for trespassing. For weeks, all Brody talked about was those dogs. Now I noticed the cages were gone and so were the dogs. Huh.

"Give it more thought before you commit," I urged Reese.

"Why are you doing it?" he asked, turning his head to look at me. "Give me the number one reason why you're so set on doing this. Because, man, I gotta tell you... from where I'm sitting, your life is damn near perfect."

I stared at the junkers parked on the neighbor's front lawn. The front porch heaved under the weight of all the shit piled up on it—an old sofa, tables with missing legs, and rust-corroded white appliances. Why did they have a freezer and a washing machine on the front porch?

"I guess it always felt like my call of duty," I said in answer to Reese's question. "For as long as I can remember, I knew it was something I was meant to do. It feels like my purpose. My responsibility to protect the people I love." It sounded corny as shit when I said it aloud but it was the way I'd always felt so I was being honest with him.

"I can respect that. But everyone is entitled to their own opinion. Their own reason for wanting to join the military."

"I never said you weren't entitled to that."

"Yeah, well, that's what you implied."

False. He'd given me a lame-ass reason for wanting to enlist so I didn't know where he got off saying that. "So what's your reason?"

He was quiet for a minute, just staring out the windshield at the mustard yellow double-wide with brown trim.

When I was about to give up on waiting for a valid reason, he admitted, "I want some direction in my life. I don't have the money or the grades to go to college and I don't wanna end up in some dead-end job, working at a plant or doing concrete work and have nothing to show for it. I want a purpose in life, you know?"

I looked at him and it felt like I was seeing him in a new light. Reese had always been the joker, and a lot of people didn't take him seriously. Until now, I hadn't either. "Yeah, I do. I get it."

He nodded and reached for the door handle.

"I'll wait until your eighteenth birthday and if it's still what you want, we'll go together." His birthday was in November. Anything could happen between now and then. But if this was something he really wanted, who was I to talk him out of it?

"Cool." He bumped my fist before he grabbed his sports bag and got out of my truck.

As I drove away, my tires spitting gravel, I thought about

how different Reese's reality was to mine. Not everyone was as lucky as me.

I hit the speed dial on my phone and waited for Brody to pick up. "What's up?"

"You wanna go for brisket tacos? I'm buying."

"Who died?"

I laughed. Asshole. "Are you in or not? I'm starving."

"I can never say no to those tacos. But we're not talking about that shit I told you."

The shit he'd told me was so fucking sick that I still couldn't wrap my head around it. He was drunk and stoned when he told me that last night and afterward, he'd regretted it. But it was out there now and he made me promise to take it to my grave. Which I would.

I wish there was something I could do to help him but I had no idea what that could be. Except to be his friend, I guess. "Didn't plan on it."

"I'll meet you there. I'm just leaving the ranch."

"See you in ten." I cut the call and tossed my phone in the cupholder. I didn't even think about Lila or the fact that brisket tacos with pico de gallo was her favorite food. I didn't think about her at all.

CHAPTER FIFTEEN

Jude

IT HAD BEEN THREE DAYS SINCE THE NIGHT LILA CAME into my bedroom, and we hadn't spoken a word to each other since then. She was either running, hanging out with her hot, bi-curious girlfriend, or working. She worked at the garden center. My mom said Lila had a green thumb and could make anything grow. I was tempted to tell her she had no idea how true that was. My dick grew every time Lila walked into a room. Which was inconvenient, all things considered.

Tonight she hadn't come home for dinner. Brody was away at a rodeo this weekend. Jesse had just come home from a track day and bragged all the way through dinner about how he was going to be the next hottest motocross sensation. And Gideon sat in stony silence, like always.

While I ate my chicken and broccoli casserole, I tuned out my dad's lecture. It was directed at Gideon, not me. "You're starting high school next week. What are your extracurricular activities? What sports will you be playing?" my dad badgered him.

"There's more to life than sports," Gideon said, spearing a piece of broccoli with his fork but not eating it.

"Sports teach you about life. They teach you how to work with your teammates. They teach you how to win and how to lose. They teach you not to be a quitter."

I finished my dinner and reached for my glass of water, guzzling the rest of it.

Setting down my glass, I leaned back in my chair and yawned, drowsy from the heat and the long week of football practice. Not to mention it was Saturday and earlier today my dad had me mowing the lawn and doing a million repairs to the house like I was his personal handyman. So I was tired and my mind was elsewhere.

"Can I be excused?" I asked, drumming my fingers on the oak table, antsy to leave now.

In our house, you didn't just stand up from the table and walk away without permission. We had the weirdest rules. Drinking was okay as long as you never got behind the wheel. Fighting was cool, encouraged even. If we had a curfew, I wasn't aware of it because it wasn't enforced. As long as we got home alive and in one piece, and we kept our commitments the next day without complaining of being tired or hungover, it was all good.

But we had to ask permission to leave the table. We had to complete all our chores on the specified day according to the chart on the refrigerator. Right next to the chart with gold stars for our major accomplishments, typically sports-related and only if we'd won. Bedrooms had to be kept tidy. Wet towels on the bathroom floor were a major offense. Dirty clothes hampers were to be put in the laundry room on Saturday morning by eight or you did your own laundry.

We were all being trained for the US Marine Corps.

My dad looked over at me briefly and nodded, giving permission to leave then re-focused his attention on Gideon who looked like he was standing before a firing squad. I felt for Gideon, I really did. It sucked being under my dad's scrutiny.

"Do you hear Jude complaining about having to go to football practice?" my dad asked Gideon as I rinsed my plate and put it in the dishwasher. "Do you see him quitting when things get tough—"

"I'm not Jude," Gideon gritted out, shooting a glare in my direction like it was my fucking fault that my dad compared us.

I didn't like it any more than he did. I hated when my dad pulled that shit and pitted us against each other like it was a competition.

"I want you to work on some drills together. Starting tomorrow morning," my dad said, his voice firm.

I didn't want to fucking work on drills on a Sunday with my brother.

Gideon shook his head and exhaled loudly. "How many times do I have to say it? I. Hate. Football."

"Do you think Jude would be as good as he is if he slacked off and didn't put a hundred percent into trying to be the best?"

I couldn't handle it anymore. I snapped.

"You need to lay off," I told him. His jaw clenched, his gaze swinging to me now. Ignoring his narrowed eyes and knowing damn well I was skating on some very thin ice, I forged on like the dumb shit I was. "He's not me. Football is not his thing. He gets straight A's. He wants to go to an Ivy League college and he's smart enough to get in." I only knew this because Jesse told me. "In the real world, that's just as important if not more important than whether or not he wants to compete in high school sports."

My father glared at me, outraged that I would dare to question him. I nearly laughed. He looked like one of those cartoon characters with steam coming out of his ears. He opened his mouth to speak but before he got a word out my mom interjected.

"Jude is right, Patrick," my mom said, sounding weary. She'd been down this road with him many times and already knew that nothing we said would change his mind. "You need to stop comparing the boys. Gideon has different interests and you have to learn to appreciate that and respect it. Not every boy wants to play football."

My work here was done. I'd said my part. Dug my own grave. Now, my mom had taken up the cause and I left her to verbally spar with my dad. On my way out of the kitchen, I grabbed a green apple from the fruit bowl and glanced at Gideon. He gave me a nod, just a tip of the chin but it was his way of saying thank you. For once, it felt like we were on the same team. And that felt pretty damn good.

But I had something more pressing to take care of right now. Taking the stairs two at a time, I closed my bedroom door behind me, cursing the fact that our bedrooms didn't have locks on the doors.

I took the wrapped gift down from its hiding place where it had been since I moved it from my truck earlier today and sat on my bed with my back leaning against the headboard, the gift in my lap. I'd had this gift in my possession for three days now and it was a miracle I hadn't opened it yet.

The wrapping paper was midnight blue with gold stars.

The gift was for me so it wasn't like I'd stolen something that didn't belong to me. I turned it over, ran my hand over it, trying to figure out what could be so important that she'd ransacked my room trying to find it.

Fuck it.

I ripped off the paper, crumpled it into a ball and tossed it aside. Then I stared at the book in my hands. A photo album? A scrapbook? Aurora Borealis on a black background graced the cover and in gold marker, it said: The Book of Jude.

I opened it and studied the collage of photos. I recognized most of them. We were nine years old in these photos.

She was so fucking cute back then. Tiny but fierce. In every single photo, we were either laughing or smiling. Jesus, I missed those times.

I turned each page slowly to reveal more memories. It wasn't just photos either. There were handwritten notes. Ticket stubs from baseball games and movies we'd gone to. Dried wildflowers that I suspected were from the time I'd picked a bunch of them in the field for her. She'd put them in a mason jar on the kitchen windowsill. Fortunes from Chinese fortune cookies that we'd laughed at. The woven friendship bracelets she'd made us that first summer.

She'd kept everything. I didn't even remember half of these photos being taken nor had I realized that Lila was the sentimental type. Guess you learn something new every day.

After poring over each photo, each memory, I turned the page and was disappointed to see it was the final one. But this, I suspected, was what she'd wanted to take back. I glanced at the door. The house was quiet. I was alone in my room.

Taking a deep breath, I read the letter she'd written me.

Dear Jude,

I've tried to write this a hundred times but the words came out all wrong. Maybe there are no right words. I guess I just have to speak my own truth and hope you can find a way to understand and forgive me.

I'm sorry I pushed you away. I treated you like crap and I ruined our friendship. At the time, it made sense to me but with each passing day, it makes less and less sense and I don't know what to do about it. But I'm going to try to explain where I was coming from.

I was scared of letting you in because you're going to leave me and you're going to become a Marine. And if I let you get too close only to lose you, then where would I be without you?

Alone. Missing you. Miserable.

After my mom died, the thought of you leaving me was too much for my heart to handle.

There's another reason I pushed you away. I felt guilty. I was kissing you on the roof when my mom died. I should have been there for her. I hate knowing that she died alone, you know?

So I pushed you out of my life. I punished you for something that wasn't even your fault.

But I've missed you every single day. I miss you so much it hurts. And I don't know how to find my way back to you. To us. To the way everything used to be.

And I think that's part of the problem. We can never go back to the way we used to be because we've changed. Life changes us. We're not little kids anymore, so nothing is as easy as it used to be. But some things haven't changed.

Even when you sometimes act like a bonehead, you're still my favorite human. You're still the first person I want to talk to when I wake up and the last person I want to talk to before I go to sleep. Whenever something happens in my life—the good, the bad, the ugly... every stupid little detail. I wish we could just hang out and talk about everything and nothing.

You're still the boy who gave me his favorite hoodie on what could have been the most embarrassing, humiliating day of my life. But because it was you, it was okay. You make everything better. Even on bad days.

You make me feel stronger and braver. You make me laugh

and smile more than anyone ever has. You make me angry and jealous and you drive me crazy because some days all I can think about is you. And that really, really pisses me off.

And I don't even know if this letter makes any sense but I guess what I'm trying to say is that I miss you. As Jesse would say, *A lot, a lot. Like, for real, for real.*

Before my mom died, she told me to be brave with my heart. She said that love makes you vulnerable, but with the right person, it also makes you stronger. I didn't really understand it at the time, but I think I get what she was saying now.

I'm not saying I'm in love with you or anything... that would be too crazy. But you make me feel weak and you make me feel strong all at the same time. So, yeah, I don't know if you've gotten this far but if you're still reading, I hope we can be friends again. I want that so much.

And I don't know, I guess what I'm trying to say is that you were my two in the morning person. You were my person and I like to think that maybe I was yours too.

I'm sorry I screwed everything up. I'm not sure if I'll even give this to you but if I'm brave enough, I will. I want to be brave.

Happy 18th Birthday.

Never yours,

Lila

I leaned my head against the headboard and closed my eyes, rubbing my hand over my chest to ease the ache.

Why couldn't she have told me any of this before it was too late? I would have understood. I would have found a way to make it right. To prove to her that I'd always be there for her. Whether I was in Texas or California or wherever I was, I would have always found a way to include her in my life. But now she'd gone and shit all over our friendship and I didn't know how to forgive her for that.

Were a few sweet words and some photos supposed to change everything? Was that what she expected to happen?

My cell phone vibrated in my pocket, interrupting my thoughts. I slid it out and read the message.

Kylie: Hey J, you wanna come over tonight? My parents will be out.

That was code for: Let's have sex.

I texted her back then tossed my phone on the bedside table and ignored the incoming messages. None of those girls meant anything to me and I'd made that clear right from the start. I wasn't looking for a girlfriend. I would never be their boyfriend. When Ashleigh realized that I would never be in love with her, she'd moved on and I'd breathed a sigh of relief when she started dating some college guy.

Kylie wasn't looking for a boyfriend. She just liked sex, so that made everything easier and far less complicated.

I read Lila's letter three more times and looked through all the photos again, reading her little notes underneath them until I knew every word by heart.

Never yours, she'd signed it.

That was where she was wrong. She had always been mine and for a while I had been hers. She'd just been too blind to see what was right in front of her eyes. She'd thrown my love back in my face just like that football jersey, and she'd walked away. I had done everything in my power to be there for her but what had I gotten for my efforts? A kick in the balls. Because that was how it felt.

This went deeper than wounding my pride. She trampled all over my heart.

Goddamn you, Rebel.

A knock on my bedroom door had me stashing the book

under my mattress. The door opened and my dad appeared in the doorway looking none too happy. He advanced into the room and I could tell that my words at the dinner table had not gone down too well.

Oh shit, here we go. No good deed goes unpunished.

"What's up?" I grabbed the tennis ball on my bedside table and tossed it against the opposite wall. It hit the wall and bounced back. I caught it mid-air and tossed it again. Toss. Catch. Toss. Catch.

"What was all that about at the dinner table?" he asked, his gaze settled on the sports trophies and medals my mom had put on the shelves to create a display. I kept moving them out of my room and hiding them in the attic but they kept reappearing as if by magic.

"Just trying to defend my brother." I kept slamming the wall with the tennis ball and catching it in one hand.

"Look at me when I'm speaking to you." With a sigh, I caught the ball in my hand and swung my legs over the bed then stood up to face him. With the two of us in this room, it felt too crowded, like there wasn't enough space or enough air for both of us to breathe comfortably. "You need to be a role model for your brothers. I expect better from you, Jude. And undermining me at the dinner table is unacceptable." He crossed his arms over his wide chest, no doubt waiting for an apology. I mimicked his stance and stared at him. I wasn't sorry and had no intention of saying it.

"Your brothers look up to you. If you say it's okay, Gideon believes it."

That was actually laughable. Gideon had never been my biggest fan and I highly doubted that he believed everything I said nor did he have any interest in following my example. Which was the whole point. He shouldn't be expected to follow in my footsteps. Gideon and I were night and day and while we'd never been close, he was still my brother so I'd always defend him.

"He's going to play football and you're going to work with him on his game," my father stated firmly, leaving no room for argument.

An incredulous laugh burst out of me. I shook my head. "I don't get it. Why is it so important to you that he plays football?"

"Because he's good. He has a natural ability just like you do."

It was pointless to tell my father that Gideon hated playing football which meant he'd half-ass it out on the field if he was forced to play. My dad would talk to Coach and get Gideon on the team and that would be the end of it. Gideon would be a Maverick, he'd wear the blue and gold jersey on Friday nights, and he'd end up riding the bench. He'd take out his anger on me because I was being forced to 'work with him.'

Gideon would start to resent my father, and me, even more than he already did. He always said that I was Dad's favorite but what he failed to notice was that it wasn't exactly a day at the beach. It came with more responsibility.

In short, this whole situation was a giant clusterfuck.

"It's for his own good. Your brother needs to toughen up and learn to start fighting his own battles. That's what real men do," my dad said before he left my room, the door closing behind him with a ring of finality.

Real men. He was raising us to be exactly like him. My mother was a saint for putting up with my father. Love. It really was blind.

After he was gone, I climbed down the trellis, strode across the field and slid open the barn door. Then I punched the leather bag hanging from the rafters until the skin over my knuckles split and bled. Because that's what real men did.

They fought and they bled and they locked down their emotions. They toughed it out and they never said die.

Real men weren't allowed to cry or complain or question the unfairness of life.

Real men were always winners. To the victor go the spoils.

By the time I left the barn after a grueling workout that ensured I didn't have an ounce of energy left in my body, it had gotten dark already. As I was crossing the field, blood dripping from my hands and sweat matting my hair to my head, I saw Lila climbing the trellis to my bedroom window. I stopped short and watched from the side of the house. She hadn't seen me standing in the shadows. But she didn't climb into my bedroom window.

She was headed for the roof.

The fuck was she thinking?

CHAPTER SIXTEEN

Lila

INSANITY. THAT'S WHAT THIS WAS. COMPLETE, TOTAL insanity. But I was determined to do it. In the dark. Without a safety harness or a rope and nothing to catch my fall.

Stay calm. Don't look down. Find your next foothold and just keep climbing.

Be brave.

Would it be worth it if I ended up dead? Or paralyzed? Or with broken limbs? I couldn't think about the risks. Not now that I was halfway there. I just had to keep going until I reached the top.

As it turned out, being vertically challenged was actually a good thing for a climber. When Jude was at football practice, I used the equipment in the gym to work on my upper body strength. I was lean and light and getting stronger by the day.

You've got this, I told myself as my chalked hands gripped the stone and I found my next foothold, pushing myself higher.

Almost there. I shuffled my feet along the drainpipe,

praying it would continue holding my weight. Reaching up, my fingertips grazed the gutter that ran along the edge of the roof. I pushed up on my tiptoes and got a better grip then dug my toe into the grout of the stone wall I was scaling and pulled myself up. That was where it all fell apart. My other foot was just dangling below me and I couldn't get a grip.

Sweat beaded my forehead and there was a pit in my stomach that turned me to ice. Panic gripped me, a shot of adrenaline rushing through my veins and making my heart pound so hard it felt like it was going to burst through the walls of my chest.

Heartless Lila. With her heart splattered on the ground next to her.

Holy shit. I was going to fall to my death. There was no safety net to catch me. Nothing to prevent me from falling and hitting the ground. I'd be toast. It was going to hurt.

Where do I go from here? What do I do? My sweaty hands slipped and my heart skipped a beat as I adjusted my grip, hanging on for dear life. I couldn't hold on much longer.

"Don't look down." His voice came from above me and I barely heard over the rush of blood to my head. I whimpered. Oh God. "Listen to me."

"Okay."

"I've got you. You're not going to fall. I've got you."

I squeezed my eyes shut, relief flooding my body.

"Get a good foothold and push up. I'll take it from there."

I couldn't even argue with him. He was leaning over the side of the roof, ready to grab hold of me and pull me to safety. It was either do as he said or risk a sudden death. Okay, maybe I wouldn't die but it would hurt like hell to fall from the second story.

I dug my toes in and pushed up and at the same time his hands wrapped around me underneath my armpits. While he pulled, I pushed, my stomach scraping against the cedar shingles until most of my body was on the roof and I was able to get my knees underneath me and roll onto my back. Then I lay there on the roof, panting from the exertion, my pulse racing and my heart pounding out a crazy beat.

And for a long time neither of us said a word. I kept my eyes closed but I could feel him next to me. Not so close that we were touching but close enough to smell his sweat and feel the heat from his body.

Once again, he'd come to my rescue and I hated that. This was something that I'd wanted to do for myself. Something I'd convinced myself I needed to do. Now I wasn't sure why it had seemed so important at the time.

Oh yeah, must have been liquid courage.

He was the first to speak. "Have you lost your fucking mind?"

I huffed out a laugh. "Nobody asked you to rescue me."

"How drunk are you?"

I shrugged one shoulder. I'd had a few peach iced teas with vodka. Buzzed but not drunk, and now I felt stone-cold sober but I didn't tell him any of this. I didn't tell him about the party at the lake or about the boy I kissed. I didn't tell him that the boy was cute but that his lips felt all wrong on mine. His touch didn't send an electric current through my body. My pulse didn't race. My heart didn't beat wildly. His lips, his hands, they weren't Jude's.

And it had made me so angry that I couldn't erase the memory of my first kiss by replacing it with something better. Because maybe there wasn't anything better. Maybe Jude was the very best and nobody would ever compare.

I didn't tell him that I saw his fuck buddy Kylie at the party either. She'd asked me about Jude and wanted to know where he was tonight. I told her I had no idea which was the truth. I also told her I didn't care which was a lie.

But why did he always go for blondes? They were always tall and willowy too, with big boobs, the opposite of me in every way. Oh right. Guess that was the whole point.

"Jesus Christ, Rebel," he said, sounding exasperated. "You've really outdone yourself this time. If you were trying to get my attention, there were easier ways to do it."

"Like what? Give you a blow job?" I laughed like that was the funniest thing I'd ever heard. My laughter bordered on manic and he waited until I pulled myself together before he spoke again. He wanted to make sure his words were heard.

"Like by doing something that didn't almost get us both killed." His voice was low and angry and maybe a little hurt, I didn't know. I couldn't tell anymore. "But yeah, another blow job would have worked. At least I'd get something out of it."

"I wasn't trying to get your attention. I don't want your attention."

"Yeah. I got that. You made that pretty clear for the past ten months."

I still had my eyes closed when I felt him leaving, taking my battered heart with him. When I opened my eyes, I was alone on the roof under a sky full of stars with only the bitter taste of regret and my salty tears for company.

I watched the stars reeling in the sky and I tried to find the brightest one. But I couldn't. All I could think about was how disappointed my mom would be in me right now.

I didn't even care if Jude had opened my present or if he'd read my stupid letter because if he had, it hadn't made one bit of difference. He was going to hang on to his hurt and anger the same way I'd held on to my guilt and fear. Nothing had changed. And I was starting to think it never would.

Instead of trying to climb down from the roof, I crawled through the attic window. Jude had left it open for me. Not to be kind but to save himself from having to rescue me again, no doubt.

The next morning I went to the climbing wall, a little bit hungover and a little bit sadder but I climbed anyway and told myself it would make me stronger and braver and I'd be able to reach for the stars on my own. Without him.

Patrick had given me the membership and the climbing shoes last Christmas after a talk we had. He asked me what would make me feel stronger and I thought it was an odd question, but a good one. I told him I wanted to learn how to climb. It had just struck me as something I wanted to get better at. Like a good life skill to have. And that was how it all started. It was my thing. Not exactly a secret. Brody knew about it. Christy knew about it. But I'd never told Jude because we didn't talk anymore.

As I was leaving the climbing wall, I pulled my backpack straps over both shoulders about to run the three and a half miles home when Brody's truck stopped right in front of me. Literally. He narrowly missed running me over. That was Brody for you. Resident bad boy and serial heartbreaker at your service.

"Need a ride, Sugar Lips?" He leaned across the front seat and gave me that signature Brody McCallister grin through the open window, his teeth so white against his suntanned skin.

I laughed. "Stop calling me that." The nickname wasn't meant to make me feel special. I'd heard him use it on plenty of girls. I tossed my backpack in the truck and climbed in, pulling the door closed. His truck smelled like horses and leather and black licorice from the Twizzlers he was eating. He was the only one I knew who liked black licorice. I'd given him a case of root beer and jumbo packs of Twizzlers for his eighteenth birthday in April. He'd given me a case of Dr. Pepper and a bag of donuts for my seventeenth birthday.

He drove with one hand on the wheel, the other one tapping out the beat of "Smack That" by Akon that was blasting from his speakers and even though it was hotter than Hades outside, his windows were rolled down and he refused to turn on the A/C. He always said he preferred to sweat than breathe artificial air. Brody couldn't bear to be cooped up and he even had trouble being in a car with the windows rolled up.

"You missed the turn," I said as he kept going straight down the two-lane highway instead of turning right. He ignored me and I leaned back in my seat, side-eying him.

"Where are we going?"

"It's my turn to buy."

"Buy what?"

"Tacos."

"You're taking me for tacos? What do you mean it's your turn to buy? I never bought you tacos."

He just laughed and ran his fingers through his longish dirty-blond hair. "How did the rodeo go?" I asked because if he was taking me for tacos for lunch, I certainly wouldn't argue with that.

"I'm the best bareback bronc rider in all of Texas, that's how it went."

I snorted. "Your head's so big I'm surprised it fits in that ten-gallon hat of yours."

"I upgraded to the twenty-gallon," he joked, and all I could do was laugh. I'd never actually seen him in a cowboy hat.

Why was it so much easier to hang out with Brody these days? I sighed loudly, the sound drowned out by his music.

When he pulled into the roadside barbecue, my eyes widened. Oh no. No, no, no.

"Take me home. I don't want tacos."

Judging by the look on Jude's face, he didn't look thrilled to see me either. His eyes narrowed to slits and he crossed his arms over his chest, clearly unhappy with this whole scenario. He was leaning against his truck waiting for Brody but instead he'd gotten me too.

Brody had tricked us.

"You're not gonna back down now, are you?" Brody asked, and I heard the challenge in his voice. His question was aimed at me but it was loud enough for Jude to hear. Which meant that neither of us were going to back down now. We'd eat tacos together if it killed us. We'd eat tacos together even if they were laced with arsenic.

Jude was the lion and I was the bull. I'd figured it out last night. Leo and Taurus. Those were the constellations he'd put on my bedroom ceiling. It was us and I couldn't figure out why he'd done it.

One time during one of our random late-night conversations I'd asked him, "Who would win a fight if a lion was pitted against a bull?" I'd fully expected him to say that a lion would always win because, among other things, he had a superiority complex and really did think he was king of the jungle.

But he'd surprised me by saying, "Depends on the circumstances. If it was a fighting bull and they were in an enclosed space, the bull would win. It would spear the lion with its horns. If they were out in the open, a lion's natural habitat, the lion would win. Lions have more grace, speed, and agility."

Who would win if a bull and a lion sat down at a picnic table outside a roadside barbecue to eat brisket tacos with pico de gallo? Nobody would win. Because lions only fought when they had something to fight for. And Jude was done fighting for me.

But after we carried our order outside and sat across from each other at the picnic table under the shade of the trees with Brody next to me, Jude bumped the tip of his sneaker against the tip of mine under the table. I thought it was accidental but I kept my foot where it was and when he didn't move his foot away I wondered if it meant something.

I looked up from my taco and met his eyes. Those blue, blue eyes like the wildflowers in the field. Our eyes locked and held and all the air whooshed out of my lungs when he reached across the table and cupped my chin in his hand, brushing his thumb across my jaw. "You're the messiest eater."

"I know," I said, my voice barely a whisper because even though he'd removed his hand and he wasn't touching me anymore, I could still feel it. And I'd heard something in his voice that was almost gentle and turned me into a pile of goo.

"About fucking time," Brody said. "Can we all be friends again? I'm getting tired as fuck of playing monkey in the middle of you two dumb shits."

My gaze swung to Brody then back to Jude. "I've missed us," I said, making myself vulnerable and being way too honest.

But that was the true definition of bravery. It wasn't about who could scale a wall or swing across a creek filled with crocodiles.

Being brave meant being honest and owning up to the things you'd done to hurt people. It was what my mom had tried to tell me but I'd completely missed the message. Until right this minute. And now I saw it all with such blinding clarity that I had no idea how I'd been so blind.

"I'm sorry," I whispered, praying he'd accept my apology. Because here I was, a girl offering up her own truth and begging him to cut her some slack. Like, please, take this heart

I'm offering you in my own two hands. Be gentle with it. Don't break it.

Would I do the same for him if the situation was reversed? I didn't know.

"You're so stubborn, Rebel. So fucking infuriating. How could you be so stupid?"

How dare he? Not like he'd been a saint throughout this whole ten-month stand-off. "You want to talk about stupid? Let's talk about Ashleigh, Megan, and Kylie. And you... my God, you are the most annoying guy. You have such a hero complex that you feel like you need to rescue me from everything."

"Oh yeah, much better to let you fall to your death. What the hell were you thinking?"

"I just panicked for a minute, but I would have been fine. I know I can do it."

"Don't even think about climbing onto that roof without me."

"I don't need you."

"I don't need you either."

"I didn't even miss you."

"You never crossed my mind."

Brody sighed and shook his head. "Oh, here we go. Feels like old times."

"Be careful what you wish for," Jude said, and the three of us laughed. I wasn't even sure what we were laughing about but it felt good. It felt like the world was right again.

———

After we ate, I rode home with Jude who took us on the scenic route, opting for the quiet back roads instead of the highway, our windows rolled down and the late afternoon sun beating down on the windshield. We weren't even heading for home. We were on my favorite winding road that took us over hills and valleys, with a view of the meadows and creeks and yucca-covered cliffs, the sky so big, a cloudless blue. And I couldn't remember the last time I'd been this happy. Just being with him again, driving nowhere, the Black Keys' "Tighten Up" playing from his stereo. It was everything.

I had no idea how I'd lived without this for so long. Without him. Because he'd always been my person. And without him, my life had been so much emptier.

"Did you mean what you said in the letter?" he asked, confirming what I'd suspected. He'd opened the gift and he'd read the letter and had waited until now to ask me about it.

"You weren't supposed to read it."

"Then why did you write it? Why did you bring it to my room if you didn't want me to have it?"

"I did want you to have it but then I changed my mind." I paused, letting the words sink in, just as if we needed a reminder of what had happened that night. I didn't think he was so drunk that he'd forgotten it. "When I went back to look for it, it was gone. And you were pretending to be asleep."

He chuckled. "As soon as you left my room that night, I hid it."

"You're a jerk," I said, but my words had no bite. I didn't really mean it. Although sometimes he was a jerk and some-times he was a downright asshole. But nobody is perfect.

"Where'd you go last night?" he asked.

"A party."

"A party. Did you let anyone kiss you?"

He probably knew exactly where I'd been last night and had gotten a full report. Or maybe Austin told Brody. They were good friends and Brody worked on Austin's family's ranch. Let's chalk it up to mistake number nine hundred and ninety-nine. I'd lost count of all the mistakes I'd made over the past ten months. "Maybe."

His left hand tightened on the wheel, and his right hand landed on the top of my thigh. "And how was it?"

I looked down at his right hand then at the one on the wheel. There were cuts on his knuckles, the skin red and raw. "What happened to your hands?"

He squeezed my thigh. "Stop avoiding the question."

"I don't kiss and tell." I laughed. I'd just given him a taste of his own medicine. He growled and squeezed my thigh again.

"You're rock hard, baby," he said, giving it another squeeze as if to test it out.

"Isn't that what I'm supposed to say to you?"

"Such a dirty mind. Where'd you get all this muscle?"

"Running. Climbing at the climbing wall. And working out in your gym."

"Yeah?" He glanced at me. I nodded. "We can start working out together."

"Let's not rush into anything."

He laughed and pulled his hand away, transferring it to the wheel so he could hang his other arm out the window and tap out the beat on the roof of the truck as "Howlin' For You" by the Black Keys started playing. I stared at his profile, at his straight nose and full lips and the chestnut hair that was tousled and messy, a warm breeze ruffling it. He didn't look like a boy anymore. There was stubble on his jaw and I wanted to brush my lips across it. Let it rough up my tender skin. I had the irresistible urge to kiss his neck. To drag my fingers through his hair and lick his abs. I wanted to bite him and leave my mark the same way he'd done to me.

He glanced at me and graced me with a slow, lazy grin as if he could read my mind and knew where my thoughts had taken me.

"So... does this mean we're friends again?"

He snorted and returned his eyes to the road. "Don't even think about friend-zoning me."

"What zone do you want to be in?"

"The one where I get to rip off your clothes and do dirty things to you with my tongue and my hands and my gigantic cock."

I rolled my eyes. "Oh please. It's not even that big."

He snorted again. "Yes, it is."

Since I had no basis for comparison, I couldn't really argue with that. And it had seemed pretty big. "You'll be lucky if I let you kiss me with that dirty mouth of yours."

"You'll be lucky if you get to find out what this dirty mouth of mine can do."

Oh my God.

What a difference a year makes.

"How is this going to work? Now that we live together." I thought aloud as we headed for home. On Sundays we had dinner as a family so we needed to get home.

"Leave it up to me. Where there's a will, I'll find a way."

Typical Jude. He hadn't changed a bit. He still thought he could take care of everything. He still needed to be in charge. But why would I fight him on something that would only benefit both of us? We were on the same team again so we'd both be winning. Why fight something I've wanted for so long?

CHAPTER SEVENTEEN

Lila

"WHAT'S HAPPENING NOW?" JUDE ASKED.

"They're having sex."

The weights clanged as they hit the rubber floor. I stifled a laugh and bit into my green apple, the tartness making my cheeks pucker as my eyes scanned the page in front of me.

"She's having sex with the dude in the kilt?" Jude asked.

"Jamie, yeah. He's a sexy beast," I taunted, the apple making a satisfying crunch as I took another bite and side-eyed him from my spot on the leather sofa. A few weeks ago, Kate got a new sectional for the family room, so we moved the old sofa into the barn. I was sitting with my back against the armrest, knees bent, paperback propped up against my thighs.

Jude scowled. "So she's cheating on her husband."

I knew his views on cheating. For him, it was a hard limit that completely broke the trust. He said there's no coming back after that kind of dishonesty. I called him a hypocrite, reminding him of all the other girls he'd been with but he claimed it didn't count because we weren't together.

"Technically, she's not cheating," I said. "She traveled back in time so it doesn't count."

"Still counts. She's still married."

I shrugged one shoulder and finished my apple, setting the core on the wood crate that doubled as a coffee table. If the barn had heat, you could almost live here.

"So, if you cheated on me while I was in a combat zone, would it count as cheating?" His gloved fist hit the leather bag with a thwack.

I hated to think of him *ever* being in a combat zone, but there was no point in dwelling on it. It was done. The day after Thanksgiving, he and Reese enlisted. That was one week ago and I was still in denial.

"It would count," I said. "That's different." I dragged my eyes away from the book to watch him. Earlier, he'd taken off his hoodie and tossed it at me so I was wearing it over my T-shirt and leggings to ward off the December chill in the air while he was only wearing black running shorts and a gray T-shirt.

Jude never felt the cold. He was always warm, like my personal space heater.

Compared to his workouts, mine were a joke, but he liked it when I kept him company and it was no great hardship hanging out on the sofa and ogling him. Every time I looked at him, it seemed as if he got bigger and stronger. He was all lean muscle without an ounce of fat and looked more like a man than a boy now.

The lit bulbs dangling from the rafters created a halo effect around him. But Jude was no angel.

"So if you traveled back in time and you cheated on me, you're saying it wouldn't count?" he persisted.

Thwack. Thwack. Thwack. The muscles in his arms flexed with each powerful punch, his eyes narrowed on the bag like it was his enemy and he was picturing the face of the guy I was hypothetically cheating with. If I ever cheated on Jude, which I *never* would, he'd rip the guy limb from limb before he walked away from me and never looked back.

I knew him so well. I knew his strengths, his faults and weaknesses, and his vulnerabilities. He liked to pretend he didn't have any weaknesses or vulnerabilities, but I knew better. Once he staked his claim, Jude was possessive and demanded unquestioning loyalty. He was generous with his heart but if you wronged him, he lashed out. His ego was as gigantic as the cock he was always bragging about, and he had a flair for the dramatic that I found wildly entertaining.

Faults and all, I loved him. Truly, deeply, madly. I didn't think there was anyone else on the planet who could ever fill his size thirteen shoes. So cheating on him had never even crossed my mind. But still, I enjoyed pushing his buttons.

"Technically, her husband hadn't even been born yet, so I don't think it should count." It was a flimsy excuse and I wasn't even sure which side of the moral debate I stood on. But it was fiction, not real life. "Chances are good that I'll never travel back in time and meet a sexy Scot so you have nothing to worry about."

His jaw clenched, unimpressed with my attempt to placate him, but he didn't comment. He just continued punching the bag to the tune of The White Stripes' "Seven Nation Army" blasting from the speakers.

"How's the sex?" he asked a few minutes later, wiping the sweat off his forehead with the back of his arm.

"Hot."

That captured his interest. "How hot?"

"Sooo hot." I fanned myself with my hand, really playing it

up. "Five alarm fire hot. Jamie has alllll the moves." I licked my lips and let out a low moan worthy of a porn star as my hand slid between my thighs. That was all he needed to hear. Getting him all riled up was child's play. He was a jealous lover but so was I, and I wasn't about to complain. Not when it benefited both of us.

Throwing down his gloves, he stalked toward me. A thrill shot through me, anticipation building. I knew what was coming and I was ready for him.

We'd been doing this song and dance for a few months, and I knew what that dirty mouth could do to me now. I knew what his hands, lips, and gigantic cock were capable of too. Well, mostly.

"You won't be needing him anymore." He snatched the book out of my hand and flung it across the room. The book hit the floor with a thud.

"Hey!"

Ignoring my protest, he grabbed my ankles roughly and dragged me down the sofa until my back was flat. Hooking his fingers into the waistband of my leggings, he slid them down my legs until they were around my ankles.

"Leave my sneakers on in case I need to make a run for it."

He laughed and tugged the stretchy Lycra over my sneakers then tossed my leggings over the back of the sofa. I drew my legs up, feet flat on the cushion and he knelt over me, nudging my thighs apart.

"Someone might catch us," I said, my hands reaching for his waistband and pushing down his shorts, freeing him from their confines, my movements hurried and with zero finesse. Fast and dirty, that was how we liked it.

"Mmmhmm." He reached for the switch on the wall, plunging us into darkness before his lips collided with mine. I held the back of his head, greedy for his kisses as his hands explored the curves and dips of my body and he slowly rocked against me. The only barrier between us was my black lacy underwear.

We were two dirty kids pushing the limits, always two seconds away from getting busted. There was a padlock on the outside of the barn door but no way to lock it from the inside.

"I feel like I need this like I need air," I murmured, my chest heaving as he drugged me with kisses that made my thighs quiver and the ache between my legs build to a dull throb.

"Same here."

His lips still sealed to mine, he slid my panties aside and dragged two fingers through my slick folds. Wrapping my legs around his waist, I rocked my hips.

"Why are you so wet?" I heard the accusation in his voice.

"From watching you, you sexy beast," I panted as one thick finger dipped inside me and his thumb rubbed the tight bundle of nerves that made heat pool in my belly and sent zings of electricity up and down my spine. "Oh my God."

"You called?"

My fingernails dug into his shoulders and my body shook with laughter. He swallowed it with a deep kiss, his tongue caressing mine while his hand continued to perform magic, breaching the tight barrier and rubbing a spot that his middle finger had found a couple months ago.

My hips bucked, my back arching off the sofa. What would it feel like if he was inside me instead of his finger?

"I'm going to—"

Just then, he removed his hand and I cursed myself for saying it aloud. My fingers tugged at the ends of his hair in desperation. "Jude."

"Just hang on, baby."

I was barely hanging on by a thread, my fingers digging into the leather cushion as he moved down my body and his mouth replaced his hand.

"Fall apart for me," he murmured, his fingers and tongue ensuring that I did just that. The orgasm built up inside me until I was writhing and moaning, my hands gripping his head and holding him to me while his tongue and thumb worked in tandem, his other hand under my shirt, squeezing my nipple between his fingers.

"Oh my God. Jude," I screamed, forgetting that we were supposed to be quiet. My thighs clenched and light fractured behind my closed lids as I fell apart.

My legs were still trembling as his flattened tongue licked between my sensitive folds, bringing me down from the orgasm that had rocked me to my core. I grabbed his head, pulling it up to mine and he kissed me hard, his tongue darting into my mouth so I could taste myself.

Pulling away from me, he sat back on his heels and my eyes lowered to his hand as he gave himself a few powerful strokes. I pulled up my shirt and sweatshirt, offering him my bare stomach and pushed myself up on my elbows. I loved to watch him lose control. His eyes squeezed shut and his muscles tensed as he leaned over me, holding himself up on one arm.

"Fuck, Rebel," he gritted out. "Look what you do to me." Warm liquid spurted on my stomach and he took a few seconds to catch his breath before he pushed himself off the sofa and stumbled around in the dark. Returning with a towel, he used it to clean me up. Then he collapsed onto the sofa and propped his feet on the crate and pulled me into his lap.

"Are you ready for tomorrow?" I snuggled into him.

He nodded, his hand caressing my thigh. "You haven't washed my jersey, have you?"

Jude was superstitious. Like, really superstitious. On game day, he always drank three Red Bulls. When he was getting dressed, he put his left sock on before his right. Before a game, he took a knee and said the Hail Mary then crossed himself three times. Now, his new superstition was that I couldn't wash the jersey he gave me because it would mess up their winning streak. "And be responsible for making you lose a game? Never. I'll wear it dirty."

He squeezed my thigh. "Good girl."

"I can be bad too." My teeth sunk into his earlobe.

"Put the fangs away, Rebel."

I sucked on it to ease the sting, eliciting a groan from Jude. He liked a bit of pain with his pleasure. "I'd love to see you in a kilt. Like Jamie."

"Is that your fantasy?" He slid his hand under my shirt and cupped my breast in one of his big, rough hands, squeezing and kneading as his lips brushed my jaw.

"Mmhmm. If you win tomorrow, you have to wear a kilt to school. For next Friday's pep rally," I added.

"Is that a dare?" His thumb brushed over the raised peak of my nipple and I sucked in a breath, squirming in his lap.

"Yep." My hand trailed down his hard chest and dipped inside his shorts, his breath hitching when I wrapped my hand around his hard length and squeezed. "You can't wear anything underneath either. You have to go commando."

"Challenge accepted." And I knew he'd do it. He'd wear a kilt to the pep rally, in front of the entire student body of 1,800, and he wouldn't be the least bit embarrassed. He'd wear it loud and proud. Jude could never resist a challenge. "Better buy that kilt, baby, because we're winning tomorrow. And *when* we win, not if, you're going to be my love slave."

"Then you'd better save your strength. I've heard the Knights have an impenetrable defense."

"I'm all about full penetration." He whipped me around so I was straddling him.

"You're all talk. I'm still a virgin." I grinded my body against his, seeking the friction, my panties soaked.

"Shut up and kiss me, wench." We kissed until we were ready for round two.

The door burst open, bringing with it a blast of cold air that chilled my heated skin. Panicked, I scrambled to get off Jude. He tightened his grip on my hips, holding me firmly in place. "Stay here."

I couldn't see who was at the door but seconds later, the lights came on and I heard her voice.

"Hey J. What's up?"

J. Ugh. I gritted my teeth and narrowed my eyes on Jude. He chuckled under his breath like this was some kind of joke to him. Jealousy reared its ugly head. In a hurry to get away, I climbed off Jude, *accidentally* kneeing him in the balls. Oops.

His face contorted and his jaw clenched, trying to ride out the pain I'd inflicted. "The fuck, Rebel?" he wheezed out.

The momentary twinge of guilt I felt was quickly replaced with satisfaction when I remembered who had just strolled into the barn.

Served him right. Pulling the sweatshirt down so it was mid-thigh, I spun around to face Brody and Kylie. Was *he* sleeping with her now? Brody was laughing so hard he was doubled over. I had no idea what he found so funny.

"Sorry to interrupt," Kylie said with a smirk that made Brody laugh harder.

Sorry, my ass. The leggy blonde carrying a bottle of vodka was a reminder of what Jude had been doing during our ten-month hiatus. She was wearing a plaid pleated skirt that barely covered her ass with thigh-high black boots over fishnets.

Under her black leather jacket, she wore a T-shirt with the name of a band I never heard of.

I hated it that she looked so cool. More sophisticated and worldly than me, even though she'd only been a year ahead of us in school.

Had she and Jude gotten dirty? What had they done together?

Kylie was a freshman in college now, so at least I didn't have to see her at school. Small victory.

I swallowed my misery. It felt like shards of glass.

Shoulders squared, spine straight, I ignored Jude who was calling my name and breezed past Kylie, shoving Brody out of my way when he tried to stop me from leaving. The scent of weed and alcohol clung to him. And that was when I realized Brody was stoned and drunk off his ass. Just another Friday night in his world. I worried about Brody. But right now, all I could think about was Jude and Kylie. Jude kissing Kylie. Jude... what had they done together?

Hands balled into fists, I trudged toward the house, the faint glow of the porch light guiding my way. My blood boiled, warming me from the inside, so I didn't even feel the cold.

Why had he slept with her but my virginity was still intact?

It was only when I got halfway across the field that I realized I'd left my leggings in the barn along with my dignity.

It was after midnight when the boy I hated to love climbed into my bedroom window and soundlessly crept across the hardwood floor. The mattress dipped under his weight when he sat on the edge to remove his high tops and then lifted the covers and slid in next to me, tucking his arms under his head. I kept my gaze fixed on the lion and the bull on my bedroom ceiling, the stars glowing bright in my moon-washed bedroom, but watched him from the corner of my eye. He smelled like fresh air, Double Mint, and woodsy scented shower gel. He smelled like home. That's what he was to me. My home. Tendrils of fear unfurled inside me and snaked their way up. They wrapped around my heart, choking the air in my lungs.

The McCallisters weren't my family. They were the people who took me in when I had nowhere else to go.

Loving Jude was dangerous. I had so much more to lose than he did. If things didn't work out between us, could we ever go back to being just friends? Doubtful. If our relationship crashed and burned tomorrow, he would still have a loving home and a family. What would I be left with?

It was nights like these, when my thoughts played on a loop in my head, that I missed my mom the most.

Next to me, Jude shifted so he was closer, so close—the heat of his body warming me as he pried my hand from their tight grip on the comforter tucked under my chin and placed it over his heart, his bigger hand on top of mine to hold it firmly in place. Underneath my palm, I could feel his heart beating in sync with mine.

"It's only ever been you," he said, his voice low and husky in the stillness of my quiet bedroom. "Only you, Rebel."

But how could that be true when he'd been with other girls? For a few minutes, we lay in silence, gazing up at the stars, his heart beating steady under my hand, our chests rising and falling with each breath we inhaled and exhaled. It was Jude's silence that spoke the loudest. And his actions. He always said that words meant nothing without actions to back them up. He could have left me to stew on this all night long but he hadn't.

"You should be asleep. You have a big game tomorrow night."

"I sleep better in your bed. Tell me you want me to stay."

What I wanted to say was that I never wanted him to leave. Not tonight. Not ever. But I couldn't say that. "You can stay. If you want."

That was the only invitation he needed. He rolled onto his side and pulled my body against his, wrapping an arm around my waist. My body fit so perfectly into the curve of his. I cursed him for being so perfect. Not perfect, as in without faults. Just perfect for me. Sometimes I couldn't believe my luck. I'd found this boy when I was only nine years old and he'd chosen me above all others.

"'Night, Lila." He kissed my hair, so gentle and loving like I was something precious to him, and I pushed aside my fears. I didn't want to keep torturing myself with thoughts of the things he'd done with Kylie that he hadn't done with me. I didn't want to think about him with anyone else. Even though he hadn't said the three words I wanted to hear, I could feel it. He *loved* me.

"'Night, Jude." *I love you. Only you.*

CHAPTER EIGHTEEN

Lila

WE WERE A UNITED FRONT OF BLUE AND GOLD, A CURRENT of electricity running through the crowd, so palpable I could touch it. Taste it. Out there under the stadium lights, Jude McCallister was a god. Tonight he was on fire.

Until it all fell apart in the fourth quarter.

"Goddammit," Patrick growled from the row directly in front of me. He threw up his hands. "What the hell was that? That's the second interception Jude threw. We were so close to winning."

"It's not all about winning," Kate told Patrick. "The boys put up a good fight. They played their hearts out and did their best. That's what counts."

He scowled, refusing to be placated. In the six months I'd been living with the McCallisters, I'd learned a lot about their family dynamics. And to say that Jude's dad put a premium on winning was the understatement of the century. He was hard on his boys but he was the hardest on Jude. I'd never noticed it before and Jude never complained, but sometimes his dad could be a bit of an asshole.

"If their defense would have gotten their heads out of their asses, maybe we could have gotten somewhere," Patrick said, snorting with disgust when he checked the scoreboard again. The digital numbers hadn't changed. Mavericks – 40; Knights – 43. "Jude's head wasn't in the game. He let that last interception rattle him."

Christy and I shared a look. She raised her brows. I was insulted on Jude's behalf and wanted to defend him. What Patrick said wasn't true. After Jude threw that interception, he didn't just lay down and die, he kept playing, giving it his all just like he always did.

Something hit the back of my head and I brushed my hand over my hair then turned in my seat to glare at Brody. He just laughed and eased another handful of sunflower seeds into his mouth then leaned forward in his seat. "Lighten up, L."

I gave him the finger and faced forward again, completely ignoring Kylie who was practically in his lap. Guess Jude and Brody were okay with sharing.

"I wonder if they had a threesome," Christy mused. I sucked in a sharp breath. She slapped her hand over her mouth. "Sorry. Did I say that out loud?"

I crossed my arms over my chest, pushing Christy's words out of my head, and watched the Mavericks lose more yards. Patrick was on his feet, shouting something at the refs. Kate grabbed his arm and yanked him back down into his seat. "Calm down," she said firmly. "It's only a game."

"It is not only a game. It's football. And it's the last damn game you'll ever see Jude play."

"It's not over yet," Jesse said, his hands balling into fists. "Jude can still do it. He can turn this around."

"Honey, it's too late—"

Jesse cut off the rest of his mom's sentence. "It's not too late," he insisted. "Jude can do it. I know he can."

I loved Jesse's blind faith in Jude and his optimism. He truly believed that his brother could turn this game around.

We were down by three with only three seconds remaining. Jude tapped his helmet, indicating that he was changing the play. I didn't know what he had in mind but it would take a miracle or an act of God to win this game.

Jude took the snap, and with no time left on the clock, he launched the ball into the sky. It was a Hail Mary pass from the midfield, an act of desperation for a quarterback with a lot of yards to cover and no other options left to him.

Twelve thousand fans held their collective breaths as the ball spiraled toward the end zone. Austin Armacost jumped up between three defenders and made the catch.

"Holy shit," Brody shouted behind me as I stared at the field, not quite believing what I'd just witnessed. "He did it. He actually fucking did it."

We were on our feet, the shouts and cheers of the crowd reaching ear-splitting decibels. Everyone knew that they'd just witnessed something amazing. So spectacular you could almost call it a miracle. A forty-five-yard pass to score the winning touchdown in the Division I semi-finals.

"He caught the ball!" the announcer shouted, his excitement so great that he kept repeating it. "I can't believe I was here to witness this. This is the stuff of legends. This is why we love Texas football."

"What a throw from Jude McCallister. Forty-five yards right into the hands of the Mavericks' wide receiver, Austin Armacost," the other announcer said.

"That's my boy!" Patrick shouted, changing his tune now that Jude was a winner.

"I told you he could do it!" Jesse screamed, punching the

air. He cupped his hands over his mouth and shouted into the crowd of screaming fans. "Yo. That's my brother. Lucky Number Seven. We're going to the state championships. Yeah baby." Jesse did a little victory dance.

I was laughing and crying, hugging Christy as we both jumped up and down. She didn't even like football, but tonight everyone was a fan.

I released Christy and searched the field until my gaze found Jude in the end zone. The players were celebrating their victory, spirits riding high as they jumped each other, thumping shoulders and pounding fists. So physical, even in their victory celebrations. They were a tangled mess of limbs and boy sweat as they tackled each other to the ground and ended up in a heap.

It wasn't every day that you got to see your boyfriend make a forty-five-yard pass for the winning touchdown. But if anyone could create magic, it was Jude. He had the Midas touch. Everything he touched turned to gold. I wondered if I was shimmering as much as the gold dusting my cheekbones and eyelids. I felt like I was lit up from the inside, so bright it was impossible to contain.

This was his night to celebrate. His night to shine. And as I stood in the bleachers on a cold, clear December night, the stars drowned out by stadium lights, I wished yet again Jude had a different dream. I wished he would come to UT Austin with me and play football. Or any other college in Texas. He could have had his pick. He could have gotten a full ride. We could have been together.

But it was useless to think of what could have been.

He'd signed a contract. Five years of his life signed away before he would be released from active duty.

Now, I watched Jude run down the field with his teammates, fists held high. His helmet clutched in his hand, hair slick with sweat, black war paint under his eyes. To me, he looked like a giant among men. Shoulders impossibly broad under the shoulder pads tapering down to his narrow waist, thighs encased in blue football pants with gold bars on the sides, he was the only player I could see on that field. I couldn't take my eyes off him.

He was searching for his family in the stands like he did after every game. When he spotted us, he grinned and held his helmet in the air. I blew him a kiss. He caught it in his hand and pounded his fist against his heart.

I love you, I wanted to shout, loudly enough for everyone in the stadium to hear it.

I loved that boy so much that sometimes it hurt.

His smile grew wider, those dimples in his cheeks making an appearance, and I was grinning back at him like a fool. Then I was laughing when Christy said, "Someone is going to get lucky tonight."

All I wanted to do was get him off that field and somewhere alone where I wouldn't have to share him with anyone. I was greedy and so selfish that way.

But I knew it would be hours before I could have him to myself.

Headlights shining, bonfires blazing, and car stereos cranked up on high, this was how we celebrated our victories or drowned our sorrows after a game. This week's field party was at Austin Armacost's ranch. We'd been here an hour, and I'd barely seen Jude. I unscrewed the lid of my water bottle and took a swig, wishing I hadn't volunteered to be designated driver.

"Are there any girls here willing to give our buddy a pity

fuck?" Tyler yelled, slinging his arm around Reese's shoulder. "Our boy's gonna be a Marine. Shipping out tomorrow."

"Shut the fuck up," Reese said, laughing. "But seriously." He scanned the groups of girls hanging out, his eyes stopping on two blondes sitting on the hood of a car, fruity wine coolers in their hands. "Any takers?"

Laughing, they turned their heads. Reese ambled over to me and Christy where we were sitting on the tailgate of Brody's truck. He and Kylie had disappeared as soon as we got here. "Christy. What d'ya say?"

She put her finger on her lips and tilted her head like she was giving it serious thought. "No."

He deflated. "Damn. I thought you were really considering it."

"I would but I have my sights set on someone else."

"Yeah? Who is he?"

"Not a he, a she."

"Damn. So it's true. You go for girls."

"I'm equal opportunity. I go for girls and guys."

"Gives you a bigger playing field." Reese settled on the tailgate next to her and I shook my head, laughing as he peppered her with questions about her sex life.

"Baby, baby, baby." Jude came to stand between my legs. "Have I told you that I love you?"

"You're drunk," I said, laughing as he nuzzled my neck. Drunk Jude was kind of adorable. "So it doesn't count."

"It counts. I love you, Lila, and I want everyone to know it." He turned around, giving me his back and spread his arms, a beer bottle clutched in one hand. "I love Lila Turner!"

"Louder for the people in the back," Tyler said. "Not sure they heard you in the next county."

"The next county," Jude scoffed. "I want all of Texas to

know it." He jumped onto the bed of Brody's pickup truck and shouted at the top of his lungs. "I love Lila Turner."

"Yeah. We know," Reese said, rolling his eyes.

"I love Lila Turner!"

"Shut up, McCallister," someone shouted.

Jude hopped to the ground and stumbled, laughing as he righted himself. "Shit. The ground was closer than I thought."

That made us all laugh.

"Is that any way to treat your QB? He's our man. Our MVP, yo," Austin said, thumping Jude's back.

"Couldn't have done it without you. You're the man," Jude said, looping his arm around Austin's neck and rubbing his knuckles over the top of Austin's head. "Who caught that ball? You. You. You. Shit. I love you, man."

I laughed as they held on to each other, swaying, and I suspected if they weren't holding each other up they'd both go down.

"So does this mean I'm forgiven for kissing your girl?" Austin asked when they let go of each other and clinked their beer bottles in a toast.

Jude snarled. "Why'd you have to bring that up? Now I'll have to punch you."

"No, you don't." I jumped off the back of the truck and tugged on the hood of Jude's sweatshirt, dragging him toward me. He spun around and pulled me into his arms, his fight forgotten in his drunken haze.

"Love you, baby." He rubbed his nose along the side of mine, the scent of beer and whiskey on his breath. "Love you soooo much."

This would have all been really great if not for the fact that the first time he'd told me he loved me was at a bonfire party after a football game when he was drunk off his ass.

Dipping his head, he kissed me on the mouth then dragged his lips across my jaw. "Do you love me, Rebel?"

I nodded.

He pulled back and studied my face intently, his eyes glassy from the alcohol but laser focused. "Tell me. I need to hear it."

"I love you," I whispered. Although I'd said the words in my head a hundred times, this was the first time I'd said them aloud.

His arms tightened around me. "Say it again."

"I love you."

"And you're gonna stay with me, no matter what happens. You're not going to fall for some college guy and send me a Dear John letter, are you?"

This was the first time I'd ever seen Jude look worried and while I could chalk it up to being drunk, I didn't think that was the case. "No. I won't do that. I would never," I assured him, my arms looping around his neck. "You're the only guy for me."

"Am I?" He was watching my face again, like he really needed the reassurance, and I sensed that this wasn't the time to tease him so I gave him what he asked for. Why lie when it was the truth?

"Yeah, you are." He lifted me off my feet and I wrapped my legs around his waist, locking my ankles together as he strode to the side of the truck and pushed me against it, my back against the passenger window.

"Even when I'm far away... you'll still love me?" he asked, kissing the corner of my mouth.

"Even then."

"Always? Forever?"

"Always and forever."

"Don't leave me again. Don't ever push me away again. If you do, my heart will break. For real, for real. Do you wanna break my heart, Rebel? Are you going to?" Vulnerability bled into his every word.

I shook my head. "No," I whispered, framing his beautiful face in my hands and searching his eyes for the truth. "Are you going to break mine?"

"Never. Promise. I swear on my life that I'll always love you. You're mine and I'm yours and that's just how it is. Just how it's always been." His words were laced with so much sincerity, it made my heart stutter and put a lump in my throat.

Maybe he was so drunk he wouldn't remember this tomorrow. Maybe our words meant nothing at all. But to me, they meant everything. We sealed them with a kiss that robbed the air from my lungs and made me wonder where he left off and I began. It felt dangerous, loving someone the way I loved him. I knew how cruel life could be. The person you loved could be ripped away from you in the blink of an eye. But I did it anyway.

I fell for Jude, and I was in so deep, there was no going back now.

CHAPTER NINETEEN

Jude

WE LOST THE STATE CHAMPIONSHIP GAME. CORRECTION. We didn't just lose. We got our asses handed to us in front of 40,000 fans. I ended my high school football career by limping off the field with a sprained ankle during the third quarter. Gideon, the little shit, smirked while I sat out the rest of the game on the bench, icing my ankle. As predicted, he'd spent the season warming the bench and half-assing his way through practices.

Thanks to our dad, my brother hated my guts to the point where he reveled in my defeat. The last game of my high school career was not one of my better nights.

I'd gotten sacked four times which had pissed off my dad to the point where he was shouting at the coaches after the game in the parking lot while the players were getting on the team bus. He was so red in the face that his blood pressure must have been through the roof. I was seriously worried he'd have a heart attack.

It took me a few days to put the loss behind me and move on. At the end of the day, there was no point dwelling on what could have been done differently. It was over, we'd played like shit and the better team won. That's how it goes. You win some, you lose some.

Now, it was Christmas Eve, the football season was behind me and I was in my favorite place on the planet. My girlfriend's bed.

Pillow-soft lips met mine and she kissed me like she always did. Like I was her oxygen and she couldn't breathe without me. Her kisses were my drug of choice and I chased the high that only she could give me. Her knees dug into my sides, thighs clenched around my waist as she grinded against my throbbing dick. Two thin layers of cotton were the only barriers preventing me from being buried deep inside her.

She pulled away from the kiss and sat up, straddling me, her palms flattened on my bare chest and threw back her head. Moonlight painted her silver, the column of her neck exposed. My fingers dug into her hips, her chest heaving under one of my old T-shirts she always slept in.

I tugged at the hem of the T-shirt. "Take it off." When we were together in her room we spoke in whispers, our voices so hushed that we had to be close to hear the words. "Let me see you."

Reaching down with both hands, she lifted the T-shirt over her head and tossed it on the floor, bared to me now except for her lacy underwear. My hands coasted up her stomach, over silky soft skin, and cupped her breasts, my thumbs brushing and squeezing pebbled nipples. The stars on her ceiling glowed above us and in the silence of her room, all I could hear was our ragged breaths and the whisper-soft moans coming from her lips.

Gripping her waist, I flipped her onto her back and knelt between her legs, pressing her thighs apart.

A sly smile tugged at the corners of her lips. "Do it," she whispered, and even though her voice was hushed, I heard the challenge in it.

"Do what?" I knew what she wanted. The one thing I hadn't given her yet. Pulling cotton aside, I stroked her with my fingers, circling and sliding, coating them with the wet heat of her arousal.

"I don't want your fingers." Impatient, she pushed my hand away. "I want you."

"It's going to hurt. I'm going to hurt you."

"I don't care." She slid her underwear down her legs and flung them across the room. I followed suit and knelt over her. Gripping her hips, I lined her up directly beneath me and rocked against her.

"Are you sure?" In response, she lifted her hips, her back arching off the mattress and I glided between her slick folds. It felt so fucking good, skin against skin, every cell in my body igniting, and I wasn't even inside her yet.

"I'm on the pill," she said, giving me further incentive to breach her tight walls.

I had never taken a girl's virginity before and I had never gone bare. But even more daunting than being someone's first was that this was Lila, the girl I loved. My heart was ricocheting off the walls of my chest as I dipped my head and kissed her hard, nudging her entrance with my tip.

She wrapped her legs around my waist and gripped my shoulders tightly. I lifted my head, looking down at her face as I pushed into her just a little bit more. Squeezing her eyes shut, she winced and inhaled a sharp breath. I was barely hanging on. But I stayed where I was and I waited for her to adjust to the pressure.

"Baby. Open your eyes." Her eyes opened and I kissed the corner of her mouth, my lips ghosting over hers. "Now breathe."

She nodded a little and squeezed my shoulders. "Okay. I'm good."

Watching her face, I inched my way inside her, more slowly than I thought myself capable of. Her muscles clenched around me tight as a fist and she clung to me. My arms braced on either side of her head trembled under the strain of using every ounce of my self-restraint.

This was a taste of heaven and of hell all rolled into one.

Tears streamed down her face and she whispered, "Don't stop." Her hands slid from my shoulders to my neck and into my hair as she lifted her hips and tugged my head down to hers. "Do it."

I dragged my lips down her cheek, kissing away her tears. I drank her pain and then I pushed all the way into her, going where no one had gone before me. With privilege came a greater responsibility and it both terrified and thrilled me knowing that she trusted me to make this good for her. I felt like I was splitting her right down the middle, cracking her wide open to create a space just for me. Buried to the hilt, I silenced her pants and moans with soft kisses. Her fingers dug into my scalp and her brows pinched together. "Shh." I kissed her on the lips and her jaw and the side of her neck. Moving my mouth to the shell of her ear I murmured. "Shh."

I don't know if I was trying to comfort her or myself but I could feel my control slipping. The effort it took not to fuck her into oblivion, not to lose myself in this moment and ride out the pleasure, was too great. My sweat dripped onto her forehead and made our bodies slick in all the places our skin touched.

"Baby. I need to—" My voice was strained and I squeezed my eyes shut, gritting my teeth.

Lila placed her fingertips over my lips. "Shh."

She angled her hips, rolling them in little circles that sucked me in deeper. My forehead dropped to hers and her soft breath mingled with mine. She held my face in her hands. "Give me all you've got. Don't hold back. I want to watch you lose control."

Lila had no idea what she was asking for or what that meant but her words loosened my resolve to be oh so careful with her. Pulling back to fill her deeper, I stroked her walls with long, powerful thrusts that she met and took, her body matching the rhythm I set.

Nothing, *nothing* on earth, had ever felt as good as being inside Lila.

"I love you."

"I love you."

Blood surged through my veins, my heart pounding. Light-headed and half-blind, warm tingles started at the base of my spine. My balls tightened and I chased the high, each stroke bringing me higher and higher until I reached the point of no return. There was no way of stopping now. Lila rocked her hips, her fingernails digging into my shoulders.

I exploded. Shuddering, I came inside her, and it seemed to go on and on. Holy shit.

I collapsed on top of her, giving her all my weight and she held on to me, both of us so still and quiet. For a few seconds, I was so boneless I couldn't even move.

Afraid I might be crushing her, I rolled off her and onto my side, propping my head on my hand and tracing her mouth with my fingertips. "Are you okay?"

She smiled. "Yeah. I'm okay." The smile slipped off her face. "I just... it was different than I thought it would be."

"Fuck." I scrubbed my hand over my face, guilt gnawing at me. "I'm sorry. I shouldn't have—"

"No." She grabbed my hand. "You were good. It's just... it was so intense, you know?"

Yeah, I did know.

"I never want to think of you doing that with anyone who isn't me. It's just so..." She stopped and took a deep breath and let it out. "It's so intimate, you know? And I hate it that you shared that with—"

"Shh. Don't say it. Being with you was like nothing I've ever experienced before."

"In a good way?"

"In the very best way. So let's just pretend we were both virgins. Because that was how it felt."

She smiled. "Really?"

"Really. I'll be right back." I climbed off the bed and pulled on my boxer briefs from the floor.

"Where are you going?"

"The bathroom. I need a towel to clean you up—"

She shook her head. "You stay. I'll go. I want you to be here when I get back."

"I'm not going anywhere."

———————

That night, she slept in my arms, her back against my chest, and her body molded into mine. I buried my face in her hair and inhaled the scent of Lila. Spring rain and honeysuckle.

It felt like only minutes later that I woke to the sound of my phone alarm buzzing. Rolling over with a groan, my hand reached for my phone on the bedside table to silence it. It was still dark outside and Lila was sleeping soundly.

I wanted to stay in her downy soft bed, with her warm body wrapped up in mine, my hands skimming over every inch of her silky soft skin.

Scrubbing my hands over my face, I yawned and sat up then grabbed my clothes from the floor and got dressed, formulating my escape plan. There were two ways to leave Lila's room. Number one. Creep down the hallway and hope nobody heard me. A few weeks ago, I'd run into Gideon coming out of the bathroom. I had a feeling he knew where I'd been but he'd just given me a blank stare and said nothing.

Number two. Exit via her window, jump down to the porch roof and slide down the pole. Then round the side of the house and climb the trellis to my room. Home free. Because of my ankle, I hadn't gone that way since before the state championship game but I was feeling confident that it was strong enough now. So I decided that was the stunt I'd perform for today's disappearing act.

I kissed her goodbye and told her to close the window after I left. Still half-asleep, she mumbled "Love you" and told me she would. I hesitated a second when her eyes drifted shut. "Don't forget to close the window."

"Baby, it's cold outside," she murmured with a little smile and a yawn. "Go. I've got you."

On that note, I was out her window and on the roof.

Ignoring the shooting pain in my ankle, I hobbled around the side of the house to the trellis and made it back to my room in record time. As I was closing the window, I heard my bedroom door open then close. The footsteps crossing my bedroom floor were too heavy to be Lila's.

Oh. Shit.

"Jude." I suppressed the urge to laugh. I don't know why I wanted to laugh. I had a feeling this confrontation wouldn't be funny in the least.

Wiping the stupid grin off my face, I turned from the window to face my dad. I raked a hand through my hair, trying to decide if he knew I'd just come from Lila's room and had any idea how long this had been going on. I quickly deduced that he wouldn't be standing in my room if he didn't know. I could come up with an excuse for climbing into my own bedroom window at six in the morning. Like, hey, I was just getting in an early workout. Didn't want to wake anyone.

Or I was playing Santa Claus and hid some presents in the barn. Which was actually true. I had hidden my presents in the barn. But I knew it wouldn't fly.

So I opted to say nothing and play it by ear, my response contingent on what he accused me of.

"Get Lila and meet me in the barn in five minutes."

My eyes widened and I drew in a sharp breath. Not what I'd expected and not how I wanted this to play out. "Can we just leave her out of this? It's not her fault—"

"I'll be waiting for both of you in the barn." He headed for the door then turned around, his voice low. "Do that ankle a favor. Use the door. And try not to wake anyone. No need to alert the entire household."

I nodded in agreement. It was the last thing we needed. But I hadn't expected him to drag Lila into this. I'd prefer that he didn't involve her and let me take the punishment for both of us. But he was adamant that she was there. Grabbing a hoodie from my closet, I pulled it over my head then crept down the hallway to deliver the good news. We'd been busted. My dad was waiting for us in the barn.

No doubt there would be hell to pay but I'd bear the brunt of it. Or so I told Lila as we crossed the field a few minutes later, our breaths coming out in white puffs of smoke, the frost coating the grass and trees glowing silver in the pre-dawn.

"We're in this together," she said. She was wearing my old baseball hoodie like a declaration of our love. "I'm just as guilty as you are so don't you dare try to take all the blame."

I grabbed her hand and tugged her toward me. Wrapping

my arm around her waist, I pulled her flush against my chest, not even caring if my dad saw us. "I forgot to tell you something."

"What?" she asked, her brow furrowed. She'd been in such a rush to get ready that she hadn't even stopped to brush her hair. I loved it like this. It was sex hair. The long waves tumbled down her back and framed her perfect little face.

"Tonight was perfect. You're perfect. And no matter what happens, or what our punishment is, it will be worth it."

She smiled, her body sagging in relief. "I feel the same way. You're totally worth it."

My hands wandered down and cupped her ass as I pressed a soft kiss on her lips. Reluctantly, I released her before this kiss turned into something more. "Let's get this over with."

Her shoulders sagged, a bit of her bravado flagging as she looked over her shoulder at the barn.

I squeezed her hand. "It'll be okay. My dad won't be mad at you."

"That makes it worse. I don't want special treatment. And I don't want you to get in trouble."

"It's no big deal. We've got this."

"Okay." She gave me a small smile. She didn't look or sound convinced but keeping my dad waiting wouldn't do us any favors. So we walked to the barn side by side and I tried to hide my limp but she noticed and shook her head with an exasperated sigh.

When we were inside with the door closed, my father gestured to the leather sofa. "Take a seat." If only he knew how much action this sofa had seen.

Lila and I sat side by side but not so close that we were touching while he stood across from us, arms crossed and legs spread slightly in a show of dominance that told us he was the authority figure with all the power. I hadn't assessed the climate yet, so I wasn't sure what would fly and what wouldn't.

"You two have put me in an awkward position."

Couldn't argue with that, so I kept my mouth shut. He didn't sound angry but he didn't sound happy either.

"I'm sorry," Lila said. "I never meant to disobey you or break your rules..." Her voice drifted off and her eyes lowered to her clasped hands in her lap.

"I was a teenager once too, believe it or not." He chuckled under his breath. My brows shot up to my hairline. Was he actually going to give us a free pass? "And that's why the rules are in place. How long have you been sneaking into her room?" he asked me.

I could lie and tell him it had been a one-off but I doubted he'd believe it. His eyes were narrowed on me, waiting to catch me in a lie. He knew the answer and this was a test. I knew from experience that lying to his face would only anger him. Whatever punishment he planned to impose would be doubled.

So I answered honestly.

"Since September." He relaxed his stance and nodded like I'd confirmed something he'd suspected all along.

"There will be no more sneaking into each other's bedrooms. Not as long as you're both living under my roof. Is that understood?"

"Yes," Lila said quickly.

My dad's gaze swung to me. Reluctantly, I nodded. "Got it."

"Having said that, I do remember what it's like to be eighteen." He exhaled loudly and rubbed his hand over his jaw, looking conflicted. "But like I said, you've put me in a bad spot. Lila is our responsibility. We promised your mother we'd look after you and treat you as one of our own," he told her.

Lila gave him a sad little smile. "Thank you. I really appreciate it."

He held up his hand. "No need to thank me. We're happy to do it. You're like the daughter we never had."

Her eyes welled with tears and without thinking, I moved closer and wrapped my arm around her shoulders. She leaned into me and wiped her eyes to keep the tears from spilling. I hated to see her cry. Hated to see her sad. But I knew holidays were especially hard for her.

"Your mom knew you and Jude were in love. Maybe even before you two figured it out," my dad told Lila, his voice softer than I'd ever heard it. He didn't want to upset her.

"What did she say?" Lila's eyes glittered with unshed tears, her voice so hopeful, always desperate to hear anything that her mom had shared with us.

My dad smiled, and it softened his features, making me wonder why he didn't do it more often. "She said that Jude is worthy, and she knew he was going to grow to be a good man." I thought I heard a hint of pride in his voice but I couldn't be sure. My mom doled out the unconditional love and praise, playing the role of good cop to my dad's bad cop. "Your mom seemed to think you'd be perfect for each other. And my wife agreed."

I'd never heard any of this. It wasn't something my dad had ever shared with me, and I doubted that he would have if Lila hadn't asked. But the fact that Caroline put her trust in me made me even more determined to be the best man for Lila.

"So maybe you can both appreciate the predicament I'm in." He scratched his head like he was truly puzzled.

Quite frankly, I couldn't see the problem. I wanted Lila, she wanted me. We were in love and sex was natural. What was the big deal? But I wasn't stupid enough to voice that.

"So now what?" I asked, putting the ball back in his court.

Let's get this over with and enjoy our Christmas. A few hours more sleep would be appreciated too. Meanwhile, I was already planning how I was going to get around whatever rules he decided to enforce.

"You have two younger brothers sleeping right across the hall from Lila. Jesse is only thirteen. I don't want him getting the wrong idea, thinking that your mother and I condone this behavior."

"Speaking of mothers, why in the world wasn't I invited to this meeting?" my mom asked as she walked into the barn, clearly annoyed that she'd been left out. She was wearing flannel pajama bottoms and my dad's fleece jacket. She wore the same ugly, tan shearling-lined boots as the ones on Lila's feet. They were all the rage and girls claimed they were like walking on a cloud.

"Patrick." She quirked her brow at him. "Would you mind explaining why you didn't wake me up?"

"It was early." My dad looked visibly uncomfortable and I coughed into my fist to cover up my laughter as he squared off with my mom. Sometimes he was so overpowering that I didn't notice how strong my mom could be when the situation demanded. She chose her battles wisely, I suppose. "I didn't want you to lose any sleep over this."

My mom planted her hands on her hips. "I'll deal with you later," she told him before turning to face us with a bright smile and a cheery voice. "Merry Christmas."

Lila and I wished her a Merry Christmas then exchanged a look.

She raised her brows. *Is this as weird for you as it is for me?*

I raised my brows. *Bizarre. But roll with it.*

I relaxed in my seat and spread my arm across the back of the sofa. Might as well settle in. "Did you bring any hot chocolate with marshmallows? Or how about some of those sugar cookies?"

My dad scowled, his voice gruff. "That'll be enough from you, smartass." He was still on thin ice with my mom and would be hearing about this for a long time to come. But I didn't think we were off the hook yet either, so I shut my mouth.

"As Patrick was saying before I interrupted," my mom said, shooting daggers at him. "We have to think of Jesse and Gideon and the message it sends." She clapped hands together. "So we've decided that if you're going to sleep together, you'll do it out in the open."

"What?" I choked out.

"You can sleep with the door open." She beamed, like she was Lady Bountiful and had just given us the best Christmas gift ever.

I sagged against the sofa. What was this insanity? "You want us to sleep together with the door open?" I repeated, just to make sure I'd heard correctly.

"We'd prefer you didn't sleep together at all until you're out of the house. But if you feel you must do it, you can do it with the door open."

Yeah, well, we couldn't do jack shit with the door open.

My dad laughed as if he'd read my mind. "Exactly," he said, making me wonder if I'd actually voiced my thoughts.

"So that's settled then," my dad said, rubbing his hands together. I got the impression that he would have preferred to have dental surgery than to have this conversation. All in all, it had gone a lot better than I'd expected. Awkward as hell, sure, but my dad hadn't been a hard ass about it. I suspected it was because of Lila. He never raised his voice to her or treated her with anything but kindness. It made me question whether it was because she was a girl or because she wasn't his daughter. Either way, it had worked in our favor.

"And no more climbing that trellis," my mom said as we walked out of the barn. She swatted my arm. "You've trampled my wisteria. I'm worried it won't come back in the spring."

"I can plant some new vines for you," Lila offered as my mom looped an arm around Lila's shoulders and the two of them walked ahead of me and my dad on what had to be the strangest Christmas morning ever. I'd taken Lila's virginity and afterwards we had a family discussion about it.

"You know when we say that you can sleep with the door open, we really mean that you won't be sleeping together at all," my dad told me.

"Yeah, I got that." A laugh burst out of me. "Well played."

"I wasn't born yesterday," he said with a chuckle and a shake of his head, pretty damn proud of himself.

But thankfully, we still had my truck, the barn, and plenty of other hidden places we hadn't even explored yet. It just meant we'd have to be more creative.

Improvise. Adapt. Overcome.

CHAPTER TWENTY

Lila

TIME WAS RUNNING OUT. I WANTED TO SLOW IT DOWN. I wanted more of it. The rest of our senior year had flown by so fast it made my head spin. No sooner had I celebrated my eighteenth birthday then it was prom night and before I knew it we were graduating.

Three days ago, we received our high school diplomas. It was supposed to be the beginning of a new adventure, but to me it felt like the end of something good. Yet another milestone that my mom had missed. Yet another step closer to Jude leaving.

Now, I stared at my phone screen, my initial excitement replaced with a stone of dread sinking to the pit of my stomach as another message came in. I'd just done laps in Christy's pool and I'd come out feeling all Zen, my muscles relaxed, but now I was all keyed up and tense. Because of a stupid text message.

"They're home," I told Christy, who was sitting cross-legged on a lounger, a bowl of cut-up fruit in her lap. It was hot as Hades out here but she looked cool as a cucumber in a black bikini and enormous black sunglasses.

"What did he say?" she asked, popping a grape into her mouth. "Did he give you any more info?"

I shook my head and tossed my phone in my canvas tote. "Nope." Gathering my wet hair into a knot, I secured it with the elastic band on my wrist and sat on the edge of the lounger across from her. "All he said was that they went camping and it was a male bonding thing. Now he said we need to talk." I gnawed on my lip, dread pooling in my stomach. It would only take a few words from him to destroy me. "Nothing good ever comes of those words."

"It might be good news. Maybe he has a surprise for you. Or maybe it's code for, I've been away for three days and I need pussy."

I laughed but it sounded feeble. "If that was it, he'd be sexting. This is not sexting. It sounds serious." I stared at the back yard where her mom was teaching a yoga class under the trees. "Ground yourself," she said as she led the group of ladies through the poses. They were supposed to be trees, standing tall and strong.

"I just don't understand why they couldn't be honest. Jude and Brody don't need to keep secrets from me," I said, absently spinning the silver charm bracelet on my wrist. It had been there since my eighteenth birthday three weeks ago. The Swarovski crystals on the silver star sparkled in the sunlight. So bright it was almost blinding.

Jude bought me a star for my birthday. An actual star that he named Star of Lila. It was one of the stars in the constellation Orion and it came with certificates and a map to find it in the night sky. When I asked why he chose Orion, he said those were the stars that guided Odysseus home. I'd resisted the urge to ask if he planned to be gone for ten years and if his journey back would be an odyssey riddled with trials, tribulations and temptations.

It was pointless to try and predict what the future held. And it was probably for the best that we couldn't see into it.

Was he going to break up with me? Would the guy who bought me a star and told me he loved me every chance he got actually do that? I didn't know. All I knew was that he'd been acting strange.

"Maybe it's exactly what he said. They went on a camping trip so they could bond. Don't make a big deal out of it. You'll drive yourself nuts."

Too late. I'd been driving myself nuts for three days. Actually, it had been longer than that. Something had been off with him and Brody for the entire week before our graduation. "I just hate feeling left out," I admitted.

"Triangles are tricky. Unless you turn it into a threesome, one man is always out."

I rolled my eyes. "It's not that kind of triangle."

Her dark brows arched. "Sure it's not. You live with two hot guys who also happen to be your best friends. Not to mention they're practically brothers." She fanned herself with her hand. "God, that's hot."

"It's not like that," I insisted.

"Yeah, okay." Christy plucked a strawberry from the bowl and bit into it. "So you don't notice the way Brody looks at you?"

"Brody doesn't..." I shook my head, disputing her words. "We're just friends. How did we even get on this topic?"

"We were trying to work out what went down on this camping trip."

I stared into the blue depths of the swimming pool as if it held the answers. "What if he's going to break up with me?"

She slid her sunglasses down her nose to get a better look at me. "Is that why you're still sitting here instead of on your way home to get dick?"

I grabbed a wedge of pineapple from her bowl, my knee bouncing as I ate it. She was right. I was stalling. If I didn't go home then I wouldn't have to hear the bad news. I could delay the inevitable. I reclined on the lounger and closed my eyes to block out the sun and my insecurities.

Fifteen... twenty minutes went by, the fruit was gone, and I was still baking under the Texas sun when Christy jostled my arm. "Go home. Get the scoop. And report back. I have to get ready for my date."

That spurred me into action. I got dressed in my loose cotton tank top and cut-offs. Stepping into my flip-flops, I fished my car keys out of my bag and slung it over my shoulder. Time to go home and face the music.

"Call me after the sex," Christy said, bundling the wet towels in her arms.

"Call me after your date tonight. And have fun."

"If we have fun, you won't be getting a call."

"Same goes for me."

"Bitch," she called after me as I skirted the swimming pool, my flip-flops smacking against the tiles.

"Hussy," I threw over my shoulder.

"Love you."

"Love you too."

On the drive home, I gave myself a pep talk. Maybe it wouldn't be bad news. Why did I assume it would be? Everything had been great for months. Our prom night was one of the best nights of my life. I wore a silver sequined halter dress with a pearl gray tulle skirt that floated around my legs when I danced. Jude wore a charcoal gray tux with a bow tie that matched the skirt of my dress. He was voted prom king, Ashleigh the queen. But we left before the announcement and only found out later via text. Jude didn't care about popularity contests. What he'd cared about was spending the night in a hotel with me.

Our relationship was solid. Jude and I were in love. Everything was good. Maybe *too* good. I shoved that thought out of my head. Pessimism wouldn't get me anywhere.

The barn doors were wide open, Eminem blasting from the speakers, portable fans on the highest setting as I lurked outside the door, undetected.

"Eight... nine... ten," Jesse chanted. "Keep going, Jude. You can do it."

Of course he could do it. I didn't know what today's goal was but Jude could do pull-ups all freaking day long. His back was to me and I watched his muscles ripple as he did chin-ups on the bar attached to the wall. Shirtless and sweaty, his hair was a tousled mess. Oh God, he looked delicious. I wanted to lick the sweat off his skin.

That's when it finally hit me. I knew what he needed to tell me. How stupid could I be not to realize it sooner? Oh, right. Denial.

How would I ever live without him? Why had I fallen in love with a guy who was always going to leave me?

Taking a deep breath, I tried to gear up for the news that would probably knock me on my ass. My gaze drifted to Brody who was punching the bag like he had a vendetta against it. Christy was wrong. Brody thought of me as a friend, almost like a sister, and nothing more. I loved Brody, but we weren't *in love*. Big difference.

Sensing my presence, Brody dragged his gaze away from the punching bag and tipped his chin in greeting. No sign of his signature grin. Sensing something was wrong, I walked inside and stopped next to him.

"Are you okay?" I asked quietly.

"Right as rain." But I could see it on his face that he was lying.

"If you ever need to talk about anything, I'm always here for you. You know that, right?"

"Appreciate it. But I'm good."

My shoulders sagged. He wasn't going to confide in me. Had he ever though? If I thought about it, he'd always kept his personal life private. For as close as we'd always been, there was a lot he didn't tell me about himself. Did he confide in Jude? I guess he did.

Jude released the bar and dropped to the ground then turned around to face me.

Jesse grinned. "Hey Lila. Have you heard—"

Jude pulled Jesse's back against his chest and clapped a hand over his mouth, effectively stopping the rest of the words from leaving his mouth. "It's not your news to share, little brother."

"Oops. Sorry."

"You're good." Jude ruffled Jesse's hair to let him know he wasn't angry before he released him.

Jesse picked up the jump rope from the floor and started skipping.

"You've got some fancy footwork there," I said, stifling a laugh when my compliment caused him to speed up. Jesse was a show-off but he was still adorable and didn't have a mean bone in his body so he got away with everything. As the baby of the family, everyone doted on him and he knew how to play on everyone's affections.

"Hey you," Jude said, gripping my hips and pulling me against him for a kiss. "Missed you."

I looped my arms around his neck and kissed him back. "Missed you more."

Brody groaned. "You two are making me sick. Get the hell out of here."

Laughing, I pulled away from Jude. We'd become one of those sickening couples and I didn't even care.

"So... what's your news?" I braced myself for the inevitable words that would come out of his mouth.

"Let me take a quick shower and then we'll go for a drive."

"A drive?" He grabbed my hand and dragged me across the field, my stomach churning with anxiety. Why couldn't he just tell me? Why prolong my misery?

Releasing my hand, he held the back door open for me. I brushed past him and stepped inside the air-conditioned house. In the kitchen, two peach pies were cooling on the countertop. Jude's favorite.

"Leave your bikini on," he called over his shoulder as he took the stairs two a time to take a shower.

Fifteen minutes later, he parked his truck on the side of the road near the swimming hole. "Why would you shower before we go swimming?" I asked as he grabbed two towels from the back of his truck and we walked down the trodden dirt path that cut through the trees.

"So you wouldn't have to smell me on the drive."

He tossed our towels and his T-shirt on a flat rock and kicked off his high tops, his eyes darkening as he stood back to watch me strip down to my red bikini. He hooked his finger in the strap and slid it up and down. "Love this little suit."

"Yeah, I know. You picked it out." My cheeks heated at the memory. Jude came into the dressing room with me.

"I have good taste." He gripped my hips and pulled me against him, brushing his thumbs over my hip bones. "Next time you need to go shopping for a bikini, I'm your man."

I tipped my face up to read his expression. "Next time I need a new bikini, will you be here to go shopping with me?"

Instead of answering, he kissed me then released me. "Let's go for a swim."

I grabbed his hand, tugging him toward me. "How about you just rip off the Band-Aid? When are you leaving?"

How much time do I have with you?

He ran his hand through his shower-damp hair and winced. "Two weeks."

I stared at him. No. He didn't just say that. He couldn't have said two weeks. I'd heard him wrong. "What did you just say?"

"Baby. Don't give me that look."

I pulled away from him and wrapped my arms over my chest. "Don't tell me how to look at you. You said we'd have a few months. You said your recruiter didn't have a slot until the fall. We were supposed to have the entire summer together. Then I'd go to college and you'd go to boot camp." I was hyperventilating. We had so many plans. We were going to make it the best summer ever. "Now it's only two weeks?"

"Yeah." That was all he said. Yeah.

"Is that why you went on that male bonding camping trip with Brody? Did everyone know? Am I the last to find out?"

"No, that's not why..." He exhaled loudly.

"Oh, I'm sorry. Am I not allowed to ask why my boyfriend deserted me for three days?"

"Don't be like that." His jaw clenched, his eyes narrowed. "The shit with Brody has nothing to do with you. It's his story to tell, not mine. If he wants to tell you, that's up to him. And I didn't desert you. I was only gone for three days."

"And now you only have two weeks and I'm working... I'll be working forty hours a week at the garden center and it's too late to take that time off. Stella's on vacation and I'm picking up her hours and..." I stopped and covered my face with my hands. It was too much. I couldn't deal with the thought of him leaving me.

Arms wrapped around me and he pulled me close. "Hey. It's going to be okay. I'm going to boot camp. I'm not dying. It's not as if the doctors have only given me two weeks to live," he joked.

"You don't know that," I said, my voice muffled by my hands.

His chest rumbled with laughter. "You're acting crazy, Rebel. Come on. Let's get in the water," he urged. "I'm sweating my balls off out here."

I snorted. "Better get used to it. Soon you'll be sweating your balls off with a drill instructor barking out orders."

How could anyone be looking forward to that? But he was. Apparently, I wasn't moving fast enough for him. He swooped me up in one swift motion and tossed me over his shoulder.

"Let me down!" I pounded my fists against his back but he just laughed and waded into the water. When he was chest-deep, he tossed me in the air like I was a rag doll.

That guy. As soon as my head emerged, I launched at him. "You're so predictable, Rebel."

"You're such a pain in the ass."

"So are you." He smiled, showing me those dimples I loved, his eyes so blue in the sunlight, his wet hair slicked back, and I had an ache in my heart the size of Texas. "The most beautiful, infuriating, stubborn pain in the ass."

"Right back at you." Instead of trying to dunk him, I looped my arms around his neck and my legs around his waist and buried my face in the crook of his neck.

"Everything is going to be okay. Promise. After you grad-uate college and after I finish the Marines, we'll have our whole lives to be together. I'll be with you so much you'll get sick of me."

"You want to spend your whole life with me?"

"Planning on it. Why? Did you have something else in mind?"

"Forever is a long time. How do you know I'm the one you want to spend it with?"

"I've always known. You're it for me."

"You might change your mind."

"Yeah, and I might get eaten by a crocodile."

I laughed. "What are you saying?"

"The odds of that happening are slim to none. That's what I'm saying. What are you saying?"

"Be prepared. I'm going to be the best Marine girlfriend in the history of Marine girlfriends."

"I don't doubt that for a minute. We good?"

I nodded and said that everything was good. What else could I do? I had to be supportive.

He was here now and we were good and I didn't want to waste another minute of our time together dwelling on how much I would miss him when he left for boot camp. I wanted to use our time to make good memories, the kind of memories we could both hang on to when we were apart. All the sweet, beautiful seemingly insignificant moments. Those were the ones that counted most and I wanted to remember every single one of them.

CHAPTER TWENTY-ONE

Jude

"ARE YOU NERVOUS?" LILA ASKED. WE'D CLIMBED ONTO the roof for old time's sake and the night sky didn't disappoint. It reeled with stars, the summer air warm and sweet and I had an ache inside my chest that felt like homesickness. Tomorrow morning I was leaving Lila.

My first instinct was to deny it and say no, that I wasn't nervous. But I opted for the truth instead. "A little bit. Are you okay?"

"No. I'm really not."

I turned my head to look at her face in the moonlight. It glowed paler, in stark contrast to her dark hair. I couldn't see the five freckles on her nose but I knew they were still there. Her answer made me question my life choices. Why had I been so dead set on enlisting? Why couldn't I have gone to college with Lila? Played football. Attended classes. Spent the next five years by her side.

"But I will be. And so will you. I believe in you, Jude. I

believe in us. We can get through anything. You showed me that."

"I love you, Rebel."

"I love you more."

"That's good because I plan to spend the rest of my life with you."

"How can you promise me forever at eighteen?"

"It's the easiest thing I've ever done. It's always been you. I've never wanted anyone but you. But..."

"But?" she said.

"But I made this decision. This was my choice. If you..." Fuck. I didn't want to say this but I had to. It was the right thing to do. I took a deep breath and let it out. "I want you to enjoy your college experience. I want you to do all the college things. Parties and tailgates and... I don't know. I want you to be happy, Lila. If you meet someone at college and you—"

She pressed her fingers against my lips, stopping the words. "Don't say it."

I wrapped my hand around her wrist and moved it. "I have to. You're young and you're... fuck, you're so beautiful..."

"You're biased."

I shook my head. "You are. There are a lot of guys out there who would give anything to be with you. And I don't want you to feel like you've missed out. Five years is a long time to wait for someone."

"Are you breaking up with me?"

I squeezed my eyes shut. "No. I'm just giving you an out."

"I don't want an out. There will never be another you. You're the only one for me, Jude."

I blew out a breath. "You say that now but that's because I'm all you've ever known. When you get to college, you'll meet a lot of different guys. Guys who—"

"I don't understand where this is coming from. You spent

years trying to keep guys away from me and now you're trying to push me to meet someone new?"

"No. I'm not trying to push you to meet someone new. I just..." I gripped the back of my neck. "I don't want you to have any regrets or to someday resent me for asking you to wait. It's a lot to ask someone at eighteen."

"Just a little while ago, you were promising me forever. Do you want to find someone new? Is that what this is about?"

"No. I don't want anyone else. But none of this is fair to you. I'll be thousands of miles away..."

"You'll be a phone call and an email away. And you'll be home on leave. You'll get thirty days a year, right?" I nodded. "And I can visit you. We'll make it work."

"But if you change your mind, I'll understand." I didn't know if that was true. I'd never questioned my life choices before. This had been my plan since I was a kid. If I was being honest, I couldn't even say why or how I'd decided it was what I needed to do. It had just always felt right. Right for *me*. I'd been selfish. So focused on what I wanted that I hadn't really taken Lila's needs into account. And now, it all hit me.

I was leaving her. Which was why she'd pushed me away after her mom died. At the time, I thought she was being ridiculous. Now I understood that it was self-preservation. It made me feel like a dumb shit for taking this long to grasp something so obvious.

"Are you having second thoughts?" she asked. "I mean, is this still what you want?"

"If I didn't, I'd be shit out of luck."

"That's not an answer."

"Yeah, Rebel. It's still what I want. But this was my decision, made solely for me, and you're being forced to go along with it. That's why I'm giving you an out."

"Wow. Okay. How big of you. You act like I didn't have a

choice. I *chose* you, knowing that this was what you were planning to do. Do you really think that if I'd wanted some other guy, I wouldn't have gone for him? Not even you could have stopped me. I only want you. And if that ever changes, which I can't see how it would, we'll take it from there. In the meantime..." She flicked my arm. "Stop being such a bonehead. We were always meant to be. Time and distance won't change that."

I believed her because I felt the same way. Maybe it was crazy to commit to someone at the age of eighteen. Maybe it was crazy to believe that we could make this long-distance relationship work. At our age, this was a huge commitment. What would make us think we could conquer all the odds? But we had faith that we could.

"You know what I'll miss the most about you?" she asked a few minutes later.

"What?"

"Your hair."

We both laughed. And then we laughed some more. I loved this girl. Every little piece of her.

"I'll see you in thirteen weeks. San Diego, here I come." She poked my chest. "So you'd better graduate. I want to see the Pacific Ocean. It'll be nice to see you too," she teased.

I don't know if she cried after I left, but as the bus pulled away the next morning she was smiling. Her smile was bright, it was beautiful, and I carried it with me all through boot camp. It meant more to me than she'd ever know because I knew she did it for me.

Over the next five years, it became our thing. She always smiled when we said goodbye and I later found out that she did it so it would be my last memory of her. We made it work. Time and distance didn't destroy our relationship.

Remaining loyal to Lila was the easy part. There was never

a question of whether or not I still loved her. I've always loved Lila, and I always would.

But sometimes love just isn't enough.

PART 2

CHAPTER TWENTY-TWO

Lila

FIVE YEARS LATER

Jude was home. It was the first thought in my head when I woke up that morning. It was the Fourth of July weekend, and he'd been back for two weeks. I still couldn't believe he was here, and that this time he was back for good. I hadn't even opened my eyes yet but I was already thinking about him. I felt the mattress dip under his weight as he shifted on the bed away from me, and when I opened my eyes and rolled onto my side, I was gifted with a view of his back.

Shoulders hunched, he was sitting on the edge of the mattress, his head in his hands. Two days ago, I woke up and found him sleeping on the hard floor. When I'd asked him why he was sleeping on the floor, he said he didn't know. He'd looked confused, like he had no idea where he was or how he'd gotten there, and that had scared me.

"Are you okay?" My voice was low and quiet so I wouldn't startle him.

"Yeah. All good."

I crawled across the bed on my knees and wrapped my arms around his middle, resting my chin on his shoulder. "Do you still have the ringing in the ears? And the headaches?"

The shoulder under my chin lifted in a shrug. On his third and final deployment, Jude had gotten a TBI, a traumatic brain injury from a bomb blast. I didn't know the details because he wouldn't talk about it.

What I did know was that his convoy had been ambushed and hit by a roadside bomb. Six Marines were killed, four wounded. Kate and I read about it in the news. We used to scour the news and hang out in the families of Marines chat rooms, desperate for information that Jude withheld from us. Whenever I used to ask him how things were going over there, he'd always say it was quiet. Nothing to worry about. Lies. There was always something to worry about in a combat zone. But it was his way of trying to protect me, I guess.

Pressing my chest against his back, I kissed the side of his neck while my hands coasted downward, over smooth skin and taut muscles that flexed under my touch. My right hand dipped inside the waistband of his boxer briefs and wrapped around his hard length.

He grabbed my hand and pulled it away. Disappointment slammed into me and I leaned back on my heels. "What's wrong?" I tried to mask the hurt in my voice.

"Nothing. I'm just not up for it right now."

"You seem like you're up for it."

Without responding, he stood up from the bed and strode to the oak chest of drawers. I stared at his back as he took out a T-shirt and running shorts and got dressed.

"Let's go for a run," he said, his back still turned to me.

"Okay," I said slowly, staying right where I was.

He sat on the end of the bed to put on his running shoes then stood up and turned to face me, his brows raised in question when he saw that I was still in the same spot on the bed where he'd left me. "Are you coming or not?" he asked brusquely.

Did he even want me to come?

It was an odd sensation to look at the man you loved but not recognize him. Maybe it was the hair. I'd never get used to that military cut and couldn't wait until it grew out. Or maybe it was his eyes. There was something in them that had never been there before. They were haunted like he'd seen too much death and destruction and couldn't reconcile with it. Instead of talking about it, he locked it down and insisted he was fine every time I asked.

"Yeah, I'm coming." I had the day off, so I wanted us to spend it together. He walked out of the room and when I heard the bathroom door close behind him, I took a deep breath and got dressed.

As he was leaving the bathroom, I brushed past him and ducked inside. Teeth brushed, hair in a high ponytail, I stared at my reflection in the mirror. You get so used to your own face that after a while, you stop seeing it but now I took a good, hard look.

I hadn't changed much. I still had a sprinkle of freckles on my nose. Same green eyes and heart-shaped face. Small nose, wide mouth. Brows a shade darker than my hair.

I'd never been the most gorgeous girl in the room but I'd always been okay with the way I looked. Jude used to tell me I was beautiful all the time. In actuality, I leaned more toward cute, and on my better days you could call me pretty. But *he* used to think I was beautiful.

Now, I wasn't sure what he thought.

When had he stopped being attracted to me? It was recent, I knew that. When he used to come home on leave, he couldn't keep his hands off me. He used to fuck me into oblivion. But in the two weeks since he'd come home, he hadn't touched me once.

With a sigh, I joined him in the kitchen. It was small and beige like the rest of the apartment. My potted herbs sat on the windowsill next to a mason jar filled with daisies, my attempt to brighten up a dull room.

"Your mom's throwing that party for you today." I peeled a banana and took a bite, watching Jude's throat bob as he drank a sports drink. He didn't acknowledge my words, and I thought he hadn't even heard me so I repeated myself.

"Heard you the first time." He tossed the empty bottle into the trash and grabbed his keys from the countertop, twirling the key ring around his finger. "Ready?"

He didn't even bother waiting for my answer. He was out the door. I finished my banana, drank a glass of water then walked out the door when I was good and ready.

Our two-story brick apartment building was plunked down in the middle of rural Hill Country, surrounded by fields and scattered houses that didn't conform to any particular design. The apartment was nothing special but our rent was cheap so we could save our money for the house and land we were hoping to buy someday.

Before we set off on our run, Jude slipped on a pair of sunglasses. It was still early, the sun hiding behind the clouds and it wasn't that bright but he was wearing sunglasses. Which was odd. Jude never used to wear sunglasses. He looked like a Marine. Like a jarhead. And I hated that he looked so different. But I knew it had nothing to do with the way he looked and everything to do with the way he was acting.

He set a punishing pace and I pushed myself to keep up. I

had a feeling we'd run until my legs were burning and I'd collapse when it was over.

I side-eyed Jude as our feet pounded the dirt road on one of his favorite routes. It was hilly, parts of it steep. Limestone cliffs rose from the ground, reaching for the clouds and thanks to all the rain we had in the spring, the fields were lush and green.

One time I asked Jude to describe Afghanistan. What did it look like? What was the weather like? Stuff like that. Always hungry for information, I used to ask Jude for details so I could try to imagine where he was when he wasn't with me.

"Depends where you are," he'd said. "The terrain can be brutal. Steep, jagged mountains with razor edges. Desert. Other places there're poppy fields and cornfields. You freeze in the winter and sweat your balls off in the summer. The sand gets in everywhere. And I mean *everywhere*. You have to watch so you don't get stung by scorpions. Not much you can do about the sand fleas and chiggers."

He told me that he'd sometimes gone for months without a shower. When he was doing Recon, they'd get dropped into the middle of nowhere, forty kilometers away from civilization and they'd have to carry everything on their backs. So on top of being in rough terrain, they were carrying upwards of a hundred pounds. He said he'd gone for weeks without dry boots because they'd been wading through mud and thigh-high water.

It sounded like hell on earth. But he'd never complained about any of that.

I stumbled and Jude grabbed my elbow, catching me before I fell. His reflexes were lightning-quick and even though it felt like he was a million miles away, his steadying hand reminded me he was right next to me.

"Keep your eyes on the road, Rebel. Stop looking at me."

He hadn't used my nickname in a while and stupidly it

gave me hope. Like we would be okay just because he'd used his childhood nickname for me. "I can't help it. You're just too pretty," I teased.

"Pretty," he scoffed. "I'm a lean, mean fighting machine."

"The fight is over," I reminded him. "You're home now."

"Yeah. Home." He said it like it was a dirty word that left a bitter taste in his mouth.

I stopped running and put my hands on my knees, leaning over to catch my breath. Sweat dripped from my forehead into my eyes and made them sting. We'd already run three miles and he'd given the impression that he wasn't planning to slow down or quit anytime soon. But more than that, it felt like he'd just sucker punched me in the gut. He'd once told me that *I* was his home and now he sounded like he wanted to be anywhere but here.

He came to stand in front of me. "You okay?" He sounded reluctant to hear my answer.

I wasn't okay. Not even a little bit. I straightened up and wrapped my arms around myself as if I needed to protect myself from him. "I miss you, Jude. I miss you so much."

He laughed like that was a joke. "I'm right here. Standing right in front of you."

"Are you though? Are you really here?"

He crossed his arms over his chest and his jaw clenched. I couldn't see his eyes behind his dark sunglasses, but I'd be willing to bet they were narrowed on me. "What's that supposed to mean?"

I stared at a two-story dark green farmhouse surrounded by live oaks that blocked the sun. Was that why the grass wasn't growing around that house? The house sat on a patch of dirt surrounded by scrubby bushes. A tire swing hung from the branch of a tree and an Irish Setter sat on the porch, wagging its tail. Like *he* was happy to be home. A wave of sadness and longing washed over me, and I couldn't swallow past the lump in my throat.

I missed my childhood. Our childhood. Our summertime. All the sweet and beautiful moments we'd shared. I missed Jude and Lila, the way we used to be. But I didn't know how to put any of that into words he'd understand. The old Jude would have understood but this cool, aloof man standing in front of me would attempt to laugh it off.

"I love you, Jude, and I've loved you for so long."

He huffed out a laugh and scrubbed his hand over his buzzed cut. "I love you too. Where is all this coming from?"

"I don't know. I just feel like..." My shoulders slumped. For five long years I'd waited for him. For five long years I'd counted down the months and days until we could be together again. And now that he was here, it felt like he wasn't really here at all. "You're so far away. So distant. And I don't know how to talk to you anymore. I feel like I can't tell you anything because I'm worried it will upset you or make you angry." As soon as the words were out, I instantly regretted them. I'd said it all wrong.

He put his hands on his hips. "What do you need to talk to me about?" I heard the accusation in his voice. "Are you saying you want to end things? Is that what you can't tell me?"

"What? No. God. Why would you even think that?"

"Oh hell, I don't know." He threw his hands in the air. "Maybe because you haven't even told me you're planning to start your own business with your little friend, Christy. You wanna talk? How about we talk about all the shit you're keeping from me."

"I'm not keeping anything from you. I'm the one who told you about the business. That was me, Jude. But I didn't think you were listening because you didn't even comment on it."

"That wasn't you. I found out from my mom."

I stared at him. He truly believed that he'd found out from his mother. "Seriously? You don't remember when I told you this? It was last week. You were playing video games."

Another thing he never used to do. Now he played those stupid video games all the time.

He looked up at the sky then back at me and I saw it on his face that he knew I was right. "Shit. I... fuck." He bit the corner of his bottom lip and I tried not to notice how sexy that little move was. In the past, I could forgive him anything when he did that. He held his hand over his forehead like a visor and massaged his temples. I wanted to ask him if his head hurt but I felt like I was always pestering him about it so I kept my mouth shut. "Sorry about that. Now that you mention it, I do remember."

A jolt of panic shot through me. What did that mean? He didn't remember but now he did? Jude had the memory of an elephant. He remembered things from years ago and could recount the memory in vivid detail but now he couldn't even remember something I'd told him a week ago?

"Jude..." I started, not sure what to say. It was pointless to keep asking if he was okay because clearly, he wasn't. "What did the doctors say when they checked your head? Did they do an MRI? Did they—"

"Lila. Stop making it sound like such a big fucking deal," he snapped. "I had a concussion. Nothing worse than the one I had when I was playing football."

I didn't believe him. He was lying. "Did you black out? Were you unconscious?"

"I'm fine. It's nothing to worry about, okay?" he said, his voice softer now like he was trying to reassure me. He wrapped his hand around the back of my head and pulled me against him. I wrapped my arms around his waist and tipped my face up to his.

When he smiled, he looked like the Jude I used to know. "Stop being such a worrywart."

"I need to look after you. You're my man."

"And don't you forget it, baby." His hands framed my face and he kissed me. "It's all good."

I had no choice but to believe him.

"Do you want to keep running?" He looked around as if he was just now noticing where we were. "I didn't realize we'd come this far. We should head back. Are you okay to run?"

I nodded but the worry was still gnawing at me. "Yeah, I'm fine. I can run distances, no problem."

"I'll slow the pace. That way we can talk if you want to."

I smiled, acknowledging that he was trying. "Okay. Sounds good."

We set out at a decent pace, more of a jog than a run and I wasn't so out of breath that it prevented me from talking. "So, tell me more about the business."

Encouraged by his interest, I told him how Christy and I wanted to open a floral design studio. All through college, I'd worked part time for a florist and for the past year I'd been working as an event planner at Sadler's Creek Vineyard. Hill Country was the wedding capital of Texas, and the floral design studio would cater to weddings and events.

"We'll have to take out some loans but I really think we can make it work. Gideon said he could put together a business plan for us."

"My brother Gideon?" Jude asked, sounding surprised, as if there was another Gideon.

I laughed. "Um, yeah, your brother Gideon. He's wicked smart and he's studying business." Gideon was going into this third year at Columbia University and was spending the summer in New York City, doing an internship at a venture capital company. But he'd flown in last night so he could be at Jude's Welcome Home party.

"Sounds like a cool idea," Jude said. "I know you'll make it a success. And I've got money in savings so you won't need to take out loans."

"Thanks, but that money is for something else, right? I mean, if you still want to do what we talked about..."

"Nothing has changed. I put a ring on it, didn't I?"

I laughed a little, rubbing my left thumb over the diamond on my ring finger. "Yeah, you did."

"There you go. I'm still going to marry you. We're still going to buy land and I'm still going to build that dream house for us and our four kids."

I laughed. "We never agreed on four."

"You'll come around."

"You still want all those things?"

"Why wouldn't I?"

"I don't know. I just... we haven't talked about it in a while."

"I've only been home for two weeks."

He was right. It had only been two weeks. I was being impatient, not to mention ridiculous. He was still Jude. Still the man I loved more than life itself. And everything was going to be okay. We just had to get used to being together again.

I was feeling so much lighter now that we'd talked, and hopeful for the future again.

"How about a race?" I asked, riding high on false optimism.

"You still think you can beat me?"

"One of these days I will, and you'll be crying the blues. I live for that day."

He just laughed. "What's the wager?"

Just then I heard a whistling sound followed by a loud pop and a crack. Before I could process that it was fireworks exploding in the field, my back hit the ground, knocking all the wind out of me. A heavy weight pressed down on me, constricting my chest and making it hard to draw air into my lungs. It took me a few seconds to realize that I was lying in a ditch and the heavy weight pressing down on me was Jude, his body covering mine as if to protect me.

"Jude." I tried to shove him off of me. He lifted his head and stared down at me. Sweat rolled off his face and onto mine. I could feel his heart pounding against my chest. He leaned his weight on his forearm so I wasn't bearing the brunt of it but he was still somewhere else, and not here with me.

"Jude. It's okay. It was just fireworks. You're okay." He rolled off me and sat up with his knees bent and his forehead pressed against his crossed arms. I sat next to him and rubbed his back because I didn't know what else to do or how to help him. His T-shirt was sweat-soaked, and I could feel his back rising and falling on each ragged breath he drew in and exhaled.

In the field across from us, a bunch of kids launched three more bottle rockets. Jude's back went rigid under my hand and the muscles tensed as if bracing himself for the explosion. I cursed the stupid kids who were doing it. But when we were kids, we used to do the same thing on the Fourth of July. We used to love it. The bigger the bang, the happier it made us.

"Are you okay?" I asked him, even though I knew he wasn't. It was such a stupid question but I was at a loss. What could you say to a man who had thrown you in a ditch to protect you from fireworks? Not much.

He took a few deep breaths, his eyes on the field and not on me. "Did I hurt you?"

I shook my head, which he couldn't see because he was staring into the distance and not looking at me. "No. I'm fine. You didn't hurt me. I'm just worried about you."

Clearly, that was the wrong thing to say. With a snort of

disgust, he got to his feet. "I don't want you worrying about me. Let's run."

Without waiting for me, he took off, running as if he had something to prove. The message was clear. I wasn't allowed to worry about him.

I wasn't allowed to mention Reese Madigan's name. I had no idea how he died. No idea how Jude had gotten shot in the head on that first deployment. When I asked, he shut me down.

All I knew was that Jude returned from his first deployment alive and in one piece but Reese Madigan came home in a flag-draped casket. As I stood in the cemetery on that summer's day four years ago, with a lone bugler playing TAPS and a Marine in dress blues handing Reese's mom the folded flag, I'd sent up a silent prayer, "Thank you, God, for not taking Jude away from me."

And that was my ugly truth. The first of many to come.

CHAPTER TWENTY-THREE

Jude

I was on my way to drunk, but not nearly drunk enough. This homecoming party was pure fucking torture. Everyone was expecting me to be happy. To be grateful that I was home, and I could resume my regularly scheduled life.

In the past, whenever I used to come home on leave, I was happy to be here. But now that I was home for good, and back with the girl I used to talk about so much the guys in my unit used to give me shit over it, I felt like I was somewhere I didn't belong anymore.

It was a shitty feeling, because I *wanted* to be happy. I wanted it more than anything.

What purpose did my life have now? Where the fuck was I supposed to go from here? Where did I fit in this world that had gone on without me, just as if there wasn't a war being fought in the middle of the desert in a godforsaken country?

Nobody cared about all the lives that were lost or all the blood that had been shed. Nobody here cared that it was still going on. They didn't give a shit. The Fourth of July was just an excuse to set off fireworks, get drunk and throw a barbecue.

Six weeks ago, I was in the rugged mountains of Afghanistan, surrounded by insurgents. Our convoy had been ambushed, our operation compromised. Six dead, four wounded when the truck in front of mine had been hit by a roadside bomb. I must have blacked out. When I came to, I was on the side of the road with no idea how I'd ended up there. Sniper rounds snapped off rocks and fizzed overhead. White phosphorous smoke filled the air and shots ricocheted off the truck I'd just been thrown from.

"We need air support." I heard Reyes shout into the radio to be heard above the din of the gunfire.

I looked to my right. "Tommy." Belly down, I dragged my body across the blood-soaked dirt and rocks. "We need to move."

"I can't move. I'm pinned down... I can't fucking move my legs."

Now I stared at the sparklers on the cake decorated with the stars and stripes. My mom was smiling as she set it in front of me on the table. "We're so happy you're home, honey."

I forced a smile. "Good to be here," I lied. And it pissed me off that it wasn't true. Why did I feel so fucking numb, like I was watching my life as if it was a movie, and I was so far removed from it that I wasn't really living it?

I was surrounded by my family. The people I loved. My dad was talking about the projects he was working on and the construction site he was sending me to when I went back to work on Monday. Gideon was talking to Lila about her new business venture. Jesse was talking about motocross with Brody who was supposed to be at a rodeo but had come home to see me. When he wasn't on the road, Brody lived in an Airstream on Austin Armacost's ranch where he still worked as a ranch hand. He was saving money to buy a horse farm and still had big dreams and plans just like everyone else at the table.

My mom asked what I'd missed the most about home and I answered, "Lila. And my family."

It was the truth and it made my mom smile.

Lila was sitting right next to me but even when she touched me, I didn't feel it. How could I ever explain this to her? I couldn't. All I could do was hope and pray that it would change. I'd only been home for two weeks. It had to get better.

I took another swig of beer and forced myself to stay at the table when all I really wanted to do was walk away and be alone. But I couldn't have walked away if I wanted to. My ears were ringing and my head was pounding so hard, my vision blurred. The ground tilted beneath me and I was so fucking dizzy I felt like I'd just gotten off a ride at the funfair and had been thrown into the house of mirrors.

I reached for Lila's hand to steady myself and clasped it in mine like it was my lifeline.

Save me, Lila. I'm drowning.

CHAPTER TWENTY-FOUR

Jude

PALE NOVEMBER SUNLIGHT SLANTED THROUGH THE cracked blinds and the pipes clanked and hissed as I moved soundlessly across the bedroom floor. In the bathroom I took a piss and washed my hands, avoiding the mirror above the sink.

I'd found something that made the good days brighter, and I reached into my hiding place and untaped it from the ceramic. Chop. Chop. Chop. Sniff. My head immediately cleared and turned the dull world into technicolor. Running my tongue over my tingling gums, I held the rolled-up Franklin to my nose and leaned over for another hit. Gnashing my teeth, I told myself that was enough. Just a few lines to give me a high without making me crash and burn. Self-control was key and I had a good handle on this.

Returning the stash to its hiding place, I wiped my nose and brushed my teeth then returned to my first love.

I *ached* for her. *Craved* her. *Needed* her. With every muscle and bone in my body. The organ in my chest beating triple time.

Lila. Lila. Lila.

My pulse skyrocketed and all the blood rushed from my head to my throbbing cock. She was still asleep, lying on her side. Sliding under the sheets naked, I wrapped my arm around her waist and pulled her flush against my body, thrusting against her, so rock hard it was almost painful.

The longer I held off, the sweeter the reward.

I rubbed between her legs, watching her sleeping face. Her mouth went slack but her eyes were still closed. That didn't deter me. She was wet. I slipped a finger inside her, feeling her, and she moaned as my thumb pressed on her clit.

"Morning," I said hoarsely, kissing the side of her neck.

"Good morning to you too," she murmured, grinding her sexy little ass against my erection.

Good. She was up for it. She let out a yelp when I flipped her onto her back and yanked and tore the cotton preventing me from being inside her. Then I buried my head between her legs and feasted, dry humping the mattress, seeking the friction for my raging hard-on while my mouth and fingers fucked her. Her legs quivered and her thighs clamped around my head as her pussy clenched around my tongue.

"Oh my God!" she screamed.

"That's it, baby." Without warning, I flipped her over and positioned her on her hands and knees, and I drove into her.

"Fuck, yes." I pounded into her, my hand fisting her hair. With the other hand, I rubbed her clit until she was meeting me thrust for thrust, pushing her ass against me. I threw back my head and roared as I came inside her. Her arms gave out and she collapsed on the mattress, her ass in the air.

And still it wasn't enough.

The sex did nothing to calm me. Two seconds after I dragged my dick out of her, I was up and pacing, pushing my hands through my hair. I needed more. I was insatiable. Firing on all cylinders. Too revved up to stay still.

"What are you doing?"

"Let's take a shower." *So I can fuck you again.*

She yawned and closed her eyes, curling onto her side like a cuddly kitten. "It's my day off. I need sleep. Come back to bed."

"Yeah, not happening." I picked her up and tossed her over my shoulder.

Turning on the shower, I gripped the backs of her thighs and lifted her up, her legs cinching my waist and her back slamming against the tiles as I rammed inside her. Her nails scored my skin.

"Fuck yes, baby," I growled. "Hurt me. Make me bleed for you."

"I don't... Jude," she panted, her fingers tugging on my hair. I was relentless, not letting up or slowing down. I needed more.

More, more, more. Of everything.

I needed to feel alive.

Her back arched and she cried out but I barely heard her. I didn't feel the sting of her nails digging into my skin. I didn't feel the pain of her teeth sinking into my shoulder. All I felt was the need to shoot my load deep inside her.

I came on a roar that ripped from my throat and I flattened both palms on the tiles next to her head to hold myself up. My head dropped to her shoulder and I tried to catch my breath.

"Let me down," she said quietly, her low voice drowned out by the roaring in my ears. She shoved my shoulder. "Jude. Let me down."

I lifted my head and blinked a few times, bringing her into focus. "You're so fucking hot, Rebel. I want to stay buried inside you. Hear you screaming my name so loud you'll wake the neighbors."

She shook her head, tears glittering in her eyes. "Who are you?"

I had no answer for her. Wrapping my hands around her waist, I lifted her off me and set her down. She stood under the spray of the shower with her eyes closed and her arms wrapped around herself for protection. From me.

Sensing she wanted to be alone, I left her in the shower.

Dressed in jeans and a T-shirt, the water in the shower was still running as I took a quick bump from my secret stash, just enough to perk me up, make a dark day brighter. I checked that my nose was clean in the mirror above the dresser before I walked to the kitchen. My stomach churned and I wasn't the least bit hungry but I wanted to do something nice for Lila. So I cooked breakfast. A peace offering. A pathetic attempt at normalcy.

By the time she joined me in the kitchen, her omelet was cold and the buttered toast was rubbery. But I set it in front of her anyway, along with the plate of bacon and a glass of orange juice. She was wearing a hoodie and sweats, her wet hair in a bun and her face free of makeup. She looked so fresh and clean, as if she'd scrubbed every last trace of me off her skin. Lila still had five freckles on her nose. And she was, to me, still the most beautiful thing I'd ever laid eyes on.

I loved her.

Irrevocably. Wholly. Madly.

And I was slowly but surely ruining the very best thing in my life.

She looked down at her plate but didn't touch the food. "Thank you."

I nodded and poured her a cup of coffee, refilling my own

mug before I sat down across from her at our small kitchen table in our cramped kitchen in our shitty apartment.

"I'm sorry." It was the only thing I could think of to fill the silence.

"I know you are." She nibbled on a piece of bacon then dropped it on her plate and I nearly cried like a fucking baby. Because I needed her to eat this fucking breakfast. I needed to do something to make everything better but I had no idea what that something was.

"Tell me something good, Jude."

I racked my brain before coming up with the most obvious answer. "You. You're something good."

She shook her head. "And what else?"

"Wild at Heart is good. You're making it a success just like I knew you would."

Six weeks ago, Christy and Lila opened their new business. My dad and I had done all the work on the cedar-shingled shed that housed their floral design studio. We knocked out a wall and replaced it with French doors. Built zinc-topped wood islands for their floral arranging. Fitted wood cabinets and shelves to hold all their supplies and tools. Poured a smooth concrete floor and clad the walls with rustic wood. It was a cool place and Lila was happy, excited about her new venture, and that's what mattered most to me. Her happiness.

"You can't think of anything that's good in your own life?"

No. "*You* are my life."

"That's what I was afraid of." She reached into the pocket of her hoodie and tossed something on the table. I stared at the pink plus sign for so long it started to blur.

"Jude?"

"Baby," I croaked. The bitter bile of self-loathing burned the back of my throat. The diamond on her finger caught the light from the kitchen window as she tucked a piece of hair behind her ear. I'd proposed to her two Christmases ago. On bended knee, I'd promised to always love her, to never leave her, and to always strive to be the best man I could be for her. I'd promised her the world and I had yet to deliver.

My eyes met hers and I saw the fear and the worry circling in their green depths on what should have been a happy occasion. I stood up from the table and pulled her out of the chair and into my arms. She held on tightly, her cheek pressed against my chest, and I closed my eyes and made her promises I prayed I could keep.

"I won't let you down again, Rebel. I promise I'll be there for you. Every step of the way." I kissed the top of her head and she pulled away, tipping her face up. "I love you, Rebel. I love you so fucking much."

"Are you happy about this? I mean... I know it's not the best timing but..."

"It's always a good time for a baby. We're having a baby."

"Yeah, we are." Worry had her gnawing on her bottom lip. "Do you think it's too much too soon?"

"No. I want it all." And I did. I wanted this baby. I wanted us to be a family. Everything would be better. *I* would be better. "But you need to eat your breakfast. I'll make a new omelet, okay? How about a stack of pancakes? You know what? I'll just make everything."

She laughed a little. "An omelet is good. Don't go overboard."

"Ask me the question again."

"What's good in your life, Jude?"

"Same answer as before. You." I dipped my head and kissed her softly. Gently. Like she was made of glass and would shatter if I pressed too hard. It was Lila who deepened the kiss and sunk her teeth into my bottom lip. My girl. She was a fighter.

"Next time you decide to fuck me, don't forget to bring me along for the ride."

"You're my ride or die, baby. I'll never leave you behind."

CHAPTER TWENTY-FIVE

Jude

I'M CROSSING A FIELD OF POPPIES IN AFGHANISTAN. I'M IN front, Reese right behind me. Up ahead, I see the boy. Today he has a cell phone in his hand. He grins at me before he darts away. I know I should report it but I don't. He's just a kid, no more than ten or twelve. Why would an innocent kid report our position to the Taliban?

Only a few minutes later, we're walking down a road when the shooting starts. I duck behind a wall, taking cover. I'm shouting at Reese but it's too late. He falls to the ground, and I leave my cover, crawling toward him. An AK is pointed at me.

I lift my rifle and get him in my sights. I pull the trigger and I shoot him. The boy's eyes widen as he falls to the ground. When I look again, it's not a boy, it's a baby. Belly down, I drag myself across the blood-soaked dirt. A bullet whizzes over my head and kicks up a cloud of dust right next to me. I don't even see the next shot being fired or where it's coming from but I feel it. My *face is in the dirt and I'm choking on it. I feel like I've been bashed in the head with a baseball bat.*

Everything goes eerily quiet but I can still hear the call to prayer from the mosque. Lifting my head, I blink the sweat from my eyes and try to adjust my blurry vision.

I'm shouting, Reese needs help, but nobody hears me.

Pressing my dirt-caked hand over Reese's neck, I try to staunch the bleeding. "Hang in there, buddy. You're going to be okay."

"Can I get a Hail Mary?" His voice is garbled. Blood runs from his mouth like a river.

"You're going to be okay." I keep repeating the words, telling him that everything is going to be okay but I know it won't.

Reese's eyes stare blankly at the blue Afghan sky.

But it's not Reese. And it's not the boy or the Talib I just shot and killed. It's a baby with green eyes and dark hair.

I get to my feet and I stagger back a step, my boot planted firmly on the ground. My blood runs cold and I'm covered in sweat. I know it was a mistake. I look down just before the IED explodes.

I jolted upright, my pulse racing and my heart pounding. Panic clawed its way up my throat, goosebumps raising the hairs on my sweat-slicked skin.

I was dying. I was going to die. All the air was trapped in my lungs and a freight trained raced through my head. I couldn't fucking breathe.

"Jude. You're okay. You're okay. It was just a dream. Breathe. In. Out. In. Out." She kept repeating it until the words reached my ears and I did as she said, trying to fill my lungs with oxygen then release it. Since when had breathing become so difficult?

I leaned my back against the headboard and closed my eyes, spent and exhausted. "Did I hurt you?" I asked when my breathing was normal again. I wasn't nineteen years old, watching my friend die before my eyes and I wasn't in Afghanistan. I was in my bed in Texas with Lila who was pregnant with my child. "Did I do anything..."

"No. No, you were just thrashing. And you... you were shouting."

Fuck. I was thrashing and shouting? I opened my eyes and scrubbed my hands over my face. "I'm sorry. Did I scare you?"

"No," she lied.

Of course you did, asshole. What kind of a psycho thrashes and shouts in their sleep? My head hurt like a motherfucker and the light made it worse but I flicked on the table lamp because I needed to see her face. I needed to see Lila and make sure she was okay.

She sat up next to me and I turned my head to look at her face. She smiled but it didn't reach her eyes. "I'm okay," she assured me. "What was your dream about?"

I couldn't tell her. My dream was too real. I never wanted Lila to look at me and see a man who killed people. I never wanted her to know about all the shit I'd witnessed or the things I'd done. Once those visions were in your head, they wouldn't go away. So I'd always kept them in a separate compartment to shield her from the horrors of war. Except now it wasn't so easily contained. It was bleeding into my real life. Instead of leaving the war behind like I'd managed to do for the past five years, it had followed me home.

My eyes lowered to her hands. She was cradling her wrist. When she saw me looking, she released it and hid her hands under the covers.

"Lila. Let me see your wrist."

She shook her head. "It's fine."

Fucking hell. "It's not fine. Let me see it."

Reluctantly, she let me take her hand in both of mine. I tried to be as gentle as I could but she winced and I could already see that it was starting to swell.

"What did I do?" I asked, my voice cracking on the words. My chest tightened and I could barely breathe. I wanted to cry like a fucking baby. Yesterday morning I saw our baby on the monitor, its heart beating steady and strong, and I'd vowed to be the best father I could be.

"You didn't do anything. I just... it was me. I fell off the bed."

"*You fell off the bed?*" Bile burned the back of my throat as my hand went to her stomach. "Are you okay? Is the baby okay?"

"I'm fine. Really. I'm okay," she assured me, placing her hand over mine.

How could she be okay? None of this was okay.

I piled up three pillows and propped her elbow on it. "Hold your arm up so your hand is above your heart. It'll help..." Help what? The swelling? The baby inside her? Her own sanity? How had it come to this? I never thought I'd see the day when I needed to protect Lila from me. "I'll get you some ice."

Thankfully, Lila's wrist wasn't sprained but she had to keep it wrapped for a few days. At night, I'd get into bed with her and wait until she fell asleep. Then I'd move to the floor or the sofa. Sometimes I'd just pace the living room or sit on our balcony until the cold seeped into my bones.

If I got a few hours of sleep at night, I was lucky. I couldn't even trust myself to sleep with her. I was trying to lay off the whiskey and the drugs she knew nothing about. Trying to be better for Lila. For our unborn baby. I'd been sober as a church mouse since the night I hurt her wrist and two weeks had gone by with no further incidents.

Until today.

I was a bomb about to detonate and I didn't fucking know how to control that or contain my anger.

"What the hell is going on?" my dad shouted. "Jude. Let him go."

I released my hold on Pete, the little shit who did concrete work for my dad, and gave him a shove. Then I turned and strode away, needing to put space between us.

"Get back here," my dad called after me. "You have a job to finish."

I turned to face him, not fully trusting myself not to plant my fist in Pete's stupid-ass face. "I need to go."

"It's two in the afternoon. You're not going anywhere until you tell me what the hell is going on with you."

"Why don't you ask Pete?"

"Dude." He held up his hands. "I was just making conversation. No need to go all mental on me."

My jaw clenched and I tried to breathe through my nose. "Just making conversation? Do you even know where Afghanistan is? Could you find it on a map?"

"Hey man, I don't get what the big deal is. You used to be a Marine, right? I mean, you're trained to kill. All I did was ask how many ragheads he killed," he told my dad. "And he slammed me against the wall, the psycho."

My hands balled into fists. The douchebag was whining to my dad. I wanted to shove his head up his ass. We'd gone to high school together and I didn't really know him then, but I knew he hung out with Kyle Matthews which made a lot of sense.

"I wasn't trained to kill," I said through clenched teeth. "I was trained to protect stupid shits like you. And they're not ragheads. They're human beings. So watch what the fuck you say."

"Okay, okay. Show's over," my dad told the guys on the crew who had stopped working to watch the drama. "Pete. Get back to work and keep your opinions to yourself. We need to get this foundation laid. And you," my dad pointed at me then used two fingers to summon me like I was a dog who had been trained to do his bidding. "Come with me."

I stared at his back as he walked away, fully expecting me to follow him. Instead, I strode to my truck and climbed in. As I pulled away, I saw him in my rearview mirror shouting for me to come back.

Twenty minutes later, I pulled off the highway and parked in front of The Roadhouse.

The scent of stale beer and cigarettes greeted me as I walked through the door, my vision adjusting to the dim interior. Multi-colored Christmas lights flashed behind the bar and a country singer wailed from tinny speakers that crackled on each note. I pulled up a stool at the bar, my arrival raising the total number of customers to four, and stared at my reflection in the Budweiser mirror behind the bar.

"Well, would you look at what the cat dragged in. You're not looking so good, baby." Colleen Madigan flipped the cap off a bottle of Bud and set it in front of me on a cardboard coaster. Reaching for the top shelf, she grabbed a bottle of whiskey and two shot glasses that she set on the bar and filled to the brim. She raised her glass in a toast. "Here's to my boy. May he rest in peace. And here's to you. Reese loved you something fierce. He couldn't have asked for a better friend."

We downed the shots and set our glasses on the bar. The whiskey burned a trail down my throat. Like battery acid. That's what lies tasted like. She refilled my shot glass and I knew she would keep them coming until I was too drunk to walk out of here.

Reese looked so much like his mother. He'd inherited her auburn hair, blue eyes, and pale freckled skin. Whenever Lila used to send me care packages, she sent one to Reese too, and she always made sure to include sunscreen. Ever since that day at the swimming hole, it had become their little inside joke.

I wanted to tell Reese's mom what really happened that day. I wanted to tell her it was my fault Reese was dead. I wasn't the hero she thought I was. The official report was that I'd gotten shot in the head trying to save a fellow Marine. A fallen brother.

Reese once told me he'd follow me anywhere. We were just kids when he said that. And then, years later, he followed me to boot camp and he followed me to Infantry School and all the way to Afghanistan.

But I'd failed him.

Now Reese was dead, and I was alive.

I was a failure.

I didn't think I deserved to be alive.

CHAPTER TWENTY-SIX

Jude

"JUDE. WAKE UP."

I pulled the pillow over my head to block out the noise and the light. Fuck, my head was going to explode. She grabbed my shoulder and shook me. I swatted her hands away then tightened my grip on the pillow she was trying to rip away from me.

"Would you just fucking stop?" I snarled. I hadn't slept in three days. Maybe a week. At this point, who was counting?

"Jude. Something's wrong. You need to get out of bed."

"What's wrong? Your little flower arrangements aren't perfect?" I mumbled.

"You asshole." She shoved my shoulder and I heard her footsteps retreating then the door slammed shut and I closed my eyes again.

How many sleeping pills had I taken? Didn't matter. They were doing their job. They kept the nightmares at bay.

When I woke up, it was dark outside and I had no idea

what time it was or even what day it was. My stomach growled and I tried to remember the last time I'd eaten.

I pulled on a pair of sweats and a T-shirt and jammed my feet in my Nikes then walked down the hallway to the bathroom. The Christmas lights from our tree glowed blue in the living room. The apartment was quiet. Too quiet.

As I washed my hands at the sink, I stared at myself in the mirror. Who the fuck was this? It didn't even look like me. I shook the water off my hands and ran them through my hair. It was still short. Lila hated it but every time it started growing out, I gave myself a buzz cut. I didn't even know what compelled me to do it. On the flip side, I hadn't shaved in at least a week and this was more like a beard than stubble.

Shit, man, pull yourself together.

A sniff test told me I smelled bad. Just rolled out of a dumpster after sleeping in it for a week bad.

I needed a shower. I needed food. But first I needed to apologize to Lila and find out what she'd wanted.

I called her name but got no answer. The apartment was small, so it took less than two minutes to confirm that she wasn't here. I picked up my cell phone from the kitchen counter and scrolled through the texts I'd missed.

The words blurred on the screen. For a few seconds I just stood there in silence, staring at my phone with my heart hammering in my ears, before a scream ripped from my throat.

"Fuuuck!"

I punched the wall next to the refrigerator. Once. Twice. Three times for good measure. Blood dripped down my arm and I barely felt the sting from my busted knuckles.

Gripping the counter, I hung my head and tried to breathe.

No. No, no, no, fucking no.

Pushing off the counter, I spun around and kicked the recycling bin, sending empty bottles and cans flying across the kitchen floor, the glass shattering on the tiles. "You worthless piece of shit."

Grabbing my keys from the counter, I locked the door behind me and jogged down the stairs.

It wasn't too late, I told myself. I could still be there for her. I could hold her hand. Help her through this. Be the man she needed.

I jumped into my truck, threw it into reverse and hit the gas. A horn blared and I slammed on the brakes, my tires screeching as I came to a full stop and checked my rearview. *Goddammit.*

I squeezed my eyes shut and took a few deep breaths before I pulled back into my spot and climbed out of my truck.

"What the hell do you think you're doing?" Brody shouted from his open window. "You almost ran her over, you stupid shit."

My gaze swung to Lila standing next to the open passenger door of Brody's truck. And God help me, she had that same look on her face as she did the morning she found out her mother had died.

In a few long strides, I was standing right in front of her. "I'm sorry, baby." I tried to pull her into my arms but she pushed me away and took a step back, putting distance between us. "I'm so sorry. I didn't know..." My voice cracked on the words. "I didn't know."

"It doesn't matter. It's over now."

It's over now.

"Thanks, Brody," she said, dismissing me. "Sorry about all that. I just..." She shook her head, at a loss for words.

"Don't apologize. Glad I could be there for you." He got out of his truck and rounded the hood, forming a circle of three. "Are you sure you're okay?" he asked her. "Do you want me to—"

"I'm okay. I don't need anything. You've done more than enough for one night."

She folded her arms over her chest and rubbed her upper arms. I wanted to wrap her up in mine and keep her warm. She was wearing my old baseball hoodie. I couldn't believe she'd kept it this long. Turning away from me, she reached into Brody's truck and came out with a towel. It was one of ours. Forest green. My mom had given them to us. "Thank you for everything," she told Brody, mustering a smile for him.

"If you need anything, call me."

I bristled at his words but I was in no position to tell him that she didn't need him, she needed me. Tonight he'd been there for her when I hadn't. And I fucking hated myself for that.

She started walking away and I followed, wracking my brain to come up with something I could do that would make her feel better. "Are you hungry? I could—"

"I just need some time alone, Jude."

"Yeah. Okay." I nodded because what else could I do? She obviously needed time to process what had just happened and had figured out that I was the last person who could help her do that.

I'd failed her.

I stood on the sidewalk and I watched her walk away from me. I was still watching as the front door of the building closed behind her. Our apartment was on the second floor, and I looked up at the blue Christmas tree lights shining through the sliding glass door. I waited for a light to come on inside but it never did.

"You fucked up," Brody said, coming to stand next to me as I kept my silent vigil outside the apartment I shared with my fiancée. My fiancée who had been ten weeks pregnant. I'd gone to the doctor's appointment with her two weeks ago. We'd listened to the heartbeat. I'd seen our baby on the monitor and I'd vowed to be the best father I could be.

Lies. Broken promises.

Who had I become? A man who wasn't to be trusted. A man who broke his promises and couldn't be counted on.

"You're so fucked-up right now, I don't even know what to say."

I laughed bitterly. "You think I need you to tell me I'm fucked up? You think I need you to point out the obvious?"

"I don't know what you need but you can't keep doing this to yourself and everyone around you. Whatever is going on with you, this shit is eating away at you. You've gotta find a way to deal with it."

That was rich coming from him. "The same way you dealt with your shit? Suddenly you're Dr. Fucking Phil?"

He just shook his head, disgusted with me. "If you need me, you know where to find me."

I didn't need him. I needed Lila. And I needed to find the guy I used to be and get him to talk some sense into this asshole masquerading as Jude McCallister.

Climbing up the stairs to the second floor, my footsteps were as heavy as my heart. When I unlocked the door and pushed it open, the chain prevented me from opening it, therefore denying me access to the apartment and to Lila. Guess that told me everything I needed to know. I could climb onto the balcony and get to her that way, but that door was probably locked too. So I sat outside the apartment, my back leaning against the door and I waited.

I kept thinking about the Christmas presents I'd wrapped and put under the tree last week. I needed to get rid of them before she opened them.

Hours later, the door opened but the chain was still on. I was just grateful that she was willing to give me this much.

More than I deserved, that was for damn sure. I scooted over and leaned my shoulder against the wall next to the door so I could talk to her through the crack.

"Jude?"

"I'm here, baby."

"It hurt. It hurt so much."

I looked up at the ceiling and rubbed my hand over my chest. I wasn't sure if she was talking about the physical pain or the emotional. Both, I guess. "I'm sorry. I'm sorry I wasn't there for you. I'm sorry you had to go through that alone. I don't—" I cut myself off before I made a lame excuse. She didn't need my pathetic excuses. They wouldn't change anything. Words were empty without actions to back them up. "Tell me what I can do for you."

"I don't know." She hesitated a moment. "Just talk to me, I guess."

"You want me to stay out here?" I hoped like hell she'd at least let me come inside and sit next to her. Hold her. Do whatever I could to try and comfort her.

"For now. It just makes it easier to talk to you."

I winced. Then I asked the question I'd been thinking since I'd read the text. "Was it something I did? Did we lose the baby because of me?" I steeled myself for her answer. I deserved every bit of her wrath and anger and blame.

"It wasn't anything you did or anything I did. The doctor said it just happens sometimes." She was quiet for a few seconds. "I wanted that baby so much."

"I know." *Me too.*

"But I think... I think I wanted it for the wrong reasons."

"What do you mean?"

She took a deep breath. "In the back of my head I kept thinking that if we had a baby, you'd want to stay. Like, maybe the baby would have made you happy in a way that I can't."

My eyes drifted shut and that vise around my heart twisted and squeezed. It took me a few seconds to pull myself together enough to speak. "I want to stay. You make me happy. You do. None of this is your fault. None of it," I stated firmly, willing her to believe it. "It's all on me. I'm the fucked-up one. You're perfect."

She laughed but I could hear that she was crying. "I'm not perfect. I say and do all the wrong things. I try so hard to be supportive but it's so hard... it's just so fucking hard. And I don't blame you. It was the war that did this to you. It messed with your head and turned you into a different person and some days... most days..." She was crying harder now and I had to fight the urge to kick down the door and break the chain that was keeping us apart. But she'd already seen what a monster I could be and this wasn't the time to force my way inside.

"Most days I just really miss you. I miss you so much it hurts. And I thought that if we had this baby, it would be like having a piece of you. The better parts of both of us in one tiny human that we could hold in our arms and watch our baby grow bigger and stronger. And I feel so cheated and so angry. I hate the US Marine Corps with every fiber in my body. I hate it, Jude. I really hate it. And I don't know what to do or how to make this better."

We'd just lost our baby, and I was losing Lila. And I couldn't handle any of it.

I was sitting outside our apartment door, three days before Christmas, at a complete loss as to what to do or how to fix this. I always used to have an answer. I always used to find a solution. Make it better. But this time I didn't know how to do that. And there was nothing worse than feeling helpless. Feeling weak because you'd let down the person you loved more than anyone else on the entire planet.

I needed to pull myself together. *"Man up,"* my dad told me last week. *"Pull yourself up by the bootstraps and tough it out."*

I rose to my feet and pressed my palm against the door. "Open the door, baby. Let me in."

"I lied. When I said I don't blame you, I was lying. I hate you right now, Jude. I can't trust myself..."

I pressed my forehead against the door, feeling like I was seventeen again, begging her to let me in. "I don't care what you do to me. You can use me as your punching bag. You can do anything you want to me. Let me in."

After a moment of silence, I heard the chain sliding against metal and she flung the door open. Gone was the sad girl and in her place was a woman I barely recognized. Green eyes flashed with anger and before the door had even closed behind me, she struck. She hit my chest, my shoulders, everywhere she could.

"I hate you!" she screamed, beyond hysterical. "I fucking hate you."

I didn't put up a fight. I *wanted* her to hurt me. I wanted her to inflict pain on me. I wanted to take her pain away and make it mine. So I didn't even feel the sting of her slaps or the smack of her palms on my chest when she shoved me.

My back hit the door and her feet stumbled. Reaching for her, I pulled her into my arms and we clutched each other tightly, holding on for life. We were on a sinking boat and we were going down.

"Why is this happening to us?" she cried, choking on a sob. "What's happening to us, Jude?"

Drowning, I held her up, trying to keep her afloat even as I went under.

I couldn't do this.

Not this moment.

Not this life.

Sobs wracked her body and I tried to hold her broken pieces together. "It hurts," she said brokenly.

"I know, baby, I know." I lifted her into my arms and carried her to the bedroom, her tears soaking my T-shirt and bleeding into my skin. They flowed like a river through my veins. As I laid her on the bed, I remembered the dream I had. The green-eyed baby with dark hair on the blood-soaked dirt road in a country half a world away.

She fisted my shirt. "Don't leave me."

"I won't." I crawled onto the bed next to her and rolled onto my side, pulling her against me. She curled into a ball, her back against my chest and I stroked her hair as gently as I could. For a long time, we were silent in our dark bedroom but I could tell by her shuddered breaths that she wasn't asleep.

"Baby. I love you. Tell me what I can do to make this better. I'll do anything."

"Put the stars back in the sky, Jude. It's so dark and lonely without them."

What do you do when you're so broken you can't find a way to put all the pieces back together, let alone put the stars back in the sky? I didn't fucking know. But for Lila, I would try. For Lila, I would do anything.

And I tried. I tried so fucking hard to be the man she needed. The man she deserved. But like most things lately, the good didn't last very long.

CHAPTER TWENTY-SEVEN

Lila

THE APARTMENT WAS DARK, THE TV BLARING AS I stepped inside. I hung my jacket on the hook in the hallway and shook the rain out of my hair as I walked into the living room.

"Where have you been?" he asked without dragging his eyes away from the flat screen on the wall.

"I went to dinner with Sophie and Christy."

"You went to dinner with your friends. And you didn't think to consult me?"

"Consult you?" I turned on the table lamp next to the sofa. Jude flinched and held up his hand to ward off the brightness.

It didn't take a rocket scientist to figure out that this was one of his bad days. I had to keep reminding myself to have patience. It would take some time to adjust and I couldn't expect everything to be perfect. But he'd been home for nine months now and instead of getting better, everything was getting worse.

Red-rimmed eyes met mine. They were so vacant. So flat and empty.

The stubble on his jaw suggested that he hadn't shaved in a week but the hair on his head was buzzed close to his scalp. I hated it. I longed to run my fingers through his hair but he kept shaving it.

He was wearing the same T-shirt and sweatpants he'd worn for the past three days. "Did you even leave the house today?"

He downed the rest of his beer and tossed the can on the coffee table with the other empties before cracking open another one and leaning back against the cushion, the remote in his hand. A crack of lightning lit up the dim room and thunder rumbled but it didn't even faze me. I wasn't scared of storms anymore. Not the ones that raged outside, anyway.

"In case you haven't noticed, it's a fucking swamp out there. Kind of hard to do roofing in the middle of a thunderstorm. Health and safety hazard, according to my old man." Raucous laughter followed that statement, although I found nothing funny about it.

"Jude," I said softly.

"Stop pretending you give a shit what the fuck I do." He waved his hand in the air. "Just go do whatever you're going to do. Don't let me get in the way. Don't worry about consulting me about a damn thing."

I took a deep breath and prayed for patience, something I'd been having to do a lot of lately. "Last night I told you Christy and I were meeting Sophie for dinner. I invited you to join us." I grabbed a garbage bag from the kitchen drawer and returned to the living room, tossing empty beer cans and junk food wrappers into it. "You weren't listening. You were too busy playing video games. This afternoon, I called and texted you to let you know where I was going, but I got no answer."

He had a weird thing about cell phones now. He hardly ever used his and probably didn't even know where it was.

"That's a fucking lie. You never told me. You didn't ask if it was okay or if maybe I'd rather you spent the evening with me. Considering you're never home. I never see you. You're too busy making your little flower arrangements. You need to ask me before you do this shit, Lila."

"I need to ask you for permission now? You didn't consult me before you took off with your Marine buddies for three days and I had no idea where you were."

"We went to a fucking funeral," he shouted. "Not like I was off fucking strippers and snorting lines. It was a funeral, for fuck's sake."

"I know that, Jude. I know." I gritted my teeth and took calming breaths so I didn't say anything that would set him off. "It's just... I wanted to be there for you. If you'd told me, I would have gone with you."

"You didn't even know him."

"I talked to him on the phone. You told me all about him. I knew you were close. I would've been there for you."

"Did you have anyone over while I was gone? Did you pick up a guy at a bar? Did you fuck him in the bed you share with me?"

My mouth gaped open. "Oh my God. I've never cheated on you, asshole."

"Oh, I'm the asshole now. You're the one who was flirting with Tyler at The Roadhouse and I'm the asshole."

"I wasn't flirting. We were just talking. He's your friend."

"About what? What were you talking about that required so much concentration?"

You. We were talking about you. And we were talking about Reese. But if I told him that, it would only upset him. "I don't even remember. We were just talking."

"I'm sick of this fucking bullshit." He hurled the remote at the wall. "I'm sick of your lies."

"And I'm sick of you flying off the handle at every little thing."

"Every little thing, huh?"

"This isn't what you promised me. This is not the life you promised, Jude. Where's that dream house you were going to build, huh? We haven't even looked at any land. We haven't even looked at any houses to buy. We're living in this shitty apartment and—"

"Oh, wait. Hold up. I seem to remember you once told me you'd live in a double-wide or a mud hut if it meant you could be with me. Change of heart, baby? This ain't the paradise you bargained for?"

"If it meant I could be with you. Exactly. The Jude I fell in love with. The Jude I have loved for so long. Where is that guy? The guy who bought me chocolate and gave me his favorite hoodie. The guy who promised to put the stars back in the sky. I don't even know who you are anymore. Jude, you need to talk to someone. You need to talk to a professional. Please. You need help."

"I don't need a professional to tell me what I already know. I'm fucked in the head. There's no fixing that. And the fucking VA hospital is useless. I tried, baby." His voice cracked on the words, his head falling back against the sofa.

"I tried," he said. "I'm so fucking sick of getting the runaround. I'm at the bottom of the fucking list." He scrubbed his hand over his face, his eyes bleak.

"I know, baby, I know." My heart was breaking for him like it had so many times since he'd returned home. "Let me help you. I can get you an appointment with a therapist. We don't have to go through the VA. Please. Just let me do this for you."

He hung his head in his hands. "I'm sorry. I'm sorry for everything. You should dump my sorry ass, Lila."

"Stop saying things like that. I'm yours. Always. I'll always be yours, Jude. We just need to... we need to get through this together, okay? We need to work through this and find someone who can help you. You can't keep living like this. Do you still have the headaches? The ringing in the ears?"

He shrugged and I took that as a yes.

"Why don't you take a shower and I'll make you something to eat, okay?"

"Stop treating me like a five-year-old." But there was no bite in his words. Only weariness and a defeat in the slump of his shoulders that scared me. I lived in fear of the day I'd come home and not find him here. Two weeks ago a guy from his unit had taken his own life. What if Jude decided that it wasn't worth it? What if he gave up the fight? Then where would I be without him?

Never in a million years could I ever have predicted that I'd have these thoughts about Jude.

He rose to his feet and I wrapped my arms around him, holding on tight, afraid to let go.

I shouldn't have gone out tonight. I shouldn't have left him alone. I held him tighter, holding on for as long as he would let me. Sometimes he didn't like to be touched. Sometimes he tried to fuck me into oblivion. I never knew which Jude I was going to get on any given day.

When he pulled away, he forced a smile that didn't reach his eyes. They looked so vacant. Like there was nothing behind them. I knew he was depressed. I knew he was in pain. But I didn't know how to reach him or how to help him.

"I love you." I kept thinking that if I said it often enough, he would start to believe it again. That somehow my love for him could be enough to save him.

"I love you too."

That was the hardest part. I knew that he did love me. But once upon a time I could envision our future, and now I had no idea what that future would look like or if we even had one. We never talked about it anymore.

My life was falling apart at the seams, thread by thread, and I had no idea how to sew it back together.

CHAPTER TWENTY-EIGHT

Jude

How fucking blissful would it be to float away on a sea of pills and whiskey?

No more pain. No memories. No flashbacks. *Peace.*

I pulled over in a ditch and cut the engine. Climbed out of my truck, weaving on my feet.

The pills rattled in my pocket as I walked into the field, a bottle of whiskey dangling from my fingertips. Stumbling, my knees hit the ground. Shit, that was funny.

I was laughing so hard I doubled over.

Pulling myself together, I fished the amber bottles out of my pocket and shook the pills into the palm of my hand. Threw them back and washed them down with the rest of the whiskey in the bottle.

Then I lay on my back in the tall green grass and stared up at the sky. The night was dark and starless. As it should be.

From somewhere far away, I heard music, a beeping sound. My eyes drifted shut.

Lila.

Lila.

Lila.

Sorry, baby, I'm just so fucking tired. So fucking weary of this battle.

Forgive me.

CHAPTER TWENTY-NINE

Jude

"JUDE, YOU PROMISED YOU WOULDN'T LEAVE ME. You promised. Don't you dare leave me."

Lila?

"I love you. I love you so much. Always and forever, remember? Come back to me. Come back to me, Jude. I don't want to live without you."

———

"Goddammit, Jude. You've never been a quitter. Don't start now."

Dad?

———

I flinched at the bright light shining in my eyes and made out the vague shape of a man standing over me.

"Jude. I'm Dr. Leighton. Do you know where you are?"

Fuck.

I closed my eyes again.

CHAPTER THIRTY

Jude

"Did you want to die, Jude? Is that what you wanted?"

"No," I lied. "I don't even remember taking those pills and I have no idea how I ended up in that field."

"I'm sorry. I know I'm saying all the wrong things. I just... I love you. We'll get through this together, okay?"

I tried to smile. "Yeah. Okay." I squeezed her hand. "You and me, baby. Forever."

"Promise? I need you to promise me, Jude."

"Promise." I'd become such a skilled liar, I was almost starting to believe myself.

Empty promises and lies. I had nothing to offer her.

I knew I had to leave her. It was just a matter of time until I did something else to hurt her.

Six weeks later, I reached the point of no return.

CHAPTER THIRTY-ONE

Lila

I BURIED MY FACE IN HIS PILLOW, MY SALTY TEARS soaking the cotton. I cried for him and I cried for the baby we lost. I cried for the boy he used to be and the future that had been ripped away from us.

I cried an ocean and still, it wasn't enough.

I waited an entire week to read the letter he left me. I don't know why I waited so long. Maybe I was scared that reading his words would make it real. If I didn't read his goodbye note, I could pretend he'd just gone out to buy coffee and cinnamon donuts and any minute he'd waltz through the front door and call out, "I'm home, baby."

Now I sat on the sofa in our dingy beige apartment and I poured myself another glass of wine. After a fortifying sip, I took a deep breath and slid the letter out of the envelope. It was written on loose-leaf pages, the edges ragged from where he'd ripped it out of the spiral notebook.

When I unfolded the letter, a check fell into my lap. I

picked it up and studied it. I knew how much he had in his savings account. It was the exact same number written on the check. As if emptying his bank account would make up for him not being here. I ripped the check into tiny pieces and tossed them into the air, watching the confetti rain down on the leather sofa and the parquet floor.

I don't want your money, asshole. All I ever wanted was you.

I started reading the letter written in his bold print. He never wrote letters in cursive and over the years we'd exchanged a lot of letters. But this would be the last one I'd ever get from him, so I read it slowly, searching for the nuance in every single word he wrote.

Dear Lila,

There are only so many times a person can say they're sorry before the words become meaningless. But I'll say it again for the millionth time.

I'm sorry.

I can't do this anymore.

I can't keep hurting you and pretend it's okay. I can't turn a blind eye, knowing that the source of all our problems is me. I used to believe that I could make you happier than any other man ever could. I used to believe that I was worthy of your love. Or, at the very least, that I could strive to be. But I'm not that man anymore. And you deserve so much better.

I promised you that I would never leave you but I have to. If I stay, I'll only destroy you.

At first, you might not see it this way but in time you'll come to realize that I did the best thing I could for you. I'm leaving because I love you. I love you so fucking much that it's killing me to watch you suffer because of me. Every day I've watched you fade until all the light in your eyes was gone, and I knew it was because of me. I did that to you. I took the light out of your eyes when all I ever wanted to do was make you shine brighter.

Ever since the day we met, I've wanted to protect you and keep you safe. But what happens when the biggest threat to your safety is the man you live with? The man who claims to love you above all others? What kind of man have I become that I would subject you to so much pain and suffering? The kind of man you don't need in your life.

All I want is for you to be happy. And the only way I know how to do that is to set you free.

The stars are still in the sky, baby. Just open your eyes and look up. On the darkest nights, they shine the brightest. And one day soon you'll see that you never really needed me to put them back in the sky for you. You're strong and brave and fierce. You're a goddamn warrior, Rebel. The real hero in our story.

I'm sorry. For everything. But I know you're going to be okay. When the chips are down, you always come back fighting. I don't believe in much of anything anymore, but I still believe in you. I will always believe in you.

Love always,

Jude

PART 3

CHAPTER THIRTY-TWO

Lila

Six Years Later

"I found someone for you." Sophie's voice came from the Bluetooth speakers as I drove, sunglasses shielding my eyes from the glare of the spring sunshine. "He's hot. Divorced. No kids. And he—"

"Not interested."

She sighed impatiently. "What is wrong with you? You need to get back out there. Is it because of Brody?"

"Is what because of Brody?" I flicked on my signal and waited for a car to pass before I turned into the Sunrise Pre-School parking lot.

"The reason you're not dating."

"It has nothing to do with Brody." I was early, so I pulled into a spot at the far end of the lot under the shade of a leafy oak and cut the engine but I left Sophie on speaker.

"Good. Not for nothing but he hooks up with women left, right and center so if he's trying to stop you from meeting someone, I'd be pissed."

Her intentions were good but this wasn't the first time we'd had this conversation. Sophie was in charge of marketing and events at her family's vineyard, Sadler's Creek, and she sent a lot of business our way. Unfortunately, she'd also taken it upon herself to play matchmaker.

Thanks to Sophie, I'd had a lot of crappy dates over the years. I was officially done with dating.

I rolled down my window to get some fresh air and leaned my head against the headrest.

"Let's go out this weekend. We'll pick up a hot guy."

"You're engaged."

"Not for me. For you. You're young, you're hot, and there's no reason for you to be single."

"I like being single."

"Yeah, well, being single is great when you're getting steady sex. Which clearly you are not."

"I don't tell you every little detail of my life. For all you know, I'm getting sex on the regular."

She laughed like that was the funniest thing she'd ever heard. I rolled my eyes. "It wasn't that funny."

Her laughter faded. "You need to let him go," she said, the concern in her voice genuine.

I knew who she was talking about. Of course I did. The funny part was that Sophie didn't even know him. Not really. The guy she'd met was not the same one I'd fallen in love with.

"I have let him go. I've moved on." I had moved on but he was always there. In my heart. In my head. In all my best memories and some of my worst ones. *He* was the reason I was single. *He* was the reason I never got past a second or third date.

"Sure you have. When's the last time you got laid?"

I grabbed my phone and took it off speaker, holding it to my ear. In retrospect, talking to Sophie on speaker phone was never a good idea. "Have you been day drinking again?"

"I live on a vineyard. What do you expect?"

A low chuckle to my left had me turning my head. Brody ambled over to my car in ripped jeans, a gray T-shirt and mud-caked work boots. He crouched in front of my open window so we were eye level, his whiskey brown eyes filled with humor.

"Afternoon, sugar lips." He gave me that charming Brody McCallister grin that made all the girls weak in the knees. Too bad I was immune to my best friend's charms.

"Stop calling me that." I laughed, shaking my head at the stupid nickname. "Sophie. I have to go."

"Fine. But I'm setting you up on a date. No excuses. Bye," she sing-songed. I cut the call and tossed my phone in my handbag, already planning how to get out of the date.

"She's right. You need to get laid."

"You shouldn't be eavesdropping." I pushed open my car door and grabbed my purse from the passenger seat, smoothing my hand over the short skirt of my floral dress.

"You should know better than to put your friends on speak-erphone," he countered.

I couldn't argue with that. My friends didn't come with filters, so I should have known better.

He raked his hand through his longish dirty-blond hair and rolled out his shoulder as we walked across the parking lot that was filling up with cars for the afternoon pick-up.

"Is your shoulder still giving you problems?"

"Nope. Right as rain."

Sure it was. Brody would die before admitting that his shoulder hurt. Over the years, he'd broken so many bones and had gotten so many stitches, I'd lost count of all his injuries. He was a bareback bronc rider, and a two-time world champion.

He also bred and trained horses in addition to rescuing wild horses.

"What are you doing here anyway?" It was my day to pick up Noah but Brody was always messing with our schedule.

"I got some new horses. Thought Noah might like to come over and see them."

Before I could respond, Carrie Dunlop breezed past us with her nose in the air. "I hope you taught your son some manners."

"Our son has perfect manners," Brody said when we reached the entrance. "It's your boy that needs—"

I elbowed Brody in the ribs to stop the words. No need to provoke her. Last week, Noah had gotten in a fight with Carrie Dunlop's son. Noah could be a perfect angel with a smile so sweet you'd never guess he had a wild streak and a temper. But man, oh man, did he ever. Secretly, I was proud of Noah. Carrie's son was a bully and picked on girls. Noah was defending Hayley, the girl he claimed to love and planned to marry one day.

Who could fault him for that?

"What can you expect? Children mimic their parents' behavior." Carrie looked us up and down with that air of superiority that always made me stabby and made Brody say things he shouldn't.

"That explains why your son always looks constipated."

Oh, my God. Carrie gasped. With a final glare aimed in our direction, she power-walked away from us in her Lululemon workout clothes, her designer handbag clutched to her side.

By tomorrow, all the other mothers would hear about this. If they hadn't already overheard. We got a few furtive glances as we stepped into the foyer. I pulled Brody aside to let the other mothers pass.

"You need to stop saying stuff like that," I said. "We're not thirteen anymore."

He just shrugged. My words would go in one ear and out the other. There was no changing Brody and it was a waste of energy to try.

"Check it out." He tapped his index finger against a crayon drawing on the wall outside the classroom that said Noah, Age 4.

His teacher had written the words to identify us. Mommy. Daddy. Grandma. Grandpa. Uncle Jesse. Uncle Gideon. MY FAMILY. There were two squares with a triangle on top and each one said HOME.

One family member was missing but I didn't point that out. Noah had never met Jude. Why should he include him in a family picture?

I studied the artwork more closely. "Why are you so tall?" I asked, incensed. "I'm the same height as Noah."

"I'd say he's got a good handle on perspective."

I burst out laughing and smacked his arm. He rubbed it as if I'd injured him.

"No mystery where he gets that fighting gene from."

I rolled my eyes. "He got that from you."

He opened the door to Noah's classroom and we stepped inside. Noah was at his cubby, getting his backpack and chatting with Hayley whose cubby was next to his. She wearing a rainbow tutu with a black T-shirt and tube socks, her brown hair in two pigtails. Her mom said she liked to get herself dressed in the morning. So cute.

When Noah saw us, he barreled toward me and I crouched down, catching him in my open arms. He smelled like citrus shampoo and crayons. I held on a little too tightly and a little too long before he started squirming and pulled out of my hold.

He patted my cheek to soften the blow of pulling away. "I love you, Mommy."

Oh, my heart. I pushed a lock of dirty-blond hair off his forehead so I could see his face better. His hair was long and wavy, nearly reaching the collar of his Dallas Cowboys T-shirt. I was trying to figure out how long I could get away with not cutting it.

"Love you too, baby." I kissed the tip of his freckled nose and stood up.

"Daddy!" Noah's face lit up with a smile that was just for Brody. As much as he loved me, he was a daddy's boy through and through.

"There's my little man." Brody scooped him up into his arms and carried him out into the hallway while I said goodbye to his teacher then trailed behind them. "How was your day, buddy?"

"Good. Real good."

"No fights today?"

"Not today," he said darkly, his eyes following Chase who was being led away by his mother.

Brody chuckled and set Noah down then held the door open for us. "How would you like to come over and see the new Mustangs I just got?" Brody asked as we crossed the parking lot to his truck, Noah's hand firmly grasped in mine to ensure he didn't dart out in front of the cars pulling out of the lot. "Then we can go for those brisket tacos you love so much."

"Yes!" Noah's grin slipped and his brow furrowed. "Mommy loves those tacos. Can she come too?"

"Your mommy is always welcome. You coming with us, Lila?"

"Please," Noah pleaded, his hazel eyes so hopeful I couldn't possibly say no. Not to mention Brody had just railroaded any plans I might have had for me and Noah. Our co-parenting plan was flexible, to say the least.

"Sure. Why not."

Noah rewarded me with a smile before he looked up at Brody. "Daddy?"

"Yeah buddy?"

"How come you don't kiss Mommy?"

I groaned. Here we go again. This was Noah's latest obsession.

"I'm scared she might punch me in the face."

"You're not scared of anything," Noah scoffed. "You're ten feet tall and bulletproof."

I had to work hard to stop the eye roll. That was the myth Brody was raising his son on, and Noah believed every word of it. Why wouldn't he? His daddy was his hero.

"I'm only scared of one thing and that's Mommy."

Noah giggled and slapped his thigh like that was the funniest thing he'd ever heard. "You should try it." He side-eyed me. "She might not punch you."

"Maybe I will, buddy, maybe I will."

Brody opened the back door of his truck and tossed Noah's backpack in the footwell while we waited patiently for Noah to climb in. The truck was so high off the ground and he was so small, but he always insisted on doing everything for himself and got annoyed when we tried to help.

I'm not a baby, he'd scoff.

I swear his first words were, "I can do it." Which meant that everything took ten times longer to accomplish. I kept silent as Brody made sure Noah was strapped into his seat and didn't say a word until the door was closed and Noah couldn't hear me.

"Stop putting ideas in his head." I kept my voice low. Even

though the windows were closed, he heard a lot more than we gave him credit for.

"The ideas are all his."

"You need to set him straight. He wants us to be a family." I glanced at Noah who was busy on the iPad Brody kept back there for him. "We need to keep explaining to him that you and I are not going to be together. Not now. Not ever."

"First of all, we have a kid together. We will always have a kid together. So that does make us a family. Doesn't matter if you sleep in my bed every night or not. I'm always going to be in your life and in Noah's life. I'm not going anywhere, Lila. I'm here for you because you're the mother of my child and because you've been my best friend for twenty fucking years. Get it through your head." He tapped my temple with his index finger to drive his point home. "I'm here to stay."

I'm here to stay. I didn't miss the implication in those words. He was here. Jude wasn't.

"You need to move on, L."

I threw my hands in the air. "What is up with everyone today? I have moved on."

"You've moved on, huh?"

"Yes."

"When *was* the last time you got laid?"

Immediately on the defensive, I folded my arms over my chest. "There's more to life than getting laid. I've been busy. I have a business to run and a son to raise and... I'm busy."

"Holy shit." He staggered backward, his hand over his heart. I rolled my eyes at the dramatic display. "You haven't been with anyone since me, have you?"

"And look how that turned out." I saw the hurt on his face from my words before he covered it up and his eyes got hard.

"Might not have been the plan but I wouldn't trade this for anything in the world."

"I know," I said, immediately chastised. Noah was the best thing I'd ever done, and Brody was a good dad. He'd stepped up, and he was always there for his son. In my book, that counted for a lot.

"I didn't mean it like that."

"Yeah, you did. But lucky for you, it's impossible to offend me."

It wasn't true. Underneath the cavalier smile and bravado, Brody was sensitive. "Your ego is too big for that," I teased, trying to lighten the mood.

"That ain't the only thing about me that's big. I'm hung like a horse and I've got some big guns."

I laughed and swatted his rock-hard chest. "Stop."

"If you ever need to scratch that itch, I'm more than happy to volunteer my services."

That wasn't happening. It had been a one-time thing. Never to be repeated. Brody and I were friends and we co-parented but our relationship had never been romantic. No need to complicate things more than they already were.

As I was getting into my car, Brody's phone rang. When I heard that he was talking to Kate and the serious tone of his voice, I paused to listen.

"What happened?" His eyes flitted to me, his expression grim.

My first thought was that something had happened to Jude. *Please God, no, don't let it be him.*

CHAPTER THIRTY-THREE

Jude

"Sounds like it's time to go home, wayward son," Tommy said, tipping his chin at the bartender who set two more beers in front of us before he moved on to a group of guys who looked like they belonged at a college frat party.

"Sounds that way."

I'd just gotten off the phone with my mom and had promised that I would. My dad was strong as an ox and stayed physically fit so it had been a shock to hear that he'd not only had a heart attack but had needed a triple bypass. She assured me that the surgery had gone well but her worried tone suggested that she needed me there. She hadn't called me until he came out of surgery which ensured that she could deliver good news. Meanwhile, I'd been sitting in a bar with no clue that my old man was in surgery.

Not sure why that should bother me but it did. Had this happened years ago, I would have been my mom's first phone call.

I took a pull of my beer and tried not to think about what awaited me back in Cypress Springs, Texas.

Memories. A cruel mistress that I'd been courting for six long years.

My gaze drifted from the Route 66 signs on the paneled wall to a brunette in cowboy boots and cut-offs sitting at a tall table by the window. When she caught me watching her, she crossed her legs and gave me a big smile. Blue eyes met mine instead of green. Her face was oval, not heart-shaped. I averted my gaze before she got the wrong idea.

I was always looking for Lila. In every bar. On every street corner.

I used to see her everywhere. I even saw her in Nepal when me and Tommy went over to Kathmandu to help with the disaster relief efforts after an earthquake. I chased the girl down the street and tapped her on the shoulder. Of course, it wasn't Lila. I'd left her in our bed in Texas two years before that.

"You're thinking about her again," Tommy said. A statement, not a question. "Ready to see her?"

"Doesn't sound like I have much choice. I'm bound to run into her." Run into her. What a fucking joke. She was as much a part of the family as I was. More so at this point.

Tommy knew all about Lila. The guys in my unit used to give me shit for talking about her so much but I never cared.

Tommy and I were together during my third deployment to Afghanistan, his second. We were the lucky ones. I'd cheated death so many times I'd lost count.

And here we were. Alive. In a bar in Phoenix, drinking beers to the tune of "Beast of Burden" blasting from the juke-box, voices escalated to be heard over the music and the ruckus of the frat boys slamming tequila shots and talking shit.

Now it was time to go back and deal with my past. I didn't

fool myself into thinking that my future was still waiting for me there. I knew it wasn't.

One day at a time. That was how I lived my life now.

Breathe in. Breathe out. And most days, that was enough.

"How long do you think you'll stay?" Tommy asked, running his hand over his sandy blond hair. He still wore it in a buzzed cut, claiming it was easier.

Even if he didn't have the eagle, globe and anchor tattooed on his bicep, you would still know he was a Marine. Tommy looked like one of those GI Joe action figures.

"My mom asked me to run my dad's construction business." She'd been hinting at wanting me to take over the business for years now. I'd been dodging it.

I didn't want to get stuck in my hometown. Not now that everything had gone to shit. What kind of fresh hell would that be?

"Maybe it's time you think about that."

"Trying to get rid of me?"

"You've been hitting it hard for years. Time to take a break. Stop and change your socks."

"My boots are dry." I took another swig of beer.

"You know what I'm saying."

"Haven't seen you taking a break."

"I live for natural disasters and chaos. While others run from it..."

"We run straight into the middle of it," I finished.

Which was why we'd set up a veteran-led disaster response organization. We worked with thousands of volunteers committed to the same goals as us. I'd always wanted to serve my country and I was continuing to do so.

Our motto at Team Phoenix was that we were there for people on their worst day. Ironic that I was there for people who were strangers to me yet I'd failed my own family and I'd failed Lila. All I'd ever wanted was to be the hero in her story. Instead, I'd become the villain.

It took me two days to organize my life in Phoenix. If you could call it a life. I hadn't accumulated much in the way of material possessions. Everything I owned fit in two duffel bags that I threw into the back of my truck.

I left Phoenix at seven in the evening and drove straight through. One thousand miles. Fourteen hours. When I arrived at the hospital, I changed into a clean white T-shirt, tossed the coffee-stained one into my duffel, and texted my mom from the parking lot.

———

The elevator opened and I stepped out of it and right into my mother's open arms. She was a world class hugger and she held on tight, not letting me go until she was good and ready. Her lavender scent was warm and comforting, a reminder that as much as life changed, some things remained the same.

When she finally released me, she held me at arm's length, her bright blue eyes studying my face before she gifted me with a brilliant smile. Other than a few more lines around her eyes and deeper laugh lines etched around her mouth, she looked the same. Her honey brown hair was cut in a chin-length bob, her skin suntanned from working in the garden.

She patted my cheek. "Aren't you a sight for sore eyes."

"I look that good, huh?"

"You look wonderful. I'm so happy you're here. I'll finally have all my kids under one roof again." At least someone was excited by that prospect. "It's been too long since we sat down to a family dinner."

Her words weren't meant to make me feel guilty, but I still felt it.

"You just missed Jesse. He went to the airport to pick up Gideon."

I saw Jesse a few months ago when he was in Peoria for a motocross race but I hadn't seen Gideon in a few years. Our lives were so drastically different that I couldn't relate. Gideon had a closetful of suits that cost more than everything I owned. According to Jesse, he lived in a 'sick' apartment in Manhattan and summered in the Hamptons.

"Now that you're here, you might be able to get some answers." My mom linked her arm in mine as we walked down the corridor to my father's room. He'd been moved out of the ICU and into a private room. On the way there, she greeted one of the nurses by name and gave an orderly a bright smile.

"I didn't come here looking for answers. I'm here to visit Dad and to help out in any way I can."

"I know." She patted my arm. "But since you haven't even let me so much as mention their names, there's a lot you don't know."

I huffed out a laugh. "I know everything I need to know."

My mom sighed. "Still so stubborn."

No comment. I wasn't about to debate the rights and wrongs of this fucked-up situation. Not when we were standing outside my father's hospital room.

"He'll be so happy to see you. They've taken him off the ventilator. He's grouchy, complaining about being stuck in a hospital, but the doctor says he's doing great." She smiled, her relief evident. "I'm going to get coffee. Give you two some time alone." She patted my arm again before she walked away, her stride brisk, her trim figure disappearing around the next corner.

Pushing down on the metal door handle, I entered my dad's room. His eyes opened and he looked over at the doorway as I moved closer to his bed.

My dad and I weren't huggers. The most we'd ever done was the one-armed hug with a back thump. Not sure that was a good idea today. Not when he had an IV in his arm and had just had his chest cut open.

"Hey old man. You'll do anything for a bit of attention."

He huffed out a laugh that made him wince and I immediately regretted my joke.

I grabbed a chair and moved it to the other side of his bed, taking a seat so I was facing the door. Still couldn't turn my back to it.

"Who you calling an old man?" His voice was hoarse and scratchy like it hurt him to talk. "I can still whoop your ass."

"Don't doubt that for a minute."

"So this is what it takes to get you home. I have to be knockin' on death's door."

"You're not even close to death's door," I scoffed. "You look like you're ready to dance a jig."

His lips tugged into a smile. My dad had a few more grays peppered through his dark hair and he was paler than normal but he still had a powerful build and he hadn't changed much since the last time I saw him a year ago. But I couldn't remember my father ever having so much as a cold or taking a sick day, so seeing him in a hospital gown, at the mercy of others to look after him, was disconcerting.

"How are you feeling?"

"Like I wanna get the hell out of here." He ripped out the oxygen from his nose, the stubborn bastard.

"Yeah. Hospitals are no fun." My eyes darted to the machine monitoring his heart, the blips and beeps reassuring me that it was still beating strong and steady. "You'll be out of here soon."

"They're threatening to keep me in here for two weeks."

"Just think of it as a vacation. Sit back and let them take care of you."

He snorted. Good luck to the hospital staff if they planned to keep him in a room for two weeks. My dad would be climbing the walls. "Good to have you home, son."

"Good to be here," I lied.

"I'm hoping you'll stay."

Those words filled me with dread. "I'm here now. Don't get greedy."

That made him laugh again and then he coughed. Shit.

"No laughing. Doctor's orders." I poured a cup of water from the pitcher on his bedside table and guided the straw to his mouth. He took a few sips then leaned back against the pillow, exhausted from the effort of taking a few sips of water. I set the cup back on the table.

"I feel like a goddamn toddler."

"You'll be fighting fit in no time."

He nodded and we sat in comfortable silence but I could tell he had a lot on his mind. "Proud of you. Proud of the work you've been doing." He cleared his throat. Paying compliments didn't come easy for him. "You've done good."

Not sure I had. I'd spent years being anything but good. "Yeah well, when you hit rock bottom there's nowhere to go but up."

"I think we both know that's not true."

He was right. In the past six years, two guys from my unit had taken their own lives. I'd come so close to becoming another statistic.

I'd been diagnosed with PTSD. It wasn't something that simply vanished. I still had triggers. I still had bad dreams that woke me in a cold sweat and made me feel like I was dying. I still had flashbacks.

I was told they might never go away. But they weren't as

frequent. In the past few years, I'd had a lot of counseling so I'd learned how to manage it better.

Every morning I woke up, and I got on with my day. Every day I made a conscious effort to be mentally healthy. That in itself was a major win.

"Do you have any regrets? About enlisting in the Marines?" he clarified. My dad and I didn't usually get into these types of conversations. We didn't talk about deep shit or philosophize about life but now he was broaching a subject we'd never discussed. "I always wondered if you did it because I talked it up so much. If you enlisted because of me."

"No. It was my choice. No regrets." Not sure if he believed me but he didn't need to be saddled with guilt for a decision I'd made.

Truth was I'd been a good Marine, and while I was in the Corps, I'd loved it. Coming home was the challenge, and it sucked that the place I'd always loved had become a battlefield. Instead of leaving the war behind, I'd brought hell to my own front door.

"It was a different time when I was a Marine," he said. "I never got sent to a combat zone. If you did it because of me, I'm sorry about that."

It dawned on me why he was talking like this. There was nothing like facing your own mortality to make you question your life choices. To study and analyze your decisions, mistakes, the wrong turns and detours that had led you to whatever place in the road you were currently at.

"I have plenty of regrets, but becoming a Marine is not one of them," I stated firmly, needing him to believe that.

He nodded, accepting my statement as truth.

A few more seconds of silence ticked by until I finally said the words I should have said a long time ago. "I'm sorry I've been gone for so long."

I didn't just mean physically gone, I had been *gone*.

"You were never a runner. Quite the opposite. If you felt you had to leave, I guess you had your reasons." I was tempted to ask my old man if he was getting soft in his old age but I sensed he had more to say. "But be prepared," he said. "Your mother won't let you get away so easily this time. She wants you to take over the business. Keeps saying it's time we took that vacation to Hawaii that I've been promising for the last decade." He paused, studying my face to see what effect his words had on me.

I schooled my features to hide my reaction. "You should take her on a vacation. You both deserve it."

"The business was always meant to be yours. It's time you step up and take over."

I was afraid this was going to happen. It wasn't only my mother who wanted me to take over the business. He wanted it too.

"You're ready to retire?"

"I'd still have a hand in the business but I don't need to be there as much as I have been over the years. It'd be good to spend some time in the garden. Maybe take up golf."

I snorted. I couldn't see my dad golfing.

"Give it some thought. No need to make any decisions right now."

The door opened, saving me from having to comment further. An enormous canary yellow bouquet entered the room. A bouquet of flowers attached to a pair of slender legs with sculpted calves from years of running. I'd be able to pick out those legs in a lineup. I knew every curve of her body. Every dip and swell. Every freckle. Every inch of silky soft skin.

Or, at least, I used to. I used to know everything about Lila Turner. Her hopes and dreams and fears. Her strengths and weaknesses. I used to be able to read her face like a well-loved book that I'd committed to memory.

She set the flowers on a table and we stared at each other across my father's hospital bed. If anything, she was more beautiful now than she'd been the last time I saw her. Dark, glossy hair fell in waves around her bare shoulders. Full, pink lips I'd kissed a thousand times.

Mine. Except that she wasn't. Not anymore.

Unlike the old days, the times I'd come home on leave, catching her by surprise twice, she didn't fly across the room and throw herself into my arms. Of course she didn't. Why would she? We were strangers now.

"Hey Lila." I leaned back in my chair, adopting a relaxed posture that belied my inner turmoil. As if this was just an ordinary day and it hadn't been six years since we'd last spoken.

"Hey Jude." She licked her lips and lifted a trembling hand to adjust her top. It was one of those off-shoulder numbers—dark blue with daisies. Her skirt was denim, and I studied the brass buttons down the front, trying to work out if they were snaps. Irrelevant. I wouldn't be ripping the skirt off her so it didn't matter if they were snaps or buttons.

I dragged my gaze away from Lila and focused on my dad, who'd been watching us with an amused look on his face. Not sure there was anything to be amused about.

"Well, I um... I need to go," Lila said, backing away toward the door.

"Don't leave on my account."

"I just wanted to drop off the flowers." She smiled at my dad. "I tried to choose the manliest ones."

My dad returned the smile, his fondness for her apparent in the gruffness of his response. "You did good, darlin'."

"I, um..." She glanced at me. Her chest rose on a deep

breath. Inhale. Exhale. "I have to get to work. I'll stop by tomorrow, Patrick. Good seeing you again, Jude."

Good seeing you again, Jude.

Her tone so formal, so polite, like we were merely acquaintances.

She left in a rush, practically tripping over herself to get out the door. When it closed behind her, I continued staring at it.

"Go," my dad said, giving me his blessing to chase after the girl I'd been chasing since I was nine years old.

I stayed seated. We weren't kids anymore.

But now that I'd seen her, one thing was certain. Those old feelings had never died. For all my fuck-ups, for all the shit I had done to her and the hell I had put her through, I had never once stopped loving her.

Question was, when had *she* stopped loving *me?*

When I came home a different man, that's when. I'd seen it in her eyes and on her face. She'd never had a good poker face. Her eyes didn't lie. I'd taken the light out of them. I had failed her in every way imaginable.

I had broken her heart and in true Lila fashion, she had come back swinging.

Fucking ripped the beating organ out of my chest and stomped all over it. She'd always been a fighter. It was one of the many things I'd loved most about her.

But never in a million years would I have thought she and Brody would betray me the way they had.

CHAPTER THIRTY-FOUR

Lila

SHELL-SHOCKED. THAT WAS HOW I FELT AFTER SEEING Jude. Nobody had even bothered to warn me that he was coming home. Maybe they weren't certain he would actually show up.

I drove past fields of wildflowers and bluebonnets, barely noticing the scenery. Spring was my favorite time of year in the Hill Country. Warm and sunny without the blistering heat of summer. The breeze whipped my hair around and I pushed my sunglasses on top of my head to keep it out of my face.

I still couldn't believe he was home.

He'd looked so good. Like he'd been lounging on a beach for the past six years. Which I highly doubted. But he wasn't the same broken man who had left me. His blue eyes were clear. They hadn't looked vacant or haunted. He wasn't drunk or high. His shoulders were broader, his body leaner, his hair longer like it used to be before he enlisted. That messy, tousled style that made me ache to run my fingers through it.

A car pulled out in front of me, and I slammed on the brakes. My car skidded to a halt, my sweaty hands white-knuckling the steering wheel. My heart was in my throat. I'd narrowly missed the car in front of me and they were none the wiser. I took a few deep breaths then pressed my foot on the accelerator, both hands on the wheel, more alert now as I drove.

God. I hadn't even been paying attention. That was what seeing Jude did to me. Made me reckless and shaken. After I'd walked out of Patrick's hospital room, it had taken me at least ten minutes to rein in my galloping heart and stop my hands from shaking.

This was ridiculous. How could he still hold so much power over me?

And there he'd been, sitting in his chair like a king on his throne, not even bothering to stand up and greet me. Not a hug. Nothing. So cold like he couldn't care less about seeing me. He'd looked almost bored.

I tugged a hand through my hair, a frustrated growl escaping my lips.

He didn't get to come back here and mess with my head. Not after the way he left me. I'd worked so hard to build a new life for myself, one that didn't include him. My life was good. I had my own business. I had my own house. Not my dream house, but my riverside cottage was an oasis. A fresh start. And most importantly, I had Noah. *He* was my one true love. My number one priority.

As much as I would love to continue driving aimlessly, I didn't have that luxury. It was wedding season and we were crazy busy, so I turned my car around and headed in the direction of Wild at Heart. My happy place.

As I walked through the open French doors of the floral design studio, I inhaled a deep breath of peonies and eucalyptus and exhaled all the bad stuff. Christy was a yoga nut and claimed it was the secret to a balanced life. But she didn't have an ex who haunted her dreams and messed with her head. She had a boyfriend who worshipped the ground she walked on.

"Hey," she said, stepping out of the walk-in cooler. Today she wore her dark hair in two buns, Princess Leia style and a khaki shorts jumpsuit that would make me look like a Cub Scout. But she managed to pull it off. Christy Rivera could make a burlap sack look chic. "How's Patrick?"

"He's, um... yeah, he's fine. Patrick is fine." God, I was the worst. I'd barely spoken to him. But it wasn't my first hospital visit. I went to see him in the ICU yesterday. Today he'd looked a million times better.

I stowed my purse in the cupboard under the wood counter and grabbed my work order for the Conrad wedding. The color palette was blush, cream and shades of green. The wedding was at an Antebellum-style plantation. The typed words blurred on the page.

Concentrate, Lila.

"Austin Wholesale just delivered our order. I did an inventory. It's all here. The mother of the bride for the Conrad wedding dropped off..."

Christy was still talking. I tried to focus on her words but I couldn't. How long was Jude back for? Was he planning to stay? Did he have a girlfriend? A wife? Oh my God. What if he was married? Surely, I would have heard about it. Right? But I couldn't be sure. Nobody in his family talked to me about him. They never even mentioned his name in my presence.

"Lila!"

My head snapped up and my gaze met Christy's. "What?"

Her annoyance morphed into concern, her dark brows pulled together in a V. "Are you okay?"

"Um, yeah..." I shook my head, disputing my own words. "No. I don't know." My shoulders slumped. I rubbed my forehead, trying to ease the tension. "Jude's back. I just saw him at the hospital."

Her jaw went slack. "Holy shit." She planted her hands on her hips. "Why didn't you lead with that instead of letting me ramble?" All I could do was shrug. "Did you talk to him?"

"Not really. We were in his dad's hospital room. It was just so hard to see him. I mean, we used to know each other so well and now we're practically strangers."

"Yeah, well, a lot has happened." She pursed her lips and I saw the judgment there. "It's been a long time."

"I know. It's just..." I shook my head again. What had I expected? That he'd pull me into his arms and beg for my forgiveness? That he'd tell me how much he missed me? "He looks great. He looks like Jude again." I didn't know if that made sense but to Christy it would. She'd witnessed the drastic changes in Jude's personality too.

"Just be careful," she cautioned. "Remember what he did to you."

"What about what I did to him?"

She waved that away with her hand like it was a pesky mosquito. "He was gone."

That was no excuse but I didn't have time to dwell on it. I needed to put it out of my head and focus on these wedding flowers. I checked the sheet again and this time the words made sense. Fourteen centerpieces. Vintage milk glass vases to be delivered by the mother of the bride. One bridal bouquet. Five bridesmaids and groomsmen. One floral arch for the ceremony.

I took another deep breath and let it out. Everything was going to be fine. Just fine. "I need to get to work."

"Okay," she said slowly, never taking her eyes off my face.

"I have to deliver and set up for that silver anniversary party. After that, I have a consultation at Sadler's Creek. Will you be okay until I get back?"

"Go. I'm fine." She gave me a skeptical look. "Really. Now that the initial shock has worn off, I'm good." I flashed her a smile just to prove it. She didn't look convinced but there were flowers to be delivered and a business to run. That had to take precedence over my fucked-up love life. Or lack thereof, as the case might be.

We loaded the refrigerated delivery truck then I waved her off and gathered the blooms I'd need, carrying the buckets of flowers and foliage to one of the two zinc-topped islands where we made our arrangements.

I got to work, prepping the stems, removing the thorns and the leaves at the bottom. For the next few hours, I got lost in a sea of peonies, ranunculus, and garden roses. The velvety frosted sage green leaves of the dusty miller and the silver dollar eucalyptus complemented the blush pink, coral, and cream petals. While I worked, I checked out my creations from all angles in the full-length mirror across from me.

Like all weddings, this one would be beautiful.

When I finished the centerpieces and bouquets, I moved them from the workspace to the walk-in where they'd stay hydrated and fresh until tomorrow morning when I delivered them.

"Are you happy, Lila?"

At the sound of his voice, I spun around, my hand over my heart. "Oh God, you scared me."

How long had he been there watching me?

He was standing in the doorway in a white T-shirt and faded denim, looking like my every fantasy. Handsome didn't even begin to describe Jude McCallister. As a teen and in his early twenties, he'd been a hot guy. But now, he was all man. Rugged and masculine and just so beautiful, I couldn't tear my eyes away. After Jude left, I'd imagined this moment so many times. How would it feel if he ever came back? Until one day I told myself to get used to the idea that he was never coming back.

"Are you happy?" he repeated, prowling toward me like a hunter stalking its prey. Graceful, powerful, unhurried. Yet his long legs ate up the distance between us in no time at all. Now he was standing right in front of me and I wasn't ready to be this close to him.

Are you happy? Under the circumstances, it was a strange question.

"That's what you want to know? If I say yes, will it ease your conscience?" I moved away from him and wiped down the workspace to keep my hands busy and my focus on anything but him. It was hard to do though. Whenever he was in my vicinity, he was *all* I could see.

"How's *your* conscience?" he asked, the accusation in his voice loud and clear. "Troubling you?"

Guess we were doing this, after all. Never one to back down, I lifted my chin and met his eyes. They narrowed on me. The anger swirling in the blue depths fueled my own. "You did the one thing you promised me you never would. You left me."

The muscle in his jaw ticked. Tiny. Imperceptible. But I saw it. "So you thought you'd get back at me by fucking my cousin?"

He said that as if it was an act of revenge. "You weren't here. You didn't want me anymore. You tossed me aside like I meant nothing to you."

He stared at me, unblinking, like he couldn't believe what I'd just said. His jaw clenched and I could tell he was working hard to keep his emotions reined in. "That's not fair and you damn well know it."

I knew it wasn't fair, and it wasn't what I'd planned on saying but the way he'd left me wasn't fair either. "Life isn't fair, Jude."

"I thought I knew you. I thought I knew your hard limits. And I thought that fucking my cousin was one of them. Brody's slept with every skank in a skirt. Did he give you an STD to go with that baby he put inside you?"

Every skank in a skirt. Well, thanks for that, Jude. "You know nothing about what happened between me and Brody."

"I know enough. He got you knocked up. And why do you think that is, Lila? How is it that he slept with so many girls yet he'd never gotten a single one of them pregnant? Until you. You ever stop and think on that? Maybe he did it on purpose."

I laughed. It wasn't even remotely funny but what else could I do? He was so far off base in his assumptions that it was laughable. "You're ridiculous. It was an accident."

"Keep telling yourself that, baby mama. How long did you wait after I left? Or wait... were you fucking him the whole time? Were you fucking him behind my back while I was in Afghanistan?"

"Don't be ridiculous. You know I never cheated on you."

"And I'm supposed to believe you. That's funny."

"I never lied to you." I looked him straight in the eye and took a deep breath, gathering all my courage. "You left me. With only a goodbye letter. I always thought you faced all your fears, turns out you run from them."

"Don't turn this around on me. You *fucked* my cousin. Maybe he was the one you wanted all along. Or maybe you just fucked every guy in town after I left."

"How dare you!" My blood was boiling. He still pushed my buttons. Besides, I'd rather get angry and argue than deal with the heartache and misery. Anger was so much easier. The cut was cleaner. Sharper.

"You were my girl, Lila. *Mine.* I never thought you'd betray me like that."

"I never thought you'd leave me but you did. And the day you walked out that door, you gave up the right to call me *your girl.* I'm not yours anymore, Jude."

"Is that right?" He advanced on me. I took a step back. We did this tango until my back hit the wall and there was nowhere left to run.

Jude placed his hands on either side of my head and leaned in. His minty breath danced over my lips. "Tell me, Lila. Should we pretend we meant nothing to each other? Pretend we didn't break each other's hearts?" His hands slid down the wall and stopped next to my hips. "Should we pretend we don't still want each other?"

I pressed my back against the wall, the violent beating of my heart so loud I could hear it pounding in my ears. "I don't," I whispered. "I'm over you."

"And I'm over you. I am so fucking over you, baby." His gaze lowered to my mouth. My lips parted, a small breath escaping. "I never think of you. You never cross my mind."

"I never think of you either." I inhaled, and it was his scent that filled my head. Cedar soap and masculinity and all those pheromones that played havoc with my senses. It's just a chemical reaction, I told myself. It means nothing. "You're nothing but a speck in my rearview mirror."

"I never think about the feel of your lips against mine. The sweet taste of you. The little sounds you made when I fucked you." His eyes were hooded and he wasn't even touching me but every word from his perfect lips sent delicious shivers up and down my spine. "I never dream of you. Never wonder if you're dreaming of me or if you've forgotten me. Do you still call out my name in your sleep?"

"Never." I'm sure I did, but there was nobody there to tell me about it.

"Liar." He dipped his head, his lips a mere fraction of an inch from mine.

Then he kissed me. Without hesitation, without asking permission, Jude kissed me.

His mouth was on mine, and I forgot to breathe. He shuddered and there was a sound from the back of his throat, a growl so deep and guttural I felt it reverberating in my core. Shivers of pleasure shot through me as he deepened the kiss. I wasn't thinking straight. I wasn't thinking at all. I pushed off the wall, erasing the tiny sliver of space between us and pressed my body flush against him, my fingers digging into his hair. It was soft and silky while everything else about him was hard, forged of steel.

His hands gripped my hips, and he lifted me up as if I were featherlight. My legs wrapped around his waist, and he spun us around, our lips remaining sealed. We were devouring one another, drowning in each other, and still it wasn't enough. I needed more.

It had been so long. Too long.

The kiss grew frenzied and wild and he set me down on the island, my legs still cinched around his waist, my skirt bunched around my hips. His tongue dragged down my neck while his hands slid down my sides. Then he ripped my skirt open and pushed aside my panties. Two fingers glided through my slick heat and I whimpered when his thumb circled the tight bundle of nerves.

"Tell me, Lila. Does Brody make you this wet? Does he make you lose your mind over a kiss?"

His words broke through and snapped me out of my lust-filled haze.

What was I doing? This man had broken my heart. Shattered it into a million pieces.

I shoved him away and hopped off the island, my shaky hands doing up the snaps of my skirt. My God. Within five minutes of being alone with him, I'd ended up half-naked and only seconds away from letting him fuck me on the worktable.

Where was my self-respect?

"Go. Away," I gritted out, adjusting my top and smoothing a hand over my crazy hair as I walked away from him on legs that were made of Jell-O. I still had to design the floral arch. I still had so much work to do today.

Get it together, Lila. Pretend he's not even there.

Turning my back to him, I gathered my supplies from the wood shelves under the windows. Pliers. Chicken wire. Zip ties. When I turned, he was right there in front of me.

"You know what's funny? I came back for you. I came back to see if there was a chance you could forgive me. I came back to see if you would give me a second chance. But I got a different answer instead."

"You didn't come back. I waited. I worried about you. Nobody heard from you, Jude. I woke up in the morning and you were gone. I found your phone smashed to pieces on the kitchen counter. I had no way to reach you. You just took off and didn't even care about any of the people you left behind." Tears threatened but I forced them back. I'd shed an ocean of tears for him. He didn't get to see me cry.

He grasped my chin and tilted my face up to his. "I came back to tell you that I couldn't live without you. I came back to beg for your forgiveness."

"What are you talking about? When was this?"

"Doesn't matter. You made your choices, same as I did."

With that, he released me and strode to the door. There he went again, waltzing away with my heart and leaving a trail of destruction in his wake.

You made your choices, same as I did.

We'd made all the wrong choices.

Goddamn you, Jude. Why did you have to come back here and churn up all these emotions again?

I hated him. I really did. I hated him so much.

If only that were true, life would be so much simpler.

CHAPTER THIRTY-FIVE

Jude

"THIS DINNER IS GOING TO BE AWKWARD AS FUCK," Gideon said, echoing my thoughts.

My mom sighed as she took the pies out of the oven. It didn't go unnoticed that they were peach, my favorite. Or that the Black Angus steaks were thick and marbled the way I liked them. Gideon had already called this dinner "The return of the prodigal son."

"Watch your language," she told him. "Get off that phone and make yourself useful." She pointed to the cabinet that held our dinner plates. "Set the table on the porch."

Reluctantly, Gideon pocketed his phone that was attached to his hand twenty-four seven and grabbed plates from the cupboard while I continued chopping cucumbers and peppers for the salad.

My mother, for whatever crazy reason, was excited about having her whole family together for Sunday dinner. And by family, she meant every last one of us, including Brody, Lila, and their son.

It had been two days since I'd seen Lila, and I had yet to see Brody. I'd be happy to keep it that way.

Jesse plucked a cherry tomato from the salad and leaned his hip against the kitchen counter, running his fingers through his light brown surfer dude hair. My baby brother was almost twenty-five but I still thought of him as a kid. He'd always been the most easygoing, laid back one in the family and time hadn't changed that. "How do you think it's gonna go down?" he asked me.

"I'm not going to say a fucking word." My gaze tracked my mom as she carried a pitcher of sweet tea to the porch. "I don't want to upset Mom."

Brody and I had unfinished business but a family dinner wasn't the time or place to get into it.

"So you don't think there'll be a fight?" Jesse asked, disappointed.

"Nobody is fighting," my mom said, the screen door closing behind her as she came back inside. "They're grown men, not kids anymore."

Gideon grabbed the utensils from the drawer and sized me up. "They're equally matched but my money's on Brody."

"What the hell?" Jesse said, scandalized. There was a good reason Jesse was my favorite. He was loyal to the core. More than I could say for Gideon or Brody. "Jude would win with his hands tied behind his back."

"There will be no fighting." My mom wagged her finger at me like I was eight years old again and had just tracked mud across her clean kitchen floor. "Do you hear me?"

"I'm not looking for a fight."

"You and Brody were always looking for a fight," Gideon said.

If memory served, it was always Brody looking for a fight. Not just with me. With anyone who so much as looked at him wrong. He'd gotten me involved in more fights than I cared to remember. I'd always had his back. He was family, and family came first. Too bad he'd forgotten that. As soon as I'd turned my back, he buried the knife in it.

Speak of the devil and in he walks. *Asshole*. He hadn't changed much. A couple inches shorter than me with a lean, muscular build and that cocky attitude that had always gotten him into trouble. Trouble I'd bailed him out of on more occasions than I could count. Obviously, he'd forgotten all about that too.

"Long time, no see," he said, that surly expression on his face that he used to reserve for teachers and authority figures.

"Was hoping it would stay that way."

At least we agreed on something.

"Brody. Play nice," my mom warned.

I laughed but there was no humor in it. "No reason to start now. Brody's always played dirty. Isn't that right?"

He crossed his arms over his chest and leaned against the kitchen counter, crossing his booted feet at the ankles. "Think what you want, cuz. You always did think you knew everything."

Son of a bitch. My hands curled into fists. It took all my self-restraint not to plant one of them in his face. He laughed like he knew what I was thinking.

If we made it through this dinner without bloodshed it would be a fucking miracle. How could my mother have thought this would be a good idea? Why had I even agreed to it?

"Brody. Carry this food out to the table." My mom's tone of voice brooked no room for argument. She shoved the salad bowl at Brody's chest. "Jude. That barbecue should be ready. Put the steaks on."

"Noah won't eat steak. Thanks to Jesse." Brody shot Jesse a look.

Noah. That was their son's name. Noah McCallister.

"Good thing he didn't ask where burgers come from. But hey, being a vegetarian is a lot healthier." Jesse patted his washboard abs. "Dad's gonna have to start eating heart healthy, you know," he told my mom. "He needs to start eating his vegetables."

My mom sighed. "You're right. I'll have to change our diet."

"Good luck with that," Gideon said, not lifting his head from his phone. He was flying back to New York tomorrow but it looked as if he'd never left the office. His black button-down was cuffed, a Rolex on his wrist, legs clad in dark denim, with expensive leather loafers on his feet.

Guess he'd gotten the life he wanted but did he look happy? With Gideon, it was hard to say for sure. He and my dad had never seen eye to eye and I sensed that he resented having to be here at all.

I took the tray of steaks and burgers off the counter and carried them out to the charcoal grill that I'd fired up earlier. The grill sat on the flagstone patio just off the porch, a temporary reprieve from Brody Fucking McCallister.

Tuning him out, I focused on the T-bones I was grilling. It was so strange being back here. Our house hadn't changed—a rambling stone farmhouse with a gabled roof that sat on three acres. I could almost envision Lila streaking across the back yard in a sunshine yellow sundress, her hair falling out of the braid her mom had put in it. Bare feet. Suntanned skin. Green eyes vivid.

My childhood memories weren't even my own. Every single good one included Lila.

"Who's that man?"

At the sound of the boy's voice, I turned from the grill and was met with a three and a half foot replica of Brody McCallister. Hazel eyes peered up at me with a mixture of curiosity and accusation. In his eyes, I was a stranger who didn't belong on his grandma's patio grilling steaks. For a moment, I was stunned into silence. I hadn't known Brody at this age, but I'd be willing to bet he looked exactly like this.

After a few awkward seconds of silence, Lila finally said, "That's your Uncle Jude."

Uncle Jude. Fuck me. Every single thing about that sounded so wrong, yet I couldn't deny it. I was the kid's uncle.

I looked down at a head of dirty-blond hair as small fists pummeled me. Like father, like son. I heard the asshole chuckling on the porch. Wasn't surprised he found this amusing.

"Noah. Stop that." Lila grabbed his shoulders and pulled him away from me. "What are you doing?"

"I don't like him." He crossed his arms over his chest and scowled at me. "He's a bad guy."

"No, he's not. He's one of the good guys." I couldn't help noticing that her voice faltered on the words. Even she wasn't so sure what to believe. It was warranted but it still hurt like a motherfucker. Once upon a time, she used to believe in me. Until I destroyed her faith in me.

The kid was right. I was a bad guy. I crouched so I was eye level with him. Not sure why I did it. Maybe it was a misguided attempt to gain his trust. To assure him that I meant him no harm.

"You look just like your daddy."

He tilted his head and studied my face, not sure if he should trust me or not. Kids were smart. I remember that from when I helped coach the youth football league in high school.

They had built-in bullshit detectors that helped them gauge a person's motives and sincerity.

"Why are you here?"

"I came to visit my family and to see your grandpa."

"And to say you're sorry?"

"Sorry for what?" I asked, curious to know what he thought I had to be sorry about. I knew I had plenty of shit to apologize for, but what did he know about any of that?

"For making my mommy cry. When she looks at your pictures, she cries and I don't like it."

My chest got tight and I rubbed it to ease the ache that his words caused. "I'm sorry I made your mommy cry. I never meant to. Your mommy is very, very special to me."

Without missing a beat, he asked, "Do you love her?"

"Noah." Lila tried to shush him and steer him away but he wasn't having it. He stood his ground and looked at me expectantly, waiting for an answer.

Kids. They just get right to the heart of the matter, don't they? "Yes. I've always loved her." It was true. No sense in lying. Lila had to know that I've always loved her. Unfortunately, love hadn't been enough to fix everything that was broken. *Me.* I'd been broken. "She was my best friend for a long, long time."

He nodded thoughtfully like that was something he understood. At the tender age of four, I wasn't sure how he could. "My best friend is Hayley. I got in a fight at school. And I'm not even sorry."

I chuckled at that one, my curiosity piqued. "What were you fighting about?"

"I punched Chase. He made Hayley cry."

"Good man. You did the right thing."

"Jude," Lila said, her voice stern but I could tell she was trying to suppress her laughter.

"He was just defending his lady love, right?"

Noah nodded. "Yep. She kissed me." He beamed. This kid was so damn cute I couldn't help but smile. Lila's son. This was Lila's son.

"Lucky you. It's good to find your one true love when you're young. Saves you from having to spend a lifetime searching for her."

He pondered that thought as I rose to my feet. My eyes met Lila's and for a moment it was just the two of us, the years falling away, those green eyes holding me captive.

"Jude," she said softly. And that was all she said but in that one word I heard everything we couldn't say.

All the years of regret, sadness, anger, and remorse came crashing down on me. I got that familiar tightness in my chest. I took a few deep breaths but it didn't help. She was still there. Still looking at me. Still making me wish that every single fucking thing could have turned out differently.

"You're burning the steaks," Brody said, his voice tight, his presence a reminder of everything I'd lost.

"Good thing it's yours then. You still take your steak incinerated, don't you?" I flipped the char-grilled steak and pressed the spatula against it. The fat sizzled and smoke filled the air. I ignored his muttered curses. Even though I preferred my steak rare, I'd eat the damn steak myself.

The dinner went about as well as anyone could expect, given the circumstances. My mom made small talk, trying to gloss over the tension. Not sure who had been in charge of the seating arrangement but I'd been placed directly across from Lila. Brody was on her left. Noah on her right. He was cute and innocent. Not his fault that his dad was an asshole.

"How long you planning to stay in town?" Brody asked me. The implication was clear. When are you leaving?

Noah was happily eating pie with two scoops of vanilla ice

cream, blissfully unaware of the tension between his father and uncle.

"For as long as my dad needs me."

"It will be a few months, at least," my mom said, sounding far chirpier than the situation demanded.

A few months. This should be fun. I needed to man up. I was here for my dad and for my mom.

With a smirk aimed at me, Brody slung an arm around Lila's shoulders like it belonged there. I gritted my teeth. I could feel my eye fucking twitching.

Lila shot him a look which he ignored. His arm stayed right where it was, wrapped around my ex-fiancée's shoulders. Even as he slid his ringing phone out of his pocket and answered the call, his arm didn't budge.

Unable to watch anymore of this, I stood up and started clearing the table, stacking plates and bowls, ignoring my mom's plea to sit down and relax. This was not my idea of relaxing. I was wound so tight I needed to punch something. Or someone.

I set the dishes in the sink and gripped the edge, my shoulders hunched, my chest rising and falling on each breath. In. Out. In. Out. My jaw was clenched so tight I was surprised my molars didn't crack.

"Are you okay?" she asked quietly, rubbing my back with the palm of her hand. Trying to soothe me, like I was a fucking baby. "Jude... are you okay?"

"Am I okay?" I laughed harshly. Was she out of her fucking mind? "Define okay."

"Could you just turn around and look at me? Please," she added, her voice tinged with worry. I hated that she felt the need to worry about me. It made me feel weak. Pathetic. The way I used to feel when I came back here seven years ago and she tried to do everything in her power to fix me. To heal me.

"Why? So I can see what I've lost? I don't need another reminder of that." Even I could hear the bitterness in my voice. I took another deep breath then granted her wish and turned around to face her.

"Brody just left. He had to check on one of his horses." That was the only reason she'd ventured into the kitchen. Brody was gone. Surprised he'd left her alone with me. Her eyes darted to the sink filled with dirty dishes. "You rinse and I'll stack?"

I scrubbed my hand over my face and laughed under my breath. Why the hell not. Let's just pretend that everything was fine. "Sure."

"He has so much energy." I followed her gaze out the window above the sink. Noah streaked across the back yard with Jesse chasing after him. "He's like one of those Energizer bunnies. Just keeps going and going." A nervous laugh escaped her lips. It was so unlike her to be nervous or act shy around me but suddenly we were like two people just getting to know each other, unsure where to even begin.

I handed her another plate to stack in the dishwasher. "He's a fast runner. Like you."

"And yet, I could never beat you."

"I would have let you win but the one time I tried that, you punched me in the face and accused me of treating you like a girl."

"I didn't punch you in the face." She laughed. "You're just making stuff up now."

"Might have been my shoulder. There was definitely a punch involved."

"Sorry," she said, not sounding the least bit sorry.

"No, you're not."

We both laughed and it eased some of the tension.

I rinsed and she stacked, neither of us talking until the job was done. When the dishwasher was filled, she leaned her hip against the door to close it. I turned from the sink, wiping my wet hands on my jeans, and took my first good look at her since she'd arrived.

"You look good, Rebel." She looked up at me from beneath her long lashes. The sun pouring through the window gave her skin a honey glow, highlighting the flecks of gold in her green eyes. Her throat bobbed on a swallow, and she licked her lips. I wanted to sink my teeth into her pillow-soft lips. Crush her body to mine and never let her fucking go.

How could I have ever walked away from the best thing in my life? Even after all these years, I still didn't have an answer. Except that I was so fucked in the head that I couldn't stay and subject her to more abuse. "Motherhood looks good on you."

Her eyes lowered to the terracotta tiled floor. "I never meant... I never meant for it to happen this way. I never meant to hurt you." She took a ragged breath and let it out as if admitting that had cost her a lot.

I never meant to hurt her either, and it killed me that I had, but it happened and there was no way to rewind time and undo the damage. "You never answered my question the other day. Are you happy?"

Unable to meet my eyes, her gaze drifted to the window. "What do you want me to tell you?"

"The truth. Is it that hard to answer my question?"

"You tell me," she challenged, her greens meeting my blues and it made me happy to see that I hadn't completely destroyed her. She was still full of fire and sass. Still so fierce and defiant. "Are you happy, Jude?"

Turnabout is fair play. I couldn't answer the question any more than she could.

"Run, Noah, run," Lila shouted.

He looked over his shoulder to see if I was gaining on him. That was his downfall. He stumbled and fell to his knees, the Nerf football still clutched to his chest. I pretended that I couldn't catch up. He was on his feet again, running and laughing. Should have known that Lila's boy would be tough. Whenever he fell down, he jumped to his feet and kept going without even shedding a tear.

"Touchdown," Jesse yelled, simulating the noise of a crowd. "Noah McCallister has scored again."

Noah spiked the ball the way I'd showed him and did a little victory dance. So damn cute. Then he flopped on the ground and panted like a dog. I loomed over him and he grinned up at me. Somewhere along the way, he'd forgotten that I was the bad guy.

"I beat you," he said.

"You sure did. You know what happens to winners?"

His eyes grew wide. "They get ice cream?"

I laughed.

"No more ice cream," Lila said. "It's time to go home for a bath and bedtime."

He kicked his feet and pounded his fists on the ground. "No!" When Lila tried to grab him, he jumped to his feet and darted away from her. "I'm not going to bed. I wanna play."

I scooped him up and tossed him over my shoulder, jogging across the field while he pounded his little fists against my back and screamed. I ignored his tantrum.

"Your old party trick," Lila said, referring to the way I was carrying her son.

"He weighs about as much as you did."

She laughed. When I reached the back porch, I spun around with my back to it. "Say goodbye to Grandma and Uncle Gideon."

The kid knew when he was beaten. I looked over my shoulder. He lifted his head and waved. "Bye Grandma. Bye Uncle Gideon."

"Goodbye, my sweet boy. I'll see you on Saturday."

Gideon looked up from his phone. "Bye buddy. Be good."

"Will you video me?" Noah asked.

"Don't I always? I miss you too much when I'm in New York."

"Yeah. It's lonely without me."

"Sure is."

Well, shit, what do you know? Gideon had a heart.

"Giddyup, horsey." Noah slapped my back as I jogged around the side of the house to the driveway.

"Stop hitting," Lila told him.

"I'm riding my horse. Go faster."

I snickered. "Your mommy used to say that."

"Oh my God. Stop." But she was laughing.

Lila opened the back seat of a blue Volkswagen Jetta and I deposited her son in his car seat.

"I can do the seat belt," she said, trying to nudge me out of the way.

"I've got it." Pulling the strap over his body, I clipped it into place. He didn't fight me on it. If anyone was worn out, it was him. I made sure he was good and secure before I lifted his hand and bumped my fist against his. "You did good out there. I bet you're gonna be a good football player."

He nodded with all the confidence of a four-year-old who still believed anything was possible. "A football player and a cowboy."

Yet another reminder that he was his father's son. "Be good for your mom." I ruffled his sweaty hair. "Cowboys and football players don't throw temper tantrums."

He nodded. "Okay. Bye."

Kids were so quick to forgive and forget. If only adults could do the same.

How in the hell had I managed to bond with Brody McCallister's son? Not at all the way I'd expected things to happen today. It helped that he wasn't here because I could guarantee that if he had been the whole evening would have been fraught with tension and more than likely, I would have excused myself and gone for a run instead of playing football with Noah.

I closed the door and turned to Lila who peered through the window, no doubt double-checking that her son was securely fastened.

"Thanks." She gave me a small smile. "Has he worn you out?"

"Nope. I could go all night long. All. Night. Long, baby."

Her cheeks flushed pink. "Oh my God, you need to stop saying things like that."

Yeah, I needed to stop and remind myself that we were no longer a couple. What the fuck was I thinking? I didn't even know what we were to each other anymore, if anything at all. For a little while, I'd almost forgotten that Noah was Brody's kid.

She glanced at Noah. "I need to get going. So I guess..." She clasped her hands and rocked back on the heels of her white Converse. "I'll see you around."

"Yeah." I stuffed my hands in my pockets to stop myself from touching her. "See you around."

She hesitated a moment, her mouth opening to say something but she obviously thought better of it because she rounded the hood of her car without saying another word.

Long after her car had disappeared from view, I was still standing in the driveway, wondering what she would have said.

I miss you, Jude. I still love you. Let's run away together and fuck each other's brains out. We'll hide away from the world and stay in bed for an entire weekend like we did when you came home on leave that first time.

Doubt she would have said any of that. In all likelihood, if she ever thought of me at all she remembered the bad shit. But before all that, there was friendship and there was love. So much love.

I shook off my memories and watched the sun set over the lush green hills, the sky painted pink and orange, the bluebonnets and wildflowers a ribbon of color in the field across our two-lane road. The air smelled sweeter here. Scented with freshly cut grass and the purple flowers of my mom's Mountain Laurel.

Home sweet home.

"You good?" Jesse asked, coming to stand next to me.

"Yeah. It's all good." It wasn't. Not even fucking close.

"It's gotta be hard though, right?"

I shrugged one shoulder. "Where you headed?" I asked, noting the helmet in his hand. Jesse had always preferred two wheels to four.

"Meeting up with Tanner and Mason. We're gonna kick back and have a few beers, shoot some pool. You wanna come?"

They were his friends from high school. I didn't really know them. When I'd left for boot camp, Jesse was only thirteen. By the time I came home, he had sponsorships for motocross and was on the road a lot.

"Nah. I'm good. Thanks."

"Sure."

He started walking toward his motorcycle then turned around. "I never thought it was right what Brody did. But I wasn't around much, so I don't know exactly what went down."

"It's in the past. Can't change it now."

"Guess not. Don't get the wrong idea. I don't hate Brody. I think he's a good guy. Just not the right guy for Lila."

Not sure that I was the right guy for Lila anymore either but I didn't mention that.

"We all love Noah."

"He seems like a good kid."

"Yeah, he's cool. For what it's worth, I think you and Brody should talk it out. We're still family. That's never gonna change."

I looked out at the road as a jacked-up truck drove past, music blasting. "Where do they live?" As if I was actually considering 'talking it out.'

"They?" Jesse's brow furrowed. "You mean Lila and Noah?"

"They don't live with Brody?"

"You thought they were together?"

"They're not?" I asked in surprise.

Jesse laughed and shook his head. "Holy shit. I love you, bro, but sometimes you're an idiot."

I scowled at him. He held up both hands. "Hey. I would have told you anything you wanted to know but you never asked."

Would I have come back sooner if I knew this? I wasn't so sure. Just because Lila didn't live with Brody didn't change the fact that they had a kid together.

CHAPTER THIRTY-SIX

Lila

NOAH FELL ASLEEP ON THE DRIVE HOME. I PUSHED HIS sweaty hair off his forehead and unclipped his seat belt. Dirt and grass were ground into the knees of his jeans and a ketchup stain decorated his blue T-shirt. His eyelids fluttered but he didn't wake up.

I gathered him into my arms and lifted him out of his seat. He was small but when he was asleep, he was heavy. Closing the car door with my hip, I hiked him up as Brody pulled into the driveway and climbed out of his truck.

"What are you doing here?" I asked when he met me by my car.

"I've got him." Without bothering to answer my question, he took Noah out of my arms. I beeped the locks on my car and followed him to the front door of my two-bedroom cottage nestled in a grove of cypress trees. Jesse called it a Hobbit house. But it was cozy and the perfect size for me and Noah.

Brody stepped aside and I unlocked the door and pushed it wide open to give him space.

"You want him in bed?" he asked as we crossed the living room.

I nodded and followed him down the hallway then ducked into the bathroom and ran a washcloth under warm soapy water.

In Noah's bedroom, Brody was undressing him on his red racecar bed that Kate and Patrick had bought for him. His room was decorated in red, white and navy, his toys corralled in canvas totes on a low shelving unit that spanned one wall. I opened the oak dresser and grabbed a pair of SpongeBob SquarePants pajamas. His favorite cartoon.

He was half-awake now, his eyelids so heavy he could barely keep them open but that didn't stop him from trying.

"Hi Daddy," Noah mumbled.

"Hey buddy. We need to get you out of this T-shirt." Noah sat up and held his arms in the air, letting Brody take off the T-shirt. He was down to his underwear now.

"I need to pee," he said as I wiped his face with the warm soapy washcloth. "Really really bad."

"Hurry," I said. He scrambled off the bed and ran to the bathroom. Noah had this habit of waiting until the last minute.

"Uh oh," I heard from the bathroom. "I missed."

Brody laughed. I sighed. I swear Noah missed the bowl more often than not. I was always cleaning pee off the floor. Off the seat. Sometimes when he was showing off, it even sprayed the wall.

It took me another fifteen minutes to finally get Noah to settle down. Fast asleep now, tucked under his navy comforter with white stars, I made sure the nightlight was on and closed his door softly before I joined Brody in the living room.

I paused in the doorway as he set a framed photo back on

the bookshelves that spanned the opposite wall. It was a photo of the three of us—me, Brody, and Jude when we were kids. We were sitting on the McCallister's back porch eating popsicles. We weren't looking at the camera and the photo caught us mid-laugh. We looked so happy. So carefree. The boys were probably telling those stupid pickle jokes they'd found so funny that summer. I was sitting in the middle, and I guess that was how it had always been.

Now I'd driven a wedge between them and I had no idea how or if we could ever come back from this.

Brody turned to face me, his back to the shelves that heaved with well-loved books and memories—framed photos and knick-knacks and the pottery bowls and vases my mom and I made the summer she was getting chemo. I crossed the hardwood floor and sat on the worn leather sofa, tucking my legs under me.

"How's your horse?"

He turned his hand over and studied the dried blood on the palm. "Got himself tangled up in barbed wire on the neighbor's property. Had to fix the fence. Those horses have thirty acres to roam free but they still try to push the limits. That's the thing about wild horses." He lifted his head, his gaze meeting mine. "As long as there're fences, they're not truly free."

"The fences are there to protect them and keep them safe."

"Yeah, well, they don't know that. They see a fence and they want to know what's on the other side. Just like we did when we were kids."

It was true. We'd always gone where we were told not to. Had always pushed the boundaries. "Why are you here?" I smoothed my hand over the crocheted yellow throw blanket hanging on the back of the sofa. "I wasn't expecting you."

His eyes narrowed on me. "I need to call ahead now to see my own son?"

"No. Of course not. I was just surprised to see you here."
He was still standing, his posture rigid, arms crossed. This
didn't feel like a social call. "What was all that at dinner?"

"What was all what?" he asked, deliberately not understanding me.

"You know what I'm talking about. Why did you put
your arm around me? Were you trying to rub it in Jude's
face?"

He threw his hands in the air. "Here we go again. It's all
about Jude."

"It's not all about Jude but that was..." I shook my head, my
gaze landing on the rustic wood coffee table in front of the sofa.
Jude made it from hundred-year-old oak. "You two were like
brothers and now you act like you hate him."

"Do I need to remind you of what he did? You expect me to
just forgive and forget? No. Not happening. And let me tell
you something." He pointed a finger at me in accusation. "If
you decide to go down this road again, so help me God, you had
better not drag Noah into your shit show."

"My shit show? Wow. Thanks for having so much faith in
my parenting skills. Noah is my number one priority and I
don't need you reminding me of anything."

"So you remember the abuse? The way he was drunk from
morning till night. You remember the drugs? You remember all
that? Because today all I saw was the Lila who still believed
that Jude hung the stars and the moon."

"Abuse?" I questioned, taking exception to the one thing I
could object to. "Are you kidding me right now? Jude did not
abuse me. None of that was his fault. He had PTSD. He had a
TBI. You know that. Jude would *never* hurt me."

No man could ever love me the way Jude had. We'd loved
hard. We'd loved fiercely. But no man could ever hurt me the
way he had either.

"And yet... he did. He put you through hell. I don't want to see you go through that again."

I knew Brody's heart was in the right place and this was his way of looking out for me but I still felt the need to defend Jude. "You saw him." I wrapped my arms around a throw pillow with a sunflower pattern. "He's doing so much better."

My words didn't sway Brody's opinion. He was a grudge holder. Jude had not only hurt me by leaving, he had hurt Brody too. He'd abandoned us without a backward glance. "He didn't come back here for you, Lila. And he sure as hell wasn't there for you when you needed him. Just keep that in mind before you go running back to him."

"I'm not running back to him." I wasn't. It was too late for us. We were irreparably broken. And as Brody had so helpfully pointed out, Jude hadn't come back here for me. He came to visit his dad, and he came to help out with the family business.

"Guess we'll see about that. Jude is used to getting whatever he wants."

That wasn't true and I couldn't understand how Brody could say that.

Spending time with Jude today brought back so many memories, churned up so many emotions. He'd been so good with Noah and for a while I'd forgotten so many things. Now Brody was here to remind me.

"Is that why you stopped by? To warn me not to fall for Jude again?"

He shook his head. "I came to tell you I'm leaving."

My heart skipped a beat. I tossed the throw pillow aside and stood up. "What do you mean? Leaving?"

"I'll be back, L. I always come back. I'm just going on the road for a few weeks. Leaving Friday."

"The rodeo?"

He nodded.

"I thought you were quitting."

"I need the money. Been thinking about it for a while. Now that I know Patrick's going to be okay, I can go." He grabbed the back of his neck, not looking at me. "I'd like to have Noah for a few nights this week. I can pick him up from school tomorrow and drop him off on Thursday evening."

I hesitated before answering. I don't know why I hesitated but Brody didn't usually spring this kind of thing on me. The whole rodeo thing seemed to have come from out of the blue. But then again, I knew he'd never really wanted to give it up. He'd given it up for Noah, and for me, I guess and now he was itching to get back to it.

"He's my son too, Lila. I should get to spend time with him," he said, mistaking my silence for refusal. "I have a room for him at my house. You know that."

"I know that, Brody. I've never tried to stop you from spending time with Noah. Of course he can stay with you."

"Good. That's settled then." He turned to go and I followed him to the door.

"You're not leaving because of Jude, right?"

He released the door handle and turned to look at me. "Believe it or not, my life doesn't revolve around Jude. You need me to stay? I will. Just say the word." His gaze held mine. I shook my head. I'd never asked him to stay. It had always been his choice.

"I don't need you to stay. That wasn't my question."

"I'm being honest. I need the fucking money. I have a shit-load of bills and a bank loan I'd like to pay off before I'm ninety."

So it really was a money issue. "You don't have to pay for Noah's daycare this summer." Not that I had money to burn but I would find a way if it meant helping him out. "I'll take care of it."

"He's just as much my responsibility as yours so fuck no. You're not going to take care of it. I'll pay for his daycare. You know I'd be happy to pay for anything that makes your life and Noah's life better."

I did know that. "You're a good man, Brody."

"Since when?"

"Since always."

"Don't get sweet on me," he teased, giving me a smile and a wink. "That only leads to trouble."

And trouble was the last thing we needed.

"You need to meet someone special. It's time you let someone in." Ever since I could remember, Brody had hooked up and moved on before anyone could get too close.

"Someone special, huh? Someone like you?"

"No. I meant..." *Someone else.*

"Yeah, I know what you meant. Falling in love... getting too close... it only leads to heartbreak." His hooded gaze held mine for a few long moments before he shook his head and walked out the door.

When the door closed behind him, I sagged against it and expelled the breath I'd been holding.

Oh my God.

CHAPTER THIRTY-SEVEN

Jude

My truck bumped along the winding dirt and gravel lane flanked by trees. Up ahead, a metal gate had been left wide open. I drove through the two stone pillars and peered through the windshield at a two-story weathered shingle house with dark green trim. It looked like a home. The kind of place where you could raise a bunch of kids. Worlds away from the life I'd been living.

Last time I saw Brody, he was living in an Airstream on Austin's ranch. Now he owned a home and a horse farm.

I pulled in behind Brody's truck and followed the stone paving slabs to the front door.

Lifting my hand, I pounded my fist against the wood. No answer. I tried again with the same result before I rounded the side of the house.

I knew this property. Thirty acres of prime Hill Country.

The summer I was seventeen and working for my dad, I worked with the crew that put a new roof on the barn. That summer Brody was working as a ranch hand and I'd told him he would love this place. One day he stopped by for lunch and climbed up on the roof with me to get a better view—beyond the barn and paddocks, the land was wild and rugged, hills and meadows and wooded areas with a natural spring lake.

"Someday I'm gonna buy a place just like this," he'd said.

The other guys on the crew had laughed like that was a joke. But I knew Brody meant it. Owning land and working with horses was all he'd ever wanted, and I knew he'd find a way to do it. That was Brody. When someone said he couldn't do something, he knocked himself out to prove otherwise.

When something—or *someone*—was off-limits, he wanted it even more.

I slowed my steps when I heard Noah's voice coming from inside the barn. Shit. I hadn't even thought he might be here.

"Can you fix him, Daddy?"

"I don't know, buddy. Some things can't be fixed."

"But you can fix anything. You can fix all the horses."

"Wish I could. He's been through a lot. That's why he gets so spooked. He has a lot of triggers and they make him relive the bad things over and over in his head."

"Triggers? Oh... like a gun?"

"What are you doing in my truck?" Brody asked, narrowing his eyes at me as he climbed into the driver's seat.

I sat up and yawned as I rolled out my shoulders. I'd slept in his truck so I wouldn't miss him when he took off. The sun wasn't even up yet.

"I'm going with you."

"I need to do this alone."

Good luck to him if he thought he could get me to leave. I settled in, preparing to be here for the long haul. "No, you fucking don't. I've got your back. I'm not letting you do this alone." *I knew he didn't want me to get out of his truck. Other-*

wise, he would have put up a fight. He hit the gas and we rode in silence. While he drove, I texted Lila to let her know I was going on an impromptu camping trip with Brody to celebrate our high school graduation.

"You wanna talk about it?"

"Nope. Wish I'd never told you."

When he told me, he was drunk and stoned, and barely coherent but it was obvious he needed to tell someone. He'd been keeping it to himself for too long. Now he was out for revenge and I wasn't about to let him do this his way. He'd end up in prison. No way could I let that happen. I had a few hours to help him come up with a better plan. One that didn't involve putting a bullet in his abuser's head.

"Uncle Jude!" Noah grinned at me and waved as I walked into the barn. Brody scowled at me but I ignored it and him.

"Hey Noah." He ran toward me then stopped short and held out his fist. I bumped my scarred knuckles against his small fist. Just a light tap so I didn't hurt him. His grin grew wider, like bumping fists had already become our thing.

"How's Hayley?" I asked.

"Good. She got a new dog. She drawed a picture for me. I drawed one for Grandpa. He said it makes him feel all better."

"You have a lot of talents. You're an artist too?"

He nodded seriously. "Yep. I'm really good." I suppressed my laughter. "Are you gonna punch Daddy?"

Tempting. "No. I just came to talk."

Noah looked at me for a minute then nodded and darted away in pursuit of a black and white border collie. "Buster. Get back here."

"If you're looking for a fight, it'll have to wait," Brody said as we walked out of the barn, our eyes on Noah as he chased the dog across the field.

"I'm not looking for a fight."

"Sure you are," he said. "You think I stole something that was yours."

"Because you did. Lila was always mine."

"If you loved her so much, you should have stuck around instead of fucking off and leaving her. Second thought, nah. She was better off without you."

My jaw clenched and I could feel my teeth grinding together. Brody had always been an asshole but he'd taken it to a whole different level when he went for Lila. I blamed him for all of it.

"When I asked you to take care of her, sleeping with her was not what I meant." Even now, after all these years, it still cut me to the core that he would do that. "You were like a brother to me. I *trusted* you. How could you do that?"

"You. Fucked. Up." He pointed his finger at me. "And you have nobody to blame except yourself."

"Why Lila? Of all the girls you could have gone for, why her?" I gritted out.

"You destroyed her and I was there to pick up the pieces. Not you. Me. I loved Lila as much as you did. Before everything, she was our best friend. And when you see a person you love suffering you want to make it better for them. That's something you should understand. Since you've always had a hero complex."

"Fuck you. Have you forgotten all the times I had your back? Have you forgotten Odessa?"

"I never asked you to come to Odessa with me. I could have handled that on my own. I had it all under control."

I laughed. "You stupid fuck. You had *nothing* under control. You would have ended up in prison. Just like your old man." It was a low blow, and I knew it, but that didn't make it less true.

"I tried to repay my debt to you. I tried to save you from

yourself," he said. "When you came back, you were so fucked up. I was dragging you home from bars when you were too drunk to even stand up. You tried to commit suicide. She was out of her fucking mind with worry. Scared to leave your side."

I was having trouble breathing. I wanted him to shut up but he kept talking.

"We were all worried about you. But we were worried about Lila too. You think I don't recognize abuse when I see it?"

"I didn't..." I took deep breaths through my nose. In. Out. In. Out. Because it was true. Whether I'd done it intentionally or not, I'd abused her.

My memories of that time were hazy. Probably because I was always drunk or high on something.

"Yeah. You can't even deny it, can you?" I couldn't deny it. It was why I left her. "She tried to hide it. Lied about it to protect you, you stupid fuck."

"Stop," I gritted out. "Just fucking stop."

"No. You need to hear this. You promised her you'd always be there for her. You broke your promises and you fucking broke her. So you don't get to come over here accusing me of anything. She's happy now. She has a son to raise and a business to run. You need to stay the fuck away from her. You don't deserve her. Not anymore. Not after all the shit you put her through."

"And you think you do? What did you think would happen, Brody? You'd get her pregnant and she'd choose you?"

"She'll always be a part of my life. We've got a son together. What have you given her besides a shitload of bad memories?"

Bastard. Red hot anger bubbled to the surface. I grabbed him by the shirt and flung him. He stumbled then righted himself and lunged at me. "That's the best you can do? Pussy," he taunted. He jutted out his chin and held out his arms. "First shot's free."

Brody had it coming.

I took the first swing. My knuckles slammed into his nose. Blood spewed all over, but I didn't stop. Another punch to the gut, and I thought he'd go down, but he didn't.

He slammed his fist into my jaw. I shook my head and tackled him to the ground, raining punches on him.

"Brody! Jude!"

Dazed, I looked over at Lila just as Brody's fist connected with my temple. Blindsiding me. Motherfucker. I rolled onto my back and we lay there writhing and panting, my hand on my head.

"Oh my God. What is wrong with you two?"

Head pounding, vision blurred, I sat up and waited a few seconds for the world to stop spinning. Then I got to my feet, weaving a little and took a few deep breaths to steady myself. The funny part? I could have beat him to a bloody pulp but I'd held back. And he'd punched me in the head. My weak spot.

Like I said, Brody had always fought dirty.

"Brody. Where's Noah?"

"Fuck," he said.

Brody put his fingers between his lips and whistled. Seconds later, the border collie raced across the field and stopped at his feet then sat up and looked at him. "Shit. Buster. Where's Noah?"

"You're asking a dog where your son is?" Lila asked, panic raising her voice a couple octaves.

"It'll be okay," I assured her. "He couldn't have gone far. We'll find him."

She shook her head and strode toward the barn. "Noah!"

The three of us separated, calling his name. I headed in the direction where I'd last seen him when he ran across the field chasing the dog that was now following close on Brody's heels.

"Noah," I called as I jogged across the field. Up ahead, I

saw a flash of red dart behind a live oak and I slowed my pace, my approach stealthy and quiet so he wouldn't run again. When I reached the tree, his head popped out to check if I'd caught him. Having spotted me, he took off again and I chased after him, grabbing him around the middle and lifting him off his feet.

"Put me down!"

I set him on the ground and turned him around to face me, keeping a firm but gentle hold on him so I wouldn't hurt him but he couldn't run away again either.

"You scared us. Your mommy and daddy are looking all over for you. Are you going to come back with me or do I have to carry you back?"

"Let me go."

"As long as you promise not to run away again."

He thought about it for a minute then nodded and I walked him back to Lila who ran to him when she saw him.

She lifted him off the ground and into her arms. His legs wrapped around her waist and she held him close, stroking his hair. "I was so scared I lost you."

Noah lifted his head from her shoulder and patted her cheeks with the palms of his hand, smearing dirt across her cheekbones. "You can't lose me. I'm your Noah."

"Yes, you are. And I love you so much."

"Love you too. Put me down."

Lila set him on the ground and took his hand. "We're going home now. Brody, get his bag please."

"Come on, L. Don't—"

"You two can finish whatever it is you were doing. He's coming home with me."

"I'm gonna stay with Daddy," Noah said.

"Not tonight. He'll see you tomorrow."

"Why can't I stay?" he asked Brody.

"Because your mom says so. That's why."

I followed Lila and Noah across the field, around the side of the house and to their car. Not sure why. I knew she didn't even want to see my face much less talk to me.

"Bye, Uncle Jude," Noah said after Lila belted him into his car seat. She stepped aside to let me say goodbye. Which was more than I deserved.

"Bye Noah."

"You got blood on your shirt."

"Yeah. I was being stupid. Fighting is stupid. It's not the right way to settle an argument. It's better to use your words."

He nodded. "That's what Mommy and Grandma say."

I smiled. "That's what your grandma always told me too. You should listen to your mommy. She's smart. A lot smarter than me."

He nodded and I tapped his fist with my bloody knuckles then backed away from the car. I glanced at Lila whose arms were crossed over her chest, her eyes on the ground like she couldn't even bear to look at me.

"I'm sorry," I said quietly. I didn't expect a response and I didn't get one. She rounded the back of her car as Brody walked out of his house with Noah's bags.

I climbed into my truck, grabbed some napkins from the glove compartment and flipped down the visor. I hated looking in the mirror. No surprise. My face was a fucking mess. I wiped the blood from my nose and tossed the napkins in the cupholder. There was no help for me now. I watched Lila in the rearview mirror. She had both hands on the steering wheel, ready to go. She was blocking me in, so I had to wait for her to pull out.

Brody stopped next to her open window and crouched in front of it. My windows were open but I couldn't hear his words from here. None of my business anyway. Whether I liked it or not, I had to accept that they were a family and I was the odd man out.

What kind of example had we set for a four-year-old? A shitty one.

I waited until I heard her tires crunching over the gravel then turned my key in the ignition.

"Just for the record," Brody told me as he passed my window. "I have no intention of forgiving and forgetting anytime soon."

"Just for the record, neither do I." I threw my truck into reverse and did a three-point turn then followed Lila down the dirt and gravel driveway. At the end of it, she turned left onto the highway and I turned right. She followed the last of the sun as it dipped into the sky while I drove away from it.

And that was how it felt. Like we'd been going in different directions for all these years and we would continue to do so.

How could we ever find our way back to each other after all that had been said and done? The best thing I could do for her would be to stay away. But now that I was back here, now that I'd seen her again, I didn't know how to do that.

Brody had been there for her when I hadn't been.

How had I failed so epically? *How?*

How could I ever fix everything that I'd broken? How could I repair the damage that I'd done? The boy who had been her best friend... the man who had loved her beyond words or reason... wanted to believe that it was still possible.

My foot was on the first step of the staircase when my mom called to me from the kitchen. Reluctantly, I walked down the hallway, the walls covered in photos that I didn't stop to look at. I'd seen them all before. Proms, graduations, homecomings, our annual family Christmas photos through the years.

As I crossed the terracotta tiles, my mom looked up from the crossword puzzle she was working on and gasped. Guess my face didn't look so good.

"Honestly. Aren't you two a bit old to be fighting?"

I pulled up a chair across from her and raked both hands through my hair. "Probably."

Tskking, my mom stood up from the table, grabbed a dish towel from the drawer and opened the freezer to get some ice for the bruising on my face.

"I'm okay," I said. "I don't need ice. Just sit down. Please."

With a sigh of resignation, she returned to her seat at the table. "Do you want some herbal tea? It might help you sleep."

"No, thanks. I'm good. Why are you still awake?" My eyes darted to the clock on the wall above the stove. It was eleven thirty and my mom had never been a night owl. After I'd left Brody's I'd gone for a drive with no real destination in mind and had ended up taking a trip down memory lane, visiting all the places Lila and I used to hang out.

"I couldn't sleep."

"Dad's going to be okay," I assured her, thinking that might be what was keeping her up, worrying.

"I know he will. But the house feels so empty without him." She smiled. "That man drives me crazy but I can't imagine my life without him."

My parents had gone through a lot of ups and downs over the years but after more than thirty years of marriage, they were still together. For better or worse. In sickness and health.

"Did you and Brody work out your differences?"

I rubbed the back of my neck. "Not sure that's possible." I knew she wanted us to be one big happy family but that wasn't going to happen.

"You two were always so alike."

I stared at her. "Brody and I have never been anything alike. We're about as different as two people can be."

She shook her head, disputing that. "You might have wanted different things in life but you were very similar. Even more so now that you're older. You both fight for the things you believe in. You're both loyal and have an innate sense of justice. And you've both experienced some terrible things in your lives."

Even though I thought she was wrong, I didn't bother arguing.

"Do you want my advice?"

"Sure," I responded even though her question had been rhetorical. My mom would give me advice whether I asked for it or not.

"You need to find a way to forgive yourself. You've always been too hard on yourself. Nobody is perfect, Jude. Everyone makes mistakes. Just try not to make the same ones over and over again."

She was cutting me too much slack. Minimizing the damage I'd done by calling it a mistake. As if I'd gotten a C on my math test instead of an A and all I needed to do was learn the material better before the next exam.

"It's never too late for a second chance." My mom rose from the table and rinsed out her mug. "Get some sleep. Things always look better in the morning." With those words of wisdom, she left me alone in the kitchen with my own thoughts.

My mom was wrong. I didn't need to forgive myself. I needed Lila's forgiveness. I had to find a way to right my wrongs.

I had to find a way to put the stars back in the sky.

CHAPTER THIRTY-EIGHT

Lila

"Prince Charming is back," Christy said, not even lifting her head from the floral arrangement she was working on. We didn't have to look out the windows to confirm. I heard the tires crunching over the gravel and I knew it was him. Right on time. The song playing from the speakers cut out and G-Eazy's "The Beautiful & Damned" filled the studio.

"Funny," I said as she slipped her phone back into her pocket and laughed.

"I call it like I see it. Fingers crossed he brought donuts today."

It had been five days since I'd gone over to Brody's to drop off Noah's special blanket that he claimed he couldn't sleep without. Five days since Jude and Brody fought. Five days since I lost my mind when I couldn't find Noah. And every morning since then Jude had come bearing gifts. Coffee and donuts. The cinnamon rolls I loved from the bakery. There was always a little note in the bag. They reminded me of the corny notes he used to leave in my locker in high school.

You look beautiful today.

I love your smile.

You're sweeter than sugar donuts.

But we weren't in high school anymore, and we had to stop acting like we were. Today I was going to ignore him. Keep working on my floral arrangements and stay focused on the work at hand. We were swamped because, after all, it was wedding season. So I'd just pretend he wasn't even there. No matter how adorable he acted or how sexy he looked in his fitted T-shirts and faded denim that hung low on his narrow hips, I wouldn't even glance his way. Nope. I wouldn't even notice the way he raked his hand through his tousled, messy hair or the way he bit his bottom lip.

I was Teflon and his charms would bounce right off me. Ping. Ping. Ping.

"Mommy!"

My head swiveled to the doorway as Noah dashed across the studio and skidded to a halt in front of me. Setting down the bridal bouquet I was working on, I wiped my hands on my shorts and pulled him toward me for a hug, my gaze narrowed on Jude as he set cardboard cups of coffee and a pie on the counter. Not just a couple slices. An entire pie. The nerve of this man.

Then he smiled and I was stunned into silence, the words of rebuke dying on my lips. It was the first genuine smile I'd seen in so long. Jude had the most beautiful smile. When he smiled, the dimples appeared in his cheeks, and transformed his entire face.

Oh Jude, you're back, I thought. I didn't know it was possible. I didn't think he'd ever come back.

"Guess what?" Noah tugged my hand to get my attention.

I dragged my gaze away from Jude and focused on Noah. "What?"

"We're going on a bear hunt." His eyes lit up.

"A bear hunt?"

Jude chuckled and my eyes narrowed on him again.

He was using my son now? How low could he sink? Brody usually had Noah on Saturdays but since he was on the road, I'd dropped Noah off at Kate's early this morning. She'd insisted. Had even called me a few days ago to make sure I would. When I'd protested that it was too much for her with Patrick still in the hospital and due to come home on Monday, she'd said, "Nonsense. I love having him."

"Jude. Can I talk to you for a minute?" It took every ounce of my self-restraint to keep my voice calm and measured. I was trying to be a responsible adult and set a good example for my son. Bad enough he'd witnessed his father and uncle beating the crap out of each other, he didn't need to see his mother screaming like a banshee. "Privately."

"I'd love to talk to you. Privately." His voice was low and intimate, making it sound like I'd asked for something else.

My hands clenched into fists and he chuckled under his breath, clearly enjoying this exchange.

"Hey Noah. Come tell me what you've been up to," Christy said, and I threw her a grateful smile. "Actually, let's grab some forks and dig into that pie."

"Pie! Yes!"

I sighed. Noah was so easily swayed. Bribe him with pie and a bear hunt and he'd follow you to the ends of the earth.

I left them in the studio and walked outside with Jude. The air was heavy, the clouds skittering across the gray sky carrying the promise of rain.

Stopping on the driver's side of his truck where we couldn't be seen from the studio, I planted my hands on my hips and squared off with him. "What do you think you're doing?"

"Spending the day with Noah. My mom went to the hospital to visit my dad. Said she has a lot of errands to run after that. So I'm just helping her out." He grinned, the picture of innocence. "It's the least I can do."

Even Kate was conspiring against me. *"The least you can do?* Seriously? You didn't even ask me if it's okay."

"I texted you. You never answered." He shrugged and leaned against the side of his truck, cool as you like, ankles and arms crossed. I wanted to punch him. Or kiss him. No, I wanted no such thing.

"You texted me?" I slid my phone out of my pocket and sure enough, there was a text from an unknown number. I didn't even have his new cell phone number. How pathetic was that?

"I used to dream about you in these shorts." His gaze lowered to my denim cut-offs. This morning when I showed up at work Christy had threatened to burn them, claiming we weren't in college anymore.

I snapped my fingers in his face. "Jude. Stay focused."

Ever so slowly, his gaze roamed up my legs and over the fitted long-sleeve T-shirt I was wearing until his eyes finally met mine. Which was almost worse than the trail of fire he'd left in the wake of his heated gaze. Our eyes locked and for a few seconds, I just stood there and stared at him, the reason for our confrontation completely forgotten.

His arm shot out and he grabbed my hand, tugging me toward him. "Lila." His voice was low and husky and reached into the deepest hidden parts of me. I unfurled like a flower, reaching for the sun as he wrapped his arm around me, a steel band holding me in place while his other hand wrapped around the back of my head and he pulled me against him, crushing his mouth to mine. His tongue parted my lips and I whimpered, my eyes drifting shut as I let him in, his tongue stroking mine and my hands fisting his T-shirt.

I needed more. Of his velvet-coated kisses and his heady scent and the feel of his hard chest pressed against mine.

My body melted into his, and I wrapped my arms around his neck, forgetting everything except for this kiss.

Oh God. This felt so right and yet so wrong. Kissing Jude felt like coming home to a place I used to know but had forgotten. A place I'd visited in my dreams and had longed to return to for so many years. And now he was here and my body responded in ways it hadn't in longer than I could remember.

But then I did remember. I pulled away, my chest heaving, and took a few deep breaths. He wasn't the oxygen I needed to breathe. Not anymore.

"Why are you doing this to me?"

He pushed his hand through his hair. "How can I not? Do you know how hard it is to be this close to you... to inhale the sweet, delicious scent of you... and *not* touch you?"

I did know because it was the same for me but I didn't want it to be. I stuffed my hands in my back pockets and took a step back, reminding myself the reason we were standing out here hidden from view. *Noah*.

I shook my head to clear it. "Jude... you can't use my son..."

"I'm not using Noah. I want to get to know him. I want to be a part of his life."

"A part of his life?" I let out an incredulous laugh. Jude was unbelievable. Maybe Brody was right. Jude was used to getting whatever he wanted and now he'd decided that he wanted to be a part of Noah's life, so of course we should all go along with it. "And how exactly do you think that's going to work?"

"I have no idea what part I'll play in his life but I'm still his uncle." He winced at the word. "I'm still family. And I..." He looked over my shoulder. "I love kids and he's a great kid. I'd never do anything to hurt him. I won't take my eyes off him." As if Noah's physical safety was the only thing in danger. "I promise you that I won't let anything happen to him."

I let out a breath. "Your promises used to mean a lot to me. You always kept your promises. Until you didn't."

Even though I knew my words hurt him, he couldn't deny it. He didn't even try. He opened his mouth to speak but closed it again as a car pulled in next to his truck. Tori, our part-time employee, stepped out of it, her eyes wide as she stared at the man standing across from me.

She was young and blonde and pretty and I watched Jude's face for a reaction but he barely looked at her. For all the crap we'd gone through and all our years of separation while he was in the Marines, I knew he'd never cheated on me. He'd always been loyal. He'd never given me cause to worry or feel insecure that he'd rather be with someone else.

"Hey Lila." She gave me a bright smile and I made the introductions. Jude scowled when I introduced him as Brody's cousin. What else could I say? Tori knew nothing about Jude.

When she went inside, he said the words I suspected he'd been meaning to say before we were interrupted. "Just give me another chance to prove myself. That's all I'm asking."

I nearly laughed. That was asking a lot. But I found myself nodding in agreement. "Guard him with your life. If anything..." I looked away then back at him so he would know where I stood. "Noah is *the* most important person in my life."

I couldn't stress that enough, and I needed him to hear it and understand it.

"I know he is," he said quietly, and I could hear the acceptance in his tone. My heart no longer beat just for him.

He smiled but it wasn't the same smile as earlier. It was sadder and infinitely more beautiful.

"Can we go now?" Noah approached the two of us but looked up at Jude.

Jude put his hand on Noah's shoulder. It was such a paternal gesture. How would Brody feel if he knew Jude was spending the day with his son?

After I said my goodbyes and watched Jude's truck pull out onto the highway, I walked back inside. Christy raised her brows but didn't say anything in front of Tori. She'd only started working for us a few months ago and knew nothing about Jude. I could see she was curious but it wasn't something I planned to share with her.

How could I even begin to explain what Jude meant to me?

"Bring him as your plus one," Sophie said as I pulled into the McCallister's driveway, windshield wipers slapping.

"Noah's my plus one."

"Fine. If you don't bring Jude, I'm setting you up with the divorced lawyer. Your choice."

"That's... ugh, no. I don't need a date for the wedding." Sophie's wedding was in three weeks. Black tie. Two hundred fifty guests. On her family vineyard. Christy and I were doing the flowers. "I have to go."

"K. Bye. And don't forget to invite him."

I had no intention of inviting Jude to Sophie's wedding. Cutting the call, I got out of my car, dashed across the front yard and up the porch steps, seeking shelter from the rain. Running my fingers through my damp hair, I knocked before I pushed open the front door. I wasn't sure why I always knocked. This house was like a family home to me. The only one I'd had since my mom died.

I followed the scent of garlic and tomato sauce to the

kitchen. Kate pulled a lasagna out of the oven and set it on the counter before turning to look at me. "Hi honey. How was work?"

"Good. It was busy but it was good. Where are Noah and Jude?" I asked, noting the four place settings on the kitchen table.

Kate pointed to the window with a smile on her face. I looked out at the back yard where a tent was pitched. It looked like the same tent Jude had once decorated with fairy lights on our camping trip. The same tent we used to have sleepovers in the summers we were just kids. Me, Brody, Jude.

"Do you need help with dinner?" I asked. "I can make a salad or…"

"All done. Go on out and see them. I know you're dying to."

I laughed because it was true. I wanted to see what they were up to. I ran across the back yard and said, "Knock, knock" before I pulled back the tent flap and ducked inside, out of the rain.

My hand went to my heart.

They were asleep. My son and the man who I had loved so fiercely. The man who had stolen my heart had his arm wrapped around my baby boy and my heart expanded like a balloon, so full it was nearly bursting.

As if he could feel the weight of my gaze, Jude stirred and his eyelids fluttered open. He scrubbed a hand over his face and tilted his chin down to look at Noah as if to make sure he hadn't neglected his duties or broken his promise to keep my son safe under his watchful eye at all times.

"Looks like you wore each other out," I said with a small smile.

"You were right about him. He never stops."

"Was he okay for you?" Noah could be a handful. Stubborn. Willful. Prone to temper tantrums when he didn't get his own way. But in my eyes, the good outweighed the bad. He was smart and funny and sweet and he made me smile and laugh every day.

"He was great. He's an amazing kid." Jude smiled as if he was proud of that, as if he had some hand in making Noah who he was. And I forced myself not to think about what it would be like if things had worked out differently and we'd had a child together.

"Hey Noah." I crawled farther into the tent and gently lifted his arm, pulling his small body against mine. I pushed his hair off his forehead with my hand and stroked it as he woke up, still dazed and half asleep.

It was easy to see why they'd fallen asleep in here. It was cozy inside, with the rain falling outside and the lighting hazy, the tent keeping them warm and dry.

"What did you guys do all day?"

"What didn't we do?" Jude said with a laugh as he sat up and raked his hand through his messy hair. I was staring again. I needed to stop this. "We played Hide and Seek. We went to the playground. We played football. We had a picnic. We went for a hike along the river. We went for ice cream. Am I missing anything?" he asked Noah.

"I can't see how you could fit anymore in. I'm tired just listening."

Jude smiled. "It was fun."

"Yeah," Noah said, fully awake now. "Lots of fun. We went digging too," he reminded Jude.

"Oh yeah, how could I forget?"

"What were you digging for?"

"Treasure," Noah said.

"Treasure, huh? Did you find any buried treasure?"

"Yep. I got lots." He emptied his pockets, turning them inside out, and set all the rocks on the floor of the tent.

"Wow. Yeah, that's... quite a treasure." I tried not to laugh but I couldn't hold it in. Noah scowled at me then stuffed all the rocks back into his pockets like I'd offended him. "Stop laughing."

"I'm sorry. I didn't mean to laugh. Those are nice rocks."

He glared at me. "They're not rocks. They're magic moonstones. When you rub them, your wish comes true."

"Is that what Uncle Jude told you?" I cocked a brow at Jude. He shrugged, the corners of his lips twitching. *Guilty.*

"Where have I heard that one before?" I muttered.

Jude laughed so hard tears sprang to his eyes.

"It wasn't that funny." But he didn't hear me because he was still laughing.

"I have to pee," Noah said, jumping up and holding himself.

"Just water the lawn," Jude said. "We all did it."

"Not me." I pulled down the zipper of Noah's jeans and Jude held the tent flap open. Noah barely made it outside the tent before he was spraying the back yard and laughing like it was the funniest thing ever.

"Your mom made lasagna," I said as we crossed the lawn to the back porch. "I think she's expecting us to stay for dinner."

"Do you have other plans?"

"No, but..."

"But what?" He wrapped his arm around my shoulders and on instinct, I leaned into him before I realized what I'd done. I ducked out from under his arm. We were no longer a couple but we were acting like one. As if on cue, my cell phone rang and I checked it on my way into the kitchen. Taking a deep breath, I swiped my finger across the screen and answered the call.

"Hey Brody. Hang on. Noah's just washing his hands."

I didn't mention that Jude was holding him up at the kitchen sink and helping him.

"Are you at Kate's?" he asked.

"Um, yeah. We're just about to eat dinner."

"Yeah, I only have a few minutes." "So Alive" was blaring in the background.

"Is that the Goo Goo Dolls?" I asked, aiming for a diversion.

"Yeah, they're performing." The rodeo world was a completely different world. But it was Brody's world and he felt at home there.

"Everything okay with you?" he asked when our silence stretched out for a few seconds.

"Yeah. I worked all day. I just got here." Jude set Noah down and gave me a look I couldn't read. "Good luck tonight. Be careful, okay? And watch out for that shoulder." *And all the rest of the bones in your body you've broken over the years.* God, who would be crazy enough to ride a bucking bronc? Brody, that's who.

"Don't you worry about me. I'll be just fine. Did you—"

"Lemme talk to Daddy." Noah reached up with both hands and I handed him the phone, biting my lip as he held it to his ear. Then he proceeded to talk a mile a minute, giving Brody the highlights of his day. Every single last one of them.

"Okay. Bye Daddy." He nodded even though Brody couldn't see him. Whatever Brody said made him nod again.

"He can't see you, Noah," I reminded him.

"I will. Love you too." He thrust the phone back into my hand and climbed into his booster seat at the table all ready for dinner now. When I checked my phone, Brody was still on the line.

"Hey. Talk to you later. We're about to eat."

"Yeah. Wouldn't want to keep Jude waiting." He cut the

call and I sighed, then pocketed my phone as Kate took the seat next to Noah, leaving me with the seat next to Jude.

Even though Brody wasn't here, I felt caught in the middle. The funny part was that if Noah had spent the day with Gideon or Jesse, Brody wouldn't have cared. But because it was Jude, he was annoyed.

I ate a bite of lasagna, which was as delicious as always, but suddenly I had no appetite.

"I'll talk to him," Jude said, his voice low.

I snorted. "Yeah, because that worked out so great the last time." I shook my head. "Just stay out of it. Everything is fine." I forced a smile for Kate. "Thank you for dinner. It's delicious."

"I'll believe that when I see an empty plate."

I forced myself to eat a few more bites when all I really wanted to do was get Noah into the car and go home. Maybe drink a glass of wine. Or a bottle.

When dinner was over, Jude walked me to my car with Noah riding on his shoulders. The rain had tapered off to a light drizzle that cooled my overheated skin. This couldn't be good, the way he was insinuating himself into our lives. After spending the whole day with Jude, Noah was already attached.

I waited until Noah was in his car seat with the door closed before I voiced my concerns. *Again.* "Listen, Jude... this is... you need to take a step back."

He crossed his arms over his chest. "Why? Because it's what *you* want? Or because you don't want to upset Brody?"

"Both."

Jude raked a hand through his hair and clenched his jaw. "Let me get this straight. You're worried about upsetting Brody but you don't give a shit how any of this affects me?"

I gaped at him. Was he for real right now? "I spent an entire *year* putting you and your needs first. Worrying about every little thing I said and did. Blaming myself for upsetting

you. I walked on eggshells the whole time you were home, Jude.
I couldn't even allow myself to grieve..." I let my words drift off.
I didn't want to get into any of this. Not now. Not ever. I took a
deep breath and averted my face so I didn't have to see the hurt
expression or the guilt on his.

"I'm sorry. You're right."

I didn't want to hear that he was sorry. I never wanted to
hear those words from him again. I brushed past him. "I need
to go."

Thankfully, he didn't try to stop me from leaving. I backed
my car out of the driveway and swung onto the road, giving him
one final look before I drove away. He was still standing in the
same spot where I'd left him. And God help me, I still loved
that man. But letting him into my life again was dangerous.

CHAPTER THIRTY-NINE

Jude

THREE DAYS. THAT WAS HOW LONG I HELD OFF BEFORE I caved and showed up at her door like a lost puppy. Lila's cottage on River Road was nestled in a grove of trees and sat on a limestone bluff. Hanging flower baskets flanked the front door, the blooms a riot of color—purple and red and fuchsia. Two Adirondack chairs sat on the front porch and I wondered if she sat out here and stargazed. From her front porch, you could catch a glimpse of the river through the cypress trees lining the riverbank. It was peaceful here, the air scented with pine and the cedar of the shingles on her cottage. The scent of cedar would forever remind me of those nights lying on the cedar-shingled roof with Lila. When I inhaled deeply, it smelled like home.

I knocked on the front door. Hopefully she wouldn't slam it in my face.

I waited a few seconds then lifted my hand to knock again.

The door swung open and she was covered from head to toe in flour. I grinned at her.

"Did you get in a fight with the Pillsbury Dough Boy?"

Looking down at her flour-covered T-shirt, she laughed. "Noah and I are making homemade pizza."

I groaned. Actually groaned. "Need some help?"

"No." But she opened her door wider, an invitation to come inside. "You do know I'm a florist, right?" she asked when I thrust the wildflowers into her hands. I'd picked half a field of wildflowers and tied them with string. It made me feel like I was fifteen years old again.

"Wildflowers picked by me are your favorite."

"They used to be," she said. "Wildflowers picked by Noah are my favorite now."

I could live with that. Much better to have a four-year-old rival than a thirty-year-old asshole cowboy vying for position. I told myself that I wouldn't think about Brody. Whenever I did, I tortured myself with the vision of them together. Which fucked with my head.

So I shoved his memory out of the way—there wasn't room for both of us—and followed her inside the house.

Noah grinned at me from his spot at the island in the cheerful sunshine yellow kitchen. He was standing on a step-stool so he could reach the granite counter. "Hi Uncle Jude. Did you bring me a present?"

"People are not required to bring presents every time they show up at your door," Lila said then muttered under her breath. "Even when they're uninvited."

I ignored her little jab and focused on Noah, my number one ally. I had a man in my corner and I wasn't above bribery to keep him on my side. "Of course I did. It's for after dinner."

He jumped off the stool and took the plastic bag from my

hand, opening the handles to look inside. His whole face lit up. "Ice cream!"

"Nothing says love like Diabetes," Lila said, filling mason jars with water to hold all the wildflowers. "You need to stop bribing us with sugar."

Love. I grinned. "Is it working?"

"No." Her back was turned to me so I couldn't see her face but to me, *no* sounded a lot like *yes*. She set the three mason jars of wildflowers on the windowsill, and I nudged her aside and turned on the tap.

"I'll have to try another tactic then." I washed my hands at the farmhouse sink, the window above it affording me a view of her garden, the last rays of evening sun painting it bronze. Flowers and plants thrived, thanks to her green thumb. Beyond her little garden a tire swing hung from the branch of an oak tree, and next to that was a wood climbing frame and a small shed. I dried my hands on a kitchen towel and turned around to face her and Noah.

"Make yourself at home."

"I will." I rubbed my hands together. "Where's my dough?"

"You weren't even invited. You can watch us."

"You can have some of mine." Noah pinched off a two-inch piece of dough and set it in front of me.

"You're far too generous. I bet I can turn this dough into a twelve-inch pizza." I indicated with my hands how big that was.

Noah looked at the dough skeptically. "How?" he asked, intrigued.

"Magic." I stole Lila's dough out from under her and started kneading it on the floured surface.

"Hey." Lila swatted my arm and tried to get it back but I nudged her aside.

"Back off, Minnie Mouse. You know you love to watch me

knead it. You love to watch my arms flex and my big hands work the dough."

"Stop it," she said, laughing. "Seriously. You need to stop."

Noah was too busy bashing the dough with a rolling pin to pay us any attention.

"Did your mommy teach you how to spin it?" I asked Noah after I'd pressed my dough into a disc shape.

He shook his head. "Can you teach me?"

"Sure can. It's all about the rotation."

"Stop showing off," Lila said as I tossed and spun the dough in the air, catching it on the backs of my fists. But she was laughing again. It was so good to hear her laugh. So fucking incredible to make her happy instead of sad.

This was how I'd always imagined our life. Full of joy and laughter and love.

———

After Noah had begged me to tell him a bedtime story and I'd complied, Lila kicked me out of his bedroom so she could say goodnight and tuck him in. It hadn't gone unnoticed that she'd put stars on his ceiling, similar to the ones I'd put on her ceiling all those years ago. Noah slept under the constellation Orion, and I took that as a sign that she had been thinking about me. That she still remembered some of the good instead of all the bad and ugly. After her comment in the driveway the other night, I hadn't been so sure that was the case.

I picked up one of the framed photos on the bookshelves and studied it. Lila was holding Noah in her arms. He must have been a newborn. So tiny. So precious. Wrapped in a white blanket. She was smiling down at her son. Brody was standing next to her hospital bed, his smile aimed at Lila. He was looking at her like she'd put the stars in the sky. And she had. She'd given him a son. And I fucking hated him for it. Hated that he got to share something with her that I never had. Probably never would.

At the sound of her footsteps behind me, I set the photo back on the shelf.

"Do you love him?" I asked, my back turned to her.

She didn't answer right away. As if she needed to give it some thought rather than gifting me with the automatic no I was praying would come out of her mouth.

Steeling myself to hear the truth, I turned around to face her. "Do you love Brody?" I repeated.

"Not the way I loved you."

Not the way I loved you. *Loved*. Past tense. "So you do love him?"

She came to stand in front of me, her gaze drifting to the photo I'd just set back on the shelf. "I love him as a friend. As the father of my son."

"What happened? How did this happen?" All the hurt and anger I'd harbored since I'd found out she and Brody had a son together, threatened to burst out of the compartment I'd shoved it into. A place I'd refused to visit or acknowledge in the years I'd been away from her. "Why him, Lila?"

She averted her gaze and let out a breath. I wasn't sure she'd answer. Maybe she didn't feel like she owed me an explanation but fuck it, I deserved that much.

"Would you prefer I'd hooked up with some random stranger? Brody was there for me. He was my friend through it all. And the night... it was just one night. One drunken night."

"It was only one night?" Only one night and the stars had aligned. She'd gotten pregnant and she'd delivered a healthy son.

She nodded. "We were so drunk, I barely remember that night."

That son of a bitch. "You were drunk and he took advantage of you?" My voice shook with anger.

"No. It wasn't like that. He would never... God. Jude. Brody is a good guy."

Debatable.

"It was one year after you left and I was..." She shook her head. "It doesn't matter. You were gone and you weren't coming back. Brody didn't do it on purpose like you seem to think he did. The last thing he wanted was a baby. He was always on the road and he wasn't looking to get tied down. But accidents happen. And no matter what you think about him, he's a good dad. He loves Noah and he'd do anything in the world for him."

I rubbed my chest, trying to ease the pain her words caused.

"I'm sorry, Jude. I know this is hard for you to accept. But I love Noah, and I can't call him a mistake. He's the best thing in my life. He's the most important person in my life." She held my gaze, wanting to make sure the words hit home. She might as well bludgeon me with them for all the times she'd already hit me over the head with them.

"I get that. I'd expect nothing less. I always knew you'd be a good mom."

She averted her gaze so I couldn't see the effect my words had on her. Lila was strong and knew how to be tough when she needed to be. She'd suffered a lot of loss in her life and that changed people. Hardened them. But underneath the tough exterior, she was still vulnerable.

I wanted to stay. I wanted to pull her into my arms and hold her. I wanted to do a lot of things but she showed me to the door.

"You need to go." Her voice was firm and I knew this wasn't the time to push my luck.

"I want to see you again. Soon." *Like tomorrow. And the day after that. And every day that followed.*

She shook her head. "This is so like you. You turn up here after six years of radio silence and you expect everything to go your way. We're not the same people anymore. You destroyed us, Jude. You broke every single promise you ever made. And I have no idea how to forgive you for that."

I had no idea how to forgive myself either, and I sure as hell had no intention of forgiving Brody. I don't care what she said. He took advantage of the situation, of her vulnerable state. There was such a thing as being a good friend, and being there for someone without having to fuck them. But Lila and I had to start somewhere and this was as good a place as any. "We can rebuild. We can start where we are. Right here. Right now. And we can find our way back to each other."

"It's too late," she said, but her voice lacked conviction and that gave me all the hope I needed that we could turn this around.

It wasn't too late. I refused to believe that. Not now that I knew she wasn't in love with Brody and had no other man in her life. "How about being friends again," I suggested. "We can start there. Come on, Rebel. I dare you."

She rolled her eyes and tried to suppress her smile. She wanted this. I knew she did. "We're not nine years old."

I snorted. "You always accepted my dares. That didn't stop when we were nine."

"Yeah, well, I was stupid. I've wised up a lot since then."

Guess we'd see about that. "See you soon."

"What the hell is this?" My dad looked down at the plate of food my mother set in front of him. Grilled salmon and a leafy green salad. To say he looked less than enthusiastic was an understatement.

"That's your dinner," she said, taking her seat at the table.

"Where's the meat and potatoes?"

Jesse snickered as he loaded his plate with salad. He'd been put in charge of the menu planning and consulted one of his nutrition apps. Jesse was a few inches shorter than my six foot three and was all lean muscle. He needed to keep his weight down for moto, he'd told me, and had become a vegetarian a few years ago, much to my father's dismay.

My mom interrupted my father's grumbling. "You listen to me, Patrick McCallister. I have a lot of plans for us. You promised me we'd grow old together and you'd damn well better keep that promise. So from now on, I'll be cooking healthy meals. Now stop complaining and eat your dinner."

My dad stared at her. Her lips pressed into a flat line, her shoulders squared, daring him to contradict her. Finally, he nodded and reached across the table, giving her hand a squeeze. "It's good to be home, Kate."

She smiled. "Good to have you home, honey. And don't you dare scare me like that again."

He cleared his throat and picked up his fork. No more words were exchanged but the message was loud and clear. Even after all these years, my parents were still in love and couldn't imagine their lives without each other.

"I'm heading out to Cali tomorrow," Jesse said. "I won't be back until the end of August when the Nationals are over. If you need a place to crash, my apartment is available. It's nothing great. But it's yours if you want it."

I had no pride. "I'll take it."

"Cool. Bonus. It's cheap and close to Li—"

"We have plenty of room in the house," my mom interrupted. "There's no need to move out. Nobody needs to live in a garage."

Jesse laughed. "If it were up to Mom, I'd still be sleeping in my old bunk bed."

Don't I know it. I was currently staying in my childhood bedroom that hadn't changed a bit since I left. Even those stupid trophies were still on the shelves. "I'm thirty years old. I need a place of my own."

Mom looked disappointed, but she'd get over it.

"Now that we've got that out of the way," my dad said. "Fill me in on what's happening with the business."

My father ran a tight ship and kept everything so organized that it hadn't been hard to pick up where he'd left off. I told him about the site inspections and updated him on the progress of the projects he'd been contracted to complete. He grilled me for twenty minutes, and I had a ready answer for all his questions.

When I finished, he nodded as if my answers were correct. I was thirty years old, I'd been in combat zones, and hadn't lived at home since I was eighteen. But he was treating me like a teenager. Some things never changed.

"Make sure you stay on top of the sub-contractors. Mike has a tendency to slack on the job. If he thinks he can get an inch, he'll take a yard. Let him know who's in charge. We can't have that brewery project running behind schedule."

I nearly laughed. The brewery project was right on schedule and Mike was a forty-year-old man who'd been working for my dad for fifteen years. He knew his shit, worked hard, and wasn't a slacker. If anything, he was the one running the show in my father's absence. But my dad had trouble letting go of the reins. He liked to be in charge which was something I understood.

"Don't worry about it. I've got everything under control." I held his gaze until he nodded.

"I'll call my lawyer. Get him to draw up the paperwork to make you a partner."

"There's no rush."

"It's better we do it now. Get it all squared away."

I rubbed the back of my neck. I was hoping to avoid this conversation for a bit longer.

I didn't think this was the right time to tell him I had no interest in taking over his business or being a general contractor. I was planning to stay in Cypress Springs but I wouldn't be stepping into his shoes. Team Phoenix was not just a hobby for me. It was my lifeblood and I had no intention of stepping away to run my father's business.

Last week when I'd driven Gideon to the airport, he told me he could help me and Tommy get more funding for our not-for-profit. I was surprised he'd volunteered to help me, considering how much he'd always resented me. He'd also confided that it was hard following in my footsteps back in high school and he couldn't wait to get away from home. I asked him if he was happy in New York. He said he felt like he could breathe easier and be his own person and I guess I could understand that too.

"Jude," my dad prompted. "Something you're not telling me?"

What I wouldn't give to tell him the truth for a change. I glanced at my mom. She shook her head, a silent plea for me to keep my mouth shut. She knew I didn't want the business but she didn't want me to tell my dad. Not yet, anyway.

The man had just come home from the hospital after a triple bypass. The doctor told my mom he needed rest and the last thing he needed was undue stress which I knew my words would cause him. I'd tell him later.

"No. It's all good."

My mom's shoulders relaxed and she gave me a smile and mouthed *Thank you*.

The next morning I moved out of my childhood bedroom and into Jesse's one-bedroom apartment above a garage. It smelled like diesel oil. The apartment was a dump but the location was ideal. Half a mile from Lila's. It was temporary but so were all the other places I'd lived since leaving home.

It felt like I'd been homeless for so long that I didn't even know what a home should feel like anymore.

That wasn't true. I knew what home felt like. My home was not a place, it was a person. My home was Lila. Being back here made me realize that I'd never gotten over her, and I never would. I was just hoping that it wasn't too late to make things right.

I needed to win back her love, her trust, and her faith in me.

And I wouldn't give up until that happened.

CHAPTER FORTY

Jude

THE MORNING SUN HAD BURNT THROUGH THE CLOUDS AND now it was all blue skies without a cloud in sight. Plumes of orange dust kicked up behind me as my running shoes pounded the dirt road that cut through lush green fields, the terrain hilly and rugged. The same road where I'd pushed Lila to the ground and threw my body over hers to protect her. Only we weren't in any danger. There weren't insurgents shooting at us. No snipers on the roof. No IED explosions. Just a bunch of kids setting off fireworks on the Fourth of July.

And I'd lost my shit.

Sometimes I still saw the faces of Reese Madigan and the other guys from my unit who had been killed. Sometimes I'd see the faces of the civilians who had been killed. Innocent victims caught in the crossfire.

I used to see that boy's face everywhere. He was smiling, excited about his candy stash and the pens we gave him. Kicking the ball around with us. He was just a boy, no older than ten or twelve, unfortunate enough to be born in a country where a war raged in his own back yard.

But now I was better equipped to deal with the stressors and for the most part, I felt more like my old self.

As I crested the next hill, I saw a figure in the distance. Even from here, I knew it was Lila. Running toward me. My heart rate accelerated, and it had nothing to do with the exertion of running.

I sped up, erasing the distance between us.

"Hey, Hot Stuff," I said when I stopped in front of her. Her cheeks were flushed pink, a sheen of sweat on her face, her hair pulled back in a high ponytail. She looked beautiful. "Fancy meeting you here."

"Right back at you." She grinned and like a fool, I was grinning back at her. Her eyes lowered to my bare chest and she licked her lips, swallowing hard. Chuckling to myself, I used the T-shirt in my hand to wipe the sweat from my face.

"Why are you here?" I asked, my gaze lowering to the sports tank she wore with her skimpy running shorts.

"Maybe I was looking for you." My smile grew wider at her admission. "Just joking," she said with a laugh, wiping the grin right off my face. "This is still my favorite place to run."

"Must be my lucky day."

"It's good to see your smile. I've missed those dimples."

"Oh yeah?" I moved closer and brushed a stray lock of hair off her face. "What else have you missed?" I just couldn't help myself, could I?

"Kicking your ass." She cocked her hip and planted a hand on it. "How about a race?"

"Oh baby, when will you ever learn? I'm the bionic man. You don't stand a snowball's chance in hell."

"Since you're so confident, how about a wager?"

"What are you willing to lose?"

"I have everything to gain." She poked my sweaty chest. "It's you who should be worried."

I snorted. "Okay. I'm game." I closed one eye and thought about what I wanted most from her. Besides everything. "When I win, I get to take you on a date."

"A date?"

"Uh huh."

"What kind of date?"

"That's for me to decide."

She considered that for a moment. "Fine. When you lose...." She tapped her index finger against her lips, thinking. "You have to be my date for Sophie's wedding."

Her date. That sounded promising. Why the change of heart, I wondered, but didn't ask. I'd take what I could get. "Done."

"Prepare to eat my dust, Devil Dog."

"In your dreams, Rebel."

"First one to reach my front porch is the winner."

"I have everything to gain and nothing to lose," I said. "Either way, I'm a winner."

I thought I heard her say "Same here" but I couldn't be sure because she'd already taken off. I took a moment to appreciate the view of her sexy little ass, before I chased after her. And just like that, my day was looking better.

To show my appreciation, I tackled her on the front lawn where I was waiting for her.

"Why do you insist on racing me? I could beat you with a one-hundred-fifty-pound pack on my back."

"Still so cocky," she murmured as my lips met hers and her arms wrapped around my neck.

Leaning my head down, I licked the seam of her lips then grabbed the bottom lip between my teeth and bit down. That's all it took for her to let me in. Our tongues danced around and I couldn't get enough. I didn't want it to end. Too soon, she pulled away and I groaned.

"I have to take a shower." She stood up and I followed. I'd always follow.

Adjusting myself in my shorts, I pulled her into my chest. "I could help you with that. I'd make sure you're good and clean. I'd soap every inch of your body and—"

She shoved my chest—still so physical—before she sauntered away. "Bye Jude."

"You owe me a date," I called after her.

She paused in the doorway and looked over her shoulder. "You owe me an entire galaxy. I'm still waiting for you to put the stars back in the sky."

Well, damn. I guess I had my work cut out for me. Was there a chance she could still love my broken, fucked-up self? The man who had lost part of his soul to a war and his entire heart to a girl?

I couldn't help the smile that tugged at my lips. I couldn't remember the last time I'd felt this hopeful. Or this happy.

CHAPTER FORTY-ONE

Lila

"ARE YOU SURE IT'S OKAY? I SHOULD TAKE NOAH HOME
and make sure—"

"Honey. He's fine." Kate put her hands on my shoulders
and turned me toward the window. Noah was eating a bowl of
ice cream on the back porch, talking a mile a minute to Patrick.
And it struck me once again how blessed I've been to have the
McCallisters in my life. They'd all been there for me when I'd
needed them. At different times in my life. In their own special
ways, they'd filled my life with love and laughter and showed
me what it was like to be part of a big, happy, rowdy family.

"He's a happy little boy. And you know why?"

"Why?"

"Because he's being raised with love. You're a good mother." Over the years, she'd had to reassure me more times than
I'd care to admit. "Your mom would be so proud of you,
sweetie."

"I hope so."

"I know so. Now go on home and get ready for your hot date."

I laughed. "It's not a hot date. This is your son we're talking about."

Kate laughed. "You two don't have to worry about sneaking up the trellis anymore."

Oh my God. I could feel myself blushing.

"He loved you something fierce. Still does."

"I don't know... I don't know how we could possibly make this work," I admitted. "It feels like it's too late."

"It's never too late for a second chance. After everything you both went through, you deserve happiness. And maybe it will help Brody too."

"Help him? In what way?"

"I think he's just waiting for you to set him free."

Her words stunned me into silence for a few seconds. "But I never... what do you mean? He's always been free."

Kate squeezed my shoulder and gave me a little smile. "I know that but I'm not sure he does. He's always been so worried about turning out like his parents. He doesn't want to let you and Noah down."

"He's never let us down."

"Maybe he needs to hear that from you. He acts tough but he needs a lot of reassurance."

My heart was in my throat so all I could do was nod. Ever since Jude had returned, I'd been hit with all these emotions.

"Okay. Enough of this. Go home and get ready for your date. Noah will be just fine."

After I hugged and kissed Noah goodbye, I left him on the porch with Kate and Patrick and drove home to get ready for my 'hot date.'

"What are you wearing?" Sophie asked without preamble.

"I don't know." I rummaged around in my closet. "My ex-fiancé is taking me on a date. What exactly should I be wearing for that?" I tossed aside a few pairs of shorts and some tank tops then sat back on my heels, defeated. "I've got nothing."

"Wear the green dress with the open back. You look hot in that."

"That's kind of dressy. I wore that to your engagement party."

"Trust me. Wear it."

"You don't think it's too much? We're not into fancy restaurants. We're more like the barbecue and six-pack kind of couple. Chances are we'll be eating in the bed of his pickup truck."

"Classy."

"That's how we roll."

"Wear the dress anyway," she ordered.

I set the phone on my dresser and switched her over to speaker so I could get dressed.

"So how's Noah dealing with the whole dating thing?"

"We're not really dating. I mean... this is.... He's too young to understand."

"If you say so but he probably understands a lot more than you'd like to think."

She was right. He probably understood more than I did because right now I had no idea what I was doing. "Am I making a mistake?"

"It's just a date."

"Dinner with Dr. What's-His-Name, the podiatrist, was just a date."

"Goldbaum. And yeah, that was just to get you back on the horse. Like a starter date."

"Like a non-starter date. I almost fell asleep halfway through his monologue which lasted the entire dinner."

There was a knock on the door and I went into full-blown panic mode. "Oh my God. He's here. He's at the door."

"Um, call me stupid but that's kind of how it works. He knocks on the door. You answer it. Then you have angry sex and order pizza."

"We're not having... I have to go."

"Have fun."

"Thanks." I cut the call and took a deep breath. Not like I didn't know Jude. Not like I hadn't known him all my life. I was being ridiculous. I smoothed my sweaty palms over the skirt of my dress and gave myself a final look in the mirror before I went to answer the door.

"Hi." I gave him a dorky little wave.

He laughed. "Hi. You look... fucking amazing."

I smiled, happy that I'd made the effort if only to see that heated look in his eyes. "Thank you. So do you." And he did. He looked amazing in a dark blue button-down shirt and jeans.

"You ready to take off?"

"Yeah, let me grab my purse." Grabbing it off the couch, I walked over to him and he took my hand and led us to the door.

"I love this place."

"Good."

We exchanged a smile and I lifted the copper mug to my lips, laughing as Jude shuddered. I had no problem drinking my Texas Mule from copper but Jude couldn't bear the thought of it. Weird the things that bothered him.

I set down my drink and watched the sunset over the hills and acres and acres of sprawling trees from our table on the deck. The restaurant was modern rustic with soaring ceilings, timber walls, and floor to ceiling windows that opened onto the deck. Romantic. Upscale but relaxed. Not at all where I'd expected to end up for our date tonight.

"Does it remind you of anything?" Jude asked, foregoing the glass and drinking his IPA from the bottle.

I'd never been to this restaurant, so it shouldn't remind me of anything, but it did. It was almost exactly what we used to talk about when we were planning our dream house. Rustic. Modern. Timber and stone. Our own treehouse, we used to say, back when we had so many hopes and dreams. We were just kids, but so in love that anything felt possible.

"It reminds me of the house you were going to build for us." I sat back as the waiter delivered our food and after we thanked him and he was gone, I picked up the conversation again. "Is that why you chose it?"

"I just lucked out."

Knowing Jude, there had been more than luck involved in his decision. I took a bite of my Gulf Shrimp and Grits. Delicious food. Perfect spot. Jude hadn't left anything to chance. And I had no idea why that bothered me when it should have made me happy.

While we ate our dinner, we made small talk. And everything was just perfect. It really was. But only because we weren't talking about anything important.

"You look beautiful, Lila."

"You don't look too shabby yourself. You clean up nice."

He looked down at the shirt he was wearing. "I bought it at the mall." He laughed a little.

"I can't believe you went to the mall. Were you okay?" I asked, remembering how hard it was for him to go to crowded places.

"I was fine."

"I had my own wardrobe crisis until Sophie told me what to wear and saved the day."

"It doesn't matter what you wear. All I ever see is you."

My gaze wandered to the scenery but I wasn't seeing it because it was the same for me. I hated that he still had this power over me. I hated that I still loved him the way I did. I hated him for leaving me.

"Hey. Lila. Look at me."

I reached for my ginger-infused cocktail and took a fortifying drink before I met his eyes across the table. "Why do you always do this to me?"

"What do I do to you?"

"You bring me to a beautiful place that looks like my dream home. The home we planned together. You make me forget for a little while. You make me... want something I can't have anymore."

"Who says we can't start over? Who says we can't have that life we dreamed about?"

I shook my head.

"Do you still love me?"

"That was never a question. I have *always* loved you." *It was you who stopped loving me.*

"Then I don't see what the problem is."

I laughed bitterly. "Seriously, Jude? After you left, I kept waiting for you to come back. Even just a phone call or a message. Anything to let me know you were still... out there, thinking of me. I had no way to contact you. You just disappeared and I didn't know where you were or if you were okay. I kept imagining the worst case scenario."

"Not a single day went by that I didn't think of you."

"Thoughts without action mean nothing. You're the one who always told me that. I get that you were going through a horrible time. I get that your head was in a bad place. But what I'll never understand is why you felt like you had to go through all that on your own. You broke your promise. And you know what? After all the sadness wore off, I was so angry at you. I hated you for leaving me. I hated you for enlisting. And that was how I got through the bad times. By being angry with you. By blaming you. And now you come back here... and you expect me to put my faith in you again?"

His jaw clenched and he looked out over the rolling hills, the beautiful scenery ruined by our ugly truths. "I'm not the same man I was when I left you."

"I can see that. But I'm not the same girl you left behind. I need to be there for Noah. I need to stay strong for him. And if I let you in again and it doesn't work out, it would destroy me. I can't go through that kind of pain again."

"So that's it?" His eyes got hard like he had any right to question me. "You're just giving up."

"This isn't giving up. It's self-preservation. How many times can one heart break, Jude?" I tossed my napkin on the table and pushed back my chair, walking out on him and leaving him alone at the table.

CHAPTER FORTY-TWO

Jude

HOW MANY TIMES CAN ONE HEART BREAK, JUDE?

That was the question that kept running through my head as I drove. I could have told her that hearts don't break. They were made of muscle. Left neglected and malnourished, muscles atrophied. But you could build them up by putting in the work, and you could make them stronger. That was what we had to do. Feed our hearts. Make them stronger.

Our love story had played out like a fucking tragedy. Redemption never came easy but I was up to the task.

Lila was silent, her posture rigid, the tension thick. But even so, I kept glancing at her. She looked so fucking beautiful in that green dress that matched her eyes, shoulders bare, and her hair falling in waves down her back. I wanted to fist my hand in it, drag her across the center console and crush my lips against hers. Slide my hand up her thigh and sink my fingers inside her. I wanted to taste her sweetness and see if it was everything I remembered. I knew it would be.

I needed to stop. This was no time to have sex on the brain, but fuck, it had been so long.

"Where are we going? This isn't the way home."

Ignoring her protests, I kept driving to the tune of The Weeknd's "Earned It." Message received. I had to earn the right to touch her again.

"Jude, just take me home."

Not like this. No fucking way. "Our date isn't over yet."

She slumped in her seat and crossed her arms over her chest, staring out the windshield as we barreled down the expressway, Austin bound. The playlist I'd made especially for her was the soundtrack of our ups and downs over the past two decades. Twenty years of love and loss, joy and pain and she was quick to pick up on that.

"You chose all this music on purpose," she accused when the Black Keys song started playing.

"Everything I do has a purpose. *You* are my purpose."

"*You* are annoying."

I laughed. She kept trying to tell me that we've changed, and in a lot of ways we had, but we were still Jude and Lila. She was still my favorite person. My favorite everything. She still loved to argue with me and fight me every step of the way, and I could still read her like a book.

Thirty minutes later, we arrived at our destination and it took me another ten minutes to find parking and practically drag her out of the car and to the entrance of the Science and Technology Museum.

"Why are we here?" she asked.

I would have thought it was obvious considering I'd just purchased two tickets for the nine o'clock star show, but apparently not. "I owe you a galaxy."

I ushered her inside the Moon Dome and we found two

reclining seats side by side that would give us a view of the entire dome overhead.

Ten... fifteen minutes into the star show, as we journeyed to the center of the Milky Way, I turned my head toward her. She met my gaze under a sky reeling with millions of stars.

"Jude," she whispered.

"Lila."

She smiled and it rivaled the stars for its brightness.

"Why do you do this to me?" Her voice was soft and this time there was no accusation in it. Without answering, I reached for her hand and she let me take it. For now, that was enough. Even though we were surrounded by people, this felt intimate. Like we were the only two people in the planetarium. I sat back and enjoyed the show, her hand clasped in mine until the very end.

When it was over, she kissed me, just a sweet little kiss that made me feel like a teenager again and I didn't push for more. I wanted her to call the shots. I wanted her to want me.

On the drive home, I drove with one hand on the wheel and the other on her thigh like it belonged there. Because it did. Even after all these years, she was still mine. As far as I was concerned, she always would be.

Like a gentleman, I walked her to her front door and waited for her to unlock it.

"What are you doing?" she asked when she got inside and turned to look at me still standing on her porch.

I tucked my hands in my pockets to prevent myself from grabbing the back of her head and crushing my mouth against hers while I slammed her against the nearest wall and made quick work of burying myself inside her. Just thinking about it and I was already at half-mast. Being a gentleman did not come without its challenges. "Waiting for an invitation."

"Damn you." She grabbed my hand and yanked me inside, slamming the door shut behind me. "I hate you. I really do."

"But you love what my hands and tongue and gigantic—"

She clapped a hand over my mouth to stop the words. "Shut up and kiss me."

Don't mind if I do. And then I was on her. Lifting her up, her legs wrapped around my waist, and the skirt of her dress bunched around her hips. I slammed her back against the wall by the front door and her lips parted on a gasp. I traced them with my tongue before sliding inside and kissed her like I was a drowning man and she was the air I needed to breathe. She clung to me, her hands squeezing my shoulders, legs tightly cinched around me, like she was afraid I'd disappear if she didn't hang on.

My lips found her neck and I rocked my hips, grinding against her. "I could fuck you right here against the wall."

"Do it," she said, a challenge in her voice that I knew so well.

Instead, I turned us around and headed for her bedroom, feeling my way in the dark while her hands gripped my hair and her teeth grazed their way down my neck. Ravenous. Greedy. Ready to devour me. I heard her shoes hit the hardwood floor with a thud in the hallway before I kicked open the door to her bedroom and laid her down on top of her bed. "Are you sure?"

In response, she lifted her dress over her head and threw it off to the side, leaving her only in a strip of black lace, affording me a view of her naked body. Her hips were fuller, breasts larger but no less perfect than the last time I'd seen her.

"Jesus, Rebel."

Hooking my fingers in the sides of her lacy underwear, I pulled them down her legs and tossed them aside. When I leaned down to suck her nipple, I saw the tattoo. A flower inked on her ribs just below her left breast. My fingers brushed over her skin, coasting up to the edge of one of the delicate petals. "When did you do this?"

"On December twenty-second. Six months after you left me."

One year after we lost the baby. An anniversary she'd chosen to commemorate by having her skin permanently marked.

"What does it mean?" I asked, lightly tracing the design with my fingertips, causing goosebumps to raise on her skin. I used to know every inch of her silky soft skin. Had touched it, kissed it, licked it, but now her body was uncharted territory, something I had to rediscover and reacquaint myself with.

"It's a lotus flower. It stands for peace, love, and eternity." She pushed herself up on her elbows and gnawed on her lip while I contemplated the meaning behind the tattoo. "Do you like it?"

"I love it." *And I love you.*

She deserved to be worshiped. To be loved wholly and unequivocally. I dropped to my knees in front of her and ran my hands up her thighs, my lips trailing to the crease of her leg. Keeping her legs pinned to the bed with my arms, I parted her lips with my thumbs, exposing the pink that glistened with her arousal.

"Tell me you want me, Lila." I lifted my head and met her gaze in the silvery moonlight, seeking her permission.

"Yes," she breathed, writhing below me. "I want you. I want this."

With my eyes locked on hers, I dipped forward to take the first taste of something I'd been denied for too long, of something that had always been mine. One shallow lick brushed her clit, and as soon as my tongue made contact, she bucked her hips against my face and moaned.

"More," she said.

Putting a hand on each knee, I pressed them flat to the bed so she was wide open to me, completely exposed. Then I sucked and bit her swollen clit, and flattened my tongue, licking her tight bundle of nerves to her even tighter hole and everywhere in between. Slit to crack. Fuck. She was so warm and soft and wet, and she tasted every bit as sweet as I remembered.

"Oh my God," she panted, fisting the sheets in her hands, her thighs trembling.

I fucked her with my mouth, and she screamed out my name, the sound shooting straight to my throbbing cock as she clenched around my tongue and dug her fingers into my scalp. I gave her a few shallow licks with my flattened tongue to bring her down from the orgasm then kissed the inside of her thigh.

She pushed herself up on the mattress and reached for me, her fingers fumbling with the buttons of my jeans while I discarded my shirt on the floor.

"Dammit. When are you going to buy jeans with zippers?"

Pushing her hand away, I laughed and did it myself, shoving my jeans and boxer briefs down with my hands while she used her feet to assist me, still such an impatient one.

I crawled up her body and palmed her tits, guiding one rosy peak into my mouth and sucking on it. Her back arched off the mattress and she grabbed the back of my head, digging her fingers into my hair. I moved up to her mouth and kissed her long and hard, letting her taste herself on my tongue while I settled between her thighs, sliding my dick between her slick folds as she grinded against me.

"You're so wet," I said hoarsely, reveling in the feel of my cock cradled in her pussy again after all these years. "It would be so easy to slip inside you."

"Do it." Wrapping her legs around my back, she angled her

hips just right, and I nudged my tip against her entrance. I wasn't even inside her yet, just the tip, but it was heaven.

"What are you waiting for?" she taunted. "Give it to me. Now."

"So greedy." But I gave her what she asked for. In one sharp move, I thrust into her, causing her to cry out, and Jesus, she was so perfect I nearly wept like a fucking baby.

How had I lived without *this*, without *her*, for all these years? *How?*

Bringing my fingers down to where we were connected, I rubbed her clit until she was writhing beneath me, begging for more, harder, faster. I stroked in and out, harder, deeper, filling her up, spurred on by the tiny whimpers and moans and the little sounds she made when I fucked her.

I pulled back to watch her face as I drove in and out of her, and I could have come on this sight alone. Full lips slightly parted, porcelain skin bathed in moonlight and waves of dark hair tumbling around her shoulders, she was my every fantasy. Over the years, whenever I'd wanted to torture myself, I envisioned her like this. How many lonely nights had I jerked off to the vision of Lila in my head? Too many to count.

Her full tits bounced as she met me thrust for thrust, her head thrown back, exposing the column of her neck that begged to be marked by my lips and teeth.

Mine.

I'd wanted to take my time with her but I couldn't hold back. I needed this. I needed her. When her legs started shaking, I pulled her close and tucked my hand under her lower back, burying my face in her neck. I breathed her in. It was a scent I remembered from so long ago. Spring rain and honeysuckle. The scent of Lila.

"Fall apart for me, Lila," I whispered in her ear, dragging

my teeth down to her earlobe and biting down before I sucked on it to ease the sting.

"Oh my God. Yes, Jude," she chanted into my ear as she clenched around my cock, milking an orgasm out of me that seemed to go on forever. I drove into her one more time, burying myself to the hilt as I spilled inside her and afterward, she wrapped her arms around my neck and held me close, skin against skin, limbs tangled and our bodies damp with sweat. I dipped my head and kissed her mouth. I never wanted to leave. I wanted to stay here in her arms, in her bed, inside her until the stars died and were reborn.

Finding my way back to Lila, being with her again like this, was worth a thousand deaths.

I was Odysseus. *Her* Odysseus. After all these long years of being shipwrecked, of fighting monsters and demons and losing battles, I had finally found my way home again. Only this time, I was home to stay.

"It's been so long," she said softly.

"Too long," I agreed. Framing her face in my hands, I kissed her lips.

I love you. Only you.

CHAPTER FORTY-THREE

Lila

"Let me go," I said, laughing, the Nerf football still clutched to my chest. "I have to check on the dinner."

"The longer it simmers, the better it tastes. Sloooow burn, baby." He gave me a playful smack on the ass before he released me but not before wrestling the football out of my hands and passing it to Noah who streaked across the back yard and tossed the ball through the tire swing, shouting "Touchdown!"

I was laughing as I crossed the back yard and went inside the kitchen, inhaling the smoky, spicy aroma of chili. Jude made it and it had been simmering in the slow cooker since this morning. Chili was his specialty, and I was still trying to coax his secret recipe out of him.

In the back of my mind, alarm bells were ringing. This was bad. We were getting too comfortable. It had been a week since our date, and we'd spent all our evenings together. We ate dinner together, took turns reading bedtime stories to Noah. I hadn't let him sleep over since our date but after Noah was asleep, we hung out. Watching movies, fucking, falling in love all over again.

So quickly, we'd fallen into a routine. Today was Saturday and I had to work, so Jude had spent the day with Noah.

While I shredded cheddar cheese and chopped green onions for the toppings, I watched him playing football with Noah. Jude was so good with him. I always knew he'd be a good dad.

Oh, my God, what was I thinking? He wasn't Noah's dad. I needed to stop picturing us as a family.

Jude's cell phone on the counter buzzed, dragging my attention away from the window.

Jude had this habit of emptying his pockets when he came home. *Home.* Not that this was home, but he'd been spending a lot of time here and he'd gotten comfortable. Reverted to old habits. So his wallet, keys and cell phone were sitting on the kitchen counter.

His cell phone buzzed with another message and curiosity got the best of me. Picking up his phone, I read the messages.

Victor: Well, fuck man, where you been? Bianca's been asking about you.

Victor: You still fighting? I've got something for you. Shitload of money riding on it. Call me.

I stared at the screen and waited for another text but none came through. What did that mean? Who was Bianca? And what kind of fighting was this guy talking about? It struck me how little I really knew about Jude's life.

We hadn't even talked about what he'd been doing for the past six years.

I glanced out the window again then back at the screen. I tried to unlock it, using different combinations of the password he used to use. My birthday. I wasn't sure why I felt so bereft that he no longer used that as his password. I shouldn't even be trying to break the code and read his messages. I set it down and picked up his wallet, turning it over in my hand. I'd given it to him for Christmas one year. The leather was cracked and worn now. I opened it, not entirely sure what I was searching for. Clues to the man I didn't know anymore, I guess.

I eased the photos out of one of the slots and flipped through them. They were all of me. God, how had I ever been that young, I thought as I stared at my senior year photo. He'd been carrying these snapshots around for years. Something fluttered to the floor and I leaned down to pick it up. It was folded into a small square and even as I held it in my hand, I knew what it was. I unfolded it and set it on the counter, smoothing my hand over the creases. As if I needed another painful reminder.

A vise squeezed my heart and I couldn't get enough air in my lungs. I sagged against the counter and closed my eyes, the photo taking me back to a place and time I'd tried to forget.

"Holy shit. That's our baby's heartbeat," Jude said in awe, like he couldn't quite believe it.

"It certainly is," the doctor said with a smile.

Jude squeezed my hand, dragging my attention away from our baby on the monitor to his face. "I love you."

I smiled through my tears and pushed aside my worries. He loved me and I loved him, and we could get through this rough patch. Together. "I love you more."

We were going to be okay. This baby would give him a reason to live. Something to fight for.

"I won't let you down, Rebel," he said as we left the doctor's office, his arm slung across my shoulders.

Before I climbed into the passenger seat of his truck, he framed my face with his hands and pressed a soft kiss on my lips.

"I promise I'll be there for you every step of the way. I promise I'll be better. For you. For our baby. We're going to be a family."

The oven timer went off, dragging me back to the present. With shaky hands, I tucked the photos back into his wallet, returning everything to the place where I found them. Taking a few calming breaths, I grabbed the oven mitts and took the cornbread out of the oven.

Then I called Jude and Noah in for dinner, and I tried to pretend that everything was okay. That another little piece of my heart hadn't just been ripped out.

How much could two people be tested? I'd gone to hell and back with this man and here we were, trying to pick up all the broken pieces and put them back together again.

Unaware of my inner turmoil, he smiled at me across the island as we ate our dinner. And oh God, that smile was so beautiful it made my heart hurt. *He* made my heart hurt. I'd been chasing his ghost for so long that some days I had to pinch myself to make sure this wasn't all just a dream. He was here. Solid and strong and capable of carrying the weight of the world on his broad shoulders again.

Noah was asleep and Jude and I were lounging on the sofa watching a movie but all I could think about were those text messages and the picture I found in his wallet. The one he'd been carrying around with him for six and a half years. The night I'd miscarried I found the presents he'd left under the tree and for some crazy reason I'd opened them. And it had killed me that he'd gone out and bought presents for a baby that would never be born. Considering that he hadn't been there for me when I needed him, I hadn't known what to make of that.

I'd been devastated and sad and so lonely and a big part of

me really had hated him for everything he'd put us through. But I remember looking at the baby presents and picturing this muscle-bound, tough-looking guy buying a downy soft, pristine white baby blanket decorated with yellow stars. And I pictured him in the bookstore buying "Goodnight, Moon." It had hurt so much to think about him doing that. I'd had no idea how to reconcile the man who sat outside the door waiting to be let in with the man who would do something so heartbreakingly sweet. That was the thing about Jude.

The good outweighed the bad, and now the scales were tipping in his favor again. But there was still so much I didn't know about him.

"I saw the texts on your phone," I said casually, my eyes on Iron Man and not on him. His feet were propped on the coffee table, my bare feet in his lap, his magic hands massaging them.

"You read my texts?" He sounded more surprised than angry. Like he couldn't imagine me snooping around and reading his messages. I guess he never realized how often I did it when we lived together. Or how I'd turned our apartment upside down, searching for the drugs he hid and the bottles of whiskey stashed in drawers and ceiling vents.

In those days, Jude was such a skilled liar. He was capable of looking me in the eye and swearing on his life that he wasn't doing drugs anymore. But what he'd neglected to tell me was that he'd stopped believing his life was worth living. One time I'd asked him to swear on *my* life. Unable to do it, he'd just walked away.

"Who's Bianca?" I asked. I was still a jealous lover.

"She's..." He winced and I knew. Damn him. "Someone I used to know."

"You slept with her, didn't you?"

He nodded and I silently cursed him for being so damn

honest. Would it have killed him to lie? I tried to pull my feet out of his lap but he grabbed my ankles and held them in place.

"Did you love her?" I rubbed my foot against his crotch, ready to kick him if necessary.

He laughed, knowing what I was thinking and kept a firm hold on my feet to protect himself. "No. I've only ever loved one woman in my life."

Slightly appeased by his response, my shoulders relaxed and his crown jewels were safe. For now. It was stupid to get jealous. Stupid to try to envision what Bianca might have looked like or what he'd been like with her. But that didn't stop me from doing it.

"Stop thinking about it. It meant nothing."

Yeah, yeah, just sex. Apparently guys could separate the emotional from the physical but I had no idea how that was possible.

But I still had questions. "What kind of fighting was that Victor guy talking about?"

He hesitated a moment and flexed his hand, studying his scarred knuckles as if they held the answer to my question. I hadn't remembered those scars and I hated that too. That he had scars I knew nothing about. Just like he had a life I couldn't even imagine. "Bare Knuckle boxing."

My jaw dropped. Shock was replaced with anger. I shoved his thigh with my foot. "What is wrong with you? You can't do shit like that with your head injury. What if... God, Jude. What if you'd gotten hit in the head?"

He shrugged. "I got hit in the head plenty of times. Didn't knock any sense into me." He was trying to joke about this, but I found no humor in it.

"It's not even legal, is it?"

"It was unsanctioned."

"So, like, some kind of underground fighting? Like Fight Club?"

He huffed out a laugh. "Not quite."

"But you fought for money?"

He nodded. "Yeah."

"Why? Why would you do that?" I shook my head, trying to understand but I couldn't. "That's just... it doesn't sound like you at all. What happened to you, Jude?"

"I was fucked-up, baby. I wanted to do anything I could to get out of my own head."

"How do I reconcile all these different people? It's like I only know a few different sides of you but not all of them. There was the boy I knew. My best friend. And then the love of my life. My... everything. You were my everything."

"And you were mine."

I pulled my feet out of his lap and tucked them underneath me. He frowned, unhappy that I'd distanced myself. Before I could scoot away, he scooped me up off the sofa and pulled me into his lap. "Stay," he said, his arm tightening around me to lock me in place like he was afraid I'd make a run for it.

I traced his squared jawline with my fingertips. He grabbed my fingers and guided them to his mouth, sucking on them while his hand coasted down my thigh. "Why do you still carry that ultrasound picture in your wallet?"

"You went through my wallet too?"

I shrugged, no apology in my voice when I answered. "I was looking for clues. I don't know who you are. Why do you keep that photo?"

"I guess it was another reminder of everything I put you through." He stroked my hair so gently it hurt. "Of how much I'd failed you. It's one of the many reasons I left and the reason I stayed away for so long."

Giving up all pretenses of watching the movie, I buried my

face in the crook of his neck and placed my palm over his beating heart. How could this man with his strong arms and broad shoulders and a heart the size of Texas have failed me? But he had.

"You said you came back. Why didn't you talk to me?"

"It was about eighteen months after I left you. It was right before Christmas." I would have been six months pregnant with Noah. "By chance I saw you coming out of that bakery you like and you were carrying shopping bags. You were with Sophie. And I sat in my truck and watched you through the windshield and I told myself, 'If she sees me, I'll go and talk to her. If she looks my way, if she gives me a sign...' Then you guided Sophie's hand to your stomach. Your very pregnant stomach. For some reason, I hadn't noticed it. I guess it was because of the dress you were wearing. You had a denim jacket over it."

I remember that day. I was wearing a dark blue maxi dress under a fleece-lined denim jacket. Sophie and I had been shopping for baby clothes.

"And you smiled. It was the same smile you used to give me when I made you happy. But I couldn't remember seeing you smile like that in so long. Not even when we were at the ultrasound. Your smile had been more worried than joyful. Like you knew, somehow, that something would go wrong."

Oh, my heart. I couldn't bear the thought of Jude sitting in his truck, having to witness my happiness when he'd played no part in it.

"And it was that smile that made me leave you again. Because you looked happy. You'd moved on. You did what I'd hoped you would. You found happiness without me. And it hurt so fucking much and I wanted to hunt down the man who had claimed you and ask him if he knew how fucking lucky he was. So I drove away and I told myself I could live without you. I told myself I'd done the right thing by leaving."

My eyes drifted shut, trying to block out the thought of what could have been. If I hadn't been pregnant with Noah. If only he'd come back sooner. So many what-ifs. But you couldn't think like that. I couldn't imagine a world without Noah and never wanted to.

Jude took my hand in his and entwined our fingers. I took a deep breath and inhaled his scent, breathing him in.

I knew there was a lot more to this story. A lot he wasn't telling me. Jude wouldn't have taken it as well as he was pretending he had.

"What happened after that?" I asked, mentally preparing myself to hear the answer.

He winced. I squeezed his hand, encouraging him to continue. "Guess I wasn't doing as well as I thought." He laughed like it was a joke but I couldn't join in. He pulled his hand away and scrubbed it over his face.

I lifted my head from his shoulder. "Jude. What happened?"

He shook his head. "A lot of shit happened, Rebel. A lot of shit that you don't need to hear about."

I wasn't letting him off that easy. "If there's even the slightest bit of hope for us, we have to be honest."

He stroked his jaw then nodded, acknowledging that I was right. "I don't remember it that well. I was at a party in Oceanside." He side-eyed me. "There was a shitload of drugs there. Let's just say I had a bad trip. I ended up in the psych ward at the VA hospital in San Diego. And in some ways, it was the best thing that could have happened. I started getting counseling. It helped. A few months later, Tommy Delgado... do you remember him?"

"Of course. I sent him care packages."

"Yeah, you did." He smiled at the memory. Jude used to tell me that I sent the best care packages and all his Marine buddies were jealous, so I started sending them care packages too.

"Anyway, me and Tommy were hanging out one day and we heard on the news that a major earthquake had struck Nepal, near Kathmandu. The damage was catastrophic. Thousands of lives lost and thousands injured. And we just looked at each and said, 'Let's go.'"

"Just like that? You decided to go to Nepal?"

He laughed. "Yeah. Just like that. We gathered a team of eight former Marines. Three of whom were medics. And we went in on a wing and a prayer."

Now, *this* sounded exactly like something Jude would do. "And what did you do there?" I asked, fascinated by his story.

"Anything we could to help. We formed a search and rescue team. Dug people out of the rubble who were still trapped. Transported people to safety. Then we stayed and helped clear the debris. When we came home we decided to set up a veteran-led not-for-profit disaster relief organization. We lead teams of volunteers into towns and cities across America that were hit by natural disasters."

"Wow. That's amazing. And that's what helped you through the bad times?" I guessed. Because I could see Jude doing that. I could imagine him leading a team and going into situations that most people would run from.

"Yeah. Pretty sure that trip to Nepal saved my life. I feel like it gave my life meaning and purpose again."

A wave of sadness washed over me. Why wasn't I enough? Why did he have to travel to the ends of the earth to find his meaning and purpose? Then he finished his story and the pieces fit into place.

"Right before I left for Nepal, I called my mom. It was the first time I'd called home in two years. I told her that I saw you a few months before and I asked about the baby. I asked if you were both okay. I guess she thought I knew... I don't know. But that's how I found out it was Brody's."

"Did that mess you up?"

He snorted. "What do you think?"

I'd take that as a yes.

"I tried not to think about it.. Because it just hurt too fucking much."

In Jude's mind, what Brody and I had done was a huge betrayal. The morning after, when I'd woken up with Brody, I'd felt so guilty. I think he did too but neither of us ever mentioned that night again. "And now? How are you doing with it?"

"I'm learning to accept it," Jude said, and that was about as much as anyone could expect.

"I just want you to know... the night I was with Brody..."

"I don't want to hear—"

"No. Please. Just listen." His jaw clenched but he nodded. "We spent the whole evening talking about you. And we were both so sad and so angry, you know? We got so drunk, Jude. And he told me..." I stopped and took a deep breath. "He told me what you did for him in Odessa. He told me what happened to him when he was in foster care."

"He told you?" Jude asked in surprise.

I nodded. "I know it was only because he was so drunk but he wanted me to know that you were there for him when he needed you. And what happened between me and Brody... that night... We were just two people who had been best friends for a long, long time. Falling down drunk and trying to comfort each other. Because we both lost you. And we both loved you so much. When I found out I was pregnant, I cried."

"Why did you cry?"

"Because you're the one who left me. But I knew I'd just

closed the door to any possibility that you'd ever come back. I knew that when you found out, if you ever did, that would truly be the end for us. And up until then, I'd still been holding out the hope that you would change your mind and that you'd turn up one day and beg me to take you back."

He repositioned me so I was straddling him and wrapped his hand around the back of my head, pulling me toward him. Our lips collided and he kissed me hard. "And here I am, doing just that," he murmured. "Begging you to take me back." He kissed the corner of my mouth. "Begging you to love my fucked-up self." Fisting my hair, he yanked it, exposing the column of my neck, his mouth moving down it, teeth grazing my collarbone.

I squeezed his shoulders and rocked my hips, grinding against his hard length as his hand found my breast, caressing it.

God, this man could make me lose my mind for him.

"You really think... you really believe we can do this?" I panted. "That we can make it work this time?"

"I wouldn't be here if I didn't." He made quick work of whipping off my T-shirt and helping me out of my cotton shorts. Not even bothering to strip off his own clothes, he unbuttoned his jeans and I pushed down the waistband of his boxer briefs, guiding his tip to my entrance.

"I've missed you so fucking much," he said as I sank down on him until I was fully seated.

"Brody will be back next week. If you want to be in my life and Noah's life, you'll have to find a way to make peace with him."

"Fuck. That works better than a cold shower."

I laughed and rolled my hips, eliciting a groan from him. "Yet somehow, you're still hard."

"For you," he murmured as his lips met mine again and his hands gripped my hips.

"I'm serious. You and Brody—"

"Stop mentioning his name," he growled. I pursed my lips and held his gaze until he sighed and then he nodded. "Fine. I'll make peace with Brody. Now can we finish what we started?"

"Mommy! I'm thirsty!"

With a groan of frustration, Jude's head hit the back of the sofa as I climbed off him and scrambled to get dressed.

"I'm coming," I yelled.

"If only that were true," Jude muttered.

Ha! That would teach him to fuck girls called Bianca.

CHAPTER FORTY-FOUR

Jude

Fuck. That's not right. When in doubt, Google it.

"Mommy can do it," Noah said. "Mommy knows how to do everything."

Pretty sure my man card would be revoked if I didn't get this right. "She does. But I've got this." Sliding my phone back into my pocket, I cracked my knuckles and rolled out my shoulders. "One more try."

He sighed. "Okay."

I untied the bow tie and started over. This time it looked halfway decent. I wet a comb and ran it through his hair then held him at arms-length. "You look handsome, slugger."

He grinned. I snapped a photo and sent it to Lila. Her response was immediate.

Lila: My baby. Why does he look so grown up? My heart can't handle it.

I bumped my fist against Noah's. "You ready to go?"

He nodded.

"Everything okay back there?" I asked him as we drove to Sadler's Creek Vineyard. The last time I saw Lila's friend, Sophie, I was coked up and drunk off my ass. I was surprised she'd even consider letting me attend her wedding.

When Noah didn't answer, I eyed him in the rearview mirror. He'd been quiet for the entire drive which wasn't like him. The kid was usually talking my ear off.

"What's wrong?" I asked. He was staring out his window, his face troubled.

"Are you my new daddy now?"

Well, shit, I hadn't seen that one coming. And I'd be damned if I didn't wish I could say yes. "No. Your daddy will always be your daddy. He's coming home tomorrow."

Happy day. I couldn't wait. But I kept my feelings to myself. This wasn't about me.

"You kissed my mommy."

"Yeah, I did. Is that okay with you?"

No answer. We were almost at the vineyard, so I kept driving. I swung a left, pulled up to the valet and put the car in park. No expense had been spared for this wedding.

After exiting the car, I handed the keys to the attendant. I opened the back door, but before I unbuckled Noah's seat belt, I probed him for answers. "Are you upset that I kissed your mommy?"

He shrugged, not looking at me. "Noah. Look at me."

"No." He kicked the seat with the heels of his feet. "I want out."

I rubbed the back of my neck and tried to figure out what to say to him. He was too young to understand the craziness of this situation and I didn't want to put him in the middle of it. I wasn't his father. I was just his uncle who also happened to be the man who loved his mother. Was it my place to tell him what the score was?

"Does it make you mad when I kiss your mommy?" I asked, trying a different tactic.

He shook his head. Relieved that it didn't make him angry, I forged on.

"How does it make you feel?" I sounded like a shrink, and fuck if I didn't hate that question. Noah obviously felt the same way. He scowled at me. How could I expect a four-year-old to have all the answers when I didn't have them either?

"I love your mom. I'd never do anything to hurt her." Lies. But that was all in the past. "And I'd never do anything to hurt you, okay?"

He relented a bit, like he was listening and absorbing the information. Processing it in his head and trying to make sense of it.

"Your dad will always be there for you," I assured him. "That won't ever change. But your mom needs friends of her own too. And I'm her... special friend." *Special friend?* I sounded like a douche. "So what do you say? Can we have fun at this party?"

He nodded and then he grinned and I let out a sigh of relief as I unclipped his seat belt. Then I texted Lila to let her know we'd arrived and we were standing outside the stone, terracotta-roofed winery that looked like a Tuscan villa.

I hadn't seen Lila since six o'clock this morning when she left for work. She and Christy had designed all the floral arrangements for the weddings so the last time I saw her, nine hours ago, she was wearing jeans, a T-shirt, and no makeup, her hair in one of those messy buns.

But now... fuck me. She wore her hair half up, half down, waves falling over her bare shoulders. Her dress was midnight blue and strapless with a full skirt that stopped just below her knee. But damn, those shoes. Black strappy high-heeled sandals with thick ribbons that tied around her ankle. I wanted to untie them with my teeth.

When she spotted us, she paused on the verandah and put her hand over her mouth as I led Noah up the stairs to meet her.

"Oh my God, you look so... you both look... you're gorgeous." Her smile was aimed at both of us.

"And you look so fu-udging beautiful." Good save. Remembering Noah, I'd caught myself just in time.

A laugh burst out of her. "Fudging beautiful?"

"Uh huh. It's the sweeter version of ducking beautiful."

"You look ducking beautiful, Mommy," Noah piped up.

I laughed.

"Thank you, honey. But let's not say ducking."

"Okay." He paused a beat. "You look fudging beautiful."

That made me laugh harder. Lila elbowed me in the ribs. "Stop."

CHAPTER FORTY-FIVE

Lila

"LET'S SAY OUR GOODBYES." I GRABBED JUDE'S HAND. "WE
need to get Noah and tell him it's time to go."

"No, we don't."

"Yes, we do. We don't have to stay for this."

"We're staying."

"Seriously, Jude. It's been an amazing time. I don't want to
ruin it." His jaw clenched. Clearly, I'd hit a nerve, but I wanted
to end on a high note and I didn't want to subject him to a firework display. "Let's get Noah and—"

"He's looking forward to this. It's all he's been talking
about. We're not going to disappoint him."

"Are you going to be okay though?"

"I'll be fine."

"Are you sure?"

"I'm okay."

"You don't have to do this."

"Lila. Stop. Noah wants to see the fireworks. We're doing this."

"You have nothing to prove to me."

He exhaled a frustrated breath. I was annoying him with my protests but I wanted him to be absolutely sure that this was something he could handle. He didn't have to be subjected to undue stress.

"I have a lot to prove, but this isn't one of them. I can mentally prepare myself for a firework display."

I hated that a firework display was something he had to mentally prepare himself for. That he had to work this hard. But at the same time, I admired his strength and all the hard work he'd done to get to this place.

So we stayed for the fireworks.

He wrapped his arms around me from behind and I leaned back against his solid chest, felt the strength in his arms and my heartbeat kicked up a notch. I didn't know how hard it was for him to do this or how much he wished he could be anywhere but here. But he did it.

When I tipped my head back to look at him, his eyes met mine, the fireworks reflected on his face highlighted the sheen of sweat. But still, he smiled and I returned the smile.

I looked over at Noah who was sitting with all the other kids in the open field, his face rapt as the fireworks exploded, lighting up the dark sky. As if he could sense us watching him, Noah dragged his attention away from the fireworks and gave us a big smile. "These are cool. Right, Uncle Jude?"

"So cool. Best thing ever."

"Yeah." Smile still firmly in place, Noah focused on the fireworks again, and a part of me wished that he could stay so young and innocent forever. That he'd never know the pain of heartbreak or the effects of war or have to mourn the death of a loved one. But that wasn't how life worked.

Noah was finally asleep and fingers crossed he was out for the count. Closing his door softly, I padded down the hallway in my bare feet, the skirt of my dress swishing against my thighs. Exhausted, I flopped onto the bed next to Jude who was lying on his back, staring at the ceiling. He was still wearing his dress shirt untucked and pants, the jacket of his tux hanging on my closet door.

"This feels like prom night," I said, rolling onto my side and propping my head on my hand.

He laughed a little. "On prom night, we barely got through the door before we were ripping each other's clothes off."

"You're right. We're overdressed."

"We were supposed to be married with four kids by now." He sounded so sad that it ripped my heart in two.

"We can't think about what could have been."

"But you do, don't you? You think about it. I never thought I'd be that guy, Rebel. I used to think that I was too strong to let something fuck with my head like that. It was something that happened to other guys, not me. And when I look back at that time, I still can't believe it was me."

I placed my hand over his heart. "It wasn't you. It was someone else. It wasn't *my* Jude."

"It was me, baby. And I'd give anything to take back all the pain and suffering I put you through."

"And I'd give anything to take away all the pain and suffering you went through. But I think... you did what you set out to do, Jude. And I was so proud of you. The few. The proud. The Marines. Semper Fi. You were my hero."

"Until I became a monster."

"Not a monster. Not a god. A mere mortal, just like the rest of us. You tried so hard but you didn't have the right support and I just wish... I wish we could have found you the help you needed. I wish love had been enough to heal you."

"Nobody could have loved me better. You're my once in a lifetime."

"And you're mine. Why does everything have to be so hard for us?"

"I don't know, baby. I guess that's just how we are. The bull and the lion."

"You're my Odysseus."

"You're my Penelope."

"So why does it still feel like you haven't found your way home yet? Why am I so scared that you aren't here to stay?"

"I don't know. What more can I do to prove it to you?"

I didn't have an answer.

"Let me show you," he said. "Let me show you what coming home feels like."

Warmth radiated from his touch and left a trail of heat in its wake. He kissed below my ear. My cheek. My jaw. Pressed his lips to the pulse point at my neck. Kissed my shoulder. My wrist.

Calloused hands, rough against my soft skin, glided up my thighs. Over my breasts. Up my neck and into my hair. His hand clasped mine and he laced our fingers together, resting our joined hands beside my head as his lips traveled from my jaw to my ear and he whispered, "Tell me this doesn't feel like home."

And it felt exactly like home because my home was him. It had always been him.

He slid inside me, and it was slow, and we were silent, our bodies saying everything our words couldn't. I curved away from the bed, the balls of my feet digging into the mattress, and he thrust harder. He groaned into my neck as he stroked in and out.

A fire ignited in my soul, burning only for him.

I touched his face and he kissed my lips, so gently, with a reverence that brought tears to my eyes. He pushed in deeper and my eyes drifted shut, a lone tear trailing down my cheek.

"Jude," I whispered. How had I lived without him for so long?

My back arched off the mattress and he kissed me again. My nails dug into his back as he stroked deeper, harder, filling up the space inside me he'd created for himself so many years ago.

"I love you."

"I love you."

All I could think about was him. All I could feel was him. All I wanted and needed was him.

"You're my home."

Forever. Always.

CHAPTER FORTY-SIX

Jude

"Is it ready to flip?" Noah tilted his head to look up at me. He was so fucking cute. In only a few short weeks, I'd gotten attached to him. I looked forward to spending time with him, as much as I looked forward to seeing Lila every day.

"Do you see the bubbles?" I asked him.

He studied the pancakes in the pan then nodded. "I see them."

"That means it's time to flip. But remember what I told you?"

"Be careful. Don't touch the pan. Cause it's hot," he repeated the words I'd told him.

"It's really hot and I don't want you to get burned."

"I know."

I stayed right beside him, ready to intervene if necessary but unlike the way he did most things, he approached this task cautiously. I wrapped my hand around his and helped him get the spatula all the way under the pancake before he tried to flip it.

"I can do it."

I released his hand and I watched him do it. The pancake was a bit burnt, which I suspected would be the case but I'd eat this batch.

I set the stack of pancakes on the island next to the bacon and Noah climbed onto his stool, all ready to dive in.

I poured a cup of coffee for Lila, added milk until it turned the color she liked it, and set it in front of her as she took her seat across from me. She looked down at the coffee then at the breakfast—pancakes, bacon, fruit that Noah and I had cut up—then finally her eyes met mine. "It's kind of nice having you around."

"*Kind of nice?*"

"Don't let it go to your head."

"Does that mean you want me to stay?" I sat on the stool next to Noah's and filled my plate with food, sending the message that I had no intention of going anywhere. I poured Noah's syrup for him, already knowing from experience that his pancakes would end up swimming in syrup if he was left to his own devices.

"What do you mean by stay?" she asked, playing coy as she speared a strawberry and guided it to her mouth.

"You know, so I'll be on hand to cook your breakfast every morning."

"Oh." She gave me that sly smile. "So you want to be my short-order cook?"

I grinned. "For the sake of keeping this PG, that's exactly what I want to be."

"There might be a job opening." She shrugged. "But I have other applicants to interview."

What a joker. "I can already guarantee that they won't have

my qualifications." I gave her some jazz hands. "Like my magic hands, for instance."

She shook her head and ate her breakfast, her cheeks flushed. As much as I appreciated seeing Lila in a fancy dress and fuck-me stilettos, this was the look I loved best on her. Messy bun with a few stray locks of hair framing her face, no makeup, and wearing a faded blue T-shirt that used to be mine.

"Nice T-shirt."

"Oh, this old thing? It's my ex-boyfriend's."

I scowled at her. She just laughed and bit into a crispy strip of bacon.

"Your mommy's a comedian," I told Noah.

"What's a median?"

"Uncle Jude thinks I'm funny."

Noah's brow furrowed. "You're not funny."

That made me laugh.

"Is Uncle Jude funny?" Lila asked.

Noah stuffed a forkful of pancakes into his mouth and thought about it for a minute before he nodded. "He tells funny pickle jokes."

Lila groaned. "Oh God. Not the pickle jokes."

I bumped Noah's fist. It was sticky with maple syrup.

Just as I was thinking that Sunday mornings with Lila and Noah were my favorite thing in the world, my newfound happiness was destroyed by a knock on the door followed by the sound of boots crossing the hardwood floor.

"Lila! Noah!" he boomed, effectively wreaking havoc on our peaceful Sunday morning.

"Daddy!" Noah jumped down from his stool and launched himself into Brody's outstretched arms.

"Hey little man." Brody lifted Noah into his arms and gave him a big hug. "I missed you."

"Missed you too."

"Noah, come back and finish your breakfast," Lila said. "Hey. We weren't expecting you this early," she told Brody.

"Yeah. I can see that." Brody set Noah back on his stool and completely ignored me as if I wasn't even sitting there. I returned the favor.

"We made pancakes!" Noah crowed. "You want some?"

"Nah, I'm good." He grabbed a strip of bacon, shoved it in his mouth, and helped himself to a cup of coffee. He knew which cupboard to find the mugs in and made himself right at home, pulling up a stool next to Lila. Driving home the point that they were comfortable with each other.

"How did you do?" she asked Brody.

"Did you win, Daddy?" Noah asked, his eyes wide, forearms planted on the countertop as he knelt on the tall stool, his rapt attention focused on the man who was clearly a hero in his eyes. The stool tipped forward on two legs. My hand shot out to steady him so the stool wouldn't fly out from under him and he'd end up face-planting on the granite. I kept my left hand on the wooden leg and drank my coffee with my right hand.

Brody shook his head. He looked like he hadn't slept in days. "Nope. Getting too old."

"Old?" Lila said with a snort. "You've only just turned thirty-one."

He huffed out a laugh. "Been doing it since I was a teenager. The best guys on the circuit now are ten years younger than me."

Lila gave him a little jab with her elbow. "Time to hang up your spurs, cowboy."

He raked his fingers through his hair and exhaled loudly. "Looks that way."

"I know you love it, Brody," she said. "But we need you to stay safe and strong. That damned old rodeo has left you with more broken bones and injuries than any man should ever have in a lifetime."

He side-eyed her. "Careful there. You're starting to sound like you actually care."

"I do care. I worry about you every time you're on the road."

I gritted my teeth, surprised that the mug in my hand didn't crack under the pressure of my tight grip. She worried about him. Like he was going off to a combat zone instead of a stupid rodeo where all he had to do was stay on the back of a horse. He did it for the glory, for the cheers of the crowd and the adoration. I knew this because I'd gone to watch him in plenty of rodeos back in high school where he'd swagger around like he was God's gift to women.

"And I always tell you not to worry," he told Lila. "I'll always come home."

The dig was intended for me. But Lila was feeding right into it. Lapping this shit up.

This was a cozy little family scene and I was the odd man out. "You done?" I asked her tersely, reaching for her plate which she hadn't touched since the cowboy swaggered in and took up residence right the fuck next to her.

"Yeah, but don't worry about the dishes. I can—"

Ignoring her protests, I cleared the dishes.

"Yeah, Mommy," Noah piped up. "Daddy *always* comes home."

I filled the dishwasher and slammed it shut with more force than I'd intended. Then I turned around to tell Lila that we needed to get out of here. Let Brody take Noah so we could spend our day together.

"Time for you to run?" he asked me. "Things aren't going your way?"

"Brody," Lila warned. "Don't start."

He smirked. "Just calling it the way I see it."

Deep breaths. He was baiting me. He'd set up this scene on purpose because he wanted me to see that they were a family.

"Don't get too attached to your Uncle Jude," Brody told Noah. "He has a habit of running away when the going gets tough."

My hands clenched into fists. That son of a bitch.

"Brody," Lila hissed. "You need to stop."

"Hey buddy, why don't you go and get ready? We'll go see the horses. Can you get yourself dressed?"

"I can do it," Noah said, hopping down from his stool and running out of the kitchen.

When Noah was gone, Brody said, "It's fun playing house, isn't it? But you've only been doing it for a few weeks. And now I'm back. You won't have Noah and Lila to yourself anymore. Let's see how you deal with that. You were never very good at sharing."

"Not when the person was mine to begin with."

"Like I said, Noah's mine, not yours. And Lila—"

"Belongs to no one," she interjected. "I'm my own person. And I'm sitting right here. I'm not a bartering chip. I'm not a plaything you two can fight over. So stop marking your territory by pissing all over it. If you can't settle your differences..." She stopped and shook her head, her eyes darting to me. "If you can't do that, none of your sweet words or anything else will make a bit of difference."

I opened my mouth to protest.

"Brody. Can you help Noah? He can't dress himself yet."

She held his gaze for a few seconds until he finally nodded. "Sure. Whatever you want, L."

After he left the kitchen, I rounded the island and reached for her. She crossed her arms over her chest, shutting me out.

As if the past few weeks had meant nothing to her. As if last night had never happened.

"I just need you to answer one question," she said, her gaze holding mine. I nodded. "Will you ever forgive me for this?"

I wanted to say that I already had, but it wasn't true. While Brody was away, I'd been able to block him out, pretend he didn't exist but now that he was back and throwing it in my face again, I knew that this was when the true test would begin.

If Brody and I couldn't find a way to co-exist peacefully, Lila would kick my sorry ass out the door faster than you could say Rebel. She'd been honest from the start, had drilled it into my head that Noah would always come first. I was not her number one anymore. And Noah was Brody's kid, not mine. So where did that leave me?

"Brody will always be a part of my life," she said. "He's not going to disappear. We found a way that works for us. We found a way to co-parent that's best for Noah. I want Noah to see that we're good friends and that we care about each other. I never want him to feel like he has to choose sides."

I couldn't argue with any of it. Everything she said made perfect sense and if Noah was my kid, I would want the same thing. He wasn't even my kid and I *still* wanted that for him. But if you ask me, this was overkill.

"Are you always going to lay it on this thick? Every time the three of you are together in my presence? Was it a test to see how much I could put up with before I cracked?"

She shook her head no. Then she took a deep breath and let it out. "I don't want to break you, Jude. I know how hard you've worked and you've come so far... I don't want to be the person who ruins all your hard work."

"I'm not that fragile. I don't break that easily." It pissed me off that she still felt like she had to worry about me.

"But you didn't answer my question." She lifted her eyes to mine. "Will you ever forgive me?"

"Will you ever forgive me?"

"I want to."

Guess I had my answer. She hadn't forgiven me yet and I was still harboring resentment over the method she'd chosen to get over me.

When Lila and I got engaged, I told her that if she ever cheated on me, that would be the end. I'd never get over that kind of betrayal. She told me that if I ever left her, there would be no coming back. Technically, she hadn't cheated on me and logically, I knew this. When I left, I'd wanted her to move on, to find happiness without me. But I still couldn't wrap my head around the fact that she'd not only slept with Brody but he'd gotten her pregnant.

Did I have any right to resent Lila and Brody for this? One could argue that I had no right.

I knew what I needed to do. I had to be the bigger man. I had to find a way to make peace with a situation I wasn't happy about. Find a way to sit down at the same table with the man who had given the love of my life something that I couldn't. It was a big ask. The situation was fucked-up. But as I knew, a lot of things in life were fucked up beyond our control.

I had two choices. Man up and accept this. Or lose her forever.

"What do I need to do in order for you to forgive me?" I asked her.

"I'm still so scared you're going to run. I'm scared that all this will be too much for you to handle and you'll leave me again. I'm scared that one day I'll wake up and you'll be gone. But I think... you have to decide if this is something you can live with. And I'm sorry... so sorry I put you in this position. But I can't go back and change what happened."

Lila and I used to believe that our love could conquer all. That no obstacle would be too great. How naïve we'd been. It was never a question of not loving each other enough. We'd never stopped loving each other.

In the end, what it came down to was whether or not we could find a way to be together without dredging up all the sins of our past. Without throwing our transgressions into each other's face every time we argued. Because we would argue. We were still the bull and the lion, and we fought as passionately as we loved.

Love tested your limits.

It was so damn easy to fall in love. So easy to love a person when times were good. The real challenge was sticking it out even when the going got rough. But I was done running. I was done trying to pretend that I'd ever find true happiness without Lila. She was it for me. My once in a lifetime love. My reason. My past, present, and my future. If I walked away from her now, I'd be a miserable bastard for the rest of my sorry life.

"I'm not going anywhere without you, Rebel. You're my ride or die. I'm never leaving you again. I promise on my life... no, fuck that. I promise on your life, on Noah's life, I will stay and I will love you until my last breath."

"And you'll forgive me for what I did?"

"I already have."

Her eyes narrowed in disbelief. Still so suspicious. Only time would heal these old wounds but we'd have plenty of time. "When did this happen?"

"Just now. I did a little soul searching. Like two seconds ago."

She laughed. "Oh God, Jude... you're unbelievable."

"Thank you."

That made her laugh harder. "I'm glad to see your ego is

still intact." The laughter died on her lips and her face grew serious. "Can you make things right with Brody?"

I raked my hand through my hair. That was a big ask. "That's what you want me to do?"

"That's what I need you to do. If you want to be a part of my life and Noah's life—"

"There's no if about it."

"If I lose you again, my heart couldn't take it."

"I won't let you down. Not again. Promise." This time, I'd keep my promise or die trying. Even if it meant playing nice with Brody Fucking McCallister. I'd do it for Lila and for Noah.

Maybe my mom had been right. I needed to find a way to forgive myself. And maybe if I could do that, I could find a way to forgive Brody for being there when I wasn't.

Taking a deep breath, I opened the door and walked into The Roadhouse. Christmas lights were still strung up even though it was May, and country music still played from the speakers but the sound quality was better and the place didn't smell like stale beer and cigarette smoke anymore.

"Well, if it isn't Jude McCallister," Colleen said with a smile. "Long time no see."

She set a beer in front of me and grabbed a bottle of whiskey from the shelf. "I'm good with the beer."

Her brows raised, but she nodded and returned the bottle to the shelf. "Where've you been all these years, sugar?"

"Everywhere and nowhere." And that at least an honest answer.

"Well, I guess that's where you had to go to find your way

back home," she said, understanding more than I'd told her. "You look good. Real good."

I tipped my chin. "Thanks. So do you." She looked the same—long auburn hair, tight jeans, and a fitted black T-shirt with Johnny Cash's face on it. "How have you been?"

She shrugged. "Can't complain. I bought the place a few years back." Shrewd blue eyes assessed me. "But I guess you know that, don't you?"

"I might have heard something about it."

With a shake of her head, she laughed. "You're a lousy liar. I've been hanging on to this for years, waiting for you to come back." She reached into a drawer under the bar and set a check in front of me. "I'm not gonna take your money, baby. You never owed me a thing."

I looked down at the check she'd set in front of me. Guilt money. The same as the money I'd tried to give Lila when I left her. "I owed you the truth." I remembered my mom's words. That I had to find a way to forgive myself. And for the most part, I had but I still felt like I owed Colleen more than what I'd given her. Which was the reason I was sitting on this barstool right now. "That story you read in the newspaper. I didn't save Reese's life. That's not how it happened. I—"

She held up her hand to stop me. "You were in a combat zone, baby. I'm not stupid. Bad things happen to good people all the time. I don't need to know how Reese died. You were there for him. Do you know how many times he used to mention you in his emails to me? You were a good friend to him. And he was proud to be a Marine and serve his country and fight right alongside his best friend. So you have nothing to feel guilty about, you hear me?"

I nodded. "Yeah, I hear you."

"Good. Now let it go. You can't hang on to all of that. Just go out there and live the best life you can. That's what Reese would have wanted. That's the best way to honor his memory."

With her words, a weight lifted off my shoulders.

"Now, what I wouldn't mind hearing are some of the good stories about Reese."

"Oh, I have plenty of them." I laughed at some of my memories of Reese. I didn't know if she'd want to hear about the time he finally lost his virginity to a stripper named Destiny and woke up the next morning with her name tattooed over his heart. But I had plenty of other stories I could share. And that's what I did. I talked about Reese for two hours and I made Colleen laugh and I made her cry and when I left, she hugged me goodbye and thanked me for sharing my memories with her.

And I guess that's all part of the healing process. You have to talk about the shit that's eating away at you, unload some of the baggage you've been carting around for too long and lighten your load.

The night before Lila's thirtieth birthday, I went to see Brody. He was sitting on his back porch, a beer in his hand, feet propped on the banister. When I made my presence known and joined him on the porch, he didn't look surprised to see me.

Without waiting for an invitation, I took a seat on the wicker chair next to him. I recognized these chairs. They used to be on our back porch.

"Was hoping you'd be long gone by now," he said, taking a pull of his beer. Still an asshole.

"Wishes don't always come true." We sat in silence for a few minutes.

"Something on your mind?" he asked finally.

I hadn't planned what I would say. All I knew was that I

had to do this for Lila. And for myself. For all of us, I guess. Here went nothing. I'd eat humble pie even if I choked on it.

"I never thanked you for being there for Lila when I wasn't." I stared out at the dark sky, the shadow of the barn in the distance, the air scented with hay and horses and the promise of summertime. Without interrupting, he waited for me to continue. "The night you took her to the hospital and sat in the waiting room for hours. And all the nights you dragged me home from bars when I was too drunk to get home on my own." I rubbed my hand over my chest, trying to loosen the tightness and cleared my throat. "You saved my life and I never thanked you for that either."

I didn't know if he would make this easy on me or give me a hard time about it. Either way, I would take whatever he dished out.

"That's why you're here? You came to thank me?"

I nodded.

"Haven't heard the words yet."

I laughed under my breath. Stubborn bastard. "Thank you." Fuck, that was hard.

"You didn't thank me when it happened because you didn't want to be saved. You were pissed at me for finding you in that field. You wanted me to let you die."

I couldn't deny it. At the time, that was true. Lila had called him, distraught when I hadn't come home, and he'd gone out looking for me. I had no idea how he'd found me, but he had. I'd been told that he found me just in time.

"Lila said you told her about Odessa."

He turned his head sharply, surprise painting his features. "I sure as hell did *not* tell her about Odessa."

"Yeah, you did. She said it was the night... you were both drunk," I finished.

"Fuck." He ran his hand over his face. "I told her?"

"How drunk were you?"

He blew out a breath and shook his head. "Honestly? I don't remember anything from that night. We drank an entire bottle of whiskey and God knows what else. Woke up the next morning and we both freaked the fuck out."

For some reason that made me feel better. "So you're not in love with Lila?"

"In love with her? I've never been in love with her. If I'd been in love with her, would I have tried to get you two idiots back together in high school?"

"Who was the idiot? You nearly broke her nose."

He laughed. "Oh man. That was funny as shit."

I scowled at him.

"Nah. I was never in love with her. For a hot minute I thought maybe... but no. Wasn't like that. I love her as a friend. But I'll tell you one thing for sure." He pointed his finger at me. "If you fuck her over again, you'll never get within a hundred yards of her or Noah again. I'll make sure of it."

"Well, then, I guess you'd better get used to seeing me around. I'm not going anywhere." Having said everything I needed to, I stood to go.

As I was walking away, he called after me. "This doesn't make us friends again."

"We weren't friends. We were brothers. We *are* brothers."

"Yeah, I guess we were."

"Still are," I reminded him.

"Yeah, yeah. Whatever you say, *Uncle* Jude. You stupid shit."

Typical Brody. He just had to get that in there, didn't he? He'd be in for a rude awakening when I became Noah's step-dad. Now all I had to do was convince Lila.

CHAPTER FORTY-SEVEN

Lila

Two Months Later

"We're going on a bear hunt!" Noah spun around and around until he got so dizzy he fell into a heap on the front lawn.

"You're so silly," I teased, tickling his ribs until he was giggling so hard he couldn't breathe. We weren't really going on a bear hunt. We were going on a Fourth of July picnic. Jude's idea. He was full of ideas these days.

We loaded the food and picnic blanket in the back of the truck and away we went.

"Where are we going for this picnic?"

"No idea. Thought we'd drive around until we found a good spot."

I snorted. Like I'd fall for that one. Jude left very little to chance. But after fifteen minutes of driving aimlessly, like we had all the time in the world, I started to wonder if maybe he'd been telling the truth. When he turned the truck around and headed in the opposite direction, I started to get concerned. Ten minutes later, we were still driving.

Maybe he wasn't okay. Maybe he was having a flashback. I didn't know what to think. I glanced at him. He looked okay. Chilled. Relaxed. His hand tapping out the beat of the music on the doorframe.

"There're picnic tables at the lake," I suggested.

"Too crowded."

"How about the state park? The one by the quarry? Or the swimming hole..."

"They'll all be too crowded," he said, dismissing my suggestions. "Don't worry." He squeezed my thigh. "I've got this."

Five minutes later, he turned off the highway and took the back roads.

"Make sure there're plenty of trees so we can sit in the shade," I said, not entirely convinced that he had any idea where we were going. He didn't even respond to my request. We were in the middle of nowhere and as far as I knew there were no picnic spots around here. Although I knew this place. It was the road we'd driven on a million years ago after Brody had tricked us into getting tacos.

It was one of my favorite Hill Country drives. Winding roads and rugged hills, green meadows and limestone cliffs. Today the sun was shining and the big sky was glaringly blue.

"Are we there yet?" Noah piped up from the back seat.

"Almost," Jude replied.

I side-eyed him. "Do you have any idea where we're going?"

"Just enjoy the ride."

No sooner were the words out of his mouth when he swung a right onto a narrow gravel road shaded by trees. Now I was sure he was lost. The truck went up a hill and at the top of it a stone and timber farmhouse with a wraparound porch came into view.

"This is someone's driveway," I said. "Turn around and go back."

Instead of turning around, he pulled up in front of the house and cut the engine. "This looks like a good spot for a picnic."

"Are you insane?"

He grinned. "Insanely in love with Lila Turner."

I rolled my eyes. "Come on, Jude. Let's go."

"What do you think of this house?"

"It's gorgeous. I love it." I did. But why was he asking me about a house? I was starving now, and kept thinking about the deviled eggs I'd made. And the sandwiches on baguettes. I needed food. "Now let's go."

He was out of the truck and rounding the hood. Opening my door, he held out his hand to help me out of the truck.

"Jude... what are you doing? I'm hungry and this is no time for games..."

His smile stopped the words in my mouth. My head swung from him to the house in front of us. Oh my God. It was so beautiful. "Is this... what did you do?"

He helped me out of the truck and unbuckled Noah from his seat and swung him up in the air before setting him on the ground. "Remember what we talked about?" Jude asked Noah, crouching so he was eye level.

Noah nodded. "I 'member." He looked up at me, a sly grin on his face.

"You're okay with it, right?" Jude asked him.

Noah nodded enthusiastically then in a stage whisper he asked, "Can I give Mommy the ring now?"

Jude shook his head and scrubbed his hands over his face

and then he was laughing. I sucked in a breath. Oh my God. Was he...

Before I had a chance to think about it, Jude was on bended knee in front of me. The driveway was gravel and he was wearing shorts. His knee would get all cut up. Not sure why that was the first thought in my head. Noah patted Jude's shoulder like he was giving him extra courage and letting him know everything would be okay.

Jude took my hand in his. "I didn't get it right the first time, but I promise you that I'll never leave you again. I'll be by your side through thick and thin. I'll walk through fire for you. Carry your burdens. Love you until I take my dying breath. And even after that, my soul will go on loving you and I will find you in the next life. Because you give me life. I live and breathe you. I have been loving you for so long. There is nothing I wouldn't do for you. And for Noah. I love you and only you." He tipped his beautiful face up to look at me, and I could barely see him through the blur of tears. "Will you marry me, Lila?"

Tears streamed down my face and all I could was nod.

Jude nudged Noah. "Psst. It's time for the ring."

My tears turned to laughter at this comedy act.

"Oh. Yeah. I got it." Noah dug in his shorts pocket and I thought it was brave and a little bit stupid to entrust a four-year-old with an engagement ring. Noah turned his pocket inside out and I laughed even harder when I saw the ring was duct-taped to the inside of his pocket.

Jude ripped off the tape to reveal a ring wrapped in saran wrap.

"This is like a military operation," I said, laughing as he finally held up a ring, triumphantly, and slipped it on my finger. Then he wiped imaginary sweat off his brow. Or maybe it wasn't imaginary. He was really sweating. And he was still down on one knee on the gravel driveway of a house he'd bought for us.

It was my dream house because it was home, and Jude was my home.

My love. My soulmate. My wish on a star. My everything.

While Noah raced from room to room, Jude led me around the house, talking about the changes we could make and how he'd build an addition. But if you asked me, it was perfect just as it was and I told him so as we stood in front of the tall windows in the living room with a vaulted ceiling and looked out at the five glorious acres of land that came with the house.

"Thank you," I said, turning in his arms and framing his face in my hands.

"For what?"

"For putting the stars back in the sky."

"You ain't seen nothing yet, baby. I'm going to give you an entire universe."

EPILOGUE

Jude

*N*INE *M*ONTHS *L*ATER
April

The florist is carrying a bouquet of wildflowers, handpicked this morning by me and Noah. We picked them from our field and tied them with string. But it's not the flowers that capture and hold my attention. It's the beautiful face of my bride as she walks down an aisle covered in rose petals, The Piano Guys' "A Thousand Years" playing in the background, the April sky so big and blue and cloudless.

She's glowing. That's the only word to describe it. The light is back in her eyes and I'd like to think I put it there. Or, at least, played some part in making her shine so bright. She takes my breath away.

Green eyes, the color of the grass in the meadow, sparkle with joy. Her full pink lips are tipped up at the corners in a smile, dark hair falling in long waves around her shoulders and down her back. When I finally manage to tear my eyes from her face I let them roam down, over the golden skin of her bare shoulders and down a deceptively simple dress that gathers around her breasts and cascades like a waterfall to her feet. The sun highlights tiny glitters of gold in the cream fabric. She looks like a Greek goddess. She looks like my every dream come true.

I've waited so long for this day to arrive, and now that it's here, I can't wait another minute.

Too slow, Rebel.

I want it all. Right now.

So I stride up the aisle to claim my bride, earning a scowl from my father who is giving her away. When she asked him if he would do the honors, I could have sworn I saw a tear in his eye. He'd deny it, of course.

"Wait until we get there," he grumbles.

"I'll take it from here," I tell him, giving him no option but to release Lila.

She just laughs and shakes her head. "This is so typical of you."

Wait until she sees the other surprises I have in store for her today.

"All your fault for looking so fucking beautiful." I grab the back of her head and pull her toward me, my other hand on the small of her back. For once, she doesn't put up a fight. Dipping my head, I kiss her in front of all our guests and she kisses me back, her arm snaking around my neck and her body flush with mine. We're so close I can feel her heart pounding and I'm almost certain it's beating at the same tempo as mine. That's how in sync we are.

"Daddy Jude is kissing Mommy. *Again*," my best man pipes up. And now everyone who is here to share our special day is laughing at five-year-old Noah's words. I love that kid. And I love that he calls me Daddy Jude. So fucking cute.

When Lila remembers that we're in a field behind our house with our family and friends seated on either side of our petal-strewn aisle and the officiant waiting to marry us, she pulls back and swats my chest. But she's smiling. One second later, the smile is replaced with a serious look.

"Are you ready to do this?" She holds my gaze, her eyes searching mine as if she wants to make sure there's no trace of doubt or hesitation. It's shocking that she could actually think there would be, but I try not to take offense. She has her reasons and if she needs reassurance, I'll give it to her for as long and as many times as she needs to hear it.

"Born ready. I've never been more ready for anything in my life." And it's true.

Only minutes later, we're exchanging our vows. I make her so many promises. I vow to love her until the end of time. I tell her that I'll strive every day to be the man she deserves. To be worthy of her. To never take her for granted and to love her through the good times and bad. I promise to keep a steady course through all the ups and downs. I'm not the least bit worried about promising her the world. I know I'll keep my word.

Now it's her turn, and I'm curious to hear what she's going to say. She looks me right in the eye, and it's just the two of us in our own little bubble. Her hands are trembling and her eyes glitter with unshed tears but her voice never quavers. It's strong and steady when she speaks.

"The first time I met you, I thought you were the most annoying boy in the world." Brody chuckles and mutters something under his breath but we ignore him. "Then you became my best friend. My fiercest ally. The boy who hung the moon and put the stars in the sky. I knew I was in love with you when

I was fifteen. The day you gave me your favorite hoodie. Years passed and the boy you were grew into the man I couldn't live without. I didn't want to imagine a life... a *world*... without you in it." She pauses and takes a deep breath before she continues. "When I lost you, I was shocked and sad and angry that the world kept spinning and life went on. Without you."

"But now I think we had to go through all that pain and heartache and separation to get to this place. It's such a good and beautiful place we're in now." We exchange a smile. Hers is soft and she wipes away a lone tear. "My love for you grows stronger and deeper every single day. And I promise you that I will love you, and only you, for the rest of my days. I promise you that I'll be by your side for the good, the bad, and the ugly and all the moments in between. I promise that I'll show you, in actions not just words, how strong and true my love ..." She freezes, and her eyes go wide.

I'm not sure what to think. Did she forget what she was planning to say? Or is something wrong?

For a second, I panic. I can't even read the look on her face and that worries me. "Rebel. What's wrong?"

Then she smiles. It's big. It's bright. It's beautiful. It's everything. She grabs my hand and guides it to her belly, flattening her palm over mine.

"There." Her eyes light up with excitement. "Do you feel it?"

I'm stunned into silence. Because fuck yeah, I do feel it. It's not exactly a karate kick. But the kid's only the size of a large eggplant. Every week, Lila updates me. Which fruit or vegetable can we compare our kid to this week? Yesterday, while she was on a spa day with Christy and Sophie, she texted a row of eggplant emojis. I was with Tommy and Brody, and my brothers doing last minute wedding preparations to the dome tent in our field where our reception will be held.

"That's what got her into this mess in the first place," Tommy said.

We'd all laughed like pre-pubescent teens sharing a dirty joke.

Now I just want to cut to the chase and start my future right here, right now. So I turn to the officiant, a woman in her fifties with the patience of a saint, and I tell her, "I think we're done here. Can you pronounce us man and wife so I can kiss my baby mama?" The poor woman just laughs and shakes her head.

"Oh Jude," Lila says, through her laughter and the tears I brush away with the pads of my thumbs. "You're unbelievable."

"Why, thank you." I give her a cocky wink that makes her laugh even harder.

I barely hear the officiant's words. All I know is that we're married and I've put a ring on it. Without waiting, I pull Lila into my arms. We kiss for a thousand years while our friends and family cheer for us.

It doesn't matter that we didn't save all our firsts for each other. She will always be my first, my last, and my only true love.

Forever. Always. My once in a lifetime. Not many people are lucky enough to find their soulmate at the age of nine, but I'm one lucky bastard. The day I met Lila, the stars aligned. And if necessary, I'll spend a lifetime putting them back in the sky for her.

———

Eight Months Later

. . .

Three months after our wedding, Levi Patrick McCallister made his grand entrance into the world. He was born on the fifth of July at one in the morning. From our hospital room, we could hear the faint sound of fireworks in the distance while Lila was in labor. We joked that he came into the world with a bang. His first name is our little inside joke. Lila made me promise to take it to my grave so we wouldn't traumatize the poor kid. But someday maybe I'll tell him that he was named after the Levi's that Lila bought me. Zippers, not buttons, for easier access. Second thought, he doesn't need to know that.

Now she's unzipping said jeans and pulling them down while I rip off her clothes. In two seconds flat, we're naked. Lifting her up, I maneuver around the mountain of wrapped gifts under the tree, soft white Christmas lights illuminating the room, and lay her down on the sheepskin rug in front of the stone fireplace. Her skin glows in the firelight and I take a moment to appreciate every dip and curve and swell of her naked body before I kiss my way up her thighs. I kiss her stomach, her breasts and the tattoo on her ribs just below her left breast. The lotus tattoo serves as a constant reminder of what we lost but it also symbolizes our rebirth. For me, it's become a symbol of hope. It blooms in darkness, delicate and beautiful, yet resilient. Like Lila.

I continue peppering kisses on her chest, neck and lips before I settle between her thighs, guiding my tip to her entrance.

Always so greedy and impatient, she grabs the back of my head and wraps her legs around my waist, pulling me closer. Our lips collide and she shifts her hips, trying to take me inside her all at once.

I tskk. "Patience."

"We don't have that kind of time."

Good point.

"I want you now. I *need* you now."

Who am I to argue with that? Her words spur me into action. In one thrust, I'm buried to the hilt and this, right here, will always be my favorite place.

Pure. Fucking. Heaven.

I glide in and out of her, and she rocks her hips, meeting me thrust for thrust. I kiss her deeply and she drags her nails across my shoulder blades. Her back arches off the plush rug and she throws back her head, exposing her neck, an invitation to kiss the pulse point at her throat. It flutters beneath my lips.

Her fingers tangle in my hair and she whispers, "I love you."

"I love you more."

We hold onto each other, our eyes locked as I move inside her, my strokes hard and long, rubbing against her clit, against her everything. We're almost there, but not yet.

"Come with me, Lila." I brush my lips over her jaw.

"I'm not letting you go anywhere without me." She grabs my shoulders and squeezes as she angles her hips to allow me to go deeper.

I slam into her, filling her up, relentless until we're both panting and a sheen of sweat coats our skin.

"Oh God, Jude..." A scream rips from her lungs and her teeth sink into my shoulder, dragging a deep groan from the back of my throat. There's no holding back now. Our pace is frenzied, graceless and lacking rhythm, driven by the primal need to lose ourselves in each other, to lose control and chase our high together.

As we hurtle into shared orgasms, she calls out my name, her thighs quivering and lips parted. I come with a vengeance that's almost violent.

With a shudder, I collapse on top of her, my forehead dropping to hers. She frames my face in her hands and for a few seconds everything is still and quiet, except for the sound of our breathing and the crackle of the flames in the fireplace.

I inhale her exhales. I live and breathe her. I can't even move a muscle nor do I want to.

"Merry Christmas, baby." No sooner are the words out of my mouth when I hear our baby's cries from the monitor. For once, his sense of timing is good but even so I groan and feel Lila's body shake with laughter. A few weeks ago I joked that we should give him a new middle name. Levi Cockblock McCallister.

"Merry Christmas, *Daddy* Jude."

And that's my cue to get dressed and jog up the stairs to rescue my son from his crib. Then I'll do everything I can to make him happy and keep him safe.

Life doesn't get much better than this. I know better than to take my good fortune for granted. Some people never get this lucky.

When I lift my baby boy into my arms, I hold him close. Maybe you have to go through hell and come out the other side to fully appreciate the little piece of heaven you've been given. I have, and I do.

"Did you know that the stars shine brighter here?" I ask Levi as I carry him to the window and raise the linen blind. I hold him in the crook of my arm so he can gaze out at the inky blue sky reeling with stars on this cold, clear Christmas Eve.

"It's true," Lila says from the doorway and then she's by my side, guiding Levi's tiny hand to her lips for a kiss.

"Mommy! Daddy Jude!" Noah races into the bedroom and skids to a halt next to us.

"What are you doing awake?" Lila asks, lifting him into her arms so he can join our little circle.

"Levi was being loud. Is Santa here yet?"

"What's that?" I point to the sky. "Is that Santa's sleigh?"

"Oh," Noah says, his eyes wide as he gazes out the window. He still believes in magic and miracles and Santa Claus. I hope a part of him always will.

Life is hard but it's these moments of joy and wonder that shine the brightest, even on the darkest nights. And I don't want to miss a single one. I have found my way home and the journey I took to get here made the reward so much sweeter.

ACKNOWLEDGMENTS

I have so many people to thank for taking this journey with me, for helping to make this the best book it could be, and for holding my hand and talking me down from the ledge when I let my crazy get the best of me. Which unfortunately was more often that I'd care to admit.

A huge thank you to Jen Mirabelli. Where would I be without you? Thank you for loving Jude and Lila as much as I do, and for believing in me and this story. You made this book so much better and I'll be forever grateful to you. Not to mention the daily chats, and for organizing all the promo and marketing. I couldn't have done any of this without you. You're amazing and I'm so glad we found each other. All the x's AND the o's.

To Aliana Milano. Thank you for beta reading, always telling me like it is, and for sending the best care packages. A day without our midnight chats is like a day without cake. You never saved me any so thanks for that. Still waiting for that birdseed salad recipe. If you ever leave me again, I'll hunt you down. You've been warned. Love you Dork.

Carol Radcliffe, thank you for the music, your friendship and your unwavering support. You are such a beautiful soul and I'm so lucky to call you a friend. #soulsister

Monica Marti, thank you for helping me find my muses and for always volunteering to read for me, even when life gets crazy busy and hectic. I'm California dreaming – can't wait to see you again. #love4evah

To Emily Meador, thank you for being such a fab admin and friend. You do such an amazing job of keeping things going in my Reader Group and reminding me which day of the week it is. Just a heads up, we'll be in Texas for the foreseeable future.

Ellie McLove, thank you for the editing and for always squeezing me in even when it's down to the wire. Which, let's face it, is every single time. I vow to do better next time.

Lori Jackson, thank you for creating this gorgeous cover. It's so beautiful I want to cry. You are such a joy to work with, thank you. Thank you to Michelle Lancaster for taking this stunning photo that graces the cover. You're a true artist.

To all the book bloggers who took the time to read and review and share, thank you so much! I appreciate you and everything you do for the indie community.

A big thank you to my family, especially my kids who put up with my crazy on the daily. We have fun though, don't we? You are my reason. Love you forever and always.

And last but certainly not least, a huge thank you to the readers. Writing is a dream come true and I couldn't do this without you. Thank you so much for reading my words. Whether you liked When the Stars Fall or not, please consider taking a few seconds to leave an honest review. All reviews are appreciated. They mean so much to indie authors.

Thank you so very much.

Emery Rose xoxo

ABOUT THE AUTHOR

Emery Rose is an emerging author of sports-themed romance. This is Emery's fourth book.